Michael D. Apperley and his wife, LuAnn, live in Belleville, Ontario. They share their home with family, friends, two cats, and a very lazy greyhound.

TO SIS FROM BROTHER

Family is the most important contributor to an individual's growth. In this, I have been blessed. My incredible wife and two children stand paramount in these reflections and my affections.

Michael D. Apperley

Eternal

Austin Macauley Publishers™
London * Cambridge * New York * Sharjah

Ordering Information
Quantity sales: Special discounts are available on quantity purchases by corporations, associations, and others. For details, contact the publisher at the address below.

Publisher's Cataloging-in-Publication data
Apperley, Michael D.
Eternal

ISBN 9781645369677 (Paperback)
ISBN 9781645369684 (Hardback)
ISBN 9781645369707 (ePub e-book)

Library of Congress Control Number: 2021908210

www.austinmacauley.com/us

First Published (2021)
Austin Macauley Publishers LLC
40 Wall Street, 33rd Floor, Suite 3302
New York, NY 10005
USA

mail-usa@austinmacauley.com
+1 (646) 5125767

Chapter 1

Most survivors thought he was supernatural. He denied it saying only, “Divinity is overrated. Humanity, now that’s hard.”

The drive into town wasn’t long and he pulled into the grocery store parking lot as the morning news ended. Oil-slicked puddles left by the dawn rain spotted the uneven expanse of pavement. The sky was clear now, the kind of crystal blue morning that promises warm spring days and eternal youth…though neither promise is kept.

As his foot touched the pavement his attention was hijacked. Arms, legs and oranges whirled in conflicting orbits until the chaos split into three divergent paths; an elderly shopper prone beside her eco bags and toppled groceries and two scruffy men running in different directions, one toward him. Consequences weighed, he placed his foot in the path of one fleeing man and his future unfolded. The fleeing man tripped and splash-landed in a puddle. He pushed himself to his knees, spitting out curses and greasy water. Rising slowly, he turned and looked at Tom with murder in his eyes.

He was a brute, his street name was Tombstone and he hurt people. Tom walked to the dripping man, a lecture on manners beginning when Tombstone grabbed his shirt front and drew back a large fist. Tombstone did not know the magnitude of his mistake. Tom locked his fingers into the hand that gripped his shirt and twisted it down violently while turning to sidestep the incoming blow. With the wrist locked, he used both hands to bend Tombstone’s palm back onto its upturned forearm, the radiocarpal joint shredding in a squishy pop. Tombstone shrieked. His forward momentum driving him to his knees, the pain screaming, *run away*. Holding the useless arm, Tom pulled up sharply and flipped the large man onto his back. Driving the heel of his work boot into the soft flesh of Tombstone’s exposed armpit and reefing up hard on the limp wrist, Tom drawled, “Suck it up princess. You’ve got some groceries to repack.”

As the brute sat hunched on the curb near the gardening section, holding his purple, swollen wrist and moaning audibly, the small crowd of witnesses kept a wary eye on him. The policeman had just finished his questioning of Tom and Mrs. Patel.

"Jesus Tom, what'd you do to that asshole's arm? His hand is floppin' round like his wrist is made of Jell-O."

"Just a wrist lock, Bear. You'd know that if you'd kept comin' to class."

Sergeant Barry Deline put a friendly hand on Tom's shoulder and replied, "It's a damn good thing you had witnesses corroborating self-defense. If not for them, I'd be takin' you in for assault instead of him."

"Kinda backward isn't it, Bear, when you hafta protect the likes of that dirt bag from folks like Mrs. Patel and me. Speaking of dirt bags, when you haul his ass to holding, you might want to spray him down and scrub him with Clorox. He stinks."

"Like what?"

"Like old road kill on a hot day," replied Tom.

"Didn't notice," said Deline eyeing Tom. "Guess the wind was blowin' the wrong way."

After the excitement at the store and the police questioning, Tom was going to be late getting back to his jobsite. *I'd better grab coffee and food for the guys or they'll bitch all day*. In all the confusion, Tom hadn't picked up the burgers and buns for their lunch. The crew had gotten used to grilled hamburgers and hot dogs on Fridays, something Tom did whenever they had a big project that would keep them at one site for an extended period of time.

As he turned into the Tim Horton's parking lot to grab takeout for his crew, he decided to be considerate and go into the restaurant instead of using the drive thru. He stepped down from his truck and noticed a raggedy group of tattooed tough guys looking him over. Three broke away and approached Tom with bad intent scribbled all over them.

"You the guy who took down Stoney!"

Tom recognized the speaker as the other punk from the grocery store. He had black lightning bolts tattooed on top of his hands running back from each knuckle. Lightning bolt looked Tom up and down and growled, "We gonna ef you up man, teach you to keep your nose outta where it ain't wanted."

Tom's half ton was behind him forcing the three thugs to approach from the front. He planted his feet shoulder width apart, crossed his well-muscled arms over his chest, tilted his head slightly to the side and chuckled menacingly, "Together or one at a time, fellas?"

Tom's absence of fear plus the knotted muscles of his work-hardened forearms stopped the trio of thugs from approaching. Tom knew right away they were all talk and that was alright with him. After less than a minute of profanity laden threats, the leader turned and walked away, his two buddies trailing quickly. *That was pleasant,* Tom thought, *I wonder what the rest of the day has in store.*

The rest of the morning went just fine. The crew enjoyed their lunch of turkey clubs, donuts and coffee and had a good laugh when Tom told them about his adventure at the grocery store. As the guys finished up the last of their coffee and prepared to go back to work, the oldest member of the crew put his calloused hand on their young apprentice's shoulder and said, "Hey Billy, has the Boss ever showed you how he makes applesauce?"

"Orly," Tom said, "Not now."

Orly Maloney was the oldest member of the crew and had known Tom the longest. He could get away with saying things to Tom that no one else on the jobsite would. "Watch this Billy," said Orly as he grabbed a shiny, Red Delicious apple from the front seat of his truck and tossed it at Tom who snagged the apple out of the air with one hand and held it out. Billy looked at Tom holding the apple in front of him. No one was saying anything. Billy looked from Tom to Orly and back. He looked at the other crew members and they just smiled and inclined their heads toward Tom. Billy then noticed the muscles in Tom's forearm start to gain definition. Blood vessels under his tanned skin began to stand out. Suddenly, white splits appeared on the red skin of the apple as Tom's fingers slowly converged. Juice ran down his hand and dripped onto the ground and white pulp pushed out from between his fingers as he slowly crushed the apple.

Tom tossed the ruined fruit into the excavation and started looking for something to clean his hands on.

"Ho-lee shit," exclaimed Billy.

"Now you know why that idiot in the parking lot didn't have a chance when he went after Tom," said Orly, "You don't do this work for almost forty years and come away a weakling."

"Billy…you don't need to swear every time you see something that surprises you," said Tom matter of factly, "Your mom is going to be awfully disappointed in us if we turn you into a potty mouth." He winked at Billy. "Okay you guys, playtime's over, everyone knows what needs to get done before quittin' time…let's go!"

Five o'clock came. They were cleaning up the site for the weekend, Tom was handing out paychecks and young Billy was impatient to start asking him questions. As the junior member of the crew, he knew he couldn't pester Tom with questions not relating to the job at hand until the drive home. He rode to and from work with Tom while he saved up for insurance after buying himself a car. Tom enjoyed Billy's company on these daily commutes, he liked the kid.

Driving home, he recounted the morning's events and had a sobering thought, bullies could be vengeful and he drove a truck with his name emblazoned on its sides in gold lettering. With a slight feeling of dread, Tom dropped Billy at his house and if he didn't quite race home, he did expand the speed limit.

When he pulled into the driveway, he could see Joy through the shier curtains pulled across the kitchen windows. Everything looked fine. He bounced up the stone steps and onto the patio where he noticed their two cats sitting on the other side of the glass door waiting for him to come in. He opened the door and stepped inside onto the granite floor. The two cats, a big orange stray that had adopted them and a small black Siamese they had purchased from the humane society, took jealous turns curling around his ankles.

"Let me get my boots off, you knuckleheads, before I trip over you."

"They're just happy to see you, Tom," Joy called from the kitchen as he walked in. "What do you want on your salad?"

He bent down slightly to nuzzle her neck and whispered, "Just you, Hon, with no dressing."

Giggling like a schoolgirl, she pushed him away and said, "Maybe later, it is Friday."

Saturdays Tom would go grocery shopping with Joy. They treated these opportunities to be together as a date, getting out of the house and spending some time together. On nice days, they would take the truck and load the groceries in the back. They would begin their trek with drive thru coffee, sipping on it while driving between their various grocery gathering destinations.

As the truck turned into the donut shop drive thru, Tom noticed the same group of raggedy guys that he had dealt with yesterday. They were just staring at the truck as he drove in to place his order so he tried not to alert Joy's curiosity by reacting to their stares. He hadn't mentioned the previous day's altercations to his wife because she would worry. Her first reaction, after asking if he was all right, would be to chastise him for putting himself in harm's way and asking, "What if they followed you home and did something?" He had no answer for these legitimate concerns, only the feeling that he had done the right thing. Tom had always believed in helping when he saw the need.

Sunday dawned bright and warm. Tom had his coffee at six while he watched the news, went upstairs, shaved and got dressed. He was just going out the door when Joy came into the kitchen. Tom swept her into his arms, gave her a smooch on the cheek and said, "See you in an hour, Hon, I'm off to church."

"Do you have some money for collection?" she asked.

"I've still got some of my allowance left," he joked as he let her go and walked out the door. Joy didn't come to church with Tom as often as she used to. Bouts of insomnia sometimes kept her up for days at a time and when she was sleeping well, Tom wasn't going to disturb her to attend the early service on a Sunday morning. He also knew, without reservation, that attending service three times a week would still leave him unable to summon half the goodness and mercy for others that his wife embodied and shared with everyone. Of all the souls Tom had met in this life, there was no one that came closer to being a living angel than Joy.

They called themselves the eight o'clockers, the hardy souls who trekked to church early on Sunday mornings. For Tom, this early morning ritual always granted him peace. The air smelled sweeter and the drive was always on roads empty of traffic. After parking he'd stroll up the sidewalk and gaze at his church, its buttressed walls of grey limestone rising out of the sweep of green lawn like strong, wide shoulders carrying the sky.

Monday morning came quickly as all Monday mornings seem to do. This particular Monday, Tom and his crew were starting early so they could meet the boom truck delivering their framing lumber. As Tom waited in the driveway for Billy to get to the truck, he thought about seeing 'lightning bolt' and his group at the coffee shop the previous Saturday. He was contemplating the nature of these fools and the paths they'd taken when Billy, with the unappreciated energy and bounce of youth, jumped into the truck.

“Hey Boss, what’s up?”

“You ready to start working on a case of tennis elbow?” Tom quipped. “Over the next ten days we’ve got about two hundred pounds of three and a half inch galvanized spikes to hammer into lumber. You ready boy?”

“Yes, I am,” Billy replied. He loved pounding nails.

As they drove out of town, Tom noticed Billy’s silence.

“What’s up kid, you not feeling well?”

“I’ve been thinking,” Billy said slowly, “About your run in with those guys on Friday.”

“What about it?”

“Well…why would those guys not stop when they bumped into that woman in the parking lot?”

Tom considered that a moment and then replied, “I don’t think it was an accident. I think they saw someone weaker than themselves and they went out of their way to hurt her. They could easily have run around her but they thought no one would bother them if they trampled her, so they did. If you can’t protect yourself, it seems no one else will either.”

“Except for you, Tom,” Billy said with deep respect.

“Billy, you would have done the same. You certainly have the skills, you prove that during every one of our sparring classes.”

“I don’t know, Boss; I hope I would’ve. Can I ask you a question?”

“Shoot.”

The question caught Tom off guard. “What do you think about God, I mean, why do you think He lets bad things happen?”

“That’s a pretty complex question, Kid. Better men than I have been trying to figure out the answer to that one for…well, a long time. I don’t have a definitive answer for you…but I’ll tell you what I think. OK?”

“OK.” Replied Billy.

“OK then.” Tom was conscious of the road as he organized his thoughts. “First of all…you gotta keep this one thing in mind; no human can understand the mind of God, so when we try to make sense of God’s purpose, we are really only fumbling around in the dark, but fumble we must because humans are cursed with trying to figure everything out. I personally think the answer hinges on the concept of free will.

“All humans exercise free will whenever they make a choice. They choose either course A or course B. If they choose course A, their life continues on in that direction, if they choose course B, their life continues in that direction. God can see the potential future of that person no matter which choice they make before they ever make the choice. In essence, He can follow your future path in either choice before you make it. He already knows where each choice will take you before you make it. Multiply that by the millions of potential choices that will be put before you in all your different potential future paths. Then multiply that by the billions of people on earth and you may have a small inkling of the power of God's mind."

"But if He is so powerful and all-knowing, why doesn't God have us make the right decision each time?" asked Billy, starting to get lost in all this metaphysical, multiverse thinking.

"Well Bill," Tom said slowly, talking while he thought it out and making sure part of his mind was on driving, "I believe God decided at the beginning to allow us to make our own choices, for right or wrong. Then throw in the fact that the devil tries to subvert our free will by trying to coerce you into always making the wrong or evil choice and you can see how complicated this gets."

"The devil?" Billy questioned, gaping at Tom with his mouth open, "Are you saying you believe in the devil?"

"Belief in an ultimate good concedes an ultimate evil."

It had been a long day and as Tom dragged one foot after the other up the stairs to bed, he understood the wisdom of living in a bungalow. Tom laid his head back on the folded pillow and pulled the sheet and comforter up. He turned and gave his sleeping wife a kiss and lay back to begin his private litany of prayer that ended his day. He asked for forgiveness of his sins; mostly his pettiness and impatience. He asked God to bless his wife and his children and to say hello to his parents. He was sure they had a place in heaven though they hadn't been religious. They had been fair and honest folks who were good to their neighbors and loved their families. When the four of them had passed away within a year, it had been devastating. They still felt the loss eight years later. He drifted into sleep before he ended the 23rd psalm.

It seemed only a few seconds had passed when Tom was yanked from sleep by a sudden noise. The numbers on the alarm clock read 4:16 so he knew he had been asleep for almost six hours. *Must've been a dream*, he thought sleepily. He heard the cats running and that brought him quickly and fully awake. Every night he closed the doors to the living hall where the stairs to the second floor were located to keep the cats from disturbing their sleep. If he could hear the cats, then the door had been opened.

Tom didn't want to alarm Joy so he slid out of bed quietly. The restored oak floors squeaked so Tom inched forward on his hands and knees. As he made his way cautiously through the bedroom door and into the big hallway, he definitely heard a chirp from the stairs. His senses on high alert, he approached the head of the stairs with extreme caution. Keeping low, he peered around the corner and down the flight of stairs. In the familiar darkness of his home, he could just make out the deeper shadow of an intruder, hunched slightly and moving slowly up the steps.

Tom watched the intruder place his foot on the next step and ease his weight forward. The trespasser was a third of the way up the stairs when he turned slightly to look back. Tom saw his chance and threw himself into the space taking the intruder low with the full impact of his weight. They hit the floor hard with Tom on top. He smashed his elbow hard onto the man's solar plexus and felt the foul breath explode from his mouth. The intruder, in an agony of pain and gasping for breath, rolled over in a desperate attempt to flee this misery. Tom wrapped his legs around his abdomen and began to squeeze. He grabbed a clawing hand and forced it back up along his spine. He could hear the shoulder separate, like pulling apart a big turkey leg.

Joy screamed and Tom turned to see her at the top of the stairs. "Joy, nine one one…NOW!" Those were his last words as his senses exploded and he was engulfed in a blinding light and a sound like someone opening a car window at a hundred miles an hour.

Gasping and gagging for air that wasn't there, mucus and spit blowing out of his mouth and nose, his eyes crusty and blind, Tom clawed his way back to consciousness. Acrid smoke and searing heat slammed his senses and the concussive blast of pain in his head forced him to vomit, spewing bile over his face and neck. Afraid of aspirating his vomit, Tom instinctively rolled onto his stomach. Vomiting had temporarily cleared his head but he could not see even though he thought his eyes were open. *Smoke*, he thought, *Stay low, crawl away from the heat.* He quickly realized the heat was coming from the floor, he had to get away, the finish on the hardwood was melting to his hands and knees and blisters were boiling across his skin.

Tom scuttled in a circle, blindly feeling for a change in floor temperature. His flailing blistered hand slapped into the bottom step and he quickly pulled himself onto the tread and immediately felt the heat lesson. *Joy! My God, Joy is upstairs*, his mind screamed and he began crawling up the stairs. The smoke was dense but the heat lessened the further he went. After an agonizing effort he reached the upper landing and tumbled into unconsciousness. Fresh drafts from an open window revived him.

"Joy!" he screamed.

"Joy…where are you!"

"Oh God," no answer.

He could just see, as through a heavy mist, tears and stinging smoke throwing a wall of fog up before him. Tom crawled forward, hands and knees wet with blood and fluid from broken blisters, shreds of skin sloughing off on the quickly warping oak floor. The heat began to build again as Tom neared the bedroom door. Grabbing the door jamb, he hauled himself up to a kneeling position. He called for Joy again as he used his blurred vision to scan the room. All his tortured eyes could see was an indistinct shape lying diagonally across the bed. The heat of the floor was increasing quickly now. The oak flooring was curling and smoking. As Tom tried to stand, he began to slip on melted skin and polyurethane. His grip on the scorching door jamb tightened as he pulled himself erect with one mighty heave. As he gained his footing and leaned to lurch forward his world erupted in a firework of sparks and exploding pieces of wood. The floor beneath his seared feet collapsed and Tom's world ended.

Chapter 2

There was something he was trying to remember, something sweet and tender something that would make him cry if he could only remember. There was a noise though, a cash register ringing, pulling him away, but from where?

The man tried to open his eyes and wished he hadn't. The brightness stabbed his brain like two hammered spikes. From a hundred miles away and drifting further he heard, "Get the nurse."

The next time he tried to open his eyes the brightness was muted. He tried to speak but his throat was glued shut and all that came out was "Guh." An angel sighed, "Shhhhh." It seemed an age later when the angel's voice purred, "Don't try to speak." A glorious feeling of cool tenderness trickled down his ravaged throat to moisten and lubricate. He began to work his lips loose and move his tongue. He suddenly realized the angel was holding ice to his cracked and crusted lips.

"More," he croaked. The angel slipped a sliver of the glorious ice into his mouth and he rolled it around on his tongue and let the melting liquid slide down his throat. His name was bliss.

Days blurred together in a timeless routine of partial sentience and floating oblivion. When awake he was oblivious and when asleep he was searching. Searching for something. It was sweet and tender and would make him cry if he could only remember. It was gone though; he'd lost it in the brightness before the ice.

He awoke to soft light and clean-smelling sheets. "Where…" his strength failed him and he couldn't finish the thought.

"You're in the hospital and you're alive."

The light in the room was blurred and softened by the light gauze bandage that loosely wrapped his face. He couldn't discern anything more than shadow shapes and soft white light. His sense of touch told him that he was wrapped in the same soft gauze that covered his face and his nose told him he was enveloped in clean. His ears acquainted his mind with the familiar voice he was hearing that he couldn't quite place. He knew he should know it.

"We're here with you, daddy, we're here in the hospital with you."

The hospital staff and his doctors were amazed that Tom was alive and recovering. He was soon able to speak with them and his family. Every day he grew stronger and soon was told what he already knew. When he was moved from ICU into the ward, his friends were allowed to come and visit. His children were amazed at the number of people who came by to keep company with Tom. They had no notion of the lives their father's had touched. Even though staying with their father was not a burden, they eventually needed to get back to their own lives, their schooling, their jobs and their loves. Over the course of several days, they each said their private farewells and left him in the caring hands of the hospital staff and his close friends.

After weeks of recovery, the day arrived to remove Tom's bandages. His doctor had been preparing Tom for this day and it was not a pleasant future the doctor was steeling him against. It had been months since the night of the fire when the doctor and two nurses came into his room.

"Well Doc," Tom said, "Let's see what we've got."

Still swaddled from head to foot, Tom had to rely on his sense of touch and his hearing to know what was happening. He could feel the doctor's gentle prodding as he began removing the bandages from his hands and arms. He could hear the nurses move about as they collected the discarded bandages. What he couldn't see were the glances darting between the three medical professionals as the layers were peeled away from his limbs. One of the nurses allowed a quick intake of air to pass her lips.

"That bad, Doc?" Tom was expecting the worst, was ready for it and he wanted to try and help the nurses and doctor through this any way he could.

"No…Tom…not really…" Doctor Bailey was struggling for words. He had never seen a recovery like this before and didn't want to relay any false hope through his demeanor. "You know Tom…I was here that night…I was in emergency when the paramedics brought you in." The doctor spoke slowly and quietly, just above a whisper, he knew Tom could hear him easily.

"When they brought you in, Tom, I was prepared to call it. I could just hear you breathing, barely, each breath torn from you, I expected each one to be your last." Doc Bailey kept speaking to Tom as he gently and with infinite care snipped away at the bandages.

"You kept breathing, shallow and raspy, but you kept it up. It took me twenty minutes just to find a spot where I could attach an IV." Dan continued snipping at the biosynthetic dressing, lightly folding back the cut dressings and tenderly removing each piece with his forceps. "We stayed with you that night and into the next day. You refused to stop breathing. We had you on Ringer's and we were cooling you but our treatment wasn't going any further. We debated airlifting you out to Sunnybrook or even Sick Kids, but we knew you wouldn't survive the transport. We decided to keep you here, pump you full of antibiotics, give you fluid resuscitation and keep you under close observation."

Doc Bailey spent the next few minutes looking closely at the skin he'd exposed. "You didn't die on us so we took the opportunity to have a deep-burn specialist come in from the University of Alberta. She observed you for a day and gave us her assessment and a course of treatment, and now here we are three months later."

Dan straightened up and was lost in thought for a minute. "How does this feel?" Dan asked as he gently probed Tom's shoulder with his index finger.

"I don't know Dan; feels like you're touching my shoulder."

"What about this?" Doc Bailey took his thumb and finger and placed them on the skin of Tom's pectoral. He gently but firmly began separating them to pull the skin tight.

"It's doesn't hurt, Dan, but it is becoming uncomfortable," replied Tom.

"You worked out didn't you…I mean before the fire?"

"Well ya, you know I helped teach a martial arts class and we did work out with the students, but that's all. I wasn't hittin' the gym or pumpin' iron if that's what you mean."

"Nurse, would you bring up the light a little. See here, do you see this?"

"See what Doc, what's the matter, what's wrong?"

"Nothing is the matter, Tom," replied Dan, "it's just that…well…it doesn't appear as if you are carrying much fatty tissue. A man of your age should have a certain percentage of body fat, a prevalent build up between muscles, organs and skin, but you don't."

The doctor and nurses continued removing the dressings from the rest of Tom's body, leaving his face and head for last. With quiet amazement they noted the complete lack of scarring on any portion of Tom's new skin. Except for a complete lack of any body hair, their patient looked as if he'd just come from a vigorous rub down at the spa.

“Tom, I haven’t wanted to say much about your recovery to this point but I don’t think I’m mistaken when I say it is miraculous.”

Head Nurse Rosa Demarco looked up from gazing at Tom’s prone figure and cleared her throat. She turned to Doctor Bailey and said, “Dan, I have been in medicine for almost thirty years. You are not mistaken…this is a miracle.”

“Well, Tom,” said Dan, “Shall we ask for one more miracle and remove the last of the dressing?”

“Sure Dan, carry on.”

Half an hour later the rest of the bandages had been removed from Tom’s face and head. Only two gauze patches rested on his eyes and overlapped at the bridge of his nose.

“Everything looks pretty good Tom, except for a bit of swelling around your face. Mostly at your lips and around your nose. It appears to be slightly swollen under the gauze at your eyes also. Nurse, would you lower the lights right down so we can remove the gauze.”

“Certainly, Doctor Bailey.”

“Okay Tom, here we go,” Doctor Bailey said quietly. “Now…as I…lift the pads off your eyes don’t try to open them right away.”

“Nurse, would you get the moistened towelettes ready please.”

“Tom…I’m going to have Rosy moisten your eyelids a bit. She’s going to gently massage the lids to remove any mucus or buildup of any kind that may have crusted your eyelids and made them hard to open.”

“That’s it, nurse…nice and gently…beautiful…thank you.”

Having his eyelids lightly rubbed like that felt wonderful. For weeks his eyes had itched and he wasn’t able to touch them. He could imagine how futile he must’ve looked trying to rub his eyes with bandaged face and hands.

“Okay Tom, I’m going to ask you to slowly open your eyes please. If you notice any discomfort or the light seems too bright, stop, alright?”

He had to make what he thought was a real effort to get his eyelids to begin parting. In his excitement, he had almost forgotten that he hadn’t opened his eyes in almost three months. The thought made him recall the last thing these eyes of his had seen, his beloved Joy laying limply across their bed. That thought brought tears to his eyes and this aided him.

“Tom…tell me what you see.”

"Everything is blurry, Dan…I can make out light and dark…I can see dark blobs moving through the light areas but that's about it. My eyes are starting to sting a bit now."

"Okay Tom…that's good for now…close your eyes and rest."

Tom closed his eyes slowly and returned to the comforting darkness.

"Tom."

"Ya Doc."

"We're going to pull the covers up now so you don't get cold. We're not going to use the tent frame but we'll lay the covers right over your skin. Would you let me know if there is any discomfort?"

"Sure Doc."

"Okay Tom, how does that feel?"

"It feels great, Dan, I feel quite comfortable without the bandages on anymore. Can I move around to get comfortable? I don't want to do something wrong. Is it healed enough to move around?"

"You move as much as you need to get comfortable. I don't think you'll do any damage to your skin. It is truly miraculous."

"Thanks for everything, Dan." Tom yawned as he said this, a wave of fatigue washing over him making him feel like he hadn't slept in days. "I think I'll take a nap now." With that Tom was fast asleep.

Tom's miraculous recovery continued and his release from the hospital came just as the news of his investigation by the Police broke. Joy's older brother, George, a very successful businessman sent his own lawyer to see Tom. After a lengthy interview he reassured Tom that he thought the chances of an indictment on drug trafficking were slim. This good news was quickly followed by a notice from Tom's insurance carrier that payment on his house insurance would be held up pending an investigation into the circumstances of the fire. Tom received a similar notification concerning the pay out of death benefits from Joy's life insurance policy. His concern for the future once his meager savings were depleted was short lived for George stepped in and forced Tom to accept his help. George would not bow to Tom's stubborn pride and finally convinced him to consider his help a loan, to be paid back when the insurance carriers finished their ridiculous investigations. The police didn't want Tom leaving town so he found himself an affordable one-bedroom apartment.

Returning to the apartment late one afternoon about a month after his release from hospital, Tom could hear the phone ringing. He reached it just before the answering machine came on. "Hello."

"Hi Tom, it's brother George…how are you?"

"Well George…alright, I guess. The case against me was just thrown out of court so that's good news. I'm just feeling a little low, wondering, you know…"

"Hey Tom, it's all right, what you're feeling is not uncommon. I was calling to see if you would come up for a couple of days. Marianne's in Vancouver with Allison helping her get settled in for her last year at Simon Fraser."

"Good for her, George. Give them my love, would you. I think I'll stick around here though, I'm not fit company for anyone."

"Tom, if you don't come up here, I'm coming down there. I don't know what your one bedroom is like but I think you'd enjoy yourself a lot more up here with me than down there with me. You know I get like a bear when I'm in a confined place."

"Dammit George…I don't want any company!"

"I'm not company, Tom, I'm family. Throw something in an overnight and get your ass up here or I swear I'm on my way. You need family now; you need to talk."

Tom had nothing to say in reply and bowed to the inevitable. "OK…you're right, George. OK then. See you in three hours."

"Great Tom…I'll have coffee and Bailey's waiting."

It suddenly felt like a weight had been lifted from Tom's shoulders. He was glad that George had insisted he spend some time with him. Right now, he couldn't think of anyone he would rather be with. Having this ludicrous charge of drug dealing finally over with gave Tom hope that he might be able to start making some sense of where his life might now be headed. He threw some clothes and his overnight kit into a bag and left his apartment. There was a late summer rain falling, little more than a scotch mist. He threw his bag into the back seat of his F 150 and jumped up into the cab. Two minutes later, he was pulling out of the parking lot and into traffic. An hour later he was on the 401 heading west. Two hours after that he reached the Bayview Avenue exit and left the 401. A pleasant drive down Bayview and he turned onto Post Road.

Just past the Bridle Path intersection, Tom turned left through the open gate and onto the cobblestone driveway of George's home.

Tom had never realized the extent of George Twittle's success until he and Joy had visited George's home for the first time. The Post Road address put the home in Toronto's exclusive Bridle Path neighborhood known as Millionaire's Row. George and Marianne's home was a sprawling five-thousand square foot, two-story home with multiple roof lines and steep pitched gables. The house was finished in the same light grey and cream-colored limestone as the roadside gates. A large three car garage extended from the side. The house was visually stunning, from the columned front entry to the black slate roof but what caught your eye the first time you drove through the gates and down the oak lined drive were the gardens. Across the entire front of the home and down each side were elevated flower beds. Each level contained flowering perennials; bushes, ivies, trees and groupings of single plants. They were organized so that as the seasons progressed the colors and perfumes were always changing but never absent. The levels of the garden were maintained and separated by stone walls of the same limestone that clad the house, with dark mulch setting off the light-colored stone. On first sighting the home it appeared as if the structure itself was rising up out of the surrounding gardens. For this reason, Marianne had chosen to call her home Stone Garden.

On Tom and Joy's first visit after the gardens were completed, Marianne had told Joy that her home in Coalmen had been the inspiration for the extensive network of raised gardens surrounding their home. She made Joy cry when she presented her with the matching twin to her own bronze plaque with the word Stone Garden scrolled across the metal face deeply etched in a flowing script. The love that Joy had for her sister-in-law was strengthened immensely when Marianne told her she would be proud if both homes wore the plaques together. One of the first things Tom did when he and Joy returned home from that visit was to embed the bronze plaque in the red clay brick of their hundred-year-old home.

These bittersweet memories filled Tom as he turned up George's driveway. The gardens were in full, late summer bloom. The hosta were flowering, the long white blooms filling the air with their sweet honey flavored perfume. Rose bushes bloomed in red and white along the specially constructed trellises that carried the colors up the home's stone walls. Sharing the trellises were the white and mauve flowers of the clematis ivies. The flowing colors had the effect of an impressionist's canvas.

As Tom turned off the ignition and stepped down from the cab of his truck, he saw George throw open the large front door and swoop down the wide stone steps, taking them two at a time. He threw his arms around Tom and squeezed him in a rib-crushing bear hug. "God Tom…it is so good to see you!"

"Good to see you too," said Tom, twisting a bit from side to side to make sure his ribs were still intact.

"Grab your stuff and let's get inside. I've got drinks set up on the back patio."

"Sounds awfully good, George."

That first evening together passed in quiet conversation. George was apologetic for not having been able to come and see more of him but Tom would have none of that for he knew George had taken care of the memorial for Joy while Tom was fighting for his life. He also knew that George had spent many days and nights with Tom's three kids, making sure that rents and tuitions were paid, making sure that the kids took care of themselves and always had a shoulder to cry on and wise council to depend on. It was also George's Bay Street lawyer that had come to Tom's rescue on more than one occasion and George would not accept any recompense from Tom. He and George had a good laugh when Tom tried to describe the look of utter horror and amazement on the faces of the prosecutor and judge when George's lawyer, Tigran Abrahamyan, first walked into the courtroom.

"I swear, George; the prosecutor did so many double takes looking from Mr. Abrahamyan and then back to me, I thought his head would twist right off. The judge at first couldn't believe that a lawyer of Mr. Abrahamyan's standing was actually in his court. He was damn near apoplectic when he found out Tigran was there to represent me. He couldn't throw the case out fast enough. I truly believe he was mortally afraid that Tig was going to make him look like a fool."

"And he would have," piped in George. "God I would have paid money and then sold seats to my friends if they had decided to continue with that farce. Did you know that Tig would only accept payment to cover his traveling time from here to Coalmen and back. That guy hates injustice more than any man I know. I think it has to do with his work trying to get official recognition of the Armenian Genocide."

"He's a good man, George."

"He sure as hell is, Tom."

"You know, George…I've met some of your friends and associates, and it occurs to me that you are fortunate in that regard. You have always surrounded yourself with good and decent people. I admire that and I'm also a little envious."

"I've had to deal with my share of scumbags, Tom, I just choose not to spend any more time with them than I have to. You're no slouch when it comes to choosing good and decent people to be close to, my sister for one."

"Being with me may not have been a wise choice for her though," replied Tom quietly, looking down into the ice in his drink.

"You can put that thought right out of your head, Tom. Joy was head over heels in love with you from the moment she laid eyes on you till…well…you know…"

"But George, we didn't have that much. We worked all the time, no fancy vacations. We had a nice home but we built that ourselves. She was so fun and beautiful…she could have married a much more successful man than I. Hell…if she'd moved up here, she probably would have had her own design firm. I let her down so terribly…I…" Tom's voice trailed off into silence.

"Tom…Dammit man! Look at me."

Tom lifted his head up and stared into George's hazel eyes. He marveled at how much George's eyes reminded him of Joy's.

"I knew my sister from the moment she was born. I knew her ups and downs, I knew when she was angry or sad, happy and content. I've even seen her with bloody murder in her eye. In all her life I never saw her happier than when she was with you."

"I don't know what to do, George. I'm lost without her. I can't figure out why this happened to us. So many things, no answers."

"Put your trust in the future, Tom. I know that sounds like a hollow platitude but I think you are going to get your answers. It's just a feeling I have, nothing concrete. You are a good and decent man Tom…follow your heart."

"That's just it though…my heart is dead, George; it won't lead me anywhere."

"Maybe not now it won't. You need to reconnect with all the things in your life that made it worth living. Bring back that love into your life that you and Joy shared."

"That love is dead and buried!" Tom couldn't believe the bitterness he heard in his own voice, he felt ashamed of his reaction.

"That's bullshit, Tom. Your children aren't dead. They need you and you need them. That's where you start to get that love back. Your friends aren't dead, Marianne and I aren't dead. We need you, Tom. Take our love and let it grow inside you. All the people you know at church and in the community, they need you Tom and they love you."

"That sounds so much like advice that Joy would have given. She loved so deeply and I think that's why she was loved so much."

"And Tom…"

"Yes."

"God loves you and that will never leave you."

Tom realized he'd been holding his breath. He let out a whoosh and then sucked in a big lungful of air. The wool that had been packed around his brain for the last few months began to clear away. "Damn George, how could I have forgotten that? I am such an idiot. Joy's love is still with me and I will see her every time I look at the kids. You've given me back hope brother, thanks."

The two men sat in comfortable silence for a minute or two. The only sounds were the clinking of ice in their glasses as they sipped at their drinks.

Uncertainly Tom asked, "I didn't know you were a religious man George. I don't think I've ever heard you speak of your faith or of a belief in God?"

"I'm what you would call a Pelagiust," George replied. "I don't go to church; I don't believe man requires a church to become closer to God. I pray for guidance every night before I go to bed and I try to let Our Father guide my steps each day."

Tom looked at George with a new understanding of this man that he had admired for as long as he'd known him. He was intrigued by what his brother in law had just told him but didn't quite know how to phrase his reply. "What do you mean by 'guide your steps each day'? Do you mean your decisions? You ask for guidance in your decision making?"

"Of course. I don't ask for specific guidance for every decision I make, the small ones, they just happen without much forethought. The larger decisions, I listen to my soul. When the decisions are business choices, I obviously do my due diligence, but then I consider how those decisions will impact all those around me. Who, if any, may be hurt? Who benefits? Are my decisions ego based? I pray each night that the guidance I receive will help me to always choose good."

"But it's easy to say you always want to choose good, but how do you know for sure what is good?"

"You know what is good, Tom. We all know what is good. We all know what is evil. Every child is born into a state of grace, free from sin, knowing instinctively what is good and what is evil. What happens to some people that turns them into the types that consciously make choices for evil, I don't know. That's a subject for another discussion, but you Tom…you are a good man and I think you've been making decisions for good all your life. It's in your nature to be good and truthful so that when it comes time to make the important decisions, for you, there is no agonizing over whether you're making the right decision, you just naturally choose the good."

It had been a long day and the subject of their conversation, although interesting, was getting too deep. He finished the last of his now diluted drink and told George he would hit the hay.

"One more thing Tom, I've got something to show you."

They got up from their easy chairs by the fireplace and Tom followed George. He walked out of the den and down the hall past the two-piece lavatory and the large laundry room. They went through a door and entered the large cloak room that was just off the oversize three-car garage. They walked past two brand new Lincolns, one a Navigator and one a Lincoln truck.

"Sweet," said Tom.

"They are, aren't they," said George. "What I want to show you is in here."

He took Tom to the far side of the garage where there was a door into the third bay. He swung open the door with a flourish. Tom walked inside and when George flicked on the light, Tom couldn't believe his eyes. There in front of him was the toughest-looking, most beautiful truck he had ever seen.

"You're looking at a prototype. It is an advanced design F150 Sabre. It's got a 6.5 liter 650 HP V10 engine with a 6-speed automatic transmission. It's a true all-wheel drive, we call it abbreviated drive, to all four wheels. The entire bottom is covered by a skid plate. This is a tank designed by Ferrari."

"My God, George…it is beautiful."

"I thought you'd like it, being a truck guy."

"What is on the body. I can't quite focus on it. Is it the lighting in here?"

"Look closely, Tom, the entire truck is a super flat, matte black. The paint absorbs light. There is not a speck of shine anywhere or a color on it that isn't black. The cab has been chopped down for a low profile, the windows are tinted in a zero-glare flat black that is the darkest you can get. It has 21-inch gas-filled Pirelli's made of soft rubber that haven't got any raised lettering on them. Pirelli hasn't even got a name for them yet."

"Why would Ford make a prototype like this? Looks to me like this truck would be invisible at night or even on a cloudy day."

"You're absolutely right. Ford has been working for the last few years to put together a beefed-up SUV for the U. S. diplomatic core. They invented this paint and it caught the interest of…shall we say…the more clandestine parts of the overseas diplomatic service."

"Wow!" And Tom meant it. "Let me look under the hood."

"Can't."

"Why?"

"There is no hood to open."

Tom walked over to the front of the truck. George was right. There was no hood to open or radiator and grill. The headlights wrapped around the entire front of the vehicle.

"This is very interesting, George, but how do you service it?"

George let Tom twist for a bit longer as they both admired the clean lines of the Sabre prototype.

"The engine uses high octane fuel, but it uses it very efficiently. This truck will run close to seventy-five kilometers on a liter of gas. Its fuel combustion temperature is about two and a half times higher than a normal engine. The gas vapor is totally consumed. There are no measurable by products of combustion. The only thing coming out of the exhaust is cool air."

"Amazing. If the gas is burned so hot, how come there's cool air out the tailpipe?"

"The engine runs so hot that it had to be constructed out of high-tech ceramics, something like the heat shield on the space shuttle. The cooling system is a high pressure closed loop system that uses liquid gas technology. There's not an auto mechanic on earth who could service this engine."

"How do you get at the engine, I mean…at some point you have to be able to do maintenance on it…don't you?"

"Very little," answered George, who was having great fun, not only because he was proud of their products in general and this one in particular but because he was seeing life in the form of curiosity coming back into Tom's face. "This particular engine configuration needs servicing about once every two hundred thousand miles."

Tom just stared at the truck, mouth open.

"We hoist the vehicle up; the skid plate drops down and then the entire engine is lowered down out of the front cavity."

"I didn't know the technology for this type of engine had been invented yet?"

"The technology was all there, the engineers at Ford had to design the engine components and systems to use that technology and make it robust enough for everyday usage. It was the paint that was the invention. It actually absorbs light. The military is looking into its applications for making vehicles stealthy."

"Can we take it for a spin?"

George chucked the key over to Tom, although they were unlike any keys Tom had ever seen.

"Go ahead, it's yours…I mean it's yours to drive for a while, you can't own it because it's not for sale."

"Quit foolin' around George, I only wanted to go for a quick spin not have you make fun of me."

"I'm not kiddin' Tom. The truck is yours for a while to test drive for us. Several of these prototypes were built, all exactly the same. The engineers in Dearborn are running a couple of these babies around a secret track somewhere but they wanted to know how these vehicles would perform being driven and handled by non-engineer types. Some of the higher volume sales organizations were given the option of test driving one of the seven or eight trucks remaining. I'm the only Canadian tester."

"Then why don't you drive it?"

"Tom, I drive to the dealership and home. I'm boring. I don't off road, I don't go on long trips. Hell, when I have to drive downtown, I get one of our courtesy vehicles to drive me where I have to go. Having me test drive this prototype would be a waste of a neat truck."

"But I only drive to and from work."

"Ya, but your drives to work are different for every job site. You drive with passengers and you drive alone. You load your truck with materials and you drive in every weather condition. You drive around Coalmen in your truck. You hate cars. You are the market for trucks."

Tom looked down at the 'key' in his hand. It was round, about one inch in diameter, and fairly weighty for its small size. It was attached to a platinum-colored Twittle Ford key chain. He closed his fingers around it and turned toward the driver's side door of this incredible machine.

"George?"

"Yes, Tom." There was mirth in George's voice.

"There is no door handle!"

"Take the initiating sensor and place it on the indented circle where the door handle would be on a normal vehicle. Now before you do that, I want to tell you something. When you put the initiating sensor on the door disc, you are accepting my offer to test drive this truck. Do you understand?"

"Do you think I'm an idiot, George? Who wouldn't give their left nut to have this truck for a while?"

"OK then. When you initialize, the truck's security and GPS computer will ask you questions. Just answer it or do what it asks."

Tom placed the sensor on the door disc. It held there with what seemed a mild magnetic attraction.

A female voice with a slight mechanical affectation said, "State your full name."

Tom looked over at George who just smiled and nodded his head.

"Thomas Michael Joiner."

The female voice asked, "Do you prefer Thomas, Tom or Tommy?"

"Tom, thank you."

"Catch, Tom." The sensor fob jumped off the side of the truck door and with incredibly quick reflexes, Tom snatched the disc and chain out of the air.

"Please press your thumb followed by your index and middle fingers of both hands onto the door disc."

After Tom rolled the six digits gently on the circular depression the driver's side door clicked once and was unlocked.

"Your prints are now recognized by the vehicle security system," the slightly mechanical female voice said. "Press any of these digits to this or the passenger side door disc and the vehicle door lock will disengage. Say, door open, specifying which door and the door will open. The door locks may also be unlocked by saying, 'unlock while specifying which door', within a fifteen-foot radius of the vehicle. Repeat instructions for opening the vehicle door. The vehicle door locks may also be engaged by doing or saying the reverse."

Tom looked at the truck and said, "Lock all doors."

There was an immediate click at both doors. Tom reached over and tried wedging his fingers in the door seam but failed to find purchase. He said, "Unlock driver's side door." There was an almost inaudible click. Again, Tom tried to slide his fingers between the edge of the door and the body without success. He said, "Open driver's door." The door swung slowly open.

George chuckled and mentioned, "If you read the operator's manual, it's six hundred pages by the way, you'll see that the doors will open at different speeds depending on how demanding your voice is."

Tom closed the driver's door, stepped back and yelled as if he was in a hurry, "Open driver's door now!" The door swung immediately open and Tom was glad he had stepped back.

"What happens if you're beside another vehicle in a parking lot? Will the truck door dent the car next to it?"

"Nanotechnology, that I do not understand, has made the paint along the entire edge of the door a proximity sensor that keeps the door from striking anything if the open command is given with no stresses added," replied George. "Climb on in."

The floor of the truck was higher than most trucks of this size because of the larger tires and heavy-duty suspension. Tom didn't see any running boards to step up onto. As he approached the vehicle's open door, he looked around for a handle possibly molded into the upper post of the windshield support to grab onto. As he got close enough to the vehicle to step up onto the floor mat by the driver's seat, he heard a very slight whirr and the entire truck dropped eight inches.

"Whoaooo!" Tom exclaimed, as he stepped back for a moment.

"How cool is that, eh?" laughed George. "The entire truck lowers for entering the cab or loading stuff into the back."

"I love it," said Tom. He went to the truck and slid smoothly and without effort onto the leather seat. The truck glided up to its original height. As soon as he settled into the plush leather of the seat, Tom could feel it moving, under him and up his back, adjusting to his contours.

The feminine voice addressed him again, "Tom…are there any modifications to the seat contours you wish to make that you would prefer to those selected for you?"

"Yes…would you stiffen the lumbar support please?"

As soon as he had made his request, he could feel the lower back portion of the seat expand into him, pressing very comfortably on his lower back.

"Noted, are there further instructions?"

"As soon as I get into the driver's seat, winter or summer, would you turn on the seat heater please?"

"Done and noted. Anything more?"

"No, thank you. George…this is the most comfortable chair I have ever sat in. I may never leave this seat." Turning back to address the truck he enquired, "How do you turn this on? There's no key and no ignition."

"Say, start engine," the vehicle's feminine voice seemed to coo at him.

"Start…engine," Tom repeated. He looked at George, "Nothing's happened George, is it out of gas?" Tom laughed at the ridiculousness of such a high-tech vehicle not starting because of something as mundane as forgetting to fill the tank.

George just looked at him and said softly, "Don't depend on your ears, Tom."

Even though Tom could hear no sound coming from the engine, he could feel the slight vibrations under and around him.

"Shift into drive, Tom, but don't go anywhere. Keep your foot on the brake."

Tom put his hand on the black metal floor shifter and pushed it forward into 'D.' The dash display lit up and a four-point racing harness dropped down to secure him into his seat. The comfort he felt was immediately enhanced by the feeling of security the harness gave him.

"I would love to take this for a spin," said Tom, smiling from ear to ear, "But I've had a couple of drinks and I'm pretty tired to boot."

"We'll take it out tomorrow Tom. Shut'er down and we'll go in and have a night cap."

Tom and George went back in and made their way to the study. They ended up talking until nearly dawn. Tom spoke of things with George that only Joy and he had ever shared. Any fears George had for Tom's emotional recovery vanished that night and he knew that all of the qualities that he loved about his brother-in-law were on their way back.

As Tom's visit neared the two-week mark, he mentioned to George that he would be leaving the next day. "I'm going to take your advice and visit Grace and her husband. They're in Barrie so it makes sense to see them before I head home. What should I do with my truck…if it's still in your mind to have me keep test driving the Sabre I mean?"

"Of course, you're taking the Sabre and don't worry about your truck. When you got here, I had one of my service reps pick it up and take it to the Oshawa dealership. They'll store it for you until you're finished with the Sabre. I figure about a year to give it a really good test. What do you think?"

"You're pretty sure of yourself, aren't you?"

"Maybe to the outside world," he winked.

The next morning dawned fresh and clear, the quintessential Southern Ontario early fall morning. Tom loaded his overnight bag onto the back seat of the Sabre's cab. George came out with his morning cup of coffee steaming in the cool air and a traveling mug of fresh joe for Tom.

"Here Tom, save you some time, sittin' in the lineup at Tim's," he said as he handed the shiny coffee mug to Tom.

"Thanks George, and thanks for everything else. I think you got me to a place where I can actually look forward to life."

"I have no doubt you would have found your way there eventually. I'm just glad you came for a visit; I enjoy your company." George put his coffee down on one of the gardens retaining walls and threw his big arms around Tom. "Remember my friend, you are a good man. Trust your heart and trust in the path that opens before you."

"Thanks brother," Tom said as he got into the Sabre. "Start engine."

Tom took George's advice to heart and over the next several weeks he visited each of his children, only staying as long as their separate circumstances allowed. With each he had the opportunity to let them know how important they were to him and how their love made his life livable. He had many little stories for each of them concerning their mother and how their lives had enriched hers.

Once home he spent some time contemplating his future. He and Joy had lost most of the value of their small nest egg of retirement savings in the last recession, and were forced to rely on the equity in their home for any calculations concerning retirement. With the home now destroyed and his insurance claim held up by the arson investigation Tom had been forced to sell the house lot. He was now using that money to live on. Joy's life insurance policy had been paid out but the thought of using money that came to him as a result of losing her was unthinkable. He had divided the small amount between his three children and told them that he and Joy had always planned to do this.

The eight o'clockers were delighted to welcome him back into their fold. Handshakes, hugs and kisses extended his welcome to the point of delaying the start of service. As the minister was one of those in the aisle hugging Tom no one took notice. He spent the next couple of weeks renewing ties with various members of the congregation over coffee or dinner.

Tom began working again, accepting small contracts he could accomplish by himself. Before he knew it, Christmas had come and gone. The holidays had been spent with George and Marianne, and as a surprise for Tom they had invited Grace and her husband along with Tyler and Lilly. Grace had her own surprise for her Father; she had just found out that she was with child. Tom was overjoyed, excited and nervous for her all at the same time. The yuletide visit was crammed solid with much laughter, talk and plans for the future.

Chapter 3

Once back in Coalmen Tom's life got back to its new normal. He worked when he could and read voraciously. Every night he went down to the dojo to work out. He would exercise and practice with the various scheduled classes and then stay late to practice by himself. Whenever one of the other black belts stayed late to work out with him, they would invariably get the mats out and work on advanced techniques. Word got out that these after class workouts were becoming the most grueling practice sessions available for serious martial artists. Tom's late workouts became a class of their own and owing to their intensity were restricted to adult black belts. By spring the unremitting training had honed his skills to a new level. He was unaware of this until one night in early April.

Tom was demonstrating to his class a technique to disarm a knife-wielding adversary. This particular night his demonstration partner was a black belt student newly attending these sessions. He was a big man, in his early thirties, who carried the nickname Rhino. He had been burning up the local tournaments and thought he was pretty good, he also thought he was pretty tough and this combination can sometimes lead to uncomfortable situations.

Rhino was to attack Tom, slowly for the demonstration, with an overhead strike as if he was slashing down with a knife. Tom crossed his wrists in front of his chest and slowly pushed the two-handed block up toward the apex of Rhino's strike. Just as Tom got to that point Rhino said, "What do you do if your opponent decides to hit you when you're blocking the strike," and as he said this he punched viciously into Tom's exposed midsection. He felt like buckling over but managed to hold himself upright as he noticed Rhino standing tall and smiling at the group. He had the distinct impression that Rhino had decided to embarrass him.

Tom addressed the class. "We demonstrate these techniques in a slow and controlled way so that students have a chance to identify the components of the move. In an actual confrontation, we don't give the opponent time to change the dynamics of our technique. Also, if it does happen, it is up to you to react to the changes in the dynamic. Here, we'll demonstrate."

He nodded for Rhino to start the move again. Rhino's arm and hand went up over his head slowly, but quickly increased speed on the downswing. Tom was ready, he sent his block up at demonstration speed so the block met the hard downward swing halfway to his chest but his wrist snap was so fast that it stopped Rhino's accelerating downward strike instantly, sending a jolt through the big man's arm. Knowing there was another midsection punch coming he twisted his right wrist and hand to grab Rhino's thick wrist and pushed it down while pulling him in. His other hand, hard as a block of wood drove into Rhino's head just behind his ear and then pushed down onto the back of Rhino's neck. Still holding Rhino's right wrist, he brought his knee up into Rhino's exposed solar plexus. Everyone heard a whoosh of air explode from Rhino's lungs as he crumpled to the mat. Tom shifted his left hand from the back of Rhino's neck to the back of the meaty part of his shoulder, while still holding onto his right wrist. He pulled in on the shoulder while pushing Rhino's arm straight back nearly dislocating his shoulder joint and forced him to flip onto his back. As Rhino rolled, Tom stepped over him with his left foot but instead of letting his foot come to rest on the mat, he swung his body around using Rhino's extended arm as his pivot point. He let his body go over backward still holding Rhino's arm, now held by both of his hands. As soon as Tom's back contacted the mat, he brought his left leg down hard over Rhino's face and elevated his hips. He wrenched Rhino's right elbow over his pelvis putting him into a painful arm bar. The more Rhino thrashed around the tighter Tom held the lock. Rhino's free hand began pummeling Tom's legs and he started shouting and cursing. Tom looked calmly down the length of his torso at Rhino and said, "I'll let you up when you calm down."

Rhino yelled, "I'm gonna fucking kill you!" His gyrations and jerking movements turned violent.

"Once more, Rhino," Tom raised his voice. "You'll have to calm down before I release you."

There was no response, only wilder exertions to break free. Tom looked down at Rhino's face. It was almost purple with rage and held an expression of animal ferocity. He had no idea what Rhino might do if released but he knew he was beyond self-control. As Tom read the situation, he had one option. With speed and strength combined in a powerful movement, Tom snapped Rhino's wrist to the floor. A muffled squelch accompanied the breaking bones and Tom could see a large lump protrude from the middle of Rhino's forearm. With a grunt Rhino passed out and Tom untangled himself and stood up.

"Listen you guys, I'd better run Rhino over to the hospital. I think we're done for tonight."

Two guys approached Tom warily and bowed. One of them spoke, "Sensei…we're friends of Greggs…er…Rhino, and we'll run him over to emerg if you want. We're really sorry this happened. We'll let him know what an asshole he's been. Will he be able to return?"

"Only if he apologizes to the class for losing his discipline. Let's see if we can use this as a teachable moment okay?"

"Thank you, Sensei," they both said as they half walked half dragged their friend out of the dojo.

The rest of the group were still milling around as Tom thought about grabbing up his bag and heading for home. The group approached and began telling Tom of their problems concerning Rhino, ending when one of the female students said, "He was making it difficult on anyone he practiced with. I was going to stop coming."

Tom was surprised by this. "Really," he said, "Was he trying to hurt his practice partners?"

Tom's apprentice from the days before the fire, young Billy, stepped forward. "I know students who refuse to practice with Rhino. A couple of months ago we were partnered up and I thought he'd dislocated my knee. You know the drill; we fake a roundhouse to the knee and then flip up to the midsection? Well, Rhino drove his roundhouse right into my knee, no fake. We were doing ten slow, no contact, so I didn't have my leg planted properly then he kicks me hard in the midsection."

"What did you do Billy; did you talk to Sensei Jim?"

"No…I waited till we were practicing spinning sidekicks and I buried one in his gut!"

"I heard about that," Tom chuckled. "He puked, didn't he?"

After much discussion concerning Rhino and the negative affect he was having on the class it was decided that Tom had acted properly and in the best defense of his students. There would be a dozen witnesses to Tom's forced self-defense if Rhino pressed the issue of his injury. As the class was breaking up and Tom was heading for the door Billy came over to him.

"Got a sec, Sensei?"

"Sure Billy…what's up?"

It seemed for a minute that Billy wasn't going to speak. He was obviously trying to frame his question but wasn't having any luck. He finally just blurted out, "How have you been training to increase your speed so much? Would you show me."

"I haven't really been doing anything differently Billy, just training more that's all."

"Naw, that's not it. You were faster tonight than I've ever seen anyone move, I was looking right at you when Rhino sucker punched you the first time. I couldn't believe you didn't go down; he hit you with everything he had. I almost jumped in between you; then stopped myself when I noticed you were still on your feet."

"I felt the punch but I didn't think it was that hard."

"You didn't see the stunned look on Rhino's face when he noticed you still standing?"

"I only saw him smiling at the group just after his strike landed."

"You started to address the class and must have been looking at them instead of Rhino. When you started talking, he did a double take. He lost the smile when his jaw dropped. That was when I knew he was trying to hurt you."

"Hmmm, I wonder why?"

"I don't know Sensei; some guys just wanna be bad asses. Rhino sees himself as pretty tough. At class a couple of weeks ago, just after the Kingston tournament, he'd been boasting about how good he was, that no one around here was much competition. Someone mentioned that you were putting on some pretty grueling sessions and that he might find them useful. He said something like, 'what could he possibly learn from a washed-up old man who wouldn't even go to tournaments anymore.' I don't know who it was, but someone else told him about the guy you subdued in the parking lot last spring, and that you couldn't really measure a person's ability until it got serious. *Serious*, he said, *I'll give you serious.* That's when he started coming out to your classes. I guess tonight was when he decided to get serious with you. Poor Rhino!" Billy laughed out loud.

"I guess I got lucky and took him by surprise."

"Are you kidding me? Rhino didn't stand a chance. After that first punch, when I realized Rhino was trying to hurt you, I moved to the front. I saw what he was going to do when you started the demo again. You managed to block his speeded-up strike but you looked like you were out of position. I saw Rhino's fist start low to strike up under your floating rib, then you…you…blurred."

"I what…?"

"That's the only way to describe what I saw. After you blocked Rhino's overhead strike you moved so fast I couldn't make out what you were doing. Then for a second I saw you hesitate when you had Rhino's arm up and over his back. Then blur, you were on the mat with Rhino in an arm bar. Then you tried to calm him down and I'm thinkin', *geez Tom don't let him up*. I didn't think all the black belts in the room could've controlled him. He went nuts, then snap, it was over."

"Truthfully Billy, I don't know what I did that was any different from what I normally do. I saw what needed to be done and just did it. I wasn't thinking about the moves, the application of techniques, everything was muscle memory, my mind was in the moment but not controlling the moment. If that is the key to my supposed new found speed then I don't think I would be able to teach it. I would advise that continual practice may be the key to this speed Billy. Know your moves so well that your body performs them without having to let your mind get in the way."

Billy thought for a minute or two before he replied, "I think you're right Sensei and I think you've moved to a level different from the rest of us. I always enjoyed sparring with you. You were…are, a smart fighter. I had to keep my wits sharp when we sparred, but I always knew I could beat you eight times out of ten. I don't think I'll ever beat you again."

That conversation stayed with Tom for many days. It troubled him. He wasn't the type of martial arts teacher that intimidated his students. He would rather inspire them to be better. After all, isn't that what teaching is supposed to be, the advancement of the students' knowledge, not preening the ego of the teacher.

Since his autumn visit with George, Tom had been feeling increasingly better, more optimistic for the future. He thought he was coming to grips with his survival and having to live his life now without Joy, though there were still questions that late at night gnawed the edges of his sleep. *Why had those men broken into his house, why was there no investigation, who were they? How had he survived the fire? Where had the drugs found in his house come from*? These questions increasingly plagued Tom's thoughts. They began robbing him of sleep, bouncing around in his head, pumping adrenaline into his tired body as he lay in bed and fought for sleep. Prayer didn't help, the questions kept coming back, overriding his attempts at calming his troubled mind. On nights when sheer exhaustion forced sleep to smother his roiling thoughts he was tormented by dreams of the fire.

It was almost a year to the day from the incident in the supermarket parking lot. The anniversary unmarked by Tom, for after nearly a week of torturous insomnia Tom was practically suicidal. He was shunning his little bedroom, trying to fall asleep on the couch with the television playing.

It was Sunday night. He had barely maintained wakefulness that morning in church and had forced himself to remain awake during the day. If total exhaustion was his only path to sleep then by God he would exhaust himself. At ten o'clock he had turned on the TV and collapsed onto his couch. He balled up the cushion and placed it under his head and pulled the blanket up over his shoulders.

He began to pray, *Dear Father in Heaven, please help me, I am so lost. What is keeping me from sleep?* His thoughts progressed, *I'm missing something. I'm missing a purpose. I have no purpose. Dear Father what is my purpose? What is it I need to do?*

He was lying beside Joy. She glowed with an inner light, so pure it almost hurt to gaze on her. Her eyes were open, she smiled at him and all his pain was gone. "I love you Tom." He heard the cats on the landing, running. He saw the shadow on the stairs, creeping. He launched himself at the shadow and they were tumbling down the stairs. Tom brought his elbow up and let it crash down onto the intruder's chest. There was a flash of light, red like reflected fire. Tom looked down at the intruder, gasping in the gloom.

"Who are you?" he screamed.

Another splash of red as flames began to curl around them. The shadows fled and Tom saw the intruder's face clearly. He screamed, "Why did you kill my life?"

The image of the big man dissolved and Tom seemed to fall forward. When Tom opened his eyes, daylight streamed through his living room window. Tom had found sleep and he had found his purpose. He ate and showered and all along thought of nothing but his dream. The man he'd tackled the night of the fire was the same man who had knocked down Mrs. Patel in the parking lot. If this was true, then he had a connection. He had never seen the parking lot guy again after the original incident, but he had seen his friend, the guy with the lightning bolt tattoos on his knuckles and he knew where he hung out. This was where he would start, he would look for him tonight.

Neither the moon nor stars were visible. The night was without light, except for the mist shrouded halogens perched atop their high poles. No hint of color possessed the buildings, or cars or even the gathered people, everything described in flat shades of grey.

Tom parked his Sabre two blocks from the doughnut shop and headed toward the sound of harsh laughter. He approached the end of the parking lot where young men were smoking, and swearing. He moved slowly from shadow to shadow with a predatory grace that allowed for no wasted motion and attracted no attention. None of the young toughs alone in the parking lot had noticed him so he stopped abruptly and nodded his head. Surprised by his sudden closeness, the young men stepped back and turned toward him. Tom saw the young thug with the lightening tattoos. "I hear they call you Bolt. I'd like a word with you."

"Fuck off old man!"

"You're quite eloquent Mr. Bolt. I'd still appreciate that word though."

"You got shit for brains mister…beat it."

Knowing exactly where this was going Tom tried one more time, "Be that as it may, I'd still like a word with you in private."

"Want to suck my dick do ya?" Gales of ugly laughter erupted. "That's gonna cost you perv. Gimme your wallet."

The five young men formed a loose circle around Tom who just stood there calmly. His breathing was deep but relaxed, his peripheral vision expanded and everything in view had a razor-sharp intensity. The strangest sensation was of time slowing, his senses were processing stimuli very quickly. "If you must," was all he said as the watery light from above now winked on several cruel blades.

One evil-smelling thug moved in from Tom's right with arrogant disregard, his knife held high, pointing at his victim's face. Tom stepped in, closing the gap quickly and grabbed the surprised assailant's wrist. He shifted his weight to his back foot pulling the young man in, snapping a wicked side kick into his opponent's exposed ribcage. The edge of his foot cracked the air like a whip. As the attacker crumpled Tom noticed pink froth bubbling from his lips.

Two from the front rushed at him screaming obscenities. With knees slightly bent and in a relaxed fighting stance he simply moved to the side and as they passed, he caved in his nearest opponent's knee with a hard downward side kick. Tom felt a big hand grab his shoulder. He threw his arm forward and up, arcing over and around his adversary's hand, bringing his arm down behind the other man's arm and then driving forward hard, hyper extending the other man's elbow until it dislocated with a pop. Tom's adversary flew forward with the momentum of Tom's thrust and fainted dead away from pain.

"Three down," Tom deadpanned looking at Bolt.

The remaining two separated. They both had their weapons, one a serious-looking switchblade, Bolt, a large butcher knife that he now began slashing through the air back and forth. Switchblade made his move when Tom was directly between them. He flew at Tom throwing his arm straight out to stab into Tom's midsection. Stepping left Tom planted his right foot and twisted his body around into a spinning back kick catching switchblade right in the midsection. Switchblade crumpled forward into the downward arcing path of Bolt's butcher knife, the heavy, wickedly sharp blade carving down across the back of switchblades neck where it joined his shoulder. His left trapezius is severed while the long blade is lodged in the cervical vertebrae. The cleaver is wrenched out of his hand as switchblade's lifeless body falls to the pavement.

Tom came silently now to Bolt who'd just witnessed his crew of four decimated in under fifteen seconds by an old man. Tom grabbed a handful of Bolt's greasy brown hair close to the scalp and holding his head firmly, struck the heel of his other hand down hard on the back of Bolt's neck just below his skull. Like a bag of hammers Bolt dropped straight down.

Tom dragged Bolt across the pavement of the parking lot, over the cement curb and up and over a small swale. They were now partially blocked from view by anyone who might drive in, looking for a late-night double/double. Tom dropped him face down into the wet grass and rolled him over with a push of his sneakered foot and knelt down beside him.

"I can't fuckin move!" shrieked Bolt, panic mounting in his voice as he realized he is paralyzed from the neck down.

Tom placed his hand over Bolt's mouth and said, "Keep quiet Mr. Bolt or I will make your condition permanent."

Bolt's eyes grew round with terror as the full weight of what had just happened began to overwhelm him and he knew he was staring into the face of death.

"Calm yourself butcher. I'm going to ask you some questions and I want straight answers. If I'm satisfied with your answers, I will realign your neck and you'll be good as new in a day or so. Do you understand what I want?"

Tom could see that Bolt was trying to nod his head but unsuccessfully. He took his hand away from Bolt's mouth and wiped it on his jacket.

"Wha…what did you do to me?"

Tom cut him off quickly, "Shut up dipshit, I'm asking the questions."

Bolt closed his eyes for a second, then opened them, resigned to answer whatever was asked of him.

"What's the name of the guy you were with, in the grocery store parking lot the day we met?"

"He's called Tombstone; he was supposed to bring a knife."

"What do you mean, supposed to bring a knife."

"I mean we were supposed to jump you in the parking lot of the store and Stoney was supposed to bring his knife and kill you but we ran into that old bitch and got separated and Stoney had wanted to kill someone with just a punch and so he was gonna try it on you cause you were just an old guy but it didn't work."

Tom stood up and turned away in confusion. *He was the target that day, but why? Why would they want to kill him? Maybe they were mistaken, maybe they thought he was someone* else. Tom knelt down again by Bolt's limp form. "Who were you trying to kill, who do you think I am?"

"You're the dude who got beat on the last city election. You started askin' a lot of questions and people got nervous so they paid me an' Stoney to finish you. I had my butcher knife with me but Stoney says he wants to cave your head in with a punch. When we saw you pullin' in we started runnin' toward you but I got tripped by Stoney and we fell into that old lady. She started screamin' and I got nervous about the hit because you saw us and I decided to take off. I didn't know Stoney wasn't behind me till I stopped runnin'."

"Who sent you, who wanted to kill me?"

“Someone, I don’t know, Stoney did the talkin’, we split a thousand bucks.”

Tom could feel adrenaline begin pumping through his body as thoughts leapt into his mind, thoughts he would never sanely consider before now. “Look scumbag, if you ever want to be able to pick your nose or scratch your ass again, you’d better remember who sent you.”

“Listen man, I don’t know who it was.”

“Where did you hookup with this guy, where were you when he paid you?”

“We were downtown at the docks, right where the pumps are where the boats get filled up.”

“You mean the finger docks by the marina?”

“Ya, that’s the place. It was rainin’ that night and we was standin’ at the pumps for a coupla minutes waitin’. Up drives this big SUV, you know, one of the big ones, like a’ Escalade or Navigator.”

“What color was it?”

“It was black or dark blue or green, kinda hard to tell at night, but I remember it had a big light over the license plate so it was real easy to read.”

“Did you read it?” Tom raised his voice in exasperation as he started to lose what little patience he had left.

“Ya, ya man take it easy. I think the letters were m…a…g or maybe m…a…y or something like that, and then a space and then zero and r and then a one. Must’ve been a date in May or somethin’.”

Tom felt his bowels loosen. The sudden realization of who was in that vehicle nearly unhinged his mind. *Could this be true, it had to be; this idiot couldn’t or wouldn’t make up something this unbelievable.* “What happened when you guys blew the hit?”

“Well the lawyer sprung Stoney the next day. He came down to the bar where I was shootin’ pool and told me we owed this guy a corpse. He said we’d pick up some help and do it when you couldn’t fight back. Stoney didn’t like gettin’ beat.”

“So what did you do?”

“Listen man, if I tell you you’re gonna kill me right here.”

“If you don’t tell me I’m gonna leave you paralyzed for the rest of your miserable life!” Tom knew what was coming now.

“Okay man okay, we came to your house that night and burned it down, but you still wouldn’t die.”

Tom could feel his eyes burning as the memories of that night came urgent and unbidden into his consciousness. “Where is Tombstone?”

“He’s dead man, you killed him. After you jumped him on the stairs, Little Stevie hit you over the head with his sawed-off baseball bat. The fire was already goin’ in the basement so me and Stevie…we dragged Stoney out. By the time we carried him back to the van he was spittin’ up blood, the next mornin’ he was dead. He howled all night, Jesus it was awful, between his busted shoulder and he couldn’t breathe from his caved in chest, I ain’t never seen or heard anyone in so much pain. When me and Stevie carried Stoney out it was Gus who went upstairs to stop your wife from callin’ the cops.”

Tom lowered his head and shut his eyes as he remembered the motionless shape lying across their bed. “Was it you who planted the marijuana and cocaine in my house?”

“Ya man.”

“Where did you get it?”

Bolt started whining now, he knew he was telling Tom too much. “Come on man, if I tell you any more, they’re gonna kill me.”

“Listen Bolt or whatever your name is, if you don’t tell me what I want to know I will make your dying last a long time. If you tell me what I want to know I’ll fix what I’ve done to your neck and you can get on a bus for T.O. or Montreal or Calgary tomorrow and disappear for all I care.”

Bolt weighed his options and decided that the death staring at him right now was more worrisome than the threat of death next week. “It was given to us by the same guy that paid us. We figured it came out of evidence at the cop shop, it still had the red and white police tape on it.”

Damn, Tom thought, *they wanted me completely destroyed*? “Okay Bolt, let’s roll you over,” Tom grabbed him by the shoulder and rolled him over onto his stomach. He grabbed his hair again close down by his scalp and with the heel of his other hand cracked him on the opposite side of the neck. Tom pushed him onto his back and lifted him up into a sitting position. “Can you hold yourself up?” he asked.

“Ya I think so. I’ve got a wicked headache though.”

“No one cares Bolt. Sit for a minute till you get feeling back in your legs and then I suggest you get out of Dodge Mr. Bolt. If I see you again you will not survive.”

Back at his apartment Tom was near despair as the night's revelations began to shred his mind. Why, he kept thinking, why would anyone, least of all the mayor, want him killed and his reputation destroyed. He had run in the last municipal election but had lost. He had made a few inquiries about the results, mostly because he'd learned that one of his opponents had overspent the provincial guidelines but he'd never pursued it. He had to get to the bottom of this, he had to find out why, but he was scared. They had tried to kill him, they had killed his innocent wife, they had made an attempt to blacken his reputation and they had tried to destroy his character. That anyone carried that much hate just for him scared Tom to his very core. He was shaking, his mind imploding, this is too much for me alone, who can I turn to?

Tom knelt down facing the couch. He clasped his hands together and leaned forward until his hands were resting on the cushions and his forehead fell to his clasped hands. "My God," he prayed, "What can I possibly do against such as this? I don't care about myself; they can do no more to hurt me. What can I do to protect my children? What can I do to preserve my friends? Dear Father in Heaven what should I do?"

Unbidden to his mind came:

Yea, though I walk through the valley of the shadow of death,
I shall fear no evil: For thou art with me;

A great calm came over him and he had the feeling that what was now to come was not his to define anymore. All of his life he had felt he was preparing for something and it concerned him that it was only his own hubris and arrogance. It wasn't until he had reconnected with his church and had humbled himself before God that he realized that all people should be prepared for something, that it was every person's task just to be ready, to be the best person they could be with the talents that God gave them. God would then decide who He needed and for what task. He lay down on the couch, put the pillow under his head and fell asleep dreaming of Joy.

Chapter 4

The next morning, he awoke refreshed and feeling that there was work to do. He must continue in the direction that Bolt's information was sending him. Before he would confront the mayor, he needed some questions answered. He drove to the Coalmen OPP headquarters. A young woman with blonde hair sat behind the desk and quickly looked up from her computer keyboard when Tom walked in.

"Yes sir, can I help you?"

"Is Sergeant Deline in please?"

"That would be Inspector Deline."

Tom said with a smile, "Is he in?"

"Just a minute sir and I'll find out." She picked up a phone receiver and spoke softly into it. "Who should I say is here?"

"Oh, I'm sorry, it's Tom Joiner."

She relayed this information, hung up the phone and said, "Have a seat over there Mr. Joiner, he'll be right out."

"Thanks," Tom said as he headed over to the vacant row of chairs and sat down.

Several minutes later Inspector Barry Deline came striding into the reception area. He took Tom's hand in his and shook it warmly while he asked Tom how he was feeling. After a few pleasantries Tom asked if they could find a private spot to chat.

"Ya, come to my office," Barry said.

They walked through a door marked 'Police Services', down a hall and into the last office on the right. Barry ushered Tom to a chair and closed the door behind him. He moved behind his desk and eased into his chair. He looked at Tom for a minute and asked, "What's up Tom?"

"I need some information Barry but I'm not sure how to ask the question." Tom tried to make some sense out of what he was actually going to ask his friend but gave up, there was no easy way. “Listen Bear, I have no way of knowing how you’re going to react to this question, so I’m just going to tell you what I know and see if you can make sense out of it…okay?”

“Take your time Tom. Does it have anything to do with the fire?”

“Yes…it does. I have found out from a reliable source that the drugs found in the debris of my house had been planted there. What I learned from this source is that the drugs came from the evidence room here in the police station.”

This brought Inspector Deline’s head up with a snap. “Where did you hear that?” he said almost rising out of his seat.

“Is it true?” Tom said.

“Who gave you this information Tom?”

“I’m not going to tell you where I got this information. Is…it…true?”

“Tom…you could be charged with interfering in a police investigation.”

“I have already been put through more than any innocent man should. Tell me the truth…is that why the drug charges that were originally brought against me were dropped, because the drugs you found in my burned-out house had come from your evidence locker?”

Barry Deline just sat there staring down at his desk. He sat there so long without a word that Tom was about to ask again. Barry got up from his desk and moved to the closed door of his office. He opened the door and looked down the hall. He closed it again and moved back to his desk.

“Barry…what the hell is going on—”

“Quiet for a sec okay.” He sat a minute before he spoke. “I don’t know where you got this information but it is correct. All house fires are investigated by the fire department to determine cause. Whenever there is a fatality involved the Ontario Fire Marshal brings in their special forensic unit and the local detachment of the police force also requests the OPP forensic team out of Toronto. On their initial investigation the OFM found the drugs, or what was left of them, in your basement. The marijuana and cocaine had been burned but not destroyed. The same with the containers they had originally been stored in. After you were charged with possession of marijuana and cocaine in amounts large enough for trafficking our new lab in Tillsonburg found dyes in the remains of the melted plastic containers that were consistent with the coloring used in police tape. It was established that the amount of drugs in your basement matched exactly an amount that was discovered missing from our evidence lock up."

"Why was none of this ever brought out? Why were the charges just dropped and the guilt by association just left there?"

"Tom, lower your voice. You cannot know any of this. If it had become a matter of public knowledge the entire force here would have been put under investigation. Every conviction we've gotten over the last five years would have been brought up for review. Every criminal from this jurisdiction now in prison would have been set free pending new investigations."

Tom's voice broke with emotion, "Barry…this wasn't right."

"No, it wasn't…but, when it was uncovered it was decided that it was in the best interest of the community to just drop the charges and not open the detachment up to investigation or allow so many criminals to be set free. Can you imagine the loss of confidence in our police force not to mention the rise in the crime rate because of all the releases?"

"So I was thrown to the wolves, my reputation destroyed by innuendo and unproven association. Did my life here not matter to you?"

"Tom…please…it was decided that the greater good had to be served. I'm sorry that it was you who was hurt." Inspector Deline wouldn't even look Tom in the eye as he finally divulged the truth to him.

"Barry…I've known you for twenty-five years, I remember when you were accepted onto the force. God Barry, it was Joy's father who helped get you on the force."

"I'm sorry Tom. I sat in on the meeting but I had no say in the matter, it was out of my hands."

A minute or two passed as Tom's stare bore in on Barry who wouldn't look at his friend.

"Tell me Barry, who was at the meeting, who was doing the talking?"

"Tom…it wouldn't do any good for you to know…it would be my career if it got out, this could be my career if anyone knew I was talking to you now."

"Fine Barry…fine. There's no need for anyone else to suffer is there?" Tom said very quietly. "Tell me one thing though, did you get your promotion before or after the charges were dropped against me?"

"Now that's not fair Tom, you know how hard I've worked at being a good cop, it's not my fault that a couple of perps were hurt during their arrests. I was cleared of any excessive use of force charges. I was cleared of all charges but they still wouldn't promote me. Do you understand Tom, I would never rise past Sergeant if I didn't play ball with them."

Tom didn't say a word. He just sat there staring at Barry, inside he felt more sorry for him than anything else. He knew he had sold his soul and not for a very high price.

Barry began to speak so quietly that Tom had to slide his chair up to his desk and lean in until his ear was almost touching Barry's lips. "The Police Chief, the Fire Chief, the head of the OPP's forensics lab, don't remember her name, the city's attorney, Lucas Collier, a couple of councilors, Calvin Alexander and Karl DeVries and the Mayor were there. Mayor Putnam was the one who did most of the talking. It was him who convinced everyone else that the safety and reputation of the city and its police force outweighed any consideration for you."

Without another word Tom walked out of the Police Station and never saw his friend again.

Tom's mind and body were vibrating. The information he'd received confirmed everything that Bolt had confessed but what should he do with it? Should he escape to parts unknown and never see another person that he knew? What about his children? Were they in danger, would they be used to get to him? He already knew. These people would eventually find out about Bolt's confession, they would eventually discover that Deline had also confessed, they would know that Tom knew. They would do everything and anything to eliminate him. Joy had already been killed in their desire to get rid of Tom; they would have no qualms about using his children or friends to finish the job. Tom made his decision. Once his mind was made up and all his questioning was put to rest, he became very calm. He began to focus on what had to be done next.

Tom knew this meant Mayor Putnam. He knew if he waited Deline's attack of conscience might lapse and he'd warn the Mayor. He turned his truck left at the next intersection and headed downtown. He pondered his impending confrontation with the Mayor, wondering how he should behave toward the man he strongly suspected of ordering his murder. He would have to remain calm and play this close to the vest until…until what? Until Mayor Putnam confessed and called the police to come and take himself away. That wouldn't happen, so what did he hope to accomplish with this showdown? He knew it was useless to get into a shouting match with the Mayor, accusing him of heinous crimes was not going to accomplish anything but get himself arrested.

His thoughts circled endlessly. *What should I do, what do I want to accomplish, what do I want to happen, what do I want…what do I want?* Something was tugging at the edge of his mind…dammit what was it! *The Lord is my shepherd; I shall not want.* Those words kept coming to Tom and had been of great comfort to him, but were they just words to be recited when under duress or did they truly contain power? Tom could not interpret how God would manifest Himself in someone's life, all he knew was how he felt. He was lost, he was out of his depth. He desperately needed guidance and his faith was telling him to let himself be guided. *Trust in God.* His days of lip service to his beliefs, no matter how sincere he had been, had just come to an end. He now knew with the full conviction of his humble faith that he was not without help and guidance. All that was required of him was the courage to continue, but did he have that quality of bravery? Could he continue? How could he not and call himself a man?

Unrestricted access to leadership, one advantage small towns have over cities. Arriving at City Hall, Tom walked up to reception and asked the woman working there if he could see Beverly Johnston, the Mayor's personal secretary. She gave Beverly a call and sent Tom up. Tom walked into the outer office that Beverly occupied as the Mayor's secretary and asked if he could see Mayor Putnam. "I know it's late and I don't have an appointment Bev, but something's come up and I just need to bend Jim's ear for a minute."

"Hang on a sec Tom. Mayor Putnam is in his office now, I'll see if he's available." Beverly got up from her chair and walked over to the Mayor's closed office door. She knocked once softly and opened the door, poked her head inside and Tom heard her say, "Excuse me Mr. Mayor, Tom Joiner is outside and was wondering if he might see you? Okay." Beverly returned to her seat. Mayor Putnam appeared in his office door and waved Tom in.

"Thanks Bev." Tom said as he walked through the door held open by the Mayor.

Of an age with Tom, James Warren Putnam was tall and slim, sporting a healthy tan combined with snow white hair. Putnam was the son of Coalmen's greatest success story. His father had become exceedingly rich selling insurance and developing commercial real estate. Before retiring he liquidated everything and placed his assets into a philanthropic trust. Upon his father's passing, James found himself the head of a multimillion-dollar charitable foundation and soon found himself Coalmen's most beloved citizen. He ran for city council winning easily but halfway through his first term ambition got the better of him and he resigned to run for Parliament. Everyone but the eligible voters of his riding thought it would be a slam dunk and after a three-month campaign Jim found himself adrift in the political wilderness. A year and a half later Coalmens' citizens were once more asked to go to the municipal polls. At this time Jim was able to convince the incumbent Mayor, a well-loved man who'd held the office for three terms, to opt out of running again. Jim won in a landslide and had held the Office of Mayor ever since.

Now, alone with him, Tom was near panic until Putnam said, "Tom, I'm guessing you've got something important on your mind...but you've caught me ready to head home, I'm expecting a call. Why don't you follow me out to the house and we can talk there."

"That'll work, thanks Jim," Tom didn't know what else to say, the ball so to speak was in Mayor Putnam's court.

Putnam opened his office door and said to Beverly, "I'm leaving now for the rest of the day Bev, take any messages that come in and I'll get them tomorrow. Com'on Tom, I'll walk out with you."

Tom and the Mayor walked out of City Hall amid small talk concerning the weather and their respective workloads. They walked to their vehicles and Tom started up his F150 Sabre. He drove out of his parking spot and pulled in behind Mayor Putnam's dark blue Escalade, stopping at the intersection. Twilight was just coming on as Tom noticed the extra bright illumination on the Escalade's bumper just over the license plate that read MAY 0R1.

For twenty minutes he followed the SUV as they drove into the Maple Ridge Hills. Jim Putnam had built his home here north of Coalmen fifteen years ago, just after his father had passed away. The beautiful ranch style home was at the end of a long private drive situated in the middle of fifty acres of wooded property. Both Tom and Putnam parked their vehicles in front of the three-car garage and walked over to the front door.

"What do you think of this location Tom? Lovely isn't it?"

"If you like seclusion," replied Tom.

Jim opened the heavy oak door and they entered into a large foyer with curved stairs ascending at one end and two large rooms opening off either side.

“Here Tom, give me your coat.” Pointing to the room opening to the right Putnam said, “Have a seat in my study Tom, I’ll fix us a drink and be there in a minute, what will you have?”

Caught in mid thought he mumbled, “Ice tea thanks?”

“Lemon wedge?” asked the consummate host.

“Sure…OK,” replied Tom.

Ten minutes later Jim was back in his office drinks in hand. “Ice tea and lemon for you Tom and Laphroaig single malt for me. Cheers.” He held up his glass to Tom and then raised it to his lips.

To be polite he took a healthy pull on his ice tea. He looked around the room for a side table with a coaster. He had to blink a couple of times to clear his eyes. It felt as if he’d been squirted with some of the lemon in his drink. His eyes began to burn and his vision blurred. “I’m sorry Jim I think I’ve gotten something in my eyes.” The burning got worse and Tom became concerned. He couldn’t see at all now and there was a rushing noise in his ears. Suddenly the floor came up and hit him on the side of the head.

Bells rang and insects buzzed and everything was grey. The fog began to lift, the bells stopped peeling and the buzzing insects turned into voices.

“What the hell are we going to do with him Jim? Why didn’t you just tell him a story to satisfy his curiosity?”

“He already knows Wayne! Deline called me before he blew his brains out.”

Tom found his wrists and ankles duct taped to an old oak chair. He saw Mayor Putnam standing in front of him, facing two Coalmen police officers. He recognized one of the officers, Wayne Kotaupolis, a large, burly guy with many years on the force but the female officer was new and not known to Tom.

“What’s going on Putnam, what do you mean Deline blew his brains out? He was fine when I left him this afternoon.”

Mayor Putnam and the two police officers turned toward Tom. Officer Kotaupolis had his billy club out and was rapping it up and down into the palm of his meaty hand. The female officer had taken off her uniform cap and her tightly woven blond braid now hung freely down her back.

Mayor Putnam addressed Tom, “I don’t know what you said to Deline… but it was enough that he obviously couldn’t live with himself. Just before you came to my office, I got a call from him saying you’d been there. Deline said you knew almost everything and he’d filled in some holes. He wanted to go public, come clean. He said now that you knew almost everything there was no use in trying to cover things up." Jim Putnam stopped for a minute and looked long at Tom. He turned toward Officer Kotaupolis and nodded his head toward the shadows. Wayne turned and walked out of Tom's line of vision. "I told Deline that he was only a cog and going public was not an option. I told him if one word of this got out, there was evidence in place right now to discredit him. He asked if what we had planned for him was anything like what we had done to you. I told him of course it was, if we can't dig up any skeletons in your closet, we will manufacture them. I told Barry that once you were in you weren't allowed out. We spoke for another few minutes and I thought I had brought him around, that is until I got a call from Kotaupolis that Deline had eaten his gun barrel. It's lucky for us that Wayne and Barry have the only offices at that end of the building. After he saw what happened he called me."

Just then Officer Kotaupolis returned into Tom's field of vision carrying something wrapped in a towel. He placed it on a side table and unwrapped the object. It was a police service revolver and Tom had a sinking feeling he knew who it belonged to.

"Wayne had the presence of mind to grab Barry's gun and lock his office before he called me. I instructed him to sit tight until I figured out what to do. Well Tom, I was in a bit of a quandary. We had a policeman's body in his own office with the back of his head missing and we had you, someone with enough plausible evidence to start an investigation and put a lot of us behind bars for years. I'll confess Tom, you had me…and then Bev poked her head in my office and said you were there and wanted to see me. Well sir, all the pieces suddenly fit and I had the perfect plan. As you were following me out to the house, I called Wayne and told him to meet us here with Deline's service revolver."

Mayor Putnam nodded toward the female officer. "Bring it over Crystal." She held the revolver by the towel wrapped barrel and tried to place the grip of the handgun into the palm of Tom's hand. He kept his fist closed. Wayne struck down hard on Tom's forearm with his fist and he felt the old wooden chair tremble under him as he lost the feeling in his hand. Wayne pried his fingers open as Tom pleaded, "Com'on Jim, what're you doing?"

Crystal placed the grip of the pistol into Tom's open palm and Kotaupolis forced Tom's fingers around the grip of the revolver and held them there. Tom tried reasoning. "Are you seriously thinking of framing me for Barry's death? You're insane."

"No," replied the Mayor, "Your prints will be all over the gun that fired the bullet that splattered Deline's brains all over the wall. We'll find the gun in a trash bin or somewhere close to the station just after Officer Kotaupolis discovers the body of his brother officer later tonight. A quick investigation will find that you shot Officer Deline with his own revolver and then locked his door and fled the building. Officer Kotaupolis and Officer Stannis here will track you down to the vicinity of my house where they will confront you trying to force your way in. That karate shit of yours scares the crap out of our people so everyone will understand the need for deadly force."

Tom didn't say anything as he digested the mayor's plan. Kotaupolis was now peeling his fingers away from the gun grip none too gently. He took the pistol and carefully wrapped it in the towel.

"What do we do now Mr. Mayor?"

"I'm off to Toronto to see Regional once I get the call. I want you two to take Tom out back and do what you have to. Then break a window or kick in a door and place Tom's body nearby. Then you'll have to move quickly. Get back to town and discover Deline's body and his gun. Check the security cam to show Tom's involvement and proceed with an APB on Tom's whereabouts. The rest you just heard me tell Tom."

Tom looked at Putnam in desperation and asked, "Why Jim, why are you doing this, what did I do to warrant all this?"

Putnam replied slowly, "I understand your curiosity Tom. You know…we couldn't have you getting an investigation started pertaining to the election."

"Why not?" pleaded Tom.

"You really don't know do you?"

"What? That Calvin Alexander over spent on his campaign."

"No," said Putnam with a laugh, "Calvin couldn't get elected dog catcher in a fair election, he could've spent a million bucks and he wouldn't have won."

Tom sat there staring numbly at Putnam, comprehension dawning.

"You're getting it now, aren't you? You were the one elected to the only seat not held by an incumbent, not Calvin. We had to destroy 80% of the returns in order for Cal to win his seat. That idiot couldn't even make the election close."

"Why was that so important?"

"He's in our pocket. He's useful. He has no idea he wasn't fairly elected so he appears honest and innocent and he will vote exactly the way we tell him to. Originally you were never factored into our plans but your campaign blew Cal and the rest of the other candidates so far out of the water that we spent the majority of our time just trying to get Cal back into contention. That's why we had Doug Blakely give Cal all those campaign spots and we had all those awards given to Cal just to make it look like he wasn't a complete moron. Even after all that, we still had to dump most of the ballots to skew the results. Can't believe people didn't get suspicious? That's why we couldn't have you questioning the results."

Jim looked at his wristwatch. "My call should be coming through soon."

"You still haven't told me why Putnam, I need to know why!"

"With Cal, added to the incumbents, we had a perfect mix that will allow us to push through our initiatives without anyone becoming suspicious. You would have thrown off the balance we required. You're too insightful and there are too many people who would listen to you if you were given a platform. We couldn't have that."

Just then the phone rang and as Mayor Putnam began to walk out of the room to get his call he said, "Sorry Tom, have to end the explanation now. Wayne, Crystal, you know what needs to be done. Wait till I'm gone."

Tom could hear Putnam's muffled voice from the other room. He couldn't make out much but he did hear Putnam say, "Ya I've stayed there before. Jarvis right. I like their roof top patio. See you there." He heard the front door open and close and soon he heard the big SUV start down the winding drive until the crunching sound of tires on gravel faded to nothing.

Crystal said, "Wayne, time to work."

"Yah," said Kotaupolis, "I'm gonna enjoy this." He tapped his police baton lightly into his open palm as he approached Tom. "You think you're so tough with that fuckin karate shit eh?" He raised the baton high and swung down with all the force his 260-pound frame could muster.

For the last few minutes Tom had been working the armrest of the old wooden chair loose. After Kotaupolis had nearly fractured his forearm earlier the doweled joinery of the armrest had separated allowing some movement. Now as the police baton whistled through the air toward his unprotected head he heaved mightily, the armrest came away and Tom got his arm up just in time.

The twenty-one-inch steel baton swung with incredible force shattered the oak still taped to Tom's forearm. He thought his arm destroyed as he and the old wooden chair were bowled over backward by the force of the impact. The ancient glue holding the chair together disintegrated and the seat pulled apart from the legs and the last remaining armrest. The chair collapsed and Tom, on his back, felt the rush of air pass him as Kotaupolis missed with a second hard swing. Tom sprang to his feet and stepped backward to avoid a third swing but his one arm and both ankles were still taped to the tangled mass of broken chair. He turned away to get some distance from the crushing arcs of the steel rod and ran smack into Jim Putnam's office desk. He ducked and hunched his shoulders as the hard-swung steel sheared away the broken pieces of antique chair still clinging to him.

Free now Tom turned and shot out a well-aimed crescent kick that broke Kotaupolis' wrist and knocked the baton away. Kotaupolis grabbed his broken wrist as Tom launched himself over the pile of splintered oak and snapped a side kick to Kotaupolis' throat.

The policeman collapsed in a heap, gasping and holding his rapidly swelling neck while Tom dropped lightly to his feet looking for the policewoman. She was standing five feet from Tom on the other side of Putnam's desk, drawing her police issue SIG Sauer P229. The semi-automatic fired a .357 shell at 1,450 feet per second with massive stopping power. Tom knew she would aim center mass and if she got a shot off the hydrostatic shock of the supersonic slug as it ripped through his abdomen could cause his brain to hemorrhage.

He dove toward the big mahogany desk. He heard the report of the first shot and felt mahogany splinters shower his back as his shoulder slammed into the heavy piece of furniture. His weight and forward motion pushed the heavy desk into her, the protruding lip of the desktop catching her at mid-thigh and pushing her legs out from under her.

She came head first over the desktop, still holding her SIG in a two-handed grip. She landed on top of Tom driving him the rest of the way to the floor and her momentum took her rolling off his back onto the hardwood. She had good training and rolled right up into a half crouch. She was on one knee, her arms out with the pistol still in a two-handed grip pointing straight ahead but in the wrong direction. She realized this instantly and sprang up while turning and brought the pistol around to bear on her target while squeezing off a round.

The muzzle flash blinded her for a moment but she knew she had missed. All she saw were shards of wood flying off the rich oak paneling that sheathed the walls of the study. Just under her field of vision she caught movement, his face was turned toward her, his eyes targeting her, he was low, just barely off the floor, supported on one bent leg as he spun, his other leg straight out approaching in a blur. The back of his calf caught her at the ankles with such force that her feet switched places with her head. The contact barely slowed Tom's sweep and as he spun, he spiraled up to a standing position.

She lay on the hardwood, dazed, her pistol still gripped in one hand. Tom walked over and kicked the gun out of her hand and it skidded to the far wall. She worked her way to her hands and knees, her head down. Tom turned toward her and as he cautiously lowered himself to speak, she reached out her left arm and wrapped it around Tom's ankles, pinning them firmly against her side. She quickly dropped her left shoulder and turned her body pushing her back against the front of Tom's legs. He was bowled over and she pivoted around, getting him into a full mount. She straddled his chest and aimed a quick punch, making contact with the side of his mouth. He felt sharp pain as his teeth cut into the soft flesh around his lips and the warm feel and rusty taste of blood leaked into his mouth. She hit him again and then her hands were around his throat. She had large hands and Tom felt her strength as her thumbs dug into either side of his trachea. Her grip got tighter and shut off the blood supply up his carotid artery to his brain. He squeezed his hands into tight fists and drove them into her exposed ribs on either side. He felt her breath blow out of her like a great bellows but her grip on his neck did not loosen. He drove his fists into her ribs again as hard as he could and then brought his hands together into the space between their two chests and drove them over his face into the gap between her arms. He exploded his forearms out against her arms and broke the grip she had on his neck. As the force of his movement pushed her arms apart, she started to fall forward onto him. Tom opened his hands and drove the heel of each palm into the sides of her head, just above her temples. She went limp and fell onto him.

Tom lay there for a minute under the unconscious woman. He could feel the blood flowing unrestricted now up his neck and his head began to clear. He rolled to his side and slid her to the floor. He spat out blood and pieces of flesh torn from the inside of his cheek. He hoped the punches hadn't loosened any teeth. *All I need now is a trip to the dentist,* he thought, replaced quickly with, *you should be worrying about a trip to the prison dentist.* That was a sobering thought as the realization of what he had been doing had a chance to sink in. *No one will ever believe that these cops were going to kill me on the orders of the Mayor. I think it's time for me to disappear.*

The policewoman was still unconscious so Tom went over to Officer Kotaupolis who lay unmoving on the hardwood floor. The officer's broken wrist, swollen and bruised lay over his chest, his undamaged hand had been clawing at his throat, he was not breathing.

Guilt clutched at him, even though Officer Kotaupolis had been happily anticipating Tom's demise. Wayne was an officer of the law and Tom was sure he had been the unselfish protector of many of Coalmen's citizens. Tom knew he had acted in self-defense; he also knew that it would be impossible to make that case with anyone, anywhere. The question now, how to make himself disappear. He would have to decide that later, the more immediate question was, what to do with the female Officer?

She was beginning to come around. Tom walked over to her as she began trying to sit up. Her tight braid had come loose in the battle and as she sat up, she began pushing the hair out of her face. She looked around and when she spied Tom standing next to her, she said, "Who are you?"

Tom had expected this and he knelt down beside her slowly and put his hand gently on her shoulder. "There has been an accident, you are all right, but your friend over there is not." Tom motioned over to Wayne with a movement of his chin so that her attention was diverted to Kotaupolis' supine form.

"Who is that?" she asked without emotion.

"That is someone you know," said Tom, "But it's not really important right now. Do you know who you are?"

"What do you mean?"

"What is your name?" Tom asked quietly.

"I…I don't know, what is my name, do you know?"

"You've suffered a blow to the head, it may take a minute before your wits return." Tom knew why she was rattled. He had aimed his strikes slightly above the temple region where the skull is a bit thicker and more resilient and had struck each side of her head milliseconds apart, setting up a bounce. He had used enough power in the strike to make her brain collide with the inside of her skull causing a concussion with its attending memory loss. Tom knew this memory loss would not be permanent.

He looked at her, "Your name is Crystal, you're a police officer. You've been in an accident. I'm going to take you into town and to the hospital. Just relax and I'll help you into my truck."

Tom draped her arm gently over his shoulder and helped her to her feet. They walked together out the front door and into the back seat of his truck. He bundled up her jacket to make a pillow and got her to lie down. He jumped into the driver's side and ordered, "Start engine." The drive back to Coalmen was uneventful. He drove into the hospital's emergency room turnaround and left the engine running while he jumped down and went around to the passenger side door. Crystal was laying across the small back seat with her head still nestled into her police jacket. She was conscious and looked up when Tom opened the back door.

"Where are we?" she asked.

"We're at the hospital Crystal and they're going to give you something to take away your headache." Tom knew her head would clear by tomorrow and Tom hoped he would be far away by then. "OK Crystal, time to get you inside." Tom took her gently by the hand and helped her get down from the truck seat. She was still a bit wobbly so Tom put his arm around her waist and helped her into the ER.

As soon as the ER nurse saw that someone was bringing in a police officer she called for an assist and ran to Tom. "What happened here?" she said in that clipped professional tone that all emergency responders develop.

"I found her walking on the highway up in the ridge hills," he lied. Tom turned his face away from the nurse as he gave up supporting Crystal and allowed the nurse to take her weight.

"Get a cart here now and notify Doctor Steve that we have Coalmen PD in distress. Where did you find her and what is your name sir?" the nurse asked as she turned back to Tom, but he wasn't there. All she saw through the sliding glass doors of the Emergency Room entrance was the reflection of the big Ford's taillights receding across the glass.

Tom drove quickly, he had to get out of town, for a while anyway. When Crystal's memories of tonight came back and the authorities found Officer Kotaupolis' body inside the Mayor's home there would be a massive manhunt for him. Tom thought his only course of action at this point was to try and find

Putnam. Toronto was far enough away for now and if he could lay hands on the Mayor he might discover where to go next.

On impulse he turned down one of the last side streets before he would pass by the local high school. This was the street where Tom and Joy had had their home. It was an old residential street where all the homes had been built before the First World War. They were good, solidly built brick and clapboard homes that middle class families had been raising kids in for a hundred years.

Tom drove to where he and Joy had shared their lives and loves and slowed the truck to a stop and got out. All that remained of thirty-five years of loving toil was a hole, partially filled in with bits of brick and stone rubble and covered by dirt. Everything that he and Joy had built together was now a partially sunken depression of mud and debris enclosed by a flimsy barrier. Even the pool in the backyard had been drained and filled. The flower beds that Joy had so lovingly cultivated had been pulled up or trampled under. There was nothing left and Tom's heart was near to breaking.

As Tom stood there in grief, he heard someone walking toward him. Turning quickly and ready to run Tom recognized his neighbor from across the street. Mr. DeGruyn and his wife had lived in this neighborhood the longest. They hadn't been close but would often wave from across the street as neighbors were wont to when people were out mowing lawns or shoveling driveways. They were a lovely older couple and over the last couple of years Tom had gone over after particular heavy snowfalls and had used his big snowblower to clean out their driveway.

Mr. DeGruyn was carrying something in his hands. It looked black in the shadows from the moonlight. The object was rectangular, roughly eighteen inches by six inches but nearly flat and looked to be heavy by the way Mr. DeGruyn was carrying it. When he got to Tom, he held out the object for Tom to take. It was the smoke grimed and dirt encrusted bronze plaque that Marianne Twittle had given to Joy all those years ago. After Tom took the plaque from Mr. DeGruyn, he brushed it gently with his hand and stared at it for a moment. Mr. DeGruyn took Tom's hand in his warm embrace and said with a slight Dutch accent, "Hello Tom. Marta and I are so sorry for what happened to you and Joy. We weren't able to come and see you in the hospital and there was only a…memorial for Joy…we weren't able to say how badly we felt…I…"

Tom put his hand on Mr. DeGruyn's shoulder and just looked at him. There were no words that either of them knew for this; they just stared into each other's souls.

"I have to go now Dieter, but thanks for coming over, and thanks for saving this," he turned over the dirty bronze plaque so the inscription faced his neighbor.

"Tom...I wanted to tell you...after the fire...before the people came and tore down what was left and drove over everything with their big machines...we...I mean the neighbors...we came and saved as many of the plants as were left. All the people around who used to walk by and admire all the beautiful plants that Joy had in her gardens, we made places in our own yards and flower gardens and saved some of what...you...had. I hope that is all right with you Tom?"

The tears began to trail down Tom's cheeks as he put his free arm around Mr. DeGruyn and hugged him tightly. "Would you please tell all the neighbors how much I appreciate them saving some of what we had?" He released his neighbor, his cheeks wet.

"Tom, I never saw you." With that Dieter was across the road and into his house.

That last comment made Tom think for a minute. If not already, by tomorrow the police will have Tom's license plate number out to every patrol car between Windsor and Cornwall. He went into the truck and rummaged around in the center console until he had what he was looking for. He took the black marker and went to the front of his half ton. His plates were white with black lettering so it was an easy matter to turn FW2 183 into EW2 188.

Tom slid back into his truck and pulled into the street.

I think I have a pretty good idea where the Mayor is going. A *roof top patio and Jarvis Street, that's got to be the Grand Hotel, Dundas and Jarvis I think. It's around eight now so I should be there about eleven thirty.*

At eleven thirty-five he was driving south on Jarvis street admiring some of the restored older buildings that dotted the city. As he drove past a beautiful stone church on the northeast corner where Gerrard Street intersected Jarvis, he caught a glimpse of the big red letters of 'The Grand' placed vertically near the top of the hotel two blocks away.

Turning off Jarvis toward the hotel entrance, Tom looked for the valet parking. Spotting a neatly uniformed young man standing officially by the curb he pulled over and stopped, quickly telling the truck's voice actuator that valet parking would be driving soon. The young man quickly came to Tom's door and held it open for him. Tom stepped down, stretched his back and looked around at the brightly lit area that served as the street entrance to the hotel.

"That is one beautiful truck sir," the valet remarked as he began his opening salvo in the battle for tips. "It's got that new matte finish on it, yes? I didn't know it was available yet?"

"I know someone," said Tom, in a friendly kind of way. This kid is good he thought. I wonder if his memory is as good. Tom reached into his pocket and pulled out a twenty, "Here kid," he said as he placed the bill into the quickly outstretched palm. "You're right about the paint, I paid a fortune for this prototype and I'd hate to have it scratched or dented. There's another one of these for you if you keep my truck close by. When I'm ready to go I'll be impatient."

"Yes sir!"

"Another thing kid, have you seen a dark green Escalade come in yet, vanity plate reads MAY OR1."

"Sure," replied the young valet, his empty hand reappearing, "that Escalade came in about thirty minutes ago, handled it myself."

Tom put a ten into the young man's hand.

"Tell your friend that he should be more generous…like you, sir. It'll take twenty minutes to get his SUV outta parking." The valet laughed as he signaled for another smartly dressed young man to come over and get the Sabre's fob. "Here's your parking number, sir, just ask for Nigel. If I'm not on station just tell whoever is here that Nigel said to be quick, they'll know what's up."

While bartering with Nigel a plan had started evolving. "Listen Nigel," Tom said as he offered the kid another ten, "I just flew in from the tar sands in Alberta, I'm sweaty and my clothes are dirty but I need a cocktail and a soak more than anything else. My friends and I like to have more than one drink if you know what I mean. I don't want to upset the straights if my friends and I get too relaxed up on the rooftop. How can we get down to our rooms…discreetly?"

"Where are you staying?"

Tom thought quickly, "We're in a couple of the Ambassador Suites."

“Very nice,” said Nigel. “Just before the freight elevators on the top floor you’ll see a set of double doors marked hotel personnel only. Here is the code to get through the doors.” Nigel handed Tom a small card containing four digits.

“Thanks Nigel,” Tom said as he started up the red tiled stairs to the carved limestone façade of the hotel. Once inside he was immediately taken by the opulence of the lobby, he was thankful he didn’t have his work clothes on. For his visit with the Mayor he had worn dark slacks, leather loafers, an overpriced golf shirt and a sports jacket. To anyone in the hotel he appeared to be a casually dressed patron arriving back after a late dinner out. The lobby was magnificent, Tom thought, as he admired the polished limestone floors, the floor to ceiling limestone columns and the paneled oculus built into the high ceiling. Tom nodded to the pretty clerk behind the counter as if he belonged there and continued toward the bank of elevators. Once inside he pressed the button for the top floor.

Tom walked down the hall remembering the valet’s instructions and found the double doors. He keyed in the four-digit code and pushed the doors open. He walked through the well-appointed change room to the stairs that climbed to the patio. At the top he found himself on a small landing with a set of curtained French doors. Moving the shiers aside he peeked out. The patio was very large with a raised area at the far end. Stairs granted access to each side of the dais but furniture, pergolas and lattice combined to obscure his view. The lower patio area appeared to be empty of any people so he cautiously moved through the doors.

As Tom made his way toward the back, he noticed elevator doors to his right. *That must be the main elevator,* he thought. He had gotten almost to the stairs when he heard the smooth hum of elevator hydraulics. Every instinct yelled hide. He scanned quickly but all he saw was a pair of half doors molded into the front wall of the raised hot tub area. He ran to them, they were locked. He saw a combination key pad beside the doors and took a chance. He keyed in his VIP code and the lock clicked open. He threw himself into the poorly lit opening and pulled the doors closed behind him.

Blind for a moment his eyes soon became accustomed to the gloom. The entire underside of the hot tub area was open to him. Just then he heard feet on the steps. As the footfalls climbed up onto the upper level Tom followed the sound with his eyes. There were only deck boards separating Tom from the new arrivals and he realized he could hear every word being spoken.

"Pauly, take Squid and Dominic, cover the stairs and the elevator. I don't want to be disturbed."

"Right Boss."

Tom could hear three sets of heavy footfalls move away.

"Do you really think bringing them was necessary?" Tom's heart jumped into his mouth; it was Putnam.

"It's necessary because I think so," replied a gravelly voice he almost recognized.

A woman's voice said, "Listen Lou, how are things going to work this summer?" He now had a name for the second voice; Lou Lamont, head of the Toronto Public Services Union. A voice familiar from numerous television interviews.

"The other councilors and I don't want to be implicated in the problems that are going to crop up over the next few months. How are we going to keep from being noticed?"

"I'll be taking care of that," replied Lou. "The 'Occupy and Lives Matter' people will be taking most of the heat. We throw in some striking workers and some police brutality…and a couple of things I've been working on, and we'll have a crisis that no one will be able to unravel. Putnam…how are things with your group?"

Jim Putnam hesitated, "The politicians, police and firemen that I've organized are ready. We didn't need that many. Recruiting the heads of municipal departments was a stroke of genius Lou. With the bureaucrats on side we can strongly influence any decision that is going to be made in half the medium sized cities across Southeastern Ontario. With these key people in place directing the police and emergency services we can begin causing problems with the Occupy and Lives Matter groups. With the Mayors and Councilors that are taking direction from us we can begin implementing some confusing emergency measures and with the bureaucrats on board we can influence the way these cities will react to each crisis. With the press complicit we control how the public perceives the mess that will come."

"Thanks Jimmy," said Lou, "I want to show you guys something." There was a lull in the conversation and Tom thought he could hear the clasps on a briefcase being released.

"Here are the planned disruption points."

Tom could here paper being smoothed out.

"The beauty of what I'm gonna show you is how simple it is," said Lamont. "This here is exactly what it looks like; tracing paper with colored points on it, but if you put it on this…" Tom could hear a heavier object like a large book being placed on the table. It was opened and then he heard more rustling of the tracing paper, "You can see exactly where and when our disruptions will take place. We can coordinate everything from this simple diagram. No computers that can be hacked, no emails that can be recovered or traced, just simple paper over a map."

"Ya, but where do we get the right map?"

"There's twenty-seven thousand copies of them at the ministry of education's Spadina warehouse. It's an old atlas that's outta print now. We've distributed copies to our operation heads. No one carries the tracing paper or the atlas together. The atlas page we use is not torn out so there's no connection between the marks and the maps. It's foolproof. Now you know how to read this, you'll be issued the atlases and the overlay. You need to know where and when things will happen. Now, before I bring you up to date on the press angle let's hear from Southwest and Northern."

"Southwest will be ready Lou, add some student protests in with the Occupy disruptions, the strikes we've got planned and the disorganization with the police and firefighters and it's going to be a real mess."

Another voice then took over, "With everything else, Northern Ontario will unleash its warriors to create havoc. We will block northern rail lines, we'll disrupt communications, we will block roads and we will disrupt logging and mining operations. There will be casualties, these white boys are packin'. If they get hurt, too fuckin' bad. These people think they own our land through the right of conquest…we'll fuckin' show them who's conquered and who ain't!"

After a short pause that signaled the indigenous leaders wrap up, Lou Lamont spoke, "I think everything is coming together. There's going to be some other activities going on you guys don't know about yet…and you don't need to know. Soon now and we'll see some extreme changes taking place or we will at least burn the system down."

"Ya man, we're gonna burn the system down, whoooooo!" Two male voices took up this chant.

“Shut the fuck up you two, this ain’t no pub crawl at your homo university. We got serious things to discuss here. Don’t make me regret inviting you along. You have nothing to say here so sit down and shut up!”

“Now…where the hell was I. Oh ya, the press? We have a couple of up and coming reporters ready to sell their souls for a scoop. You know about the month end meeting. You all know how important that’s going to be and you all know who’ll be there. I’ll give you this opportunity now, to go over anything that could provide problems for us later on. I don’t want crap being brought up in front of the others that might make any of us look bad, especially me.”

There was a pause in the talking and Tom figured the leader of the group was looking around at each of the individuals at the table.

Putnam spoke. “I’ve had a slight problem in Coalmen. I’ve taken care of it but thought I might mention it in case it makes the news. Remember last year we had to monkey with the election results to keep someone off council. We tried to ruin his business and hoped he would just leave town. Well he was more stubborn than we thought. He got wind of some things we were doing to him and he was getting a high-priced lawyer from Toronto involved so we tried to eliminate him. His wife was killed but the stupid bastard survived. Million to one I was told, miracle and all that. He was low priority, but we were still working on a way to eliminate him. Earlier today one of my cops committed suicide after talking to this guy. I got him out to my house and had a couple of loyals shoot him, then frame him for the murder of the cop who committed suicide. That should tie up all those loose ends.”

While Putnam had been speaking, he had been pacing nervously, not knowing how his news would be perceived. All eyes were on Putnam so when a breeze ruffled the sheets of tracing paper and the top half dozen sheets slid off the table and floated to the decking no one noticed. Two of the thin sheets slipped between the gaps in the decking and Tom quickly grabbed one, folded it into quarters and slipped it into his pocket.

“Are you sure this is all packaged up tight, I get worried around miracles?” There was nervous laughter from the group as Lamont made his observation.

“Positive,” Replied Putnam.

“Good,” said Lou, “Let’s call this meeting adjourned and have some drinks…Shit! Where did they go?” Lou had just realized his papers were askew. He grabbed them all up and after counting proclaimed, “We’re missing two.”

Putnam said, “What’ll we do if they end up on the street below?”

“Nothing,” growled Lamont, “They’re worthless paper to anyone who doesn’t know what they’re for. Remember, that’s the beauty of this system.” Lou looked around for a second and whispered to Putnam. “Hang back with me for a second.” Louder now he addressed the group, “You guys go down to the suite and get us some drinks goin’. Pauly, Squid, Dominic, you fellas find those two papers.”

When they were alone Lamont spoke to Putnam, “Well Putnam, I spoke with Beal about your suggestions.”

“What did he say?” Tom could hear the suppressed excitement in Putnam’s voice.

Lamont took a minute to reply. “He will consent to you attending the next couple of Downfall meetings. If he thinks you can make a contribution to our overall goals, he’ll promote you to regional commander.”

“That’s your position isn’t it?” replied Putnam.

“I’ll be moving up to district commander if you work out, so don’t fuck it up for me!”

“District Commander eh?” mused Putnam, “I wondered who would be promoted to district after Clayton Chow died. Tough for the organization when the District Commander for Ontario gets lymphoma and dies.”

“You can’t be repeating this Putnam, but as the new Regional Commander for Southern Ontario and the GTA you’ll have the clearance to know this. Chow was getting too big for his britches. He wanted command and when he was told he wasn’t ready he threatened to go public with what he knew. Fuckin’ politicians. Anyway, Beal talked to his superiors in L A and the next thing we know Chow had lymphoma. They made him aware that if he was still thinking of going public then his family and his wife’s family out to second cousins and that shit would pay the price for his betrayal. He caved and they let him die after only a month instead of punishing him further with a lingering death.”

Tom could hear Putnam shudder.

Lamont let this morsel of insight worm its way into James Putnam’s mind. He wanted Putnam to understand at his core just what he had become a part of. Once you were in, there was absolutely no getting out, ever! Even the grave could not release you from your obligations.

"You remember that next month is our Territorial meeting," continued Lamont. "We'll be unveiling to the Regional Commanders what is going to be happening across North America. As the acting District Commander, I got the heads up on what's coming."

"Tell me Lou," Putnam replied excitedly.

"OK Putnam, don't get your knickers in a knot. Here's what I know in a nutshell…remember Putnam if it comes back to me that you leaked any of this to anyone, I will kill you myself! Now, where was I…oh ya…over the next year the elected governments of the States and Canada will be pressured to the breaking point. The end of this summer and into the fall our groups, composed mostly of low-level malcontents, intellectual mercenaries and home-grown terrorists, will begin their programs of disruption. Throw into that mix the Presidential election this November and the pot will really start to boil."

"What if the wrong guy gets elected?" queried Putnam.

"There is no wrong guy," said Lamont. "No matter which candidate wins we have people that will offer proof of wrongdoing and election fraud. The losing party will cry foul and it will throw the new administration into complete turmoil. There will be riots in major cities and they will reach a time of great crises. In our own Parliament we have agents within the major parties who will bring about a vote of no confidence. The Governor General will be forced to call an election. We will do the same here as in the U.S. We will have innuendo and then proof of voter fraud and the supporters of the three main parties will be at each other's throats. We will institute violence and riots in major cities. This will all happen in late winter early spring. In some places martial law will be instituted, the National Guard will be brought in and here the War Measures Act will be passed. By the summer the lid on this pressure cooker will have to be screwed down tight."

"Wait a sec," jumped in Putnam. "How do you know this is all going to play out like you think? We've had contested elections in the past and they didn't lead to a breakdown in the system."

"We've been practicing this for a long time Putnam. Each time we've done this we've put the brakes on before we tipped the system into crises. Each time we do this we bump up against the system a little harder to get a feel for how much pressure we need. We've been working out the kinks, and now we're ready. Our meeting next month with the Territorial Commanders of both the

U.S. and Canada and all their Sub Commanders will flesh out this plan for us and also bring us up to speed on what the final push will be."

"What is that?" asked Putnam.

"I don't want to spoil the surprise," growled Lamont, "Let's go get some drinks." Lamont and Putnam left the balcony and all Tom could hear were the heavy footfalls of Lamont's goons.

"Hey Pauly, I see one of dem pieces of paper. They must've blown between the boards." The three were coming around to the double doors that opened into the underside of the raised deck. Tom knew that a cursory search would uncover his hiding spot within minutes. He heard the little doors open.

"Dominic, go in there and get those papers."

"Aww Pauly, I'll get my trousers dirty."

Tom heard the large man grunt as he got down on his hands and knees to crawl into the gloomy mechanical area.

"Which way Pauly?" whined Dominic, "Can't see nuthin'."

"Go to your left…no your other left. That's it, I think straight ahead from there."

"Think I see 'em Pauly…ya, got it."

"Keep lookin' Dominic, Mr. Lamont says there's more'n one down there."

"Aw c'mon Pauly, my knees is gettin' wet, there's lots of puddles down here. Hey Pauly…there's someone here."

Tom's black loafer had been at the edge of the compressor and as he tried to wedge himself tighter into the small hiding space his foot had slipped on the slick concrete and moved out just as Dominic's gaze had glided past.

"Grab 'em Dom!" Yelled Pauly. "Squid you get in there and give Dom a hand."

"Sure Boss."

Dominic grabbed Tom by the ankle and started pulling on his leg. "Hey, easy buddy, lighten up, I'll come peacefully." Tom crawled out of the maintenance area and when they were both out, he said, "Jeez you guys, what's the beef. My wife sent you here to find me?"

Pauly looked him up and down and said, "What was you doin' in dare?"

Putting on an air of guilty confession, he said, "Well I got a bit hosed earlier and my wife wanted to go out for dinner and I was in no shape so she got pissed and I retreated up here to the patio to hide and sleep it off. When I heard the elevator coming, I thought it was her and I slipped under there so she wouldn't find me."

"How'd you get in there?" asked Pauly.

"I've this code for several VIP areas and I tried it, it worked."

Pauly seemed like he might be starting to believe Tom's jury-rigged story.

"What did you hear from down there?" asked Pauly.

"Nothing," lied Tom, "Asleep."

"I think we should take him down to see Mr. Lamont," said Dominic.

Pauly scolded, "No names you idiot!"

"Hey I don't want any trouble."

"I think you should come with us," said Pauly.

"Look fellas, why don't you just let me go back to my room. I didn't hear anything and I never saw you fellas." Tom started backing away from the three large men to give himself some room. He stepped back and put his hands behind him to feel for the lip of the raised deck. His jacket pulled tight and brought the pocket where he'd stuffed the tracing paper into prominence.

"Pauly, look it," said Squid.

They reached into their pockets and retrieved small black pouches. Tom instantly realized they were ballistic nylon bags, partially filled with lead shot attached to a flexible handle. *Crap*, he thought, one swing *can remove half your face and there are three of them coming at me.*

Squid sprang forward, nimble for his two hundred and ninety pounds. Tom pulled his chin in, arched his back slightly and shifted his weight to his back leg, just quickly enough to allow the hard-swung blackjack to miss his nose by a hair. Squid was not used to missing and his forward momentum threw him off balance. As he stumbled forward Tom sent a hard sidekick into his backside that accelerated him headfirst into the skirt of the raised deck. There was no give to the vinyl cellulose matrix of the composite lumber that was used in the front molding of the deck. Tom could see Squid's neck compress and knew that if he wasn't partially paralyzed, he would at least be out of the fight.

Tom backed up quickly to roll onto the raised deck as the two came at him. The back of his legs touched the deck but when he began his roll, he became tangled in a bar stool. They grabbed his ankles and yanked him mightily from under the furniture and off the raised deck. Tom landed hard and his chest was stomped on. His lungs felt crushed, his breath coming in short gasps, ragged and painful. Dominic's massive hand clamped onto the top of Tom's hairless head and he was hauled upright.

"Hey Pauly, he ain't dead."

Pauly looked over at Dominic and then at Tom, "Ya Dom, he ain't dead. Ever happen before?"

Dominic thought for a second, "No…that stomp usually just crushes 'em and they die."

Tom didn't like the subject or tone of this discussion. Wobbling on his tiptoes now, Dominic's powerful fingers digging painfully into his skull, he knew his face and neck were terribly exposed. He had no idea how long this discussion would hold Dom and Pauly's attention.

He threw a right cross at Dominic's temple and felt solid contact. He might as well have punched a steer. The big man turned his gaze away from Pauly to stare at Tom. Balanced on his toes, Tom threw a hard right at the hinge of Dom's jaw, then drew back his right and in tandem with his left he delivered a double shuto to each side of the big man's neck. This should have dropped a mountain gorilla, but Dominic just looked at Tom and smiled. Tom felt Dominic's left hand tighten on his head, felt the bones of his skull compress, saw the man's huge right hand form an even bigger fist and begin to draw back. In desperation Tom started attacking the big man's throat. He knuckle-punched the larynx, he drove haitos into Dominic's carotid artery, and he punched with all his might onto the button of Dominic's iron chin. Dom unclenched his fist and brought his right hand back to try and defend himself, he was tiring. Tom's heels touched the ground. Using all his strength Tom drove a palm strike straight up into Dominic's nose. He felt the cartilage of Dominic's nose implode and felt the sharp bone of the nasal passage drive into the heel of his palm like a spike hammered into a two by four. Tom wrenched his hand free flinging blood off his palm from the gaping wound. There was too much blood. He looked up, Dominic's nose was gone, replaced by a gore filled depression that was erupting blood. His eyes, crossed at contradicting angles were bleeding. Where his nose should have been there was a thick clot of blood and mucus blown out over his face like an impact crater. In the middle of this dark tear there was a stream of blood and something else gushing down his face and onto Tom. Dominic was dead, he just hadn't fallen over yet. Tom caught movement just at the edge of his periphery and made to evade. His ankles were suddenly locked up and he couldn't move. As if watching the last three slides in a power point presentation, he saw dead Dom's knees buckle, he saw Squid with his arms tightly wrapped around his ankles and he saw four massive knuckles quickly filling his view.

Tom's eyes wouldn't open. It felt like he had a thick layer of wool wrapped around his face but his cheek was being stung by bees. He tried to evade the little buggers but they kept finding his cheek and stinging. He thought about swatting them but his arms were pinned.

"Wake up buddy…we want to talk to you."

The bees were talking to Tom.

"I think you killed him Pauly," said Squid.

"Not…dead," mumbled Tom, "Get bees off."

"What the fuck…bees? C'mon buddy, open your eyes."

Tom slowly opened his eyes and his head started to clear. His face felt like it had been crushed in a vise and he could only see clearly out of one eye. When he breathed liquid bubbled in his nose and it felt like an axe, embedded in his chest, was being twisted.

"I think he's coming round Squid, don't let go of his arms!"

Tom saw Pauly's face, in and out of focus but close to his. Pauly slapped Tom's cheek one more time for good measure, then said, "Okay buddy, who are you and what you doin' here?"

"Putnam…following…Putnam." This was all Tom could get out, he couldn't breathe and he could feel his guts beginning to roll over.

"Stay with me buddy, what…is…your…name?"

Tom stayed conscious just long enough to realize he was throwing up. He heard a muffled growl of revulsion as Pauly jumped back. Then he saw the strangest thing. A round piece of wood appeared at the side of Pauly's face, then Pauly's head snapped to the side and everything faded out.

He was on his knees when he regained his senses, his face and chest plastered to the floor in a pool of vomit, his arms down and to the side and his rear stuck in the air. His mind chuckled, remembering the joke about the guy who wanted to be buried with his butt sticking out of the ground.

Tom heard noise and activity. He heard a man running and cursing and he could hear a woman's voice yelling. Tom leaned and let his hips fall sideways to the floor. From this angle he could see Squid stalking someone, he was moving forward swiping his blackjack back and forth. A young woman dressed in dark clothing was slowly and deliberately backing up while not taking her eyes off Squid. She was smoothly rotating a six-foot rod with one hand in front of her as she held her other arm out to the side for balance.

From his prone position he saw Pauly lying just a few feet away. Pauly's face was crimson streaked. His eyes were open and his big right hand wiped the blood away. He swore silently and grunted, both at the same time as he awkwardly pushed himself to his knees.

"Christ!" he muttered as he tried to brush blood and vomit from his jacket.

"Got you bitch!" Squid shouted. He made a violent swing with his outstretched blackjack. The girl backstepped nimbly and Squid's exertion toppled him forward. The maple bo arced upward instantly smashing into Squid's jaw like an uppercut with an anvil, the blow pushing Squid upright, looking skyward. In an instant the bo changed direction and the long slender shaft came crashing down on Squid's forehead. His knees buckled and he fell face forward, his limp arms making no move to break his fall.

While Squid received this vicious beating, Pauly was on his feet. Blackjack out, he was hunched over, trying to silently approach the young women from behind. There was no way Tom could get up and tackle Pauly. Just trying to raise his head made him almost pass out. Pauly passed Tom's prone form. Using his hands and arms Tom turned himself clockwise so his feet were just ahead of Pauly as he crept away from Tom toward the woman. On his side, Tom hooked his right foot across the top of Pauly's trailing left ankle and with great effort drove the leading edge of his other foot into the back of Pauly's knee. With the last of his strength he cried, "Bo fighter!"

The young woman pirouetted away from the fallen Squid. Her head led her body as she spun gracefully on a perfect axis and her eyes transferred the image of danger to her brain faster than her body was spinning. She brought her maple bo up and around in a two-handed swing and caught the hobbled Pauly across the temple. Pauly's head snapped to the side and slammed onto his shoulder with a sickening sound as the hardwood staff shattered on impact. Tom let his eyes close, his energy sapped he could feel reality slipping away.

Tom felt gentle hands raise his head, his eyes were still closed but he could feel his head being cradled. "Oh God you stink!" she said trying to hold her nose.

"Ya," he mumbled, "It's hard holding anything down when a battering ram pounds your guts." Tom tried to sit up but couldn't. His head swam and he thought he may throw up again and that would be too embarrassing.

"Lie back down," she said, laying a cool hand soothingly over his forehead as she gently but firmly guided his head back down onto her lap.

"Who are you, why are you here?" Tom knew he sounded erratic but there were just too many questions.

"Okay Tom, one at a time."

"Hey…how do you know my name?"

"Shhhhh…settle a bit and I'll try to explain." She sat there for a minute while she gathered her thoughts and Tom had a chance to study her face. She was pretty, on the younger side of thirty. Her hair was dark, but it was hard to tell because it was pulled back into a very tight pony tail. Her eyes were dark and appeared deep set in the harsh light. What made an impression on him though was her skin. Maybe it was because she wore a sheen of perspiration or maybe she was flushed from fighting, but Tom thought she glowed with a suffused light.

She cleared her throat and started speaking in a low whisper, "My name is Laura…if you are who I think you are, you will find out the rest of who I am. I know your name because we have met before."

"Really," said a bewildered Tom, "I'm sure I would remember you if I'd met you before. Are you a friend of Gracie's, from school maybe…you're too old to be a friend of Lilly's?" Tom was babbling now, maybe it was time to shut up and let the young woman speak.

"We met at a martial arts tournament ten years ago. I was sixteen and a new brown belt. My dad was my sensei and had just started bringing me to tournaments. The black belts were performing their katas and dad wanted me to see them. He especially wanted me to observe you. He had seen you the year before when you'd won the Canadian Men's Open Championship and had been impressed with your style, he said your intensity was towering."

Tom remembered that tournament. It was the biggest tournament he had ever been in and he had won both kata and kumite in his division. He also remembered being nearly knocked cold by a fire-breathing twenty-five-year-old who was impatient to be awarded the overall championship.

"After you won the gold in black belt kata, my dad brought me over to meet you."

"Jorry…Jorgen Hoching…are you little Laura Hoching?"

"Yes," she smiled.

Tom struggled to sit up; his head had cleared a bit. "Let's move up there," he said, nodding to the covered hot tubs. She helped him to his feet and he felt her strength. They made their way slowly to the hot tubs and Tom pulled the cover back from one. He gingerly went to his knees, fearing he may just topple over. He dipped his hands into the lukewarm water and splashed it onto his face, scrubbing the partially dried vomit from his skin. After repeating several times, he removed his jacket, pulled his golf shirt over his head and lowered it into the pool of water to rinse it.

"I think the jacket is ruined, but if I can rinse the smell out of my shirt, I might be able to wear it out of the hotel without drawing attention." As he was speaking, he started to turn toward Laura. He stopped when he noticed her staring at him. "What's the matter, am I bleeding?"

"No," she said, still staring at him, "It's just that…I read the article about you from your hometown paper…it was picked up by the Post. The article said you were so badly burned that at one point the doctors didn't think you would survive, but I don't see any scarring. Your skin looks pretty healthy, well…the skin on your chest and back anyway. Are the scars on your legs?"

"There was no scarring," said Tom softly, memories threatening to come tumbling forward. He shuddered, "My doctor said it was a miracle. The Canadian Journal of Medicine said it was an impossibility. There's been a gag order put in place to silence my doctor or they're threatening to have his license revoked. I spent three months in the hospital completely swaddled in bandages. When Doc Bailey unwrapped me, he couldn't explain my recovery. All the hair on my body was gone. Even my eyelashes were gone. But my skin was fine, actually better than fine. I'm sixty, my skin was saggy, pouches under my eyes, loose skin at my neck, you know…like a favorite old suit that's now too big. Well when they took off the bandages it was as if my insides had filled the suit back up again to its original fit. Eventually my eyebrows and eyelashes grew in, but so far nothing else. Doc Bailey wanted to take me down to some burn lab in the states to try and get some answers but I couldn't. There were trumped up drug charges that were pending and I was having problems with the insurance companies that held my policies. I had a lot to deal with."

Tom had wrung the excess water out of his shirt and pulled it back on. He pulled at the sleeves and collar to try and get the shirt to lay right but it was still damp and clung to him annoyingly.

"I know Tom; I've been keeping up with your story since it first came to my attention. I think that's why I was here tonight."

"What do you mean by that?"

"I was here following Lamont and his merry band of jerk offs. Look Tom, I don't know if Lamont is going to miss these three goons or not, but I think we should get out of here before someone comes looking for them and finds us instead."

"Good idea," said Tom. "Let's check something first." Tom grabbed his own soiled sport jacket and pulled his wallet and credit card holder from the inside pocket. "Oh ya," he exclaimed, "Mustn't forget this." He pulled the folded piece of tracing paper from his side pocket.

"What's that?" asked Laura.

"Later." Tom then proceeded down the stairs and over to Pauly's body. "Here's one less dipshit to populate this world," he said as he knelt down by the large man's dead carcass. He opened Pauly's jacked by the lapel and reached inside to the breast pocket.

"Nothing," said Tom, "I guess in their line of business they don't carry too much identification." They searched the other two thugs and came up with nothing. "I think we better hide these bodies."

"Let's put them under the raised deck," said Laura, "Do you think you can do that? I mean…can you exert yourself without keeling over…they are pretty heavy." Laura's voice trailed off as if she thought she may have offended Tom's masculinity or something.

"Thanks for the consideration Laura…I actually don't feel too bad. My head has cleared some and I don't think my ribs are broken, although I don't know how they couldn't be, Dominic's foot should have broken my ribs and ruptured every major organ I possess. Why I'm not dead I don't know."

Ten minutes later they had the bodies of the three killers pushed under the deck. Tom was about to close the little doors when Laura said, "What do you think we should do about this?" She was pointing at a blood pool left when Dominic's ruined face had ploughed into the rubberized coating of the rooftop floor. There were also small puddles of blood where Squid and Pauly had met their fates.

Tom looked around quickly, "There's a hose just behind the doors, if it's turned on, we're in business."

Tom reeled out ten feet of the black rubber hose and turned the knurled brass nozzle. A rush of water poured forth and Tom aimed the stream at the pools of blood. He directed the water to push the blood toward the roof scuppers and the rain handling system drained the fluids away.

"I think that will pass a cursory inspection. We don't have time to do any more." With that Tom coiled up the hose, threw it underneath the raised deck and closed the double doors.

"Any idea what we should do now?" asked Tom.

"I have a place, we can talk and grab a bite. You hungry?"

"Hadn't thought about it but ya, I'm famished," he replied.

"Good," she said, "Let's go then." Laura led the way to the elevators. Once they were in the lobby Laura said, "You get the truck; I'll meet you out on Jarvis."

Nigel was good on his earlier promise and had Tom's big F150 within minutes of Tom handing him the valet card.

"Enjoy your stay in Toronto," said Nigel with a smile, as he closed Tom's driver side door. He placed the last twenty that Tom had given him into his pocket as Tom cinched up his seatbelt.

"Take care Nigel," he said as he pulled away from the side street curb.

Laura was waiting for him just before he was ready to turn onto Jarvis Street. She jumped up into the truck's cab and said, "Just drive. We're going up to Gerrard Street; turn right when you get there. It's only about another block and a half."

Tom drove quietly, all his senses focused on the street as a wail of sirens grew quickly out of the indistinct hubbub of noise that is a city. They were descending rapidly out of the north and approaching Tom's location. With no time or opportunity to veer off Jarvis he kept moving north with traffic. "Laura," Tom said slowly, "If they're coming for me, you sit tight. I'll run…tell them I held you hostage. If they catch me, I'll tell them the same thing."

"Hush Tom…look."

Three police cars were screaming past them with their sirens blaring and their red and blue lights flashing. They careened into the Grand Hotel and Tom lost them in his rear-view mirror.

"They must've found them," said Tom.

The short drive to Gerrard Street produced no more sirens and as Tom turned right, he saw the beautiful stone church that he had noticed earlier.

"Look at the stonework on that old church," Tom remarked to Laura, "I wish I had a chance to take a closer look."

"Well well," replied Laura, "I guess I'm in the wish granting business tonight. Turn into this street."

Tom put on his signal and turned left onto Horticultural Avenue.

"This goes into Allan Gardens, doesn't it?"

"Yes, but we're not going that far. See those townhouses ahead?"

"Ya."

"Drive around to the back…ya right here, turn left then right, stop."

Laura jumped out of the cab and ran over to the garage door at the back of the first townhouse. She flipped up the cover and entered her code. The garage door opened and he backed smoothly in, then saw Laura wave for him to leave the truck and come outside.

"Aren't we going inside?" Tom asked.

"No, we keep this townhouse as a front. If we're discovered here then it takes our enemies' eyes off where we really are."

"What're you talkin' 'bout Laura? You're sounding very cloak and daggerish."

"Quiet Tom," Laura exclaimed gently but firmly. "All these questions and more will be answered, but not right this minute and not here."

She reached up and grabbed Tom by his shirt front. Without another word she started walking toward the church with Tom in tow. They approached the north side of the large stone building and Tom noticed the church parking lot was hidden from street lights. Laura gave a quick look around and then proceeded behind a buttress in the wall and Tom saw a steel door labeled, Custodian. Laura unlocked the door and they walked through into the basement of the church. Undeterred by the darkness Laura walked purposely forward still holding onto Tom's shirt front. They came to a door which Laura pulled open and she and Tom stepped inside. Tom thought he could make out panels and meters on one of the walls. "Is this a utility room?" he asked.

"Shhh," was the reply. Laura went to the far wall and moved her hand to the top right corner. Tom heard a soft click and the wall pushed away. They stepped inside and Laura pushed the wall back into place. "Follow me," she instructed.

The corridor they followed was comfortably wide and Tom noticed the floor descending slowly. They went through two more doors during their hike but Tom had no idea how long they'd been in the basement of the church when they came to a third door and Laura flipped the top of a keypad open. She keyed in several numbers and then said, "Laura Hoching…nineteen." There was a hiss and the door opened. Tom walked through the doorway and into another era.

Chapter 5

The panorama before him had such a richness of color and texture he felt home. The room entered and warmed him, it balanced him; his heart broke to think he would ever have to leave. It was so much more than just a room. The space before him was large, he estimated two thousand square feet, about half the size of a basketball court. There were no interior walls, just one open space. Because of the size of the room it was hard to discern the height of the ceiling, but if Tom had to guess he would say fourteen feet.

The floor was made of large slabs of polished limestone with brass splines set between the generous blocks of stone. The light reflecting from these polished floors was a soft creamy gold. Large oriental carpets lay upon these stone floors but not in such abundance that the warm light from the stone was dimmed. On the walls to a height of six feet was the most beautiful hardwood paneling Tom had ever seen. The wood itself had to be mahogany, just by its color alone. It was finished to bring out the deep reds and purples of this most richly hued wood. The recessed panels each were long and narrow, two to a vertical section running all around the walls. Every ten feet or so there was a tall pilaster, shaped as a fluted column out of the same warm tropical timber reaching all the way to the ceiling where it bloomed into a Corinthian capital. From each capital there ran along the ceiling to the capital on the opposite wall the primary beam of a coffered ceiling. The primary trays were approximately ten feet by ten feet in size, having the secondary beams and trays laid out inside these in an alternating square and octagonal pattern. The plastered walls and ceiling above the mahogany paneling were painted in a muted cream. The entire atmosphere of the room could only be described as golden. The only illumination that Tom saw were sconces on the walls, one in the middle of each section of open wall between the mahogany columns and several reading lamps. Some on tables or desks situated around the room and some stately brass or platinum floor lamps nestled in beside overstuffed and extremely comfortable looking leather armchairs.

At the far end of the room were very long and solidly built mahogany tables placed slightly in front of floor to ceiling bookshelves. The tables were strewn haphazardly with books and magazines and reading lamps. Comfortable looking leather chairs, some in a deep rich hunter green and others in burnished brown surrounded the long tables and at the end of one table bathed in the light from a single lamp sat an elderly gentleman, reading.

"C'mon Tom, I want to introduce you."

Tom followed her and the seated man turned toward them. Tom wanted to look at the beautiful finishes of the room, but he couldn't take his attention away from the man they were approaching. He stood as they got nearer, he was tall, slim and ramrod straight. His medium length hair was pure white and very thick. His face was lined with age and worn with care but the twinkle in his piercing blue eyes and the half smile on his lips were those of a younger mien. His entire bearing portrayed a distinguished and stately manner.

"Tom, I'd like you to meet Gordon Bernard."

"Pleased to meet you sir." He extended his hand.

"Tom…It is so good to finally meet you. I have been looking forward to this for some time."

As Tom took the older man's hand in his firm grasp, he could feel that firmness reciprocated and felt a tremendous strength residing there. He knew instinctively that he was now under this man's protection and for a while he would be safe. The realization of just how unsafe and alone he had felt for the last twenty-four hours suddenly engulfed him as the growing fatigue caused by this accumulated nonstop stress washed over him and he almost stumbled.

"Here Tom…please sit down," Gordon said as he gently guided Tom to one of the leather armchairs. "You have had rather a busy twenty-four hours, haven't you? Laura my dear, would you be so kind as to put on a pot of tea please. Earl Grey I think…Tom, is that all right with you?"

"Yes, thank you," said Tom. "That would be terrific." Laura seemed to disappear between the book cases and Tom realized there must be more rooms back there.

"What kind of a place is this?" Tom asked with unconcealed wonder in his voice.

"If you're up for it, I'll answer any questions you have Tom."

"Where are we Mr. Bernard and who are you? How do you know me and why have you been looking forward to meeting me?"

"Those questions will encompass some rather lengthy explanations, but let us start by having you call me Gordon, all right?"

"That's fine Gordon, thank you."

Gordon sat for a moment looking at Tom. There was great compassion in his eyes and a melancholy note in his voice when he started to speak.

"You have been through a great deal recently. You have lost your wife, your home, your livelihood and your earthly reputation."

These words clamped Tom's chest like a tightening vice. He couldn't breathe, his throat shut and his eyes began to burn with a thousand unshed tears. He tried to speak but only croaked, "Why?"

"Tom…you were in their way."

"I don't understand."

"You will Tom, soon enough."

Just then Laura reentered the vast library pushing an exquisite silver cart with a matching silver tea set. On plates was freshly sliced bread and preserves.

"It'll just be another minute or two to steep. Have I missed much?"

"No," replied Gordon, "I was just about to tell Tom about our sanctuary."

"Good," said Laura, looking at Tom.

"It is a long story Tom and has many branches that we may or may not touch on tonight, but given your condition I will be as brief as thoroughness allows. Two centuries ago the War of 1812 commenced. The Americans had an eye to expanding into the British colony of Upper Canada. York, the future city of Toronto, became their opening target. The British regulars, under Major General Sheaffe, had the local militia dig supply depots throughout the area for the safe storage of arms and material. The large excavations were dug deep, lined with unmortared rubble stone and floored with compacted sand over course gravel."

"Excuse me gentlemen…the tea is ready. Here Gordon. Tom, how do you like yours?"

"Just a bit of sugar please…thanks."

With the three now sipping tea and munching on slices of bread with fruit preserves, Gordon continued his tale.

"The history books call it the Battle of York, but it wasn't much of a battle. In April of 1813, Fourteen American naval vessels crossed the lake and landed their invasion force of seventeen hundred infantry. They easily handled the 600 defenders. The Americans had their victory and then proceeded to loot and burn the town and any of the British supply depots they could find. A week later on May 8 they sailed away. The supply depot that had been dug and maintained at the eastern boundary of York was missed by the marauding Americans. This eastern limit would later become Jarvis St.

"The militia emptied the depot and the British regulars took the majority of the supplies and marched off to reinforce Kingston. It was decided that the large and well-built depot excavation would be camouflaged and left for possible future use. Huge pine trees, eight feet in diameter, were felled from the surrounding forest. Their branches were removed but the timbers were not sawn or dressed. They were set side by side across the excavation, and then chinked with plant fiber. Earth was piled and leveled over the timbers and sod was laid over this. The empty depot was never used again and was quickly forgotten as the sod grew and saplings took root in the soil covering the roof of the large excavation."

Gordon took a sip of tea and continued with the tale of York's phenomenal growth and its evolution into the city of Toronto, how that growth expanded the city's limits until the hidden military depot became Toronto real estate.

"By the 1870s the population of Toronto had mushroomed to sixty thousand and one of the city's Baptist churches, located on Bond Street, was bursting at the seams. It was decided by the congregation that it was now large enough and prosperous enough to have a full-sized church constructed of stone. Several successful and wealthy businessmen belonging to the congregation purchased a plot of land on the northeast corner of Jarvis and Gerrard Streets. This plot coincided with the location of the old military supply depot. The forgotten depot was still roofed by perfectly preserved pine logs covered over by twenty feet of earth compacted by sixty years of rain, snow and frost. The excavation for the new church's foundation was dug directly over the old depot."

At this revelation Tom asked, "Did the excavation break into the old depot?"

"No," replied Gordon, "The existence of the subterranean supply depot remained unknown. What is of interest to us here is that one of the stone masons hired to work on the foundation of the new church, was one Gordon

Bernard Senior. His wife had just born their first child, named after the father; Gordon Bernard."

Tom was just about to sip the last of his tea but stopped abruptly and slowly peered at Gordon. He didn't say anything at first, just looked at Gordon, waiting for an explanation. As Gordon calmly returned the look without speaking further, Tom finally asked, "Have I heard you correctly? Are you saying your father worked on this church in the eighteen seventies? Are you saying you were born then?"

"Eighteen seventy-five to be precise, end of June actually."

"My God Gordon…that would make you…"

"Tom," Gordon said softly, "You do not need to remind me of how old I am. I have lived in three consecutive centuries."

"This is unbelievable," Tom forced the words out. "This is impossible! No one has ever lived that long." Tom lapsed into brooding silence.

"Do you think I am lying to you?" asked Gordon without accusation. "Do you think that Laura found you, saved your life, brought you here to this secret and unknown place to meet me so that I could lie to you concerning my age?"

"It doesn't make any sense," countered Tom. "Of course, you wouldn't do all this just to make up a story concerning your great age. I don't disbelieve you Gordon. if I'm to believe the rest of your tale, then your claim must be true. It is just that this is outside of any logic that I have ever believed in or trusted."

"What about your belief in God Tom?"

"What do you mean?"

"There are many people who would say that belief in a God is a thing that defies logic. You and I along with a great many others believe, defying all logic that says otherwise." Gordon knew he was close to losing Tom. He was staring straight ahead with a glazed look, his head shaking slowly from side to side.

"Tom…just for now, suspend your desire for credence."

"I can do that."

"I would like you to listen to me for a little while longer, accept my words and the story they tell at face value, for now. If at the end you decide that I am not being honest with you, you are free to leave."

"I want to believe you. I believe truth is spoken freely here, it's just that the logical side of me is having trouble catching up to the spiritual side of me."

"I would suspect your sanity if you told me anything else," said Gordon. He looked over his shoulder to a curtain on the other wall that was between two fluted mahogany columns. "I want to show you something Tom." Gordon stood and moved toward the wall that held the closed curtain. Laura, then Tom stood to follow Gordon. When they were standing in front of the golden curtain, Gordon reached up and took a tasseled rope in his hand.

"What is your Psalm Tom?"

"Excuse me," Tom said, not understanding.

"What is the Psalm that has helped you throughout your life? What is the Psalm that you clung to when you first comprehended what had been done to you and your family? What Psalm came into your mind when you implored God to guide you?"

"The twenty third." Tom was numb. How deep was this man's understanding?

"Say it Tom, recite the twenty third Psalm!"

In a barely audible voice Tom started, stumbling at first but gaining coherence with each word, strength coming to him as he spoke:

"The Lord is my Shepherd; I shall not want
He maketh me to lie down in green pastures:
He leadeth me beside the still waters.
He restoreth my soul:
He leadeth me in the paths of righteousness for His name' sake.
Yea, though I walk through the valley of the shadow of death,
I will fear no evil: For thou art with me;
Thy rod and thy staff, they comfort me.
Thou preparest a table before me in the presence of mine enemies;
Thou annointest my head with oil; my cup runneth over.
Surely goodness and mercy shall follow me all the days of my life,
And I shall dwell in the House of the Lord forever.
Amen."

As Tom finished the last line Gordon pulled the rope and the curtain opened, revealing a large, roughhewn stone tablet set into the plastered wall. On it were carved the same words that Tom had just recited by heart, the same but different.

In a beautiful combination of young and old, male and female, Gordon and Laura began to recite the words as carved in the stone:

The Lord is my Shepherd,
I shall not want for He maketh me.
To lie down in green pastures he leadeth me.
Beside the still waters he restoreth my soul.
He leadeth me in the paths of Righteousness,
For His names sake I walk through the valley of the shadow of death
I shall fear no evil for thou art with me;
Thy rod and thy staff, they comfort me.
Thou preparest a table before me.
In the presence of mine enemies Thou annointest my head with oil.
My cup runneth over for surely goodness and mercy shall follow me.
All the days of my life I shall dwell in the House of the Lord.
Forever.

A profound silence fell as Gordon and Laura finished reciting the Psalm. Tom was at a complete loss and did not know what to say, didn't even know if he should say anything. Over the years he had recited this Psalm seven or eight thousand times and had never suspected the order of the words could change. This made no sense whatsoever. Tom's thoughts refocused as he noticed Gordon and Laura looking at him. They were smiling and calmly looking at Tom, waiting patiently for him to make a reply.

"This makes no sense Gordon. Why would anyone change the arrangement of the twenty third Psalm?"

"We've often pondered that very question Tom, but not in the way you mean. This is the original version that King David wrote."

Tom was done. If these people were lying to him, if there was any falsehood in these two, he could not feel it. Maybe it was because he hadn't slept in close to thirty hours. Maybe the more surreal something was the more he was inclined to believe it. Who could have predicted two days ago that he would be the cause of someone's death, be saved himself from certain death by a young woman he had met ten years before and be led into a secret underground citadel that had been excavated under a church a hundred years ago, and Oh…let's not forget the one hundred- and forty-year-old man. He turned around and sat down in the closest armchair he could find. Gordon and Laura came over and sat beside him.

"Okay you guys, that may just be the straw, but please explain this one to me now if you wouldn't mind and then I think I need to get some sleep."

"Of course," said Gordon. "This one is quite straight forward."

Tom laughed.

"You know the story of King David of ancient Israel."

"Sure," said a deadpan Tom, "David and Goliath."

"Good," Gordon continued, "David became King of Israel and Judah in 1010 BC. The language spoken during this time period was an ancient form of Hebrew and the written alphabet of this language is called today Paleo Hebrew. When King David eventually wrote his psalms, they were written using this alphabet. Once he achieved his rule, King David proceeded to take the loose kingdom of Israel and Judah and forged an empire. David was a warrior king, a warrior for God. This is important to remember for we believe it is at the heart of the Twenty Third Psalm. We believe that David wrote this psalm shortly after the events that produced the legend of David and Goliath. He is a young shepherd who becomes an armor bearer in the army of King Saul. Before a battle with the Philistines in the Valley of Elah the Philistine champion named Goliath challenges whoever the Israelites would send out to meet him in single combat. David volunteers and the rest is the legend.

"Now Tom, think about the psalm. *The Lord is my shepherd*, David, having been a shepherd all of his young life, knows how a shepherd cares for his flock and will protect each one of them. *I shall not want for He maketh me*, David knows also he has been fashioned by God and has all the attributes and abilities that will be required of him to fulfill God's desires for him. *To lie down in green pastures he leadeth me*, as a young shepherd David has spent his life leading his flocks to safe pastures where they can safely feed and rest. As a devout young man David realizes that God, as his shepherd does the same for him. *Beside the still waters he restoreth my soul*, the best pasturage has water. To a desert people water signifies life. David gives thanks to God every time he finds water and shows the connection between the restoration of his soul and the finding of water, what we believe may be a reference by David to baptism. *He leadeth me in the paths of righteousness*, David is saying that he believes that God knows the best path in life for him, and by extension all of us, and that if he follows the path God lays out for him his life will have true meaning. *For His names sake I walk through the valley of the shadow of death*, for his God and his faith David volunteers to meet Goliath in single combat in the Valley of Elah. The enormity of David's trust in his belief of God's path for him cannot be overstated. Here he is, a young shepherd boy, newly elevated to the position of a king's armor bearer, walking out into the middle ground between two opposing armies. There, waiting for him is the Philistine champion. Reported to be seven feet tall he is massively muscled and encased in the finest armor that the Philistines can afford. He would cast a huge shadow. Contrast this death dealing behemoth with David, a scrawny teenager who just recently called home the hills and fields surrounding Bethlehem. *I shall fear no evil for thou art with me*, here again is David's stated faith; that no matter the situation God will never leave him. *Thy rod and thy staff, they comfort me*. The rod or scepter and the staff of a monarch are symbols of governance and rule. David writes of the comfort that he derives from God's rule over his life. Even if Goliath destroys him there is no fear or shame because David has trod His path. *Thou preparest a table before me*, wherever David's life will lead him he knows that God has gone before him and prepared the way. All David needs is the courage to go forward. *In the presence of mine enemies Thou annointest my head with oil*, surrounded by Philistines and standing in Goliath's immense shadow David knows God's plan for him is not over and he shall come out of this confrontation victorious. *My cup runneth over for surely goodness and mercy shall follow me*, David is overjoyed with this realization and he knows that after this victory he will be the one chosen to dispense justice and mercy for his people. *All the days of my life I shall dwell in the house of the Lord*, he reaffirms his promise that no matter the content of his life going forward from this day, he will never lose his trust in God. *Forever*, puts the seal to his oath."

Tom mused for a second and then said, "That is a fascinating interpretation of your version, and it makes a lot of sense, but how can you be so sure that this recitation is the original version of the Twenty Third Psalm?"

"There is, living still in the Middle East, a tribe that retains a form of Paleo Hebrew as the root of their modern written language. They number less than a thousand people now and are named the Samaritans. It was the Samaritans who first translated King David's original writing of the Twenty Third Psalm into some of the modern languages that are in use today, mainly Arabic and Kurdish. That is why our tablet reads in English and not some forgotten dialect of ancient Hebrew. This tablet was carved in seventeen forty-four from an earlier tablet that had been presented to a group we are descended from. That particular tablet was carved in fifteen oh eight."

"So…" Tom hesitated, "This tribe spends its time translating old Hebrew writings?"

"No," replied Gordon, "They are an unbroken linguistic line going back to the time of King David. When they recite or record writings from the early periods of the Hebrew empire, their portrayal is correct."

"How did you find them?"

"It took four hundred years of civil war and military defeats to destroy David's kingdom, during which time large portions of its citizens were killed or dispersed. The culture was lost and the language that King David had written his psalms in ceased to be used. It was sixteen hundred years before anyone from the west heard it in its original form. In the late eleventh century during the First Crusade, a Benedictine Monk named Ademar de Fleury, found some of David's psalms in their original Paleo Hebrew being translated into Arabic. He managed to save the documents from marauding Frankish knights. He was a scholar and master of languages and studied the ancient documents. In 1099 he disappeared into the desert. Thirty years later the monk reappears as a nameless wandering prophet in the City of Turbessel. The wandering monk had undergone an epiphany while lost in the wilderness and had begun a system of beliefs he called 'The Shepherd's Path.' The Monk found a following in Turbessel and an end to his wanderings. Eventually he accepted twenty-three disciples into his service and trained them in his beliefs. Once trained they were sent out to find their own paths with orders not to proselytize. They were to accept followers of all faiths they believed had been directed to them by God. They were never to exceed twenty-three followers.

"By 1144 Turbessel was being torn apart by Muslim incursions and its demise was inevitable. De Fleury decided to leave for Jerusalem before Turbessel fell. He wasn't afraid of the coming violence, he had followers and friends of all faiths. He was concerned that many people in their desperation and fear of turmoil would try to make him out to be a Messiah that would save them. You see Tom…Ademar de Fleury had been forty-eight when he left France in 1095 to join the armies of the Crusade."

Gordon stopped speaking. He had noticed Tom's head begin to nod, not in agreement but in total exhaustion.

"I'm going to try and conclude this chapter quickly Tom. I cannot imagine your fatigue. De Fleury and some of his followers left Turbessel in May and made their way to Jerusalem. They lived and worked and remained anonymous. De Fleury continued to teach any and all candidates that found their way to him. The monk was still in Jerusalem in 1192 when Richard of England met the Muslims under Saladin. The battle for Jerusalem never took place for Richard realized that even if he managed to defeat Saladin and capture the city, his forces would never survive Saladin's siege. He and the Kurdish leader made truce to allow his forces safe passage out of the Holy Land and make Jerusalem a safe city for Christian pilgrims. Twenty of de Fleury's disciples left with the retreating army and made their way back to England. De Fleury remained in Jerusalem and it is here that our manuscripts lose track of him. Some say he is still alive and in the ancient City of God. Our chronicles go on to chart how the 'Shepherd's Path' took root in England and spread from there. The Path also took root in France, the Holy Roman Empire, Lithuania, Poland and the territories of the Teutonic Knights. From those core areas it filtered out into the rest of the world."

Tom stretched mightily in the big comfortable armchair and took in a large lungful of air. He let his breath out slowly and said, "This is a truly amazing tale Gordon, and defies belief. Throughout history there have been myths and stories of secret organizations, have you guys ever been part of those legends? Has anyone, anywhere on earth ever suspected that you exist or is there any investigation anywhere trying to uncover your group?"

Gordon gave Tom a big smile and replied, "We are undiscoverable. I realize this sounds arrogant…but you have to keep in mind that we don't pursue membership. Outside of the people that we know as part of our group we never, and I repeat, never speak of our group and its mission. The only persons who ever find their way to us have already been chosen to find us. As far as my personal experiences go and as far as my reading of our chronicles has taken me, no one who has ever found us has left."

"I think I'm toast Gordon. I need some sleep. Is there somewhere here that I might grab a couple of hours of sleep?"

"Sure is Tom," Laura replied, pointing the way back through to where the kitchen was, "I'll show you."

"I might not be able to sleep after hearing all you have told me, but I'm glad you did. Goodnight Gordon."

Laura led Tom through the opening into the very large and well-appointed kitchen. There was a wide hallway leading off the opposite end and they proceeded down this hall. They stopped at a door halfway down and Laura turned the knob to allow Tom to enter.

"You'll find a washroom at the far end of the room. Fresh towels in the linen closet along with soap and a drinking glass. You should be able to find everything; the rooms are not that large."

"Thanks so much," Tom said, "You really saved my bacon."

"Goodnight Tom, sleep as long as you can." With that Laura closed the wooden door quietly and moved off down the hall.

Tom was pleased to see the bathroom contained a small shower. When he got in, he decided an eternity under this soothing stream of hot water would still not be enough. He got out and was drying off in front of a large wall mirror when he started inspecting his naked torso for damage. There were some splotchy brown and blue areas but the tenderness associated with touching a bruise was surprisingly absent. "I guess those guys didn't hit as hard as I thought," Tom mused. He lay down on the bed and bunched the pillow up so that it supported his neck and thought, "What a night, I sure hope I can sleep." The gentle arms of Morpheus encircled him and bore him to a dreamless sleep as his head touched the pillow and his eyelids closed.

The heavenly smell of coffee greeted Tom's journey back to wakefulness. *Joy must have gotten up before me*, Tom considered dreamily for a second before reality slapped him. He recovered quickly though and was warmed by the thoughts of where he was and the incredible insights revealed to him the night before.

I wonder what time it is?

Tom turned on the table lamp and got out of bed. He put on a robe and slippers that he found placed by his bed and wandered out into the hallway. The intoxicating smell of freshly brewed coffee and hot buttered toast made his stomach gurgle. He poked his head into the large kitchen and saw Laura standing over the work island spreading jam onto a piece of toast, a steaming cup of coffee next to her.

"Is there enough of that for another cup?" he said hopefully.

"I just made a full pot," Laura mumbled around a mouthful of toast.

Tom grabbed a big mug from a rack of cups hung by the fridge. He poured the steaming liquid into the mug and looked around for cream.

"Cream's in the fridge and if you want it sweet, we have honey, coconut sap or agave nectar."

Tom opened the fridge door and grabbed a big pitcher of cream, whistling.

"You're awfully chipper," she said, "For a guy who had the crap beat out of him two nights ago."

"Two nights ago, how long was I asleep?"

"You've slept for eighteen hours, it's four in the morning the day after you got here. Are you hungry, I can fix you pretty much anything you would like."

"I'll just start with coffee for now thanks. Why are you up at four in the morning?"

"Gordon and I have been doing shifts so that one of us could be here when you woke. Gordon thought, and I agree, that a friendly face would help you adjust if you had problems…you know…when you got up."

"You guys have been nothing but thoughtful and kind to me since you first brought me here and I want you to know how much I appreciate it." Tom took a long slurp of his coffee and let out a satisfied, "Ahhh."

"There's nothing like a good breakfast to cure jet lag, waking up in an unfamiliar place or interrupted sleep patterns. All of the food we have brought in is organic. Nothing pasteurized, homogenized or processed. Gordon has believed all his long life that food should be consumed in as close to the condition that it came out of the ground at harvest as possible. The twenty-three members of our Shepherd's Path group include a dairy farmer and two market garden farmers who already believed the same thing. Every couple of days we have fresh produce brought in and we freeze some of the seasonal stuff for the winter."

"Do you have any problems delivering into the church basement?"

"The church caretaker is one of our members and schedules our ins and outs during the daytime so as not to attract undo attention."

Laura walked over to the large stainless-steel side by side refrigerator freezer and opened one of the doors. She began pulling out food items.

"We have free range chicken eggs, homemade cheddar cheese, organic mushrooms, garden fresh bell peppers and anything else you might like in an omelet. We will even grease the cast iron skillet with fresh churned, unpasteurized, unsalted butter."

"That sounds too good to turn down, can I help with anything?"

"You just sit and have another cup of coffee. You don't know where anything is yet and if you haven't cooked in cast iron before it can be tricky."

As Laura began moving about the large kitchen Tom marveled at her grace. Every motion was fluid with no wasted energy. In the nonstop crush of life-threatening activities and then the brain numbing revelations made known to him two nights ago he had had little time or opportunity to actually see this young lady who had so recently entered his life. She was an incredibly lovely young woman. Of medium height, he could see that she had long legs and arms. She had a nice figure that Tom knew would attract many admiring looks from young men her own age but he also knew her strength and skills. Woe be to any young man who thought he might be able to take advantage of this seemingly sweet young girl. Her hair was chestnut with streaks of light brown and her eyes were hazy blue, almost dark grey. As she prepared Tom's breakfast, she hummed a nameless tune. Tom suddenly felt a lump in his throat as he realized he could have been the cause of this marvelous young woman's death. He also realized how much he missed his own daughters.

"Laura…I didn't have a chance to ask you how your father is?" He knew immediately the answer was not one he wanted. She stopped in mid stride and took a second to answer. She was looking downward when she said, "Dad was killed by a hit and run almost three years ago. He was out shoveling the driveway, the police said the vehicle had to plow through a snow bank to hit him, they never found the driver."

"I'm sorry Laura," Tom responded his heart saddened. Tom was pulled from his reverie when he realized Laura was talking to him. "…was a member."

"Excuse me Laura, I was thinking about the last time I saw your Dad and I missed what you were saying."

"You know Tom…I had always known how much my Father thought of you, I wonder if part of that was because he knew the quality of person you were and that you might eventually find your path to us."

"I don't understand what you mean Laura," queried Tom, not knowing what she had said before this.

"Dad was a shepherd," said Laura. "I didn't know. About a month after his death I was attending church and was overcome with sorrow and had to leave the service. I came downstairs into the basement where there is a washroom and I met Gordon in the big meeting room. He noticed right away that I'd been crying and we began to talk. He quickly discovered who I was and decided that my feet had been set on the path to finding him. He told me that he had been a close friend of my fathers and convinced me I needed to see the sanctuary. I came down here and was told the same story as you were. There is still much more to the story but you were too tired last night for the full rendition. It didn't take too much to convince me, I was probably being groomed for this since I was a little girl. You see my mother had been killed when I was a very young child. Dad had told me she had been shot accidentally during a holdup in a convenience store. It was soon after that he began to teach me karate and jiu jitsu. He had instilled within me that God was always looking out for me, that if I trusted in the Lord that He would guide my steps. I think he was right."

Tom got up from his stool and gave Laura a hug. "Thanks for telling me this Laura." He sat back down and Laura went on preparing the breakfast. They ate in a comfortable silence, each knowing that they were with someone they could rely on under any circumstance. After helping Laura clean up the dishes Tom asked, "Do you know where my clothes are? I'd like to have a shower but I don't want to walk around all day in a bathrobe and slippers."

"Oh, here they are. Gordon asked the caretaker to include them in with the church laundry. They have one on site in the attached hall. They cleaned, dried and pressed everything."

"Thanks so much." Tom was elated; he hadn't been looking forward to walking around in clothes that had a faint odor of vomit mixed with dried blood and bits of brain.

Tom had his shower, used the kit he found in the vanity to brush his teeth. He put on his clean clothes and walked back into the kitchen. There he met Gordon who was just getting himself a cup of coffee.

"I think I'll have another," Tom said as he reached for a cup. "Where's Laura?"

"She's just now gone off to have her own shower and get dressed," replied Gordon. He took a sip of coffee and said to Tom, "I have been drinking coffee most of my long life and I have never grown tired of it. I tried smoking and got tired of it, I even drank a bit but became bored with that, but I've never lost the taste for a good cup of coffee."

"I know what you mean Gordon. The construction industry runs on coffee. I think I would have taken it intravenously if I could have figured out how to do it."

They both chuckled over their shared love of a good brew.

After a short time of silence Gordon injected, “Laura told me you were asking about her father.”

“Ya…I knew him years ago, really fine man. She has had a rough time of it, losing both her mom and dad like she did.”

“Their deaths were not accidents Tom.”

Tom looked up at Gordon quickly, not knowing why but dreading what was coming.

“Jorgen’s wife Pam was shot in a bungled convenience store robbery. The bullet, we believe, was meant for Jorgen. The police investigating called it an accidental homicide committed during a felony robbery. There was little Jorgen could do.”

“Why do you think their target had been Jorgen? It sounds like you’re talking about a botched assassination.”

“You’re quite right Tom. Jorgen was eventually assassinated by a hit and run.”

“Why?” asked Tom.

“Think about the history I revealed to you. Think about the young King David. Many of us in the Shepherd’s Path become warriors of God. We go forth and battle evil. Here again we don’t go looking for battles, the fight is brought to us. Take your fight with Lamont’s thugs the other night. Laura was there following Lamont to gather information on his whereabouts and what his plans might be. You were there following Putnam and trying to find out what he was all about. You were both brought to battle, unwillingly. That is what we do. We gather information on certain persons of interest to try and confound and confuse the forces of evil.”

“Are you saying that you battle demons?”

“We try not to. In all our history, whenever one of our shepherds has been forced into battle with a true demon, they have lost. Humans cannot battle demons and survive. We battle humans who have been corrupted to evil.”

“But how do you know who your enemy is?” Tom asked. “You say they are humans who have been corrupted, corrupted by whom?”

“The first humans, corrupted to evil, are unknown to history, having been turned so long ago. We believe servants of the twisted lord, demons if you will, burst upon early man and contrived to destroy many with fear and turn what remained to evil by daunting command, subverting God’s path for humanity right from the outset of our evolutionary journey. Demonkind thought free will made humankind weak. They used the fear of the unknown to cause suspicion and strife, guessing that only the most savage and fierce humans could survive. Early man's psyche was more resilient than they assumed for man refused to be destroyed by the fear of the unknown. Humankinds' burgeoning awareness of his place in nature and time made him believe that tomorrow could be different than today, could be better than today, and that gave rise to the idea of hope. Demonkind assumed that because man possessed free will it would be easy to coerce him to choose evil, but they erred in believing evil an easier choice than good. Free will can also make a conscious being very stubborn and many early humans perished fighting for hope and against being forced to choose evil.

"You see Tom, along with hope, mankind also learned love, fighting head to head against the forces of the Twisted Lord. Protecting the weaker in their midst taught the strong of body and spirit how to love their community. This became the ideal of duty and the giving of yourself for no reward. It showed mother and father how to love their children. It showed leaders how to love their followers. The desire to protect is at the heart of all love. The strife also showed the weaker how to love those that protected them. As love for their protectors was learned, faith in those above them was born and ultimately faith in God. The amazing thing about the Twisted Lords desire to subvert mankind to his will is that it created man's greatest virtues, hope, faith, duty and love.

"You must remember Tom that all this did not happen overnight. Our early ancestors fought the creatures of evil for thousands of years and lost millions. After the Twisted Lord and his minions realized that fighting humans directly had only strengthened us, they decided on a different tact. They left us alone and watched and humanity forgot. With no great adversaries to unite against and left to our own devices we slowly learned about greed and envy and lust. From these vices we learned how to hate. As the millennia passed and these vices came to prominence the forces of evil recognized their opportunity. They finally understood how to corrupt man to evil. The carrot, instead of the stick. Their agents identified those humans who had learned the lessons of vice and they promised them riches or power or the favors of the opposite sex to do their bidding. After a time, it was easy for the Twisted Lords servants to use corrupted humans to do their recruiting for them. Evil could now step to the side and let humans corrupt humans. This was a time of great upheaval in mankind's history. It was the time of the ancient empires. The Sumerians and Egyptians coalesced and were the first that could be considered expansionist empires. The Babylonians rose from the ashes of Sumeria along with the Assyrians. The Hittites wandered onto the historical stage during this period along with the Indus River cities. The Shang and Chou dynasties of the Asian empires prospered and then vanished. The Chaldeans, Medes, Cimmerians and Scythians all thrived for a time and then were eventually overrun. Toward the end of this era of warring civilizations and empires bubbling and roiling to prominence there came into being the domains of the classic Greek city states, the Persian Empire, Judea and the Sinhalese in India. China in this period was ruled by feudal kingdoms but was united to a point by its single ethnicity and a powerful administrative bureaucracy. This period was roughly twenty-six centuries ago. What happened in these regions over the short span of the next hundred years is truly amazing. Important religious reforms and right living philosophies appeared across this band of civilization existing and extending from Central Europe to Eastern China. Pythagoreanism and Rationalist Philosophies in Italy and Ionia. The Yahwists in Judea and the religious reformer Zarathrustra preaching his philosophy known as Zoroastrianism. Siddhartha Gautama founded Buddhism and also in India at this time Jainism was becoming established. In China, Lao – Tzu founded Taoism and Kung Fu – Tzu taught morality and ethical behavior which became known as Confucianism. Our belief is that during the time of great human expansion and unceasing turmoil, caused by the age of ancient empires, God had been carefully planting the seeds of the soon to be great belief systems. These kernels germinated during these hundred years of religious and philosophical fervor and went on to eventually become the great beliefs we have now that nurture and give hope to billions of people."

"But we are Christians Gordon. Are you saying that all other religions and belief systems pray to our God?"

"He is not *our* God Tom," Gordon said emphatically, putting stress on the exclusionary meaning of 'our', "But we are *all* his children."

The wisdom inherent in that line struck Tom like a two by four to the forehead.

"God put the idea of religion into our thoughts to ease our burdens in a troubled world. These religions and philosophies at their root are also blueprints for how to live a good life. That is what God wants for us, to lead good lives, to love our families, to love our neighbors and to have that love returned to us."

"So what happened?" Tom shook his head, "This history is hard to wrap my head around. I know you don't have the answers, how could you?"

"You're right Tom, who among us can fathom the mind of God. I can tell you though that all the strife and hate that pits man against man, faith against faith and nation against nation can be laid at the feet of the Twisted Lord. As for the idea that all religions worship the same God. Well…how many divisions are there in the Christian faith and we all supposedly worship the same God."

As he was finishing up that last thought Laura came strolling into the kitchen tousling her rich chestnut hair with a towel.

"Lord that feels good!" She looked at Tom and said, "Cleanliness really is next to Godliness."

Addressing Gordon now she asked, "Have you told Tom about rotting souls yet?" She walked to the coffee pot and poured herself a cup.

"What's this about rotting souls?" asked Tom.

"Do you recall Tom, near the beginning of our conversation you asked, 'how do you know who is your enemy?' I answered in the larger context and described the forces arrayed against mankind. Laura's point is to the very real knowledge that there is a way for us to know categorically who our enemies are. The souls of humans long in the shadow of evil begin to disintegrate. The soul, which belongs to God, is very resilient but can be weakened after long years of neglect. Feelings of hate, greed and lust will further weaken a soul, but what begins the decay is the putting into action of these thoughts and feelings. Murder and rape and theft can quickly begin the destruction of a soul if it has been weakened in this way. This growing putrefaction of the soul gives rise to an odor of spoiled meat. The stronger the odor, the longer the soul has been under assault. This is usually only evident to one who is on the shepherd's path or close to it."

"You're saying you can smell evil?"

"In a word…yes. Some of us do smell the odor more strongly than others; generally, it is in proportion to how long you have been associated with The Path."

Tom nodded his head thinking back to his encounter with Tombstone in the grocery store parking lot. He'd also smelled something a bit off when he was held captive at Putnam's house but had chalked it up to the earthy smell of fertilizer on farmers' fields.

"Tom," interjected Laura, "Remember the papers you found the other night, have you shown them to Gordon yet?"

"Oh no…I left them in my pants pocket. I hope they didn't go through the wash."

"Ah…not to worry Tom." Gordon opened a drawer and retrieved a small zippered bag. "Bill went through your pockets before your clothes were laundered. Here are your vehicle ignition fob, your card holder and two pieces of tracing paper."

"Ah great," replied Tom. "I overheard Lou Lamont telling the rest of his group that this tracing paper had the locations and dates of the disruptions they're planning. This tracing paper is laid over a map and the colored dots coincide with a point of action. He didn't explain how to decode the symbols though."

Gordon asked, "What map are they using?"

"All I heard was Rand McNally."

"Well isn't that fortunate," Gordon said. "I'll be back presently."

As Gordon exited Tom turned to Laura and asked, "Has there been any news concerning the three bodies we left on the roof of the Grand?"

"Gee Tom, I don't know. I haven't had a chance to watch any news on TV or even look at a newspaper." Laura picked up a TV remote, "I'll turn on the news." Tom noticed a flat screen over the big double sink where a window might have been in an above ground structure. The big screen brightened as cable news was doing the weather report. Once wrapped up the two anchors chatted about the early spring weather and how it would affect the Poverty Coalition protestors who had taken over St. James's Park on the anniversary of an earlier rally. Laura and Tom continued watching until Gordon returned carrying a black and yellow textbook.

"Here we go I think," said Gordon as he opened the atlas and started leafing through the pages. He came to the Canadian section with its provinces and stopped at the page that had a large map of Ontario.

"Put the tracing on here Tom and see if it matches up."

"I don't think this will work," replied Tom, "The tracing paper looks to be twice the size of the map."

Gordon flipped the page and found a larger map of Southern and Central Ontario with far more detail than the previous one-page map.

"This is more like it," said an excited Gordon.

Tom took one of the tracings and folded it along the already present crease. He then placed the fold where the two pages joined. He opened the tracing until it covered the two pages.

"Something's not right," he said. Tom studied the layout for a second and then cursed under his breath. He lifted it out of the crease and turned it one hundred eighty degrees. He put the fold back into the middle crease and opened the tracing back up. There were dots of different colors placed at various locations on the map that corresponded with place names. Laura pointed to a large multi colored dot resting over Toronto. "Look here," Laura said as she took a pencil and used the sharpened end as a pointer. She touched the tracing paper on the lower right quadrant of the quartered circle, the pie shape was blue. Under the magnifying glass they could see a short series of letters and numbers, s j p followed by A10 – 1 underneath. A red pie shape above that had the letters r c and the numbers 1 + 5. Laura removed the pencil from the tracing paper and tapped the eraser against her lower lip.

"What are you…" Tom began until Laura shushed him.

"Gimme a sec…Holee crap."

"What is it Laura?" asked Gordon.

"I don't know," Laura said slowly, still deep in thought, "It almost seems too simple."

"Don't over think it," interjected Tom. "I heard Lamont say they were keeping things very simple. No computers, no emails, everything just basic. Without the map, the dots on the paper are meaningless."

"Alright," Laura started, "We just heard on the news that the Poverty Coalition had started their occupation of St. James Park yesterday. Do those initials there, s j p mean St. James Park? Today is April ninth. Do the letters and numbers there, A10 mean April 10th? No clue what the minus one means though."

"That's brilliant Laura," cried Gordon. "Something is going to happen tomorrow at St. James Park. Look here," Gordon fanned his hand over the entire tracing paper covered map. "Nowhere else are there letters before the numbers on the second line. Look, above this blue pie shape is a red pie shape that's labeled r c and then below 1 + 5. Right next to it on the upper left quadrant are the letters c h and then under that 1 + 27. When the D Day landings took place in 1944 the D stood for the exact time that the landing craft were to hit the beaches of Normandy. Operations scheduled to take place after that hour were designated D+. If it was for the next day it was D+1 or a week later it was D+7. Don't you see the 1 + means how many days after April 10th. On April fifteenth something will happen at the designated location r c. On May 12th something will happen at the location designated as c h. What's still missing is the meaning of the different colors."

Tom suggested, "Laura's right, the letters are the specific locations where these events will take place. Look at the size of the colored dots and the scale at the bottom, some of these dots are covering a hundred square kilometers. This multi colored circle covers the entire GTA. I'd say that the letters here are the first letter of each word in a location or a landmark, s j p means St. James Park, so r c would be some well-known spot in the city. Any ideas? You guys know the city better than I do."

Frustrated Laura grumbled, "It could mean anything. It could be the initials for a restaurant or a department store or stand for Roman Catholic. In a city the size of Toronto r c could stand for a hundred thousand different things."

"I don't think so."

Laura and Gordon both turned toward Tom. While they had been mulling over this riddle, Tom had glanced over at the muted TV. The network's sports segment was airing and Tom found himself looking at the baseball scores from around the major leagues and the list of upcoming Blue Jay's home games at, "Rogers' Center," repeated Tom, "On April 15th the Blue Jays will be playing a home game against the New York Yankees at...Rogers' Center, r c. These locations we're looking for are large, well known places. They'd have to be for the proposed actions to be significant."

"That's it then!" cried Gordon as he patted Tom on the shoulder. "Well done!"

"c h...City Hall!" Laura jumped off her stool and looked more closely at the map. "We should be able to figure out where all the disruptions are going to take place."

"Well the four in Toronto anyway," said Gordon. "These other places spread out over Southern and Central Ontario might be more challenging." Gordon stopped and looked at Tom. "I don't know if you realize Tom what an extraordinary find this map is. Along with gathering information it is our mission to disrupt, disturb and disorder the actions of the servants of the Twisted Lord, to keep them off balance. Something big is coming if I read this map correctly."

"I recall Lamont saying something about burning the whole system down when I was listening under the patio. Wish he'd said more. What do you think he meant?"

"Over the course of mankind's history, the agents of the Twisted Lord have brought down many systems, from a group of farmers organizing into a community to an empire spanning continents. It could mean a non-government type of system such as a religion or guild. When a system is organized, if it becomes successful it creates a stable and productive environment where ordinary people feel safe. That safety promotes harmony and harmony allows people to grow to their potential. When humans are unafraid and allowed to work toward their potential, civilizations flower and people produce wonderful things. You may be familiar with this idea as, Life, Liberty and the pursuit of Happiness. I believe the system under attack is the United States, and by extension Canada and the democracies of Europe."

Tom held up his hands to interrupt, "Excuse me Gordon, but that's a little hard to believe. How could a group such as Laura and I fought the other night hope to bring about the destruction of the United States? America has been around for more than two hundred years and is the most powerful country in the world. It's not possible."

"Think Tom. To fully grasp the scale of what we are talking about you must first understand the enormity and complexity of what we are dealing with. Lamont and Putnam are only a tiny cell of an organization that has been here on earth in one form or another for close on three hundred thousand years. Did you not understand Tom, that when we were discussing the events that led ancient humankind to discover the virtues of hope, faith, charity and love that we were speaking of very ancient times and very ancient man…Tom…we were speaking of *Homo sapiens neanderthalensis* and their forced evolution. The war with evil and its consequent culling of huge numbers of humans and the forced changes in the way ancient man thought provided the impetus and direction for the next step in our evolution to becoming what we are now, *Homo sapiens sapiens.* Understanding the time scale involved here will put into perspective the vastness of our enemy. You say impossible to bring down a country as powerful and significant as America and I answer that they have already accomplished this, more than once and to political entities larger and more peaceful."

Tom sat on the edge of his seat. Uncharacteristically he believed without reservation the ideas that Gordon was pouring into him. Throughout his life Tom had been a skeptic. It had taken him many years of internal argument to come to grips with the idea of faith and its existence and many years after that to realize he could have it. His hard-won faith let him know that Gordon spoke the truth and all he had to do was listen. He suddenly felt connected to a consciousness that spanned the ascent of human endeavor from the beginning. A broad smile suffused his face. Gordon paused in his narrative to look closely at Tom. He turned to Laura and quietly observed, "He's beginning to understand Laura."

"Your understanding of mankind's history boggles my mind," Tom said, "but it has the feel of truth. Even though I have never heard this chronicle taught as history or even mentioned as legend it makes so much sense to me. Humanity in all its glory and all its absurdity is slowly inching its way to God. And with all of the roadblocks and wrong turns we throw in our own way it is our battles against evil that ultimately put us back on the right path."

Gordon grabbed Tom by the shoulders and squeezed. "Welcome Tom. I believe you have just become one of us. I never doubted for a moment."

"Thank you, Gordon, but I still have questions."

"When you cease having questions you stop learning and learning brings you closer to God."

"All right then Gordon, what large and peaceful political entity was brought down by these forces of evil?"

Smiling Gordon replied, "How about the Roman Empire?"

"That'll fill the bill," Tom said, sitting back down on the kitchen stool. "I'd always thought the Roman Empire was a voracious empire expanding through war to the detriment of its citizens."

Gordon began, "In 1778 a British historian named Edward Gibbon published *The History of the Decline and Fall of the Roman Empire*. It is said to be one of the greatest historical works ever penned. I presume you've heard of the *Pax Romana*?"

"Yes," replied Tom.

"The period of Roman history described by the *Pax Romana* was roughly two hundred years. It began around 30 BC and continued roughly unbroken until the beginning of the second century AD. Gibbons judged this period as the time when humankind was happiest. It is also the time when Christ walked the earth and the first tendrils of Christianity were spreading their message of peace and brotherly love throughout parts of the Roman Empire. This period also encompasses the reigns of the five 'Good Emperors': Nerva, Trajan, Hadrian, Pius Antoninus and Marcus Aurelius. I bring these Emperors up because they planned their own successions. They would 'adopt' promising candidates for succession and groom them to be leaders. Before they retired or died, they would appoint one to be their successor. This worked well for eighty odd years, bringing only the best forward as candidates and not relying solely on the father's good genetics. That is until Marcus Aurelius broke with this tradition and had his son Commodius succeed him. Commodius was not a good ruler and after him Rome was never again to have long periods of good government combined with extended periods of peace."

"I'm not following Gordon; how does this end the Roman Empire?"

"Let us remember the point I made previously Tom. The forces of evil are extremely patient, none of the changes wrought against human civilization happens quickly. By the year 248 AD, Rome had existed for one thousand years. During that thousand years of Roman expansion a certain stability and tranquility had settled about the Mediterranean world. Art, science, literature and philosophy flourished. If long periods of peace and good government continued, this Roman progress in the life of the mind would invariably connect with the spreading peaceful philosophy of Christ's teachings. Unfortunately, we will never know where this combination might have taken mankind. After the era of the five good Emperors, governments and politicians of Rome became increasingly corrupt, more concerned with accumulating wealth and power. As Emperors came and went with rapidity, opposing factions in the government bureaucracies tore away at the once stable Roman system. It was also at about this time that the first organized persecutions of the then passive Christians began. Can you see the pattern emerging here Tom?"

"I believe so," answered Tom. "If I understand you correctly…evil, whether a true demonic entity or a bent human…what?" Gordon and Laura had both just audibly gasped, uncoupling Tom's attention from his thoughts. "What is it you guys?"

Gordon asked him, "Why did you say 'bent humans'?"

"Well," responded Tom slowly, trying to organize his thoughts, "I have heard you refer to the devil, at least I think you mean the devil, as the Twisted Lord, so it made sense to me that the humans he corrupted would be bent, why?"

Gordon just stared at Tom, so Laura answered, "We have been calling the corrupted humans, bent, for as long as I can remember."

"Even longer than that," interjected Gordon. He continued to look at Tom, "Quite amazing, I think. Please Tom, do continue."

Tom was silent for a minute, trying to find his train of thought. "I think that the corruptive forces of evil were never asleep. They were, are, always searching out ways and means to bring people over to the dark side."

Laura giggled and Tom said, "Caught that reference did ya?"

"Yes, I did Tom but I don't think Gordon did. He doesn't get out a lot."

Gordon just sat there allowing the two youngsters to have their connection. "Do go on please Tom," he said.

"Certainly," Tom replied. "The Twisted Lord, must have recognized the danger to his plans if the philosophy embedded in early Christianity were to meld with a stable, robust, peaceful, intellectually enlightened Roman empire. The Romans may have developed a society and a government that saw a strong economy and a prosperous and satisfied citizenry as something to show off. The diplomacy of prosperity rather than the spear point. Given enough time I bet it would've worked out."

"We think it might have done just that," said Gordon.

"Anyway," continued Tom, "The corruptive influence was stepped up and Rome's rulers forgot about the importance of honor and duty in leadership and the populace of the empire turned away from the virtues of honest work and responsibility. The early Christians were targeted for harassment and their early philosophy of love toward all was crushed under official persecution. With the path toward peace and love disrupted the Roman Empire tottered on, slowly devolving into weaker and weaker ciphers of its old glory, never recapturing its vitality. That's how Rome was brought down."

"To paraphrase Professor Higgins 'By God I do believe he's got it.'"

Smiling, Tom asked, "I do get how the Roman Empire could be brought down by corrupting its leaders. Rome was autocratic. The power of leadership was corralled at the top. The regular citizen was disenfranchised from any decision making, they had no path to power. There is no comparison between that system and the ones we enjoy now that are represented by the United States. Evil can't just corrupt some Senators or Congressmen or the President and destroy the US; their democratic system will allow the people to vote them out."

"You are absolutely correct Tom. Lincoln summed it up quite nicely in his first inaugural address when he said: 'While the people retain their virtue and vigilance, no administration, by any extreme of wickedness or folly, can very seriously injure the government in the short space of four years.' The key to the truth of that observation are the words: 'while the people retain their virtue and vigilance."

"I understand your point Gordon. In their undying and unremitting assault against humanity the forces of evil have corrupted to their cause enough regular people to bring down the government."

"You're almost there Tom. You remember when I mentioned that free will made humans stubborn and that the servants of the Twisted Lord found that it was not as easy to get people to choose evil as they'd assumed. Well that has held true throughout our history. Our souls that have been given to us by God provide within us a longing for good. That doesn't mean that the desire for good can't be overcome by the desire for earthly riches or power, but we begin life knowing that good is the right choice for us. The numbers of people that can be directly corrupted by these dark forces is a number quite a bit smaller than what you would probably think. If the forces of evil could target and corrupt to their wills even one tenth of one percent of the world's population our struggle would have been lost ages ago. What they have learned to do is use the 'bents' to subvert and subsume society's ideas of what is virtue and what is not. This has been one of their hardest tasks and they have been working toward this end for several generations of man. It has only been in the last eighty to ninety years that the pace of their subversion has accelerated to the point where they feel they are ready to strike."

"Okay Gordon, I'm not following you. If their corruption success rate is less than one tenth of one percent, that would still make it possible to have a force of nearly seven million people. That is quite an army!"

"It would be, except it is impossible to organize. There are varying degrees of this type of corruption. Some bents go eagerly and fully to evil, others go but with reservations. Some are corrupted to lie, others to cheat and steal and still others to murder. As your path crosses with those of the 'bent' you will be able to discern more and more how far into hell they have been drawn. The corruption success rate is fairly even throughout most of the world. The percentage of bent in the population of China is no higher than in France, or India or Iran or Canada. The majority of humans bent to corruption, stay where they are most useful. Also remember, their greatest weapon is secrecy, therefore their leaders are mindful against concentrating large numbers of bent together."

"So what you are saying is that relatively small numbers of bent humans are trying to pervert our ideas of virtue to upend society."

"That is right. It takes different forms in different parts of the world, but the end goal of the bent and their masters is the same; chaos, war, hate. Humanity devolved to our animal instincts. Here in North America where we have had a hundred and fifty years of peace…Yes?"

An astonished Tom had interrupted Gordon by throwing both hands up, palms outward. "How can you say that Gordon? We've had two world wars, the Korean War, a war in Vietnam, Iraq and Afghanistan and countless other skirmishes around the globe."

"Again Tom, you are quite right. My point…that the continent of North America, where we live, where our homes are…has not experienced the devastations and deprivations of war since the American Civil War. The cycles of war bred revenge and resentment have almost been broken here. Do you not see Tom…that North American society…with the United States as its largest component, is experiencing the same nexus that Rome had during the *Pax Romana*.

"But why us, why the United States. How is America any more important a target than say, Victorian England? They had long periods of peace where their only strife was colonial wars."

Gordon went to take a sip of his coffee and realized his cup was empty. As he slid off his stool and walked over to the coffee pot he asked if either Tom or Laura wished another cup. After everyone poured, Gordon began his answer.

"In 1789, when George Washington was inaugurated as the first President and the United States began with its republican form of government, it was unique on the face of the earth. Humanity, embodied by those early Americans, was finally experimenting with free will as the ruling component of their country's ideals. For two and a quarter century that ideal was working better than its framers envisioned. Was the country perfect, of course not, but it gave its citizens the idea that they weren't limited. Their beliefs were their own, not to be marginalized by a state sponsored religion. Their diligence and industry belonged to themselves, they weren't serfs tied to the land. Theirs was a classless society where upward mobility was allowed and generally praised. These attributes of American society catapulted the country into prosperity. It also produced a revival of religious thought. These ideas of freedom and liberty have made it the main target of the Twisted Lord. Because that country and what it represents for humanity was so successful, the powers of darkness, human and spiritual, have combined to try and take it down. We are living now during a time that could be called the *Pax Americana*. Only future histories will tell us if we're at the end of it, or are on the threshold of a greater outcome. No matter which though, we still have a job to do."

"And that is?" asked Tom.

"Mankind's knowledge of rightness can be eroded over generations of small attacks by a patient, ever cunning, deathless enemy. Our mission is to offer continuity of conscience to a short-lived humanity."

Just then a doorbell sounded. "We have company," said Gordon. "I should go and meet them." He jumped down from his stool and made his way out of the kitchen and disappeared into the huge study.

"You have a door bell?" chuckled Tom.

"No," replied Laura. "We have a system of motion and heat sensors which trigger a chime down here when one of our entrances is accessed…Tom, isn't that you?" Laura was staring at the muted television. He turned and looked. Sure enough, there was his picture just above the shoulder of the newscaster.

"Turn the sound on," Tom said.

"…tario Provincial Police say the man is armed and dangerous. Do not approach. If you see this man anywhere you are to call the number at the bottom of the screen. To recap, Tom Joiner of Coalmen Ontario is wanted for questioning in the killing of two Coalmen OPP officers and the wounding of a third. In other news…" Laura hit the mute button.

"Did you see that picture," she said, "It doesn't really look like you."

"Ya I know," considered Tom. "Years ago, I used to write a weekly op-ed column for our local paper. That was the photo they used with my byline. My hair and mustache were still black and I weighed thirty pounds less than I do now."

“I don’t think anyone would recognize you from that picture.” Asserted Laura.

“Any up-to-date photos of me were destroyed in the fire. My doctor obviously wouldn’t give them his photos of my recovery…either that or the OPP didn’t ask him for recent pictures. They don’t want anyone finding me, which means they want to find me themselves and make sure I can’t attend a trial.”

“That makes sense Tom.”

From the entrance to the kitchen Gordon said, “Tom…there’s someone here to see you.”

Tom turned.

“Twittles!” squealed Laura and launched herself off the stool and into George’s open arms. After being nearly crushed by George’s bear hug and still holding onto his large arm Laura turned toward Tom and said, “You were right George, he came.”

Tom was stunned. George approached and they threw their arms around one another. George said, “I knew you were headed for the path when you visited last fall.”

Tom just stared up at George. Everything seemed to fall into place. The advice George had given him, the truck with the stealth abilities he’d forced on him. “How long George?”

“Have I been part of the path? It’s been a long time eh Gordon. What do you think, twenty, twenty-five years?”

“It’s been thirty-two years George, just after you purchased your first Ford dealership,” replied Gordon.

“Well I’ll be…” said Tom. “This has got to be the most interesting three days of my entire life.”

“You know what they say,” laughed George, “Lord keep me from living in interesting times.”

They all laughed. To Tom it seemed as if a circle had closed with the arrival of George. They chatted amiably and drank coffee for the rest of the morning. George filled Tom in concerning the news coverage. “The talking heads are theorizing that it was Tom’s loss in the municipal election that drove his feeble mind over the edge.”

Around noon it was decided that they could all do with a bite to eat. They worked together making lunch and were soon sitting down to hearty roast beef sandwiches. For the first time in hours there was a lull in the conversation. Tom turned to Gordon, "You'd started telling me some of the history of your place here and when you spoke of your birth, I forced you to digress. Would you finish the tale?"

George said, "It's been years since I last heard the tale. Where exactly did you get to Gordon?"

Swallowing his last morsel of sandwich and washing it down with some chamomile iced tea Gordon replied, "I had just arrived at the point in the story when my father began work on the stone foundation of the church. That's where Tom hijacked my story with his doubts."

Tom noticed a big smile on Gordon's face and knew Gordon was making light of his doubts.

"How do you feel now Tom?" George asked looking over at him.

"It's an incredible story, and I'm moved at your trust in telling me."

"Ya…but do you believe us?"

"More than I don't George."

"Good," said Gordon, "Then I shall resume. As I told you previously, I was born near the end of June in 1875. My father was a stone mason and had been hired on by the company that had been contracted to lay the foundation of the church. It was promised to this company that if they could keep the foundation costs on budget and their work was satisfactory that they would be awarded the contract for the stonework on the exterior of the church building. By the time the masonry work on the church was completed my father had become a crew foreman. He was an ambitious and hardworking young man and afterwards went out on his own. He was quite successful as a masonry contractor, specializing in jobs that required finesse and imagination.

"In 1893 an early contributor to the Jarvis Street Baptist Church named William Elliot passed away. It was suggested by some in the congregation that Mr. Elliot should be interred under the church. Before the church fathers would begin fundraising, my father was asked to do a site study. I was eighteen at the time and learning the trade from my father. It was during the exploratory excavations of the soil under the church basement that my father and I discovered the log covering of the original military supply depot. My father was an avid amateur historian and was especially interested in the history of Toronto and the battles that took place in and around York during the War of 1812. He knew exactly what we had uncovered. The immense pine logs were virtually untouched by the passage of eighty years. I asked my father if he would reveal his discovery to the church fathers and he replied, 'What the passage of time and the natural decay of the world had failed to reveal should be left a curious secret, known only to us two.' He winked at me and laughed and said that we now knew something that no other living soul suspected and that maybe someday it would be of use to one of us. My father was very wise.

"We covered in our small excavation and it was as if we'd never been there. Six months later the idea of interring Mr. Elliot in a basement crypt was abandoned and a year after that my father was killed when scaffolding that he was working from collapsed. He was a few months shy of his fortieth birthday." Gordon stopped his narration.

"I'm sorry to hear that," said Tom quietly. "It sounds to me like you were close to your father."

Gordon looked up with a sad smile and said, "No more and no less than any other young man with his father. My heart was never really in the building trades. My father understood this but never the less undertook the task of teaching me a trade. With kindness and a firm hand, he had begun my education as a stone mason. It wasn't until after he was gone and I'd gained some wisdom of my own that I understood his qualities. After my father's death it didn't take me long to decide that I didn't want to work with stone, so I joined the army. I was crazy about horses and wanted the cavalry. It seemed a glorious way of life, riding in formation all day wearing a sharp looking uniform. After our initial training we were sent out to join our new regiment. We were called the 1st Hussars. Fourteen of us were sent to join 'A' Squadron, 1st Battalion of the Canadian Mounted Rifles. In March of 1900 we were sent to South Africa and attached to the British Expeditionary Force fighting the Afrikaners during the Boer War. It was great sport until two of my mates were picked off by Boer sharpshooters. The Boers were excellent marksmen and perfected a hit and run style of warfare that had Colonial Command on the ropes for many months.

"During one of these hit and run strikes, three of us were separated from our main force and spent several nights in the bush. On the first night we were riding down into a narrow valley when we smelled smoke on the wind. We galloped along the small river that formed the floor of the valley hoping we were smelling the cooking fires of our main force. What we found was a small farm that had been attacked. The house and barn were no more than embers and the livestock had been carried off. We found the owner, a grizzled old Afrikaner, pinned to the ground by a short spear. We tended to him the best we could and he told us they had been attacked by Kaffiri, a none too polite term the Afrikaners used for the Bantu and Zulu that populated the region. He asked us to look for his daughter. She was his only surviving family member and offered us a reward to look for her. He directed us to dig by a small copse of trees behind the smoldering barn and then died. We buried him in a shallow grave and then reconnoitered the area for his daughter. We searched for her the rest of the night but found nothing. After sleeping for part of the morning we went to the copse of trees and following the deceased farmer's instructions we dug up a small but very heavy chest. We broke open the lock and found the chest full of small, crudely poured gold bars. At the time we figured that each bar probably weighed about a pound. We counted 60 bars in the chest, and we found five more chests. We couldn't believe our good fortune, but soon remembered our promise to the old farmer. Each chest was loaded onto a pack horse and we spent the next three days looking for the lost girl. We never found her but we did find our squadron in the course of our searching. Once back at our regimental camp we made inquiries about the farmstead and any reports of Bantu attacks in the region. There were none.

"Our regiment's deployment ended after a year and we were shipped home. We had continued to inquire about the farm and the possible survival of the girl, but we had no name and only a guess at the exact location of the farm. A week before we were to ship out the three of us made a decision about the gold. We knew that if we turned it over to the civil or military authorities it would disappear into whatever bureaucracy took charge of it and the girl, if ever located, would never see any of her father's estate. The farmer had also offered the gold to us to search for his daughter. Therefore, it was decided that we would convert a portion of the gold to pound sterling and leave a retainer with an agency that we knew would continue the search. We contracted their services for ten years. At the end, if the girl was not found the three of us would divide evenly what was left. Four days later one of our group was kicked in the head by a startled stallion and died. That meant that there was now only two of us left, myself and Lawrence McGregor. We called him Larky; he had a beautiful singing voice. We made a promise to each other that if one of us should perish before the ten-year search was completed that the survivor would make sure the deceased's heirs would receive his share. If the deceased had no heirs then the half share would revert to the surviving member. We made arrangements with a shipping company and had the crates of gold shipped home and put into storage. The crates were marked 'samples – meteor fragments.'

"When we returned to Toronto I mustered out and spent the next nine years traveling the country, working as a mason. My mate from "A" Squadron and I kept in touch and the reports from South Africa kept coming in. There were a couple of leads over the years but nothing came of them. About six months before the ten-year search was finalized, I received word that Larky had taken sick. He had contracted influenza and it had turned into pneumonia. He lingered for a month and then passed away. He left no family behind. Of the five good friends that I had made during our early days in the cavalry I was the only one left. "I was not ready for my reaction upon learning of Larky's passing in 1911. The news affected me tremendously. The five of us had been best friends in our youth and as we grew and matured I had naturally assumed that we would all settle down and have families and our circle would remain constant; and now thirteen years later I was the only one left and none of those departed had left any family to remember or mourn them. They were good men and fine soldiers; they had worked hard and wanted to help better this world. My father had also been a good man who had worked very hard for his family and community. Now, they were all gone and mostly forgotten. I felt very lost. I abandoned the gold to the security of the storage firm and tried to flee my melancholy. For three years I traveled the rails, drinking and getting into fights and other troubles. In early 1914, I found myself just outside of a little town called Andalusia in Southern Alabama. I made the acquaintance of a preacher there when he saved me from drowning. I was drunk and stumbling along the edge of a small but fast flowing creek in dense forest when I tripped and fell in, hitting my head on a rock. The preacher had been meditating in the woods and heard my splashy entrance. He found me quickly, fished me out and resuscitated me, then spent the night in the woods sobering me up. The next day he brought me to his campsite where he and twenty-two of his "flock" were trying to construct a meeting place. They had no experience and the design of the shelter was quite extraordinary. To them my expertise in building and especially my experience as a stone mason was a tremendous asset. I worked with them for three months and in return was fed and allowed to camp on their property and later to occupy their new building. They had sufficient funds to purchase the required building materials but if I had not come along, they never would have completed their task.

“The Preacher seemed to have taken a liking to the ne’er-do-well he’d pulled from the drink. He was genuinely interested in my story and would ask about my family, or my military service, or my travels and then listen. These quiet conversations soon turned into long discussions concerning life and death and our personal feelings on the meaning of life. He soon told me of the Shepherd’s Path. Like you I was incredulous, but stayed to hear more. Over the course of a few nights’ conversations he told me his story and the story of the Shepherd’s Path. His understanding of the course my life had taken to bring me to him was undeniable. The other members of his flock shared their tales with me and theirs were just as convincing. I gave myself over to their cause and continued to help them complete their meeting hall. The reason behind their need for hidden shelter became quite clear after I learned of their purpose. The shelter’s entrance was difficult to make out by any casual observer and this was important to them, for secrecy was a life and death matter. Their group had been drawn together in southern Alabama because of the renewed stirrings of the Ku Klux Klan.”

“My God Gordon…you actually knew men who battled the KKK?” asked an amazed Tom.

“Well…yes. They didn’t call themselves Klan yet, but they were the beginnings of the second Klan movement. They were mostly disgruntled southern white men who had been sympathetic toward the first Klan before it dissipated during the late 1870s. These home-grown terrorists gave themselves various names, they were the Red Shirts in Mississippi and the White League in Louisiana and the Carolinas. Their goal was to get Democrats elected through violence and intimidation against black and Republican voters and thereby regain political power in the South. They succeeded for the most part and between 1874 and 1900 they managed to put Democrats back into power in the Deep South and overturn much of the progress in racial equality that Republican legislators had accomplished.

“These groups had petered out after accomplishing their goals but there was always a core of poor, bitter white men who were dissatisfied with their lot. As the new century came in and civil rights organizations such as the Niagara Group and the fledgling NAACP worked to have the exclusionary election rules in the South changed to let more blacks and Republicans vote, the Southern Democrats began agitating for the reformation of the secret societies that had put them back in power and, they hoped, would keep them in power.

"During the months before I had been rescued by the Preacher, there had been several cases of deadly violence against several black families and prominent Republican candidates in Covington County Alabama. The Preacher had begun the idea of building a concealed headquarters for their chapter of the Shepherd's Path. Their goal was to protect the civil rights organizers from harm while also disrupting the organizing of the new hate groups and the implementing of their policies. They would be anonymous in working toward their goals so they required an anonymous location to meet, plan and store materials. We had begun with a small watertight cave beneath a small stream and behind its subsequent waterfall as it flowed over the side of a hill. We excavated the cave to widen and lengthen its interior. Mortared stone walls within had strengthened the sides and ceilings to lessen the chance of cave ins. Waterproofing and plastering had made the interior comfortable and dry. Judicious design using baffles and flues allowed them to use a wood burning stove in the kitchen without the telltale chimney smoke to give away their location. The later installation of a small generator allowed them to power a few electric lights."

"Is that what gave you the idea for building this place?" asked Tom.

"Yes, but not until much later." replied Gordon. "It was getting on into summer and The Path members were doing their work of gathering information. They had infiltrated a hate group that was posing as a gun and saber club and had learned their first operation was going to be an attack on a white teacher who was secretly teaching black families to read and write. The Preacher could only observe and record what would happen, there were over fifty armed and hooded men going to the teacher's house and there were only twelve of us available at the time. I was the only member of the group with military experience, the other members had rifles, everyone hunted, but they weren't fighting men, by training or inclination.

"We had thought about warning the teacher but we only learned of the planned attack the day it was to take place. There were few phones in Covington County, so there was no chance to get word to them. We followed the hooded gang for what seemed like hours and finally came to the end of the country lane where the teacher's house sat. They surrounded the small house while sitting their mounts and called the teacher out. Two men dismounted and grabbed the teacher before he had a chance to react. They pushed him off the low porch and two other men began beating him with the butts of their rifles. While they were doing this his wife and son ran out, they were grabbed and held and forced to watch. We heard a shot from inside the house. Almost immediately the remaining mounted men opened fire on the house with every rifle and pistol they'd brought. Windows were shattered and bullet holes began to appear in the clapboard walls. The hooded men soon stopped firing and while some kept watch the rest rode forward and pitched their torches into the home through the broken windows. The wooden building ignited quickly and you could hear the screaming. Several people, I could only see their silhouettes against the bright flames, tried to escape through the front and back doors but mounted men cut them down.

"We were hiding in the woods that bordered the homestead and I was circling the yard through the screen of trees in an impotent rage. If I'd shown myself, I would have been killed. If we'd fired through the trees we would have been located and killed. I found myself at the back of the house where the woods came closest to the building. There was only one rider visible where the trees indented back into the woods slightly. He raised his rifle and I saw a child trying desperately to push open a shutter that closed off an unglazed basement window. The hooded man waited, waited for the single-minded desperation of the poor child to force it into exposed helplessness where his bullet would rip the little body of life. I wasn't going to let that happen. I picked up a small branch lying on the forest floor and threw it with all my strength at the rump of the horse. I couldn't miss a target that big and on impact the horse kicked out. The rider fired but missed the child. As he tried to settle the bucking horse, I was on him and bore him to the ground. I beat him to death with my bare hands. I never removed his hood and when I finished it was soaked red. I didn't see the child but I've always hoped he or she escaped. That child would have been the only survivor of the hell on earth the teacher's house became that horrible night.

"We were all shaken by this. The magnitude of the hate we saw was almost incomprehensible. I told the Preacher that his men would have to become more involved in stopping this evil. He wrestled with that for days until coming to a decision. Returning violence back upon these men was not why they had been brought together he told me. There was a reason why they were so diverse, why they were shopkeepers and doctors and bankers. The twenty-three men of their group were of many different races, religions and walks of life and a part of almost every strata of the Covington County community. There was very little that went on that they didn't hear about or have firsthand knowledge of. Their task was not to fight the battles, but to know where and when battle would take place. It would be for others to do the fighting. As a military man I knew the value of good intelligence so I understood the Preacher's reasoning. If I understood the Shepherd's Path, I knew that should violence be necessary the means for it would make its way to them.

"I also knew that it was time for me to make my way home. In Europe war had broken out and Canada was in desperate need of trained fighting men. I said my goodbyes to the Preacher and his flock and made my way north. Two weeks later, by the time I reached northern Alabama and was making my way into Tennessee, I heard news concerning Covington County. Seems a small group of men, numbering close to two dozen 'Negros and Republicans', and belonging to what was then called Loyal Leagues had broken up the large gathering of a local gun and saber club. Three white men had been 'murdered' and the rest of the gun and saber club disbursed with injuries. Warrants had been issued for the members of the Loyal League but they had disappeared into thin air. No one had been able to identify any of its members so arrests weren't anticipated. I was now more than convinced of the truth inherent in the Shepherd's Path."

Gordon finished speaking and was silent for a few moments.

Tom asked, "Were you able to find out how things went with your friends in Alabama?"

"I never heard from them again but I am certain they continued to do their work, tirelessly and unselfishly. I also firmly believe that without the cells of the Shepherd's Path working against the bent, that civil unrest through racial violence would have torn the United States in two. It wasn't until after the war that I was able to put some of the pieces of the bigger picture together.

"In 1915 director D.W. Griffith wrote and produced a silent film that dealt with the Civil War and Reconstruction called, *The Birth of a Nation*. It was rooted in extreme racism and portrayed black men as unintelligent and sexually aggressive toward white women. It glorified the founding of the first Ku Klux Klan and is credited with inspiring the formation of the second Klan movement. It was the first motion picture ever screened at the White House;

the President was Woodrow Wilson. The iconic image of a burning cross that came to symbolize the KKK was first pictured in Griffith's film. The stated goal of the Klan and their Democrat allies was to deny blacks equality in the life of their country, accomplished by extreme violence meant to terrify and subjugate minority populations. They wanted to deny Blacks, Jews, Catholics, sympathetic Whites and trade unionists any kind of political input. This Nadir of American race relations had the potential to destroy the coming *Pax Americana* we spoke of earlier. Hatred in all its forms is the work of the bent and their masters. The work of the Shepherd's Path in this turmoil is still ongoing."

"It's unfortunate you were never able to make contact with the Preacher and his group again. From listening to you speak of them I think they meant a lot to you."

"They did Tom…the Preacher saved my life and put me on the path. I do know one thing though."

"What's that," asked Tom.

"I will be with them again." Gordon winked at Tom and he knew that Gordon was offering him comfort for his own loss.

"What happened once you got back?" asked Tom.

"With my Boer War experience, I was offered a commission and posted as an instructor. The last thing I wanted was to be an instructor so I refused the commission and in November 1914 was attached to the 7th Canadian Mounted Rifles. In June of 1915 we set sail but by the time we reached France, the cavalry had been turned into mobile mounted infantry. No more massed formations, they had been cut to ribbons by machine gun fire. We were reorganized into smaller mobile units that could move quickly to plug holes, carry orders between units or just go where the fighting was fiercest. I was at Willerval with the Canadian Light Horse in 1917 when the Battle of Vimy Ridge commenced. We paid a terrible price but we earned the fear and respect of the Germans. Kaiser Wilhelm II called the Canadians the 'storm troopers' of the British Empire. The German High Command even changed their battle plans when they found out that Canadians would be manning positions they had targeted.

"The war in France was awful, the carnage and the waste of life, it was easy to see that this type of conflict, on a global scale, was exactly what the twisted lord had in store for humanity. I knew what I had to do. I had purpose in my life once again.

"With the war's end in nineteen eighteen the government wanted to demilitarize quickly so we were all shipped home and I found myself back here. I thought I needed to take action, but soon realized I had no idea what that entailed so I decided to make myself ready for whatever came my way. I thought of the cache of gold. If a course of action became evident, I would need resources. This wealth had been placed in my control and I decided it was time to put it to work. I needed to know its value so I went to different assayers in towns throughout rural Ontario and Quebec. When I returned home, I calculated the gold's value at roughly $125,000.00 dollars. If you compare the buying power of a working man between 1920 and now that gold, in those terms, would have a worth of almost 62 million dollars."

"Wow," exclaimed Tom, "That's a lot of cheddar."

"Indeed," smiled Gordon. "I spent the next several months liquidating some of the gold bars. Again, I took my time and spread the bars around so as not to bring attention to myself. Once I had some capital to work with, I began searching."

"For what?" asked Tom.

"I was searching for pathways. Things that might lead me to my purpose. I know this sounds quite mysterious; all I mean is that I was looking for things that just felt right. For instance, I had been born into an Anglican family. I had not been a church going man but once home from the war I had a very strong feeling that I should join a church. I was out strolling one beautiful spring day, no apparent destination in mind, when I realized that I was on the sidewalk in front of the Jarvis St. Baptist Church. In a rush of memories, I saw my father and his work as a young mason. I recalled his later career and how he and I had dug in the basement of the church and the secret we shared. I thought of the Preacher and his sanctuary where he and his flock worked in anonymity. I walked into the church and became a member. I also began searching for the company that had employed my father during the construction of the church. Snider and Sons Builders had been around since the 1840s and was still owned by a great grandson of the original founder. The company had fallen on hard times so I approached the owner who was hesitant at first to sell. I made him a fair offer and promised to keep all his employees on. I infused some cash and new direction into the company and it soon became a going concern. One of my foremen was a member of the Jarvis St. Church and became the first person I ever told about the Shepherd's Path."

"How did that go?" Tom asked.

"As I mentioned before, I have never known the Shepherd's Path revelation to be rejected. Persons who cross our path are watched. If they display potential for inclusion, we still do nothing but watch. Until they intersect with us in such a way that it becomes virtually impossible not to reveal The Path to them, we don't. We had been watching you for a long time. George first brought you to our attention soon after you and Joy were married. Totally independent of that, Laura's father Jorgen brought your name to me as a person of interest. He was not surprised that we already knew of you. So you see Tom, we knew your qualities for many years and George desired nothing more than to bring you to The Path, but it could not be until the night you and Laura met. It's called the *Intersection de la Voie*. It is different for everyone."

Gordon paused for a long moment as if to organize his thoughts after an interruption. "To continue, the company did well in the boom times of the post war period. We expanded, we vertically integrated, buying lumberyards, sawmills, door and sash fabricators and large tracts of land for the lumber rights. My foreman and fellow Path member Salvatore Lombardi, we called him Stoney Lonesome, became the head of the construction company. He knew every man on his payroll and that soon grew to over a hundred. Over the years ten of Stoney's tradesmen came to the Shepherd's path. By the early 1930s we had purchased close to a dozen different businesses. We operated a cement plant, an import export brokerage firm, a law office, a paper mill, various retail stores and a heavy machinery operation that specialized in deep foundations. There was no logical reason why I purchased these concerns. They weren't added to the growing list of businesses we owned because I had a vision or desire to form a conglomerate. They were purchased because at the time it felt like the proper thing to do. That was my philosophy…my understanding of 'The Path.' First of all; do no harm, second; be patient, third; act when the opportunity feels right. Now that is an oversimplification of my reasoning but it is sufficient for now. When the depression hit, we found ourselves in a unique position. None of our expansion was accomplished using borrowed money. We were paying cash for everything and we had money in the bank. All of our business operations were affected by the depression, but we were able to keep every man and woman who was with us when the depression hit.

“As the years went by our business interests were profitable enough to keep all our people well paid. Our Shepherd’s Path cell always had twenty-three members and we continued our work of gathering information. We watched our governments, kept track of social trends, and plotted technological advancements, especially in entertainment and communications. We kept a record of all prominent people, what they said, how they backed it up and how their lives were lived according to their public offerings. We were looking for evidence of the bent.

“In 1938 the Jarvis St. Baptist Church suffered a devastating fire. I gave the church a sizable donation toward its rebuilding fund, with the proviso that Snider and Sons Builders be allowed to rebuild and refinish the church basement. I used this as an opportunity to build our sanctuary.

“Over the years our construction operations had outgrown Snider and Sons Builders, and the original business I had purchased in 1920 was inactive. The ten tradesmen that belonged to ‘The Path’ were employees of Snider and Sons and were subcontracted out to our other businesses. All of our ‘Path’ members were also employees of Snider and Sons Builders, even though they may be employed elsewhere or even own their own businesses. This was done so that we could financially assist if necessary any of our ‘Path’ members with something as simple as a pay cheque. This could then be easily explained to family and friends as a second job. We also covered our ‘Path’ members with life insurance and occupational insurance to help provide for their families if something untoward should happen to them. We were still only gathering information at this point but no one knew if or when our operation would be forced to change and maybe take on more hazardous work. After the fire in 1938 it seemed like a good fit for Snider and Sons to do the work of rebuilding the church basement. Only ‘Path’ members worked here so secrecy was not an issue. To seal the deal and give us autonomy at the work site, Snider and Sons would be completing the project for the Jarvis St. Baptist Church free of charge as a donation to the church from the owner of the company. Everything went according to plan and within eighteen months we had the church basement restructured and rebuilt. We also had our new sanctuary, pretty much as you see it here, completed below the church basement in the old military supply depot that was dug in 1812.”

“I just love that story,” said Laura. “It’s like reading an adventure novel.”

“I don’t think there are many authors alive today that have half enough imagination to write such a tale,” said George. “The sheer scope of the story almost defies credulity.”

“I said almost the same thing when Gordon first began the history,” exclaimed Tom. After several moments silence Tom asked, “What happened after you finished building this sanctuary?”

“Now that is a tale that would take weeks to tell you,” murmured Gordon. In a stronger voice he continued, “Suffice it to say we have survived till now.”

“Hmmm,” mused Tom, “Survived till now…when did you realize you were living longer than most?”

“Right around the time we completed this sanctuary believe it or not. Our group finally had a permanent home, we had our work before us and, most importantly, we still had our anonymity. One of our Path members brought up the question of that very anonymity to the group several months after we had moved in, so to speak. It was the summer of 1940 and the country was in the calm of the ‘Phony War’ in Europe and newspapers here at home were looking for material to fill their front pages. One of our members, who happened to be a journalist, became aware of a story concerning our business operations. A colleague of hers was doing a series of articles dealing with companies that had weathered the depression and were poised to do well during the coming war. He had made the connection linking many of our businesses and had become overly curious about the variety of business operations that we controlled. He was perilously close to uncovering the ties between our working businesses and Snider and Sons, the umbrella company that employed all The Path members. That would bring the church and the work we had done here within the orbit of his curiosity. This would not do. We began divesting ourselves of the various corporate holdings we controlled. We sold out to competitors or entities looking to enter those markets, or we shut down businesses altogether, whichever harmed employee interests the least. One of our members was a partner in the law firm that we not only owned, but that was contracted to do all the legal work for all of our businesses. Names of corporate officers or owners were changed to non-entities and dates of sale were changed to wipe out all links between our holdings. This was all very illegal in a corporate sense, but caused no harm in a moral sense. As this was being done, I was also having my identity erased which was much easier to do in those days. As far as our country and its government were concerned Gordon Bernard Junior had disappeared after he was honorably discharged in 1919.

"During this process it had occurred to me that I was turning sixty-five. I did not feel sixty-five, I was told I did not look sixty-five. My hair was the same color as in my youth, I was not stooped and I had the energy of a younger man. People refused to believe I was over thirty. It came into my mind at this time something the Preacher had told me when I was with his group in Alabama. The Almighty would use your talents that had been inherited at birth if you were needed in his work. Often those talents or traits you were possessed of would be augmented to help you in your labors. I did not know if I came from a long-lived family or not, but obviously our creator, to whom we are all tasked, had need of my continuing energy and vitality. Since then I have never given it a second thought. There is also the legend in our group of Ademar de Fleury, which tells us that he is still alive in the Holy Land and that would make him almost a thousand years old. Keeping me alive for 146 years pales in comparison." Gordon laughed and with that brought his incredible tale to an end.

"I am getting hungry," George said. "I know that must sound quite mundane Tom after the fantastic things you've recently heard, but men…and women…must eat."

"I'm all for that," said Laura with much enthusiasm. "It feels like we haven't eaten all day."

"I'm not really that hungry," interjected Tom, "It'll be dark soon, I'm going down to St. James Park to see this poverty Coalition group."

Laura looked over at Tom and added, "I'm going with you Tom. Let's make a couple of sandwiches and we can take them with us."

"Sounds good," replied Tom.

While they made their sandwiches, Gordon showed George the map and tracing paper which they took into the library to study.

"Good luck with the ciphering," Tom yelled as he followed Laura up the stairs. They exited the basement and in a few minutes were strolling down Jarvis Street eating their sandwiches.

"It's only five or six blocks," said Laura, "we should be there in no time."

The late afternoon sunshine was bright and warm, and the trees that lined the street were shimmering in the pale green of spring. Tom could smell the unbounded energy of new growth in the air and was reminded of how much he and Joy had loved springtime. He remembered this sadly and it was as if he was remembering someone else's life. Laura noticed his melancholy and guessed its reason. She moved to his side and wrapped her arm in his. She looked up at him and smiled. Tom took great comfort in her nearness and hoped she did also. *We're just two orphans* Tom thought as they strolled along. It occurred to Tom that he knew virtually nothing about this young woman who had saved his life.

"What do you do Laura?" he asked. "Do you still go to school?"

"Yes," she replied, "U of T."

"What are you taking?"

"When Dad died, I was in my third year, Bachelor of Science," she answered. "I took the rest of that year off. Dad's estate was in good order and between his life insurance and savings I was pretty comfortable. I was living in Mom and Dad's house and not doing much of anything until I met Gordon. Once I realized how well Gordon had known my Dad, I asked what he thought I should do. He urged me to finish my schooling. He made the case that Dad would've wanted me to get my degree no matter what. Of course, he was right so I went back and got my degree. I applied to the Faculty of Medicine and was accepted. I'll be finishing my second year of preclerkship and next year I start working in hospitals and clinics. I think I might specialize in emergency medicine but I'm not sure yet…it depends on…" her words kind of trailed off.

"Depends on what Laura," asked Tom. "Course maybe it's none of my business. If I'm prying just tell me to mind my own business, OK."

Laura hugged Tom's arm harder, "I think of you the same as Gordon and my Dad. I feel like I've known you most of my life, I just didn't want to think I was boring you."

"Far from it. Tell me what's going on."

"There's someone I'm close to at med school but I don't know if there's a future with him. Depending on what he takes and where he goes it might have a bearing on the decisions I make. Also there's The Path to consider." She fell silent.

"I don't think inclusion in The Path excludes having relationships. Look at your parents, your Dad was a member but your mother wasn't."

"That's true," she said, "but it does complicate things."

"I think things will work out for you the way they're supposed to," said Tom. "I mean, think about it, our whole philosophy of The Path says for us to keep faith with God and walk the path He puts us on. Who is this young man, have George or Gordon met him?"

"Oh yes, they've met him."

"And…?"

"They both think he's pretty great. He's a year ahead of me. He'll be going into residency next year and then he'll have to pick a specialty. We started U of T at the same time but I fell a year back after Dad died. We knew each other when we were younger, our Dads were friends and we all studied martial arts together."

"Did he stay with it?" Tom asked.

"Oh yes, he's quite good," Laura replied with a mischievous grin. "I was hoping you would join me in our class tomorrow so you can meet him."

Tom was surprised. He hadn't anticipated taking part in any normal activities, considering the things that had been happening to him lately. "I don't know Laura, what if we're in a life and death struggle again?" He smiled.

"Make you a deal Tom…if it's life and death, we'll beg off class, if not we'll go…OK?"

"You got it. What's this lucky fella's name?"

"Agamemnon de Lisser," she laughed, "His mother believed in mighty names."

"That's a handle and a half," mused Tom.

"His friends used to call him Aggy until one day shortly after he'd started med school. Someone shouted out 'Hey Aggy' and all the other students thought he was a transfer from the agricultural program at Waterloo. Now everyone calls him Memmy…here we are."

Tom and Laura stopped at the intersection of Adelaide and Jarvis and looked over at St. James Park. It sparkled like a pale emerald in the late afternoon sunshine. Just above the tree line he could see the domed cupola of St. Lawrence Hall and at the far western edge he could just make out the copper spire of St. James Anglican Church, a green finger pointing to heaven.

As the park came into focus, he began to notice elements out of context. There was an ugly snow fence twisting around the park, the slats looking like the stop motion rambling of a drunken sailor. Behind the awkward barrier and the first outliers of trees there appeared to be ramshackle shelters thrown up by squatters. Blue, orange, green and milky tarps thrown over cords strung between trees, large cardboard boxes with rectangular openings hastily cut in their sides and sheets of old plastic hanging horizontally from strung wires to form partitions.

"We won't be able to hop that snow fence easily," said Tom. "I wonder where we can get in."

Laura was looking up and down the street. There was garbage everywhere. It was pushed up against the snow fence on the park side, but every once in a while, a breeze would push paper or fast-food containers over the fence and onto the city sidewalks. "These protestors have only been here a couple of days and already this place looks like a pigsty. Let's go this way." She pointed west.

"Sure," replied Tom, one way looking as good as another.

As they walked slowly down the street, they continued to look into the park and at the snow fence to see if they could gain access.

"I wonder who erected the fence?" said Laura. "I don't think the city would, unless they were worried about crowd control. The protestors would never get a permit to erect the barrier unless they had someone in City Hall who could make it happen without any attention being drawn to them. Why would they want a fence…unless they're hiding something." After a moment of reflection Laura snapped her fingers, "The map's legend dated tomorrow for something to happen here didn't it Tom?"

"That's why we're here."

"Then they're restricting access to the park grounds because whatever is going to happen tomorrow is being set up tonight."

"Sherlock Holmes got nuthin' on you Laura."

The sun was getting low on the horizon now and the shadows cast by the city's tall buildings were stretching outward.

"It'll be dusk soon, Good time to do some snoopin' eh?"

"Here," said Laura motioning down an alleyway, "The fence runs between the trees and this parking lot, we may be able to get over it farther in, at least we won't attract attention." She flashed a smile at Tom, "C'mon."

They turned left and continued into the parking lot. The shadows here had taken over and it was evening dark. They advanced further into the gloom, moving slowly and were near the Cathedral Church when they came upon four, scruffy young men. Any light from nearby streets was cut off by two large buildings and the trees of the park, making it secluded and dark, perfect for an entrance into the park secured by four guards.

"Get the fuck outta here," snarled one of the four.

Tom sized up the quartet quickly. One, tall and slim with a bad case of acne, Two was overweight and sitting on a concrete curb, a container of chocolate milk in one hand and a cigarette in the other. Three, talking, was bigger than the others and thought he was in charge. Four, with his back to them was just zipping up his fly. "Do you smell anything Laura?"

She lifted her nose in a parody of a dog sniffing the breeze, "Only the aroma of roasted chestnuts and urine."

Number four now turning toward them had finished with his fly and had one hand cupping his crotch. "I knew you was scopin' my stream sweetheart…you want some of this…dontcha bitch!"

As four swaggered over to Laura the leader walked toward Tom, "You," he pointed his finger at Tom, "Get lost old man, we'll take care of the tart."

He closed the gap between himself and the unmoving Tom. "I said move out gramps!" He reached out his right hand and gripped the lapel of Tom's windbreaker. Tom reached over the hand and wrapped his fingers around the meaty part of Three's palm. As soon as his fingers found their purchase, he clamped the palm fast and tight and worked his thumb into the tendons on the top of the hand. Surprise and pain flashed across Three's face. Tom waited one moment to see uncertainty creep into his eyes before he turned his hand upward, wrenching the offending hand off his lapel and bending it down and away.

"Stop!" The kid screamed as he desperately tried to relieve the excruciating pain radiating from his wrist by rotating his body in the same direction that Tom was twisting. He was down and his back was exposed. Tom's left arm encircled Three's neck and he squeezed. He let go of the misshapen wrist and brought his right arm up behind his opponent and pushed his forearm down on the back of his neck. Three went to sleep quickly and Tom laid him down on the pavement.

Tom looked around for the others and saw Laura standing next to him. "Where'd they go?" he asked. Laura pointed two fingers toward the church grounds and one finger back the way they had come.

"As soon as you put screamer there in a wrist lock, they took off. They're not much for backin' each other up."

"Let's get in before they come back with friends."

They walked through the break in the barrier and started down one of the diagonal paths that led to the park's bandstand. They looked around as they walked, the grass on either side of the walkway had been churned to mud, lower limbs of trees had been hacked or broken off and used as kindling and everywhere you looked the view inside the park was blocked by hastily erected makeshift shelters. Overall hung the stench, acrid smoke mixed with the smell of unwashed bodies and undiluted human waste.

Tom looked at Laura, “Is that the smell of the bent or is it just filth?”

“I’m not a hundred percent sure,” replied Laura, “There could be bent here but the garbage and filth would mask their smell.”

There were people everywhere, squatting in the mud around smoking fires of green wood, lying on benches covered by pieces of creased plastic or standing in small knots passing a bottle or a joint around. There were sign carriers running up and down the paths yelling out slogans and trying to get the attention of anyone from the media. They continued walking and observing, mostly where they were stepping, and Laura said to Tom in a lowered voice, “There sure doesn’t seem to be anything in here they’d want to keep hidden.”

“Let’s keep moving toward the center of the park Laura.”

“Sure Tom, do you have an idea?”

“Not exactly…but what do you do when you have a particularly nasty bit of garbage to throw out?”

“I don’t know Tom, do you mean…you double bag it?”

“Exactly! This human refuse is the next barrier, the second layer of the double bag. I think what we’re looking for is near the middle of the park.”

They continued working their way deeper into the park grounds. The amount of hanging plastic sheets and tarps became more numerous and this seemed to thin out the numbers of roaming people. As they worked their way through more and more sheets of plastic it occurred to Tom that they were passing through concentric rings of barriers that must radiate out from a central point.

“These people are going to a great deal of effort to hide any views of the center of this park.” They crouched down and passed under another layer of tarps. They stood up and looked around in the darkness and Tom whispered, “I think we’re here.” About ten feet in front of them they could see a large circular tent like structure. It was obvious the way the hanging tarps circled around the tent that Tom’s observation of concentric rings was correct.

“That’s like the Yurt library the original Occupy people had,” observed Laura in a hushed voice, “But this one’s bigger I think.”

They walked to the wall of the yurt and pressed their ears to the fabric, hearing muffled voices coming from inside. Tom got his pocketknife and gently pushed the well-honed blade through the fabric of the wall. He made a three-inch vertical cut and opened the incision to peer inside. He saw a small chamber with a wooden floor, one wall had an opening in it covered by a loosely hanging flap and it was vacant. Tom enlarged the cut and motioned Laura to wriggle through. After he watched her feet disappear, he followed. They crept over to the covered opening in the wall and listened intently. They could no longer hear any voices so he slowly pushed aside the canvas covering. They were looking down a corridor. Three canvas coverings identical to the one he had just pushed aside were spaced at short intervals along the length of the fabric hallway. They moved silently along the hall, stopping at each flap to peer inside. The first one they looked into had a small table with a black and yellow book on it and a Coleman lantern set to a low flame.

“Looks like the high school atlas,” Tom said, turning to Laura.

“Let’s have a look and see if it’s the same one we have,” She whispered.

“Better not,” advised Tom, “We don’t have a lot of time. Someone could come through that entry flap any second.”

They continued on to the next panel, nothing there. Just as they approached the last curtain, they heard approaching voices. They quickly bolted into the last chamber, tripping over something on the floor. They scuttled over to the corner farthest from the flap trying not to breathe. The voices were getting louder, two men arguing.

“I told you never to let that book outta your sight. Do you know what would happen if we lost it?”

The second voice answered sarcastically, “What’re they gonna do, torture us? You really that scared of Lamont? I know he tore into us the other night but he can’t really touch us…can he?”

“It’s not Lamont that creeps me out OK, it’s that other guy. You ever look into his eyes?”

The second voice derided, “Fuck me man, you are such a pussy.”

“Fuck off you douche, just get the atlas.”

Tom could hear the footsteps of the two men enter the table room through the flap. Their voices became slightly muffled but they could still be heard. “When are we gonna dispose of the sack in the other room?”

“When we get the word from Lamont. We’re supposed to meet him at that oyster bar across Adelaide around eleven.”

Tom looked at Laura and mouthed, ‘What time is it?’ She hit the illuminate button on her watch. The digital display read 07:46PM.

“Grab that book and let’s ditty mou outta here.”

“Hey Ricky…did Lamont ever find the guys that killed his muscle?”

“I don’t think they caught him yet, but they think they know who mighta dunnit.”

“You mean they think it was one guy who killed those three meatheads? I wouldn’t wanna meet him in no dark alley.”

“Ya, Lamont says he thinks it was the same guy that killed the two cops in Putnam’s little butt fuck town. They’re leanin’ pretty heavy on Putnam to come up with this guy. I think they’re gonna put some talent on that asshole’s tail if Putnam doesn’t produce him pretty quick.”

Tom could hear them leave the table chamber and start down the short canvas corridor toward the exit.

“What do you mean ‘talent’?” asked the second voice.

“You know, the ones we’re not supposed to know about, the ones that Lamont is always saying he’ll set on us if we fuck up.”

“Oh shit.”

That was the last of the conversation Tom heard as the two voices trailed off into the night. He looked over at Laura who was already looking at him.

“I guess they’re onto me,” he said softly. “Do you know what he meant by ‘talent’?”

“Demons,” Laura said, almost a whisper.

“Are you kidding me?”

“Tom…I’ll let Gordon explain when we get back. Right now, we have other things to concern ourselves with.” Laura nodded her head at the body laying on the floor next to them. She moved over to the prone figure and placed her fingers on the neck just below the hinge of the jaw. “There’s a strong pulse,” she said as she looked intently at the face of the woman lying there. “I think I’ve seen this person before.”

“Who do you think it is,” asked Tom as he went over to the flap and peered out into the yurt’s corridor.

“I think she’s a City Councilor. I’m not sure of her name or her ward but I’ve seen her face on the local news and in the Star. She’s an advocate for the Poverty Coalition. That would explain why she might be down here…but I’m not sure why she’d be trussed up and unconscious.”

Tom thought about what Laura was saying as he gave the corridor another look. “I would hazard a guess that whatever their plan is for her, she’s not gonna like it. I think they’re going to harm her in some way to cause a riot with the people she’s trying to represent, the people in this park right now.”

“What do you think we should do?”

“Let me think for a minute.” Tom knelt down beside the unconscious woman and began to undo her bindings. “She needs medical attention,” Tom finally said. “Is there a hospital around here?”

“Ya, Saint Mike’s up the street.”

Tom started lightly slapping the unconscious woman on her cheek. He lifted her by the shoulders into a half sitting position and gently shook her. “Hold her upright for me,” he asked Laura. She knelt down and supported the woman’s unsteady body. Tom rubbed her hands and moved her arms up and down. He patted her cheeks again and called softly to her but couldn’t get any response. “Lay her back down.” He breathed out through his nose, “If it’s only eight o’clock now and those two don’t find out what they’re supposed to do with her till eleven, then they’ve probably got her knocked out pretty good. Do you think you could get her over to Saint Mike’s by yourself?”

“It’s only three or four blocks…ya, piece of cake.”

Tom recalled her strength. “I’m going to track down frick and frack and see what they have planned for tonight. It might help us decipher the map.”

“OK, then I’ll get back here as quickly as I can.”

“No! Listen, if I can’t find them, I’ll go back to the church. If I do find them my questions won’t take long to ask, and if everything goes to hell I’ll be getting out of here as fast as I can, so whatever way this turns out I’ll be gone before you have any chance of getting back here.”

“Fine,” she said, but it wasn’t.

Tom placed his hand gently but firmly on her shoulder. “You don’t like leaving anyone without back up do you?”

"Tom," She looked in his eyes and he saw truth reflected there, "You are the sharp end of the spear. I know this. We are approaching a collision and I don't want you to be alone."

"I'm not alone Laura, none of us are."

She gave him a hard punch on his arm and laughed, "You idiot, you know what I mean."

Tom smiled back at her, "Of course I do and I'm thankful for that. Now, get that woman to the hospital and I'll see you back at the church."

"I'm on it." She put the prone woman's arm over her shoulder, grabbed her around the waist and in one fluid movement stood and brought her passenger up with her. "One thing though, meet back at the townhouse where we parked your truck. That way if you're followed no one connects us with the church."

"Good. I'll lead the way out."

They made their way out of the big yurt and into the maze of hanging tarps and plastic. The unmistakable earthy perfume of pot smoke was heavy in the air. Tom was out in front and after he passed a group, he heard one of them say to Laura, "Hey man, you guys all right?"

Before Tom could stop and turn back, he heard Laura reply, "Bad trip man, I don't know what she's on but I gotta get her to a hospital. You wanna help?"

"No man, just askin'."

A second voice piped up, "I'll give you a hand. Where you takin' her?"

"Saint Mike's, to emerge and then skeedaddle."

"Cool…let's go."

That's good, Tom thought, she'll have help now and if there's any trouble she can take care of herself. Without looking back Tom headed off into the maze of plastic partitions.

He knew the park wasn't large, but after fifteen minutes of aimless searching he was considerably disoriented. He could see the tower of the cathedral, but little else over the obscuring tarps so he decided to head for the tower and use it as a base marker to come up with some kind of logical search pattern. After thirty minutes of a somewhat more orderly hunt he still hadn't spotted the duo. He decided to abandon his pursuit and turned around to look for the tower and his exit route. Thirty feet back, down the path he had just hiked, the two were sitting down at a bench. As he strolled back toward them, trying not to raise their suspicions, he noticed one of them pull a lighter from his jacket pocket along with what Tom could only imagine was a joint. Sure enough, as the young man lit the end it flared up and he had to blow the flame out.

He had heard their voices twice before now, but this was the first time he had gotten a clear look at their faces. They were nice looking young men, a bit scruffy, but all in all not that different from most other male university students. These two had probably been seduced by promises of better grades or a more lucrative career than their fellow graduates. Who knew what they had been promised, it didn't matter to Tom. They had thrown away their humanity when they became willing accomplices to torture and murder.

As Tom approached them, they looked up at him with casual disdain. They were the power brokers here, they were the ones who knew what was really going on. This man crossing their path was useful to them only because he swelled their ranks by one. They expected him to lower his head in deference and keep moving on. They were a little annoyed but not alarmed when the stranger stopped in front of them.

"Which of you is Ricky?" Tom asked in a subdued tone.

They looked at each other in surprise and then back at Tom. In a surly voice dripping with impatience the man on Tom's right said, "Who wants to know?"

"I do," replied Tom in such an honest and matter of fact way that the answer was drawn from Ricky almost unconsciously.

"I'm Ricky," countered the man to Tom's left, suddenly becoming aware that the man facing him did not recognize his authority or power. He rose menacingly from the park bench. He was a head taller than Tom but gave up thirty pounds of muscle.

Tom ignored the rising Ricky and looked down at the other fellow seated on the bench still holding the joint in front of his face as if he'd forgotten it was there. "I'm the guy you don't want to meet in no dark alley." It took a minute for this to register.

"Shit," was all Tom heard. Ricky made to bolt to his right and his friend began to rise from the bench to run left. Tom shot out a front kick that caught Ricky's buddy square in the chest and sent him and the park bench sprawling backward. As he did this Tom also reached out and grabbed the back of Ricky's coat collar. Tom's leg recocked, he shifted his hip, jerked back on Ricky's collar and swept across the back of his calves with a downward arcing roundhouse. Ricky's legs snapped forward as his upper torso was yanked back and this put him on the ground with enough force to knock the wind out of him. He lay there sputtering, unable to rise.

Tom left Ricky where he lay gasping and went around the overturned wooden bench and grabbed the other by the throat. He applied just enough pressure to get his index finger and thumb in behind his trachea.

"Whoa…whoa man…what do you want?" said the young man, the strain on his windpipe evident in his voice.

"Your name for starters." replied Tom.

"Ya…ya…OK man…take it easy, that really hurts…whatever you want man."

"This is nothing," Tom growled as he moved in closer and tightened his grip slightly, "Test me, I will rip your throat out."

"Ahhhhhhhh," the man's scream was cut off.

Tom let off a bit and said sternly, "Quiet!" Tom kicked at the overturned bench with his heel to set it on its legs again. He pulled the gasping youth none to gently over to the front of the bench and pushed him down onto it, releasing his grip on his throat. "What is your name?"

"Oh God…oh God…what are you gonna do to me man…don't hurt me man…I don't know anything."

Tom lashed out and slapped the hysterical youth hard across his cheek. "For the last time boy, what…is…your…name!"

"Sean…my name is Sean."

"OK Sean. That wasn't so hard was it? Now…tell me about your plans for the woman you have drugged in the tent?"

"Don't say nuthin'," Ricky coughed from the ground.

Tom bent over and grabbed Ricky by his medium length blond hair and pulled him almost to his feet. He slapped him and pushed him down onto the bench beside Sean. A thin bubble of blood popped from the corner of Ricky's mouth. "Shut up!" Tom directed at Ricky. He looked at the two of them sitting there like truant schoolboys brought before the headmaster.

"You two haven't really done anything yet, have you? You didn't kidnap and drug the Councilwoman, she was brought to you, you were to keep her under wraps until Lamont told you what to do with her." The surprised looks on their faces told Tom everything he needed to know. "You two organized this little shindig though, didn't you?" Tom said as he swept his hand around the wrecked park.

They both nodded. Sean said, “They taught us how to set up a protest in our Poli Sci class. Peaceful or reactionary violence, whatever intensity you needed.”

“Nice,” responded Tom, “Taxpayer dollars and your parents’ tuition money at work eh? What were you gonna do if Lamont said kill’er?”

Ricky stared glumly at the ground while Sean stammered, “We…we really hadn’t thought that far ahead. They dropped her off a couple of hours ago and told us to meet Lamont at eleven…across the street…at the oyster bar.”

“Who is she?” Tom asked impatiently.

Ricky answered slowly, “She’s Glenda Purdy, city councilor for this ward. Lamont’s guys picked her up at her Regent Park office.”

“Names not familiar,” said Tom, “Besides the fact that she’s a councilor do you know anything about her?”

They started squirming and Ricky whined, “Ah c’mon man…why not just let us go eh, we’ll get outta here…we won’t tell nobody nuthin’. Look man, we didn’t know what we were getting’ into…if we tell you anything more, they’ll kill us man…”

“Tell you what Ricky, why don’t I show you what I’ll do using Sean here, then you can decide who scares you more. The guy who’s gonna hurt you now, or the guys who aren’t here?” Tom cracked his knuckles for effect. Sean started to moan softly, he knew he didn’t want to be the recipient of any more of Tom’s persuasions.

“Quit moanin’,” Ricky hissed at Sean as he rose, “What’s he gonna do to us if we yell and scream and attract witness…” He didn’t have a chance to finish his thought as Tom grabbed him by the collar and yanked him in while punching down into his face. The front knuckles of Tom’s fist caught Ricky just below the nose and his upper lip exploded into fleshy pulp and thick blood. As he spiraled down into unconsciousness Ricky blew out his breath and his two front teeth. Tom released his collar and Ricky slumped back down onto the park bench, his head lolling back, leaking blood and spittle down both sides of his mouth and a dark stain spreading over the crotch of his hundred- and fifty-dollar jeans.

“Oh fuck man…did you kill him?”

“Not yet,” Tom replied quietly. “OK Sean, your turn, ready to talk?”

“Ya man…you bet. She’s Glenda Purdy…oh ya…you know that already. She’s some advocate for the poor and homeless, used to be some professor over at York University, wrote some books on social engineering we had to read, helped out with Occupy and the G20 riots. She's worked with Lamont lots before on stuff, that's why his guys had no problem getting her in their car and then dosin' her."

"What did they give her to knock her out?"

"Don't know man. Just know they dropped her here and told us Lamont would see us later."

"She's one of you," said Tom, "She works with Lamont to cause trouble, why would he want to kill her?"

"I don't know man…"

Tom was quiet for a minute, trying to think this thing through. *Maybe I should meet Lamont at eleven* he thought. *No, I'm getting' too recognizable.* "Get your friend and get outta here," he said to Sean, "I would suggest you both move as far away from Toronto as possible."

Before Tom finished Sean jumped up and took off down the sidewalk leaving the insensate Ricky. *So much for friendship,* Tom thought. He checked to make sure Ricky wouldn't choke on his own blood and then started walking toward the Anglican Church tower and the way out of this labyrinth.

He left the park the same way they had come in. He had walked a couple of blocks north on Jarvis and was just crossing Shuter Street when he noticed Laura leaning against a chain link fence guarding a parking lot.

"Hey there, been waiting long?"

"Long enough, I was considering going back to the park to look for you. Find out anything interesting?"

The two fell in together and began walking back up the street toward the church. "A little. How did you make out with Councilwoman Purdy?"

"So that's her name. Huh. I got her to emerge and then took off before the nurses cornered me."

"What about the guy who volunteered to help you?"

"Oh you heard that did you? You didn't turn around when I stopped to talk to that group so I didn't know if you'd heard the conversation."

"Ya…I'm not deaf yet," Tom said laughing.

"He made a pass at me the first dark alley we came to. Wouldn't take no for an answer."

"What'd you do?"

"Let's just say he won't be able to stand up straight for a couple of hours."

Tom caught her meaning immediately and grimaced. “What a scumbag.”

“What did you expect, look where he was.”

“You’re right of course…did you expect that to happen?”

“Kinda. This isn’t the first time that sort of thing has happened to me, or to friends of mine. That’s one of the reasons I’ve stayed with martial arts all these years…I can say no without concern.”

Tom didn’t know what to say so he kept quiet. They made the church quickly and once safely down and inside they found Gordon at one of his tables reading. He turned to them and said, “George left earlier. He has some things to take care of before this situation here gets any more serious. How are things at the Park?”

“The park has been damn near destroyed!” Tom was surprised at his vehemence. “These spoiled kids have no idea what they are destroying. They are wanton and reckless and have no reason for their actions.”

“Their leaders have the reasons Tom and they are unleashing their minions. Please, tell me what you learned.”

“The protest is a front. The park has been turned into a duck blind and overrun by kids who don’t realize they are being used. Two college kids, Sean and Ricky, put the protest together but are ignorant of its purpose also. Earlier, City Councilwoman Glenda Purdy was picked up from her Regent Park office by Lamont’s men and drugged. Laura and I saw her bound and unconscious in their headquarters tent. We freed her and Laura took her to Saint Mikes. After that I went looking for Sean and Ricky. After a little persuasion they…ah, opened up. They had been instructed to meet Lamont at eleven where they would be given their instructions. They had no idea what Lamont wanted them to do with Purdy and they told me they hadn’t given it much thought. If instructed to kill her, I think they would have bitched and moaned but in the end, they would have done it, they are terrified of Lamont and his superiors.”

“Interesting,” said Gordon. “What did you mean when you said the park had been turned into a duck blind?”

“The real hunters are hidden and surrounded by decoys,” replied Tom, “And their targets are the news media.”

“Quite,” Gordon speculated. “What did you take from all this Laura?”

“Well,” She said slowly, “I missed Tom’s interview with the Gomers but I did see the condition of the park and Purdy bound and unconscious. Tom has it right. I think Purdy was to be killed. Some organization or political party that is opposed to her beliefs would be blamed and then the riot would start. This is just the beginning of a year of unrest and violence; I don't think they are ready to bring out their big guns yet."

"I think you are both right," Gordon smiled, "Well done. Had you thought about following them at eleven to see what Lamont would do?"

Before Tom could reply Laura said, "I don't think that's such a good idea, they suspect who Tom is and they probably have an idea of what he looks like."

"How do you know this?"

"We overheard Ricky and Sean just after we discovered Purdy in the tent. They said if Putnam couldn't deliver Tom, they would bring in some 'talent.'"

Gordon's looked up quickly, "What did you say!"

"You heard me correctly," she said quietly, "Talent."

Tom looked from one to the other and when they remained silent, he asked, "What does that mean?"

Gordon sighed and explained, "Many of the bent use the term talent to refer to demons. From the little we understand of the inhabitants of their world there are several orders of demons. We suppose these different orders serve different uses. We know of two types that from time to time have interactions with humans. There are the alpha types, these are the beings who are sent to deceive us and lead the bents. They appear and act completely human. These are almost mythological creatures as we only suspect their existence and have never really gone up against one that we know of."

"I'm confused then," said Tom, "You told me once that no human can defeat a demon. It sounded to me like you had tangled with these creatures before."

"As far as I know, and my knowledge of our orders history is not absolute, there have been only a handful of human, demon interactions since the monk Ademar de Fleury walked back out of the desert wilderness. Most of these collisions occurred early in our history and none of them ended well. These particular demons are different than the alphas I just told you about. These demons appear in human form but they don't have the cognitive abilities of the alphas. This order of demon is brought in by the alphas when they require wet work to be performed. I believe that Lamont's superiors will request these things be brought in to locate and kill Tom if Putnam can't accomplish the job with his own people."

"Gordon…I've been wondering…my wife is gone but I still have children. Would Lamont and his thugs try to get to me through them? Are they in danger…shouldn't I be protecting them, instead of being here with you?"

Gordon thought for a moment and then asked. "How would you protect your children Tom? Would you gather them together and tell them they are in danger? They would ask, from what? You would then be forced to explain why they are in danger and from where that danger arises. Do you think they would believe you?" He waited for a moment as Tom struggled with these questions. "Even if your children believed your explanation, what could you do, where would you go? Tom…your best chance of protecting your children is working with us. Please don't forget…there is a power that looks over us and cares for us and protects us. We don't always understand the ways and means of that power but as few humans in history have ever conclusively known, we know that power exists."

"You're right of course. I couldn't protect my children from this danger. I guess they were put in danger the day I confronted Putnam."

"We are all in danger Tom, and by that I mean every human on earth. If the twisted lord's plans for humanity ever come to fruition there will not be a safe place anywhere. The world will be torn by bloody conflict; war, civil strife, rioting. In short…the apocalypse, writ large and lasting ten thousand years. I told you earlier that you had come to our attention years ago, that we watch people that interest us, the good and the evil. The bent do the same. What I'm trying to say to you is that the qualities that attract our attention also attract the attention of the bent and their masters. You and your children came to the attention of Lamont and his predecessor long before your confrontation with Putnam."

Tom sat in silence for a minute. "I don't think I've recovered fully from the last couple of days. Would you mind if I headed off to bed?"

"Not in the least Tom, sleep well."

"Thanks Gordon…g'night Laura."

"Sleep well Tom. Don't forget you're going with me to work out tomorrow night and meet Memmy."

"Wouldn't miss it Kid." With that Tom was off to the shower and a good night's sleep.

His body and mind still exhausted, Tom didn't awaken until nearly noon the next day. As he sat on the edge of the bed feeling more refreshed than he had in months he marveled at all that had transpired in four short days. He rubbed at his eyes with the heels of his palms and then dragged his hands down his cheeks. His face felt different, it was rougher than normal. He rubbed his palm across his chin. It was scratchy. He rose from his bed and strode into the bathroom. He flicked on the light and closed his eyes until he could stand the brightness. His reversed image stared back at him from the mirror. *Whadauno*, he mouthed as he took a closer look. His whiskers were back. He'd have to start shaving again. He peered up and got a real surprise. His hair was back, very short hair, but it was all back and all black. *This is truly amazing,* he thought. He looked down and saw that the hair on his forearms was beginning to grow back and even the fine hairs on the first phalanges of his fingers was there. The hair was coming through on his legs and he pulled open the waistband of his boxers, "I guess I'm battin' a thousand."

Tom couldn't account for his renewed hair growth but he didn't care. It was coming back in and that was fine with him. It would at least confuse anyone looking for a bald man with no eyebrows. Maybe he would grow his moustache back, or a goatee, or maybe even a full beard. Na, he reflected, Joy had never liked him in a beard. His thoughts were on his grooming then as he got into the shower. Half an hour later he walked into the big kitchen to find Laura, Gordon and a man he didn't recognize just sitting down to lunch.

Gordon smiled at Tom and said, "Tom I'd like you to meet Bill." Bill stood and the two men shook hands. "Bill has been taking care of us and helping to keep our presence secret for more years than I can count."

"I'm happy to meet you Bill," said Tom. "George has told me you are his friend and that makes you family in my book."

"Thank you, Tom, I have the same regard for people who are friends of Georges."

Tom looked around and asked if there was coffee.

"In the carafe Tom, sit and I'll get you some."

"Thanks Gordon." Tom stuck out his chin and gave everyone a look at both profiles. "Notice anything different?"

"Your hair is growing in!" cried Laura, "Oh isn't that marvelous. In a couple of days no one from around here will recognize you."

Gordon handed Tom a cup of steaming coffee and said softly, "It's quite amazing really. Just last night we had talked about you being recognized if you had tried to tail Lamont, and here you are this morning…your appearance changing." He shook his head slowly as he returned to his seat and his sandwich. "Pardon me Tom, may I prepare you a sandwich?"

"Thanks, but no Gordon. I'll sip this delicious coffee and maybe make myself some toast."

Gordon sat staring at Tom for a minute with a slightly crooked smile on his face.

"Have I dribbled coffee down my chin?" Tom laughed as he noticed Gordon looking at him.

"Do you recall our conversation of last night and your concern for your children and what could be done to safeguard them?"

"I certainly do, we figured I could best protect them by staying here and battling against the forces of evil. You know, it almost sounds comical when said like that."

"You're right Tom," agreed Gordon. "The Twisted Lord and his earthly minions have always tried to embarrass people who spoke the truth or make the uttering of deep truths sound comical. That way the average person actually stops thinking in terms of absolutes, especially the absolutes of good and evil. I digress. George called this morning with some interesting news."

Tom gave Gordon a tentative look.

"Everything is fine Tom. First off, Grace's husband Trevor has been transferred. The software company he works for has sent him and his family to Austria. He has been given a promotion and has been tasked with overseeing the startup of an R&D unit and labs there. His employer has purchased their home from them so he wasn't stuck trying to sell their home from Europe."

"Wow," interjected Tom.

"That's not all, Tyler has been sent to his company's field office in Indonesia. He will be studying natural gas plumes in the Pacific, and Lilly has graduated early from RMC and will be posted to an Intel unit working somewhere near Cheyenne Mountain in the US."

This is unbelievable, thought Tom. "How do you know all this?" he asked.

"George has been keeping a very close watch on your children. It would surprise you also Tom to know just how many people around the world your brother in law has contacts with. One of his tasks within our order is for him to know people. He knows the bad ones we have to watch and he knows the good ones that may be of help to us. Our order has profited from George's associations. If George had been more mercenary, he could well have been a billionaire by now using the information he has gleaned over the years from the people and organizations we have asked him to keep tabs on."

Tom sat there for a few minutes letting this latest news ferment in his mind. Other things he'd known and felt about George were in this mental mash as well as ideas he'd only just learned, especially the information that had been presented to him concerning The Path. "I don't think amassing wealth was ever a consideration of George's was it. He was never troubled by the need to have more than other people. His personal path led him to you out of his own quest for finding good people."

"You see your brother George very clearly now don't you Tom? When you begin to see people, really see them, the good ones have a purity of purpose that can't help but make you want to change for the better, to be more like them."

Quietly Tom remarked, "I have always thought highly of George and had always worked hard at trying to be more like him."

"It may surprise you Tom, but George has often talked of his efforts to be more like you."

Tom suppressed the lump in his throat that was forming by quickly swallowing a mouthful of coffee. He thought he would change the subject so he asked the obvious question. "Has there been anything on the news about our rescue of Ms. Purdy last night?"

"First thing this morning," mentioned Bill. "She gave an interview from her hospital room; her private hospital room mind you. Even though she is an advocate for the poor she doesn't think much of sharing a ward with them." Bill chuckled. "No suspects yet, but Purdy mentioned she had received some threatening correspondence from a right-wing group that she wasn't at liberty to name. There was no mention of Lamont or anything concerning his limo being the last thing she remembers before waking up in the hospital with an IV in her arm."

"Do these people not understand who they are allied with?" Tom shook his head slowly from side to side as if he was having a hard time understanding their stupidity. "They will be used, until dying is their only use."

"There were other items mentioned Tom that weren't connected to the Purdy story," said Laura. "An unidentified man who was part of the Poverty Coalition's takeover of St. James' Park was found dead on a park bench this morning. The TV news said that he had been in a fight but the injuries he had sustained were not the cause of his death."

"So what killed him?" Tom asked.

"They said there were no signs of a mortal wound anywhere, except that his core body temperature was lower than the lowest air temp recorded last night."

"Holy crap!" said Tom, "The kid was alive and breathing when I left him. Damn…what do you think happened?" Tom looked at each in turn.

"We know what happened Tom and we're grateful that you got out of there when you did."

Tom looked intently at Gordon.

"A demon must have come looking for…what was his name Tom?"

"Ricky."

"Thank you…a demon must have come looking for Ricky. It must have found him shortly after you left and questioned him. They interrogate strictly by intimidation and fear, a fear so deep that some have lost their sanity during questioning. As punishment for talking to you the demon would have frozen Ricky's heart. From this we may conclude that Lamont has grown impatient with Putnam and has considered you a big enough threat to call on their aid."

"This is not credible," Tom grimaced. "Why would they freeze his heart?"

Gordon replied softly to Tom's anguished question. "Don't assume that any kind of humanity dwells there. It is a demon, a beast of evil, placed in human form by its master but having no human attributes. It may speak but does so rarely except to give orders. It has nearly superhuman strength but delights in killing with intense cold."

"What do you mean, how do they kill with cold?"

"They steal the heat of life from your flesh." Gordon looked over at Bill who looked down at the floor and sighed audibly, then rose from his chair. He unbuttoned his shirt to reveal his chest. Tom could see a wound, hand shaped over Bill's heart. It was raw, red and white patches of skin holding open sores and partially healed splits.

"I was almost killed by a demon," Bill started slowly. "Nearly sixty years ago. I was just a kid, fifteen at the time, I was a caretaker in one of the last residential schools for young native kids. I was cleaning, down in one of the sub basements when I heard some noise. I went to investigate, we always had problems with rats, and I saw this large man speaking harshly to the headmaster. I asked the headmaster if everything was all right and this thing was on me, fast. I was scared out of my mind. I heard this thing in my head asking what I knew and who did I spy for? It quickly understood I knew nothing. It ripped through my coveralls and then it felt like I was hit on the chest with a sledge hammer. The next thing I remember is seeing Gordon's face." Bill looked at Gordon.

"We were investigating the administrators of this residential school and our sudden appearance took them by surprise. The headmaster fled and the demon, not ready to be revealed, followed. That's how we found Bill, delirious with fear and pain lying on the floor. We brought him back with us hoping he would recuperate. Over the next eight months he came close to death on several occasions. He was paralyzed from the neck down; his breathing was uncontrolled and sporadic and his heart kept stopping. We could not keep him warm. He was in and out of consciousness, sometimes raving, lost and alone. We could not improve his condition no matter what we tried. Our order at the time included a very capable physician but he was unable to make Bill comfortable. We knew we could not help him, neither could we abandon him. We knew he'd been attacked by a demon but had no idea how to help ease his pain. He wasn't dying, but he wasn't alive. One night I couldn't sleep. I was having a hard time coming to grips with the utter hopelessness of Bill's plight. He was in so much pain and I could do nothing for him. In desperation, and more to ease my own disquiet I held Bill's hand and recited the 23rd. When I finished, I sensed Bill's breathing had eased and I began to recite the history of The Path. When I finished several hours later the little apartment was full of our people and Bill was awake. He remembered every word I had said and he has been with us ever since."

Bill closed his shirt up and redid the buttons. He looked at Tom and said quietly, "I am never free of pain, the lesions never heal and I am always cold."

"I'm sorry," said Tom.

"I'm alive," said Bill, his voice getting stronger, "And I carry with me a reminder of who and what we are preparing to battle."

"Do they use any other weapons, other methods of interrogation. I don't even know the right questions to be asking you. What should I know if I come up against one of these things?"

Gordon's terse reply, "Run."

At first Tom thought Gordon may have been joking but the look on his face belied that assumption. Gordon, Laura and Bill were deadly serious.

"There is no way we know of to survive a direct confrontation with a demon. Bill was lucky the demon didn't want to be discovered at that particular time. That is the only reason the demon didn't finish the task. If Bill had been a member of The Path, or if the demon had known we were of The Path, it would have stayed and killed us all. To hunt us down and kill us is one of its functions.

"Then why doesn't this Twisted Lord flood the earth with these demons and hunt you all down, for that matter why not hunt down and kill all good people?"

Gordon took a moment. It was logical to assume that a supernatural being who was immortal and the foe of God would be almost all powerful, but this was not the case and he had to explain this properly to Tom. Gordon had to clarify the Twisted Lord's limitations but he did not want Tom to underestimate their adversaries. "The Twisted Lord is but a mockery of our God, a cipher born in envy and evolving to jealous hatred of all the living works of God. This description should not in any way lessen your fear of this being. It is less than God but many times more powerful than anything you can imagine. The Twisted Lord cannot create from nothing. It can create evil from good, it can corrupt anything, but it cannot create life. Therefore, the Twisted Lord only has the shadow things it began with, a finite number, so it can't flood the world with its beings, it must corrupt and distort what it can and kill what it can't. It feeds on discourse and strife and feels pleasure in the destruction of God's works. We may only imagine what a world it controlled would be like, we do know it is always trying to achieve this."

"So you know very little it seems," said Tom in a subdued voice. He was suddenly feeling very exposed knowing these things were searching for him by name.

Gordon placed his hand on Tom's shoulder and when Tom looked up into his eyes Gordon placed his other hand upon Tom's chest over his heart. "We are only human Tom and even though we may only understand things as humans, we know about God, we know of His love for us, we know that nothing we do against the forces of evil is without value, we know these things Tom and it gives us courage to continue."

Tom placed his hand over Gordon's and took a breath. "Thanks for that…I know I'm not alone." Tom moved over to his stool by the counter and had another sip of his coffee. "It's cold," he said as he poured the dregs down the sink. "Was that it for news?"

"One other item," replied Laura. "A missing person alert for one Sean Pollik. A student who supposedly went missing three days ago. Do you suppose that could be the other guy you spoke with?"

"Not enough information to go on. I should've gotten his last name. The way he took off though, I would imagine he's halfway to Saskatoon by now."

Laura began singing, "Runnin' back to Saskatoon…Ya Burton." She looked around sheepishly. "Sorry guys, I thought everyone was getting' a bit down."

"When you're right you're right Laura. Gentlemen and lady, I'm going to shave, I hope I haven't forgotten how, then I'm going to make myself some lunch. Then…if I'm not mistaken, Laura is going to present me to her beau and work me till I'm ragged in her martial arts class."

"It's actually Memmy's class tonight," chuckled Laura, "and he will work us hard."

As the day waned Tom tried not to dwell on the evils that filled the world or the demons that were hunting him, but those thoughts were never far from his mind. He looked for Laura later that afternoon, his mental struggles had wrung him out and he contemplated forgoing their planned work out. When he found her in the massive reading room, she took one look at his haggard face, "No! You're not going to renege on your promise. I want you to meet Memmy and the work out will be the best thing for you, get your mind off what's troubling you."

"You're probably right," Tom replied tiredly, "But don't be embarrassed if I drop out of the opening workout."

"You won't," and she laughed.

"Laura," said Tom. "I don't have a gi."

"Not to worry, I still have dad's stuff at home. We'll find something to fit."

"When do we leave?" Tom asked.

"We should take off soon if we're to run by my place."

"I'll get my keys and we can take the truck."

"Great," said Laura, "I love your truck!"

"Well…it's not really mine, it's George's."

“You needn’t worry that George will ask for the truck back while you still need it.”

“I didn’t consider how much the truck has helped me until, in hindsight, I realized that its stealthiness probably got me from Putnam’s place to the hospital and then out of town to here without being noticed by the police. Isn’t that a lot like George himself…you don’t realize how much he’s helped until after.”

“That’s our George,” chuckled Laura, her quiet laughter a tinkling sound that filled Tom with hope. She yelled out, “See you later Gordon,” as they exited the sanctuary.

It wasn’t a long drive and the traffic wasn’t heavy. They drove onto the bridge over Rosedale Valley Road and continued north until Laura pointed right and told Tom to turn. A few houses in she had him pull up to a beautiful two and a half story red brick and granite home. “Sorry, no driveway, you’ll have to park in front.”

“Looks like lots of people park on the street here,” said Tom, looking around at the splendid older homes in this neighborhood.

“C’mon,” said Laura, jumping down out of the truck.

“Engine off, door locks and security on,” Tom instructed the Sabre as he exited the truck and followed Laura up the carved granite steps to the arched double doors of the stately home.

Once inside the entry hall Laura said, “Wait here a minute while I run upstairs and get your gi and grab my bag. Look around if you want, Dad would have loved for you to see his house.”

After a minute or two Tom yelled up to Laura, “Where exactly are we going, where are the classes held?”

“At the GSU Gym on Bancroft Street.” Laura yelled down, “I’ll be down in a sec.”

Tom wandered about and found himself in Jorgen’s study. There were framed photographs all over one wall and Tom noticed that most of them contained people dressed in karate gis. He looked closer and saw that many of them were of Laura at different ages and belt levels. Near the end of the martial arts pictures he came upon a series of photos showing him competing. The last three were pictures taken at the Canadian Open Karate Championships, the last competition Tom ever entered. He had become the oldest participant to ever win the gold. The final seconds of the bout were captured in the three photos.

Tom noticed his blank, almost otherworldly lack of expression portrayed in the pictures. As he stood peering at this series of photos Laura came into the room.

"Kokoro wa hanatan koto wo yosu."

Tom looked around at Laura.

"It means; Be ready to free your mind. Dad used to study those pictures. He told me once that they illustrated the perfect state of mind for someone in martial arts trained combat. A mind that concentrates on nothing but is aware of everything. Dad was crazy to accomplish what you demonstrated when those pictures were taken. He was never able to get to that plateau, but he always said that for him, it was the journey that was important."

Tom didn't know what to say. He had read of the Zen philosophy inherent in the practice of karate but had never thought anyone would hold him up as an example. "I tried never to think too much when I sparred, I figured the training should take over. Make sense?"

"It does. When I'm using my bo I never think about what I'm doing, the bo just seems to go where it's supposed to. Here you go." She tossed a duffel bag at him which he caught easily. "Let's go."

Twenty minutes later Tom was in the men's change room at the GSU gym putting on Jorgen's gi. It fit very well. Heavy, black cotton trousers cinched in with a satin drawstring. The top was heavy cotton also but white with the traditional string ties on either side. After arranging the two pieces till they felt comfortable he reached into the duffel bag and pulled out an old limp belt that must have been thirty years old. The black had been washed almost entirely out of the old belt and it was a mottled grey in color. He stared at the belt for a moment or two and then gingerly looped it around his waist two times and tied it in the traditional knot. Just as he walked out of the change room door, he saw Laura a couple of feet ahead of him. She was wearing a red top with white trousers and her belt, being newer, was all black. She was carrying her bo and turned smartly when he said her name. "Laura…about this belt."

She just looked him up and down and gave him a thumbs up.

"You do me a great honor Laura, letting me wear one of your dad's old belts."

"It's his oldest Tom. You're wearing the belt given to him by his sensei the night he earned first dan. I think it's like forty years old."

"Thanks Laura," Tom said maybe a bit too seriously.

"Dad'd be pleased if he knew you were wearing it." She looked into the gym and waved, "C'mon, there's Memmy."

Tom walked into the gym just behind Laura and looked around. The hardwood floor glistened under numerous coats of urethane. An abstract jumble of multicolored lines played over the floorboards defining the limits and courts for several different sports that competed for space here. Laura headed toward center court where a group gathered around an imposing figure. His dark hair was curly and close cropped and twilight eyes were set in a handsome face, he stood a full head above the students surrounding him. Broad shoulders tapered to a narrow waist, supported by long, straight legs. He had a ready grin for everyone and as he turned toward Laura the brilliant white smile he uncovered was enough for Tom to realize the depth of his feelings for her.

"Hello Barbie," he said in a rumbling baritone.

"Oh Memmy," she said as she swatted him playfully on the shoulder. He leaned forward and kissed her on the cheek. Laura turned to Tom with a radiant smile and said, "He calls me Barbie because he says I look like the dolls his sisters played with when they were kids."

"The most beautiful Barbie Doll ever created," the liquid baritone purred.

"Tom…this is my dearest friend in the world. Memmy…this is my dad's friend Tom. You must remember my father speaking of Tom."

For just an instant Tom thought he saw a dark tick in Memmy's glance. "Yes, I do," said Memmy addressing Tom. "It is a pleasure to finally meet you Tom." Memmy extended a very large hand to Tom who took it immediately. The grip was firm without being intimidating. "I'm glad you could make it out tonight. I think you'll enjoy the class."

"I'm sure I will," replied Tom, forgetting the tick and deciding he liked this fellow already.

"What do you think Laura, should we get this class started?" rumbled the voice.

"Can't wait," came her eager reply.

"Line up!" Boomed Memmy and everyone began to hurry to their customary places. Tom didn't have a customary place so he just stayed next to Laura. As one of the senior black belts in the class, Laura stood in the front row of students. The higher your rank, the closer to the front you stood. This allowed the lower ranked students to watch the higher belts as they went through their workout and practiced techniques as a group. After everyone settled into their places and quiet descended, Memmy began, "Welcome everyone. We have with us tonight a guest of Sensei Laura's. His name is Tom and he was a friend of Sensei Laura's father. He is a black belt of long standing and has been champion of many tournaments. I'm going to ask him if he would run us through a workout. Tom…would you lead the workout please?" Memmy walked over to Tom to take his place next to Laura and Tom walked to the front.

"Thank you, Sensei." Tom bowed low to Memmy who returned the bow. Tom noted the time on the wall clock and asked Memmy, "How long do you usually run the warm up?"

"Your call Tom, we have a pretty hardy group here who like to sweat." He grinned mischievously. Tom could see students in the middle rows turn to whisper to each other, likely assuming this should be a pretty easy warm up. Tom liked that and decided to do a work out that would test their fitness.

After thirty minutes there were only two, Laura and Memmy, who had kept up with Tom. His vigorous routine overworked every major muscle group in combination with achingly long joint stretches. He looked over at them and said, "Well done you two." He bowed to Memmy and said, "Sensei?"

Memmy looked at Tom as if in a daze. He shook his head once slightly and bowed to Tom. "Thank you, Tom." Tom and Memmy changed places and Tom was back beside Laura.

She elbowed him lightly and whispered, "That was the best warm up we've ever had…thanks Tom."

"That was great, wasn't it," Tom replied feeling his heart pounding strongly in his chest as his breathing started to return to normal. He returned his attention to Memmy who was looking out over his class.

"We will spar now, everyone take a minute to recoup and then get your gear on." The class began to break up for the moment and Memmy motioned to Tom, "May I have a word?"

"Sure." Tom said as the two men moved toward the change room, away from the resting class.

When they were out of hearing Memmy rounded on Tom and in a low voice growled, "What the hell was that Tom! You come into my class and try to kill everyone? I don't know who the hell you think you are but you can't do that here!"

Tom was instantly defensive. He couldn't believe Memmy's reaction to the intensity of his warm up. Did Memmy not realize that everything Tom did during a class was geared toward teaching students how to better themselves in the practice of martial arts? The thought held him for a moment before he calmed down and realized that; no, Memmy didn't know how Tom taught. He knew nothing of Tom except that he had crashed into Laura's life four days ago and now he was probably her main topic of conversation. Like a flare the insight lit up Tom's awareness…Memmy was jealous. This magnificent man was so head over heels in love with Laura, so vulnerable to her every word and action that he probably didn't even realize he was overreacting to Tom's display of teaching authority.

He stepped back and bowed, "Sensei…it is a teacher's responsibility to his or her students to awaken within them not only a desire to learn, but an awareness of what they do not know. Your students, as young people, surrounded as they are by other young people within this academic environment, immersed in a culture that worships youthful vitality…they are unaware of the…pressure…that one as aged as I am, can place on them if he wishes." Memmy's eyes went wide and he straightened up even more than he had been. "Sometimes Memmy, a demonstration of strong fatherly affection is necessary."

Memmy looked long at Tom. It was not a battle of wills but a need to understand that held Memmy. Finally, he relaxed and said, "I did not realize that fatherly affection could be so intimidating, or that pressure from one as aged as you would be so exhausting." He smiled, "I thank you and my class, in time, will appreciate your lesson. Would you spar with us?"

"No doubt!" said Tom. The two men walked back into the gymnasium. Laura looked over to Tom, mild interest in her eyes and Tom gave her a wink to allay any concerns.

"Line up!" instructed Memmy. "Black belts take up positions around the perimeter of the dojo. Kyu belts divide yourselves up evenly beside the black belts. You'll spar with each black belt for three minutes, then at the whistle you will move to the next black belt and wait your turn. Black belts…you will score your kyu belt opponents and at the end of class the best two kyu belts will spar. Sensei Laura and I will judge. Kyu belts must wear all protective gear, black belts…gear is optional. No contact to head or below the belt, light contact only, to midsection. Remember, clean technique. Okay, find your places."

Tom decided he should only need hand protection and was able to borrow Memmy's sparring gloves. He picked a spot to spar near the back of the gym. Most of the higher kyu belts gathered at his location. Memmy came over with a couple of yellow belt students and told them to start with Tom. He allowed one of the blue belts to stay and then made the others divide themselves around the room. He told them as they left, "Don't worry, you'll all have your three minutes with Sensei Tom."

With a blast of Memmy's whistle the sparring started. There were no surprises for Tom, the yellow and orange belt students were hesitant at first and he had to let them know he wouldn't abuse them. Tom guided them through certain sparring techniques and combinations and allowed them to practice these on him. The green and blue belt students were more confident and came at him with dogged determination. He had to stop them occasionally and let them know where they were leaving themselves vulnerable in their desire to score points. He also had to demonstrate how easily a veteran black belt could pick them apart. He did this with fluid ease but without too much bruising of youthful egos. He had to be a little more careful with the two brown belts. They had been decently trained but were still too eager on the offensive. It was simple for Tom to sit comfortably in a back stance and let them try to get to him. He would explain this technique before Memmy blew the three-minute whistle for the change so that each of them knew why they couldn't get close enough to strike. There were many bows and thank yous from the students.

Before the sparring in the round finished Tom noticed one of the grad students from the front office come into the gym and start speaking with Memmy and Laura. He was too far away to hear anything so he returned his attention to his last student. A minute later Memmy blew his whistle and Tom's sparring partner bowed, thanked him and walked back to the front. Tom was just about to follow her when he saw Laura coming toward him with a troubled look on her face. "What's up?" he asked.

"Henry, from the Student Union office, told Memmy and I that a couple of metro's finest were here asking questions about a person of interest. They had that old newspaper photo of you. They gave him a copy to circulate."

"Damn!"

"It's Okay. Henry didn't recognize you from their picture and neither did anyone else in the union office. I think the authorities must be trying to link you with the disappearance of the two douche bags from the protest at St. James Park."

"You're likely right. What do you think we should do?"

"We could probably walk right out and no one, not even the police, would recognize you. You do look a lot different than you do in that photo. The only problem is…there might be something in the vicinity that will know you no matter what you look like, if you catch my meaning."

"I do."

"See those stairs?" Tom looked where she was pointing and nodded his head. "Go down and you're in a storage room. Look to your right and you'll see a door that exits into an outside stairwell. It's the same stairwell we're parked beside. Go out and get in your truck. I'll say our goodbyes and grab our clothes and be there in a minute."

"Good thinking," he said as he moved toward the stairs. No one saw him depart as everyone's attention was on Memmy. Tom moved quickly down the old concrete steps to the basement. Minutes later he was outside climbing into the Sabre. He sat there for several minutes, hunched down, keeping a low silhouette. Laura came around the front of the building carrying their two duffel bags. Tom saw she had changed. She opened the passenger door, threw the two duffel bags in the back and climbed into the seat. "No one's out front. We can go."

"Engine on," Tom said, and he felt more than heard the engine purr to life. "Where to?"

She looked at Tom, "What do you mean…home I guess?"

"Which home? Your dad's or the church, and should we drive around a bit first to see if anyone's following us?"

"Good point, I think we should drive around a bit. Go back onto Huron and turn right onto Russell. Russell takes you over to Spadina Crescent; it's like a big roundabout."

Tom eased the Sabre out onto Huron Street heading south. A minute later he turned west onto Russell and in another minute, he was merging onto Spadina Crescent going north. Laura started looking around, to the back and to the sides. "It's only fifty along here so I should be able to spot anyone trying to stay with us."

“Don’t be too conspicuous, you’re boppin’ around like a bauble head doll. Adjust the side view mirror and the big makeup mirror on the visor so you can see everything to the back. Keep your head looking straight while you move your eyes from road to mirrors. I’ll go a little slow. If you notice a car staying with us and letting everyone else pass then we may have a tail.”

After fifteen minutes of driving Laura said, “I haven’t seen any vehicles that stayed with us for more than a minute. I’ll keep watching, you head to Mount Pleasant Road. We can turn down there and either stop at my place or go on to the sanctuary.”

“I’ll leave my sweaty gi on until we get back to the sanctuary and then I’ll shower there,” said Tom. “Did you want to drop anything off at your place?”

“Everything I need is at the sanctuary, but I’d like to stop at the house and pick up some photo albums of dad’s. I think you might get a kick out of them, you’re in a lot of the tournament albums.”

“I’d love to see them,” Tom replied.

“Here’s Mount Pleasant, hang a right.”

In ten minutes, they were almost to Laura’s street. “I’m gonna turn at South Drive and follow it around. I’ll park just down the street from your place, across from that big Georgian style home. I want to sit there for a minute before you go in.”

“Okay,” said Laura. “I haven’t seen anything following us. Not one vehicle stayed with us for more than four or five blocks.”

“I know,” said Tom, reflecting on their night so far, “But having my photo shopped around and finding out I’m being hunted has me spooked and edgy. I’m going to be extra cautious if you don’t mind.”

“No problem,” came the reply, followed by a giggle.

Until that little giggle Tom had almost forgotten how young Laura was. *A lot’s happened in her young life*, he thought. *Losing both parents so young could’ve really messed her up. It’s a good thing she’s still able to see the humor in situations.*

They came to a slight bend in the road and decided to park in the empty driveway of a darkened house. There was only one other car on the street, a large black sedan parked across from Laura’s house. After fifteen minutes they’d observed no activity on the dimly lit street. “Okay Laura, I’ll wait here and watch, go to your house, get what you need and then we can head back.”

As she exited the Sabre Laura said, "I'm just going to grab the photo albums; I shouldn't be more than five minutes."

Tom watched as she sauntered down the street toward her house and then took the steps up to her front door two at a time. The key went in the lock and she disappeared inside. He couldn't see if she turned on any lights because the view of her living room windows was blocked by a tree and a high cedar hedge. When they'd left the gym, they were just losing the light but now the night was complete. The moon was obscured by clouds and the solitary streetlight on Meredith Crescent was out. The only illumination the street received came from the nearby intersection.

Tom thought about how much he had enjoyed the class that night as he waited for Laura. He realized how much he missed teaching and it easily led to thinking about his former life and how he longed for that normalcy. His musing evaporated, *Where was Laura? This was taking too long.* A lifetime of dividing hours into tasks accomplished and yet to be done had left him with an acute internal clock. He reached into the back of the cab and unzipped his duffel bag. He pulled out his pants and T shirt and quickly changed into his own clothes. He grabbed his loafers and slipped them onto his bare feet. As he slid out of the truck he whispered, "Doors lock, security on." Tom walked to the rear of the Ford and across its back to get onto the sidewalk. The truck was now between him and Laura's house so he could observe the building without being seen from an upper window. All seemed quiet but he was worried now. *Am I just being paranoid?* Tom didn't even have to answer that question, being paranoid was going to keep them alive.

He stood up straight but kept his head down and his face in shadow. He walked slowly down the street toward Mount Pleasant Road. As he passed Laura's house, he glanced sidelong at it. There were no lights on, only a subdued glow from inside the living room. She could be on her way out this second. He would give her until he reached the end of the street and then he would have to investigate. Seconds later he came to the busy intersection, he crossed Meredith and started down the sidewalk that fronted her home. When he reached the wrought iron fence at the side of her neighbor's driveway he slowed and looked around. Nothing moved. He slipped up beside the iron fence until he was hidden from anyone's accidental gaze by a large tree. He crouched down and made his way carefully to the front corner of the big brick and stone house. This early in the year the gardens hadn't sprouted so Tom was exposed as he inched his way to the living room window. He didn't care at this point; he had to see inside the house. He raised his eyes just above the level of the sill and peered inside. Most of the room was obscured by the drawn drapes but he could see a sliver of living room floor bathed in the light of an overturned lamp. A sneakered foot stepped over the lamp and disappeared. He could sense movement just beyond his limited vision.

What now, he thought. *Get in the house stupid and get your friend!* Tom hurried between the closely packed homes and entered the back yard. He searched quickly and found a basement window. Jorgen had bolted a frame containing metal bars on the outside of this window. Tom grabbed two of the bars and looking Heavenward strained mightily to spread them. They wouldn't budge. *What were you thinking Tom, God would suddenly grant you the strength of Samson.* He gave one last desperate pull on the bars and again they failed to part. He shook the bars in desperation and noticed the rusty screws move in the old concrete of the foundation. He stopped trying to pull the bars apart and simply pulled the framework out. He laughed quietly. *There's always a path to where you need to get, it's just not always the one you think it is.* Tom laid the metal frame and bars on the grass and looked at the basement window. It was a fairly new vinyl side slider that had been recently installed. He jiggled and pried at the fiberglass mesh screen until he forced it out and then pushed sideways against the glass of the window and slowly it moved. He pushed a little harder and the thermopane slid all the way over to the stop. *Damn*, he thought surprised and relieved at the same time, *once Jorgen installed the bars he must not have been as vigilant about locking it.*

Tom pushed his way head first through the window. As soon as his head and torso were all the way in and he could feel his balance shifting he reached back to the window sill with his hands, grabbed firmly and slowly flipped himself through and in, like a slow-motion gymnast. Landing softly, he immediately crouched down and looked around the dim, unfinished basement to get his bearings. The creaking of the old floors alerted him to movement above. As his eyes adjusted to the dimness, he could make out the basement stairs. He made his way to them avoiding boxes and the usual basement clutter. He could hear male voices. He inched up the worn wooden treads, noticing they had no backs on them. They moved a bit as his weight shifted from tread to tread but were surprisingly quiet. The door above was slightly ajar, as if someone had just been in the basement. He got to the door and turned his head ninety degrees so he could look out the opening.

Laura was bound hand and foot and was sitting on a chair looking up at a man who's back was to Tom. Standing beside him was a very large, middle aged man dressed in black. He looked like the kind of guy who would have a pistol in a shoulder holster. The man facing Laura was doing all the talking, "You'll tell us where that prick is when we're done with you bitch." He leaned toward her and grabbed her hair in his fist. "Maybe I'll give you a ride to, that'll loosen up your tongue. Once I start bangin' you, you'll tell me anything I want just to keep me around." Laura spit in his face. The man lashed out with a right and caught her across the cheek. A cut opened and quickly welled with blood.

The large man put his hand on the other's shoulder and said in a menacing voice, "Easy there stud, we have quicker ways to make her talk. Go out to the car and get my kit. We'll pump her full of horse tranks and smack and she'll be beggin' to tell us stuff."

Tom jumped off the side of the old wooden stairs and grabbed whatever he could find off the floor that would fit in his hand and threw it at the window. He'd grabbed an old golf ball and it cracked the glass. "What the fuck was that?" Tom heard. He quickly moved under the stairs. "It sounded like it came from the basement. You stay with her…I'll check it out and be quiet." Tom could hear heavy footsteps coming to the basement door. He looked around for a weapon, all he saw was a water-stained box of Scrabble. The door above his head creaked open, a dim light bathed the opposite wall and the tops of the stairs. A heavy foot tortured the top step followed by another foot on the next tread down. The large man descended slowly, two hands on a revolver held out in front of him. "Give it up right now asshole or I'm gonna put one in your guts." When the man stepped down onto the fourth tread Tom struck. He drove his foot up toward the bottom of the fourth tread in a powerful kick. He used all the force he could put into the kick and gave his whole torso a quick snap to add a whip crack at the top of the kick just as he made contact with the dried-out timber of the tread. The step exploded kicking out the man's foot. He lost his grip on the pistol when his back crashed down onto what was left of the basement stairs. Stunned, he lay with his back to Tom who reached around and encircled his neck between two treads. Tom tightened his hold and the big man began to struggle. Tom grabbed his own right wrist with his left hand and pushed while squeezing his arm tighter. The big man struggled harder, his body bouncing up and down on the ruined stairs, his arms flapping and his hands trying to grab anything that would give him leverage to struggle more. Tom leaned back and pulled with all his strength and felt a pop. The big man stopped moving.

"What the hell is going on down there?" Tom heard from above. "McPhee! McPhee…answer me dammit!"

Tom started up the stairs. "McPhee's got a lot of answering to do, none of it to you though." Tom reached the top of the stairs and walked through the basement door and into the front hall. Just to his left was the living room where Laura was tied up. Her captor was standing behind her, one hand tangled in her auburn hair and the other pressing an eight-inch switchblade to her neck. "I see you've given up your butcher's knife Mr. Bolt." Tom had seen the lightning bolt tattoos on the fingers of Laura's assailant and a lot of things began to make sense. "Do you remember what I said to you the last time we met?"

"Fuck you, asshole…I'm the one with the knife to your girlfriend's neck. One more step and she bleeds!"

Tom looked down at Laura. She stared back at him, clear-eyed and calm. "What happened after I left you at the doughnut shop, Bolt?"

"What the fuck do you care man?"

Tom was desperate to keep Bolt talking, "I don't really; I just want to know how you caught me."

"It was pretty easy actually. You guys always think you're so fuckin smart, with your bullshit fuckin karate. Putnam found me the next day. Seems he wasn't too worried that we'd spoken. Seems like it helped him with a plan he was hatchin'. Anyways, I didn't hear nuthin' till that night when he grabs me up and we drive here to Tranna. I was here with Putnam when I saw you leave that fancy fuckin hotel with this quiff. I watched you get yer truck and then pick up princess here at the corner. Later Putnam and this other guy, Lamont I think, come out of the hotel maddern my ole lady when she's got no smokes."

Tom could sense that Bolt was warming to his story. He was loosening up; the knife wasn't pressed into Laura's jugular as firmly. Tom knew he could move closer if he was careful, just like closing on a sparring opponent. Dance a bit and ever so slowly move closer until you're countered, then you know how close you may get to launch your attack. He shifted his weight from side to side as if he was tired or cramped, using each movement to close the distance.

"I told them I saw you. I thought Lamont was gonna punch ole Putnam in the nuts. He yells at Putnam, says, I thought you took care of that fucker. Putnam goes purple but got nuthin' to say. Lamont asks me what I saw so I told him I saw you get in your truck and then stop to pick up this chick. He tells me to describe her so I tell him what she looks like. He keeps pestering me with questions about her and finally he snaps his fingers and says he knows the bitch." He nods down at Laura. "McPhee and me was stakin' out this house when you guys came by earlier. We called Lamont and he told us to sit tight. We got bored and hungry but we couldn't leave or that Lamont guy would have his pet skin us alive." Bolt shuddered. "We were fixin' to go back to the car when in walks this one and we grab her." Tom was now only six feet from Bolt. "Hey," Bolt yelled, startled by Tom's nearness. He pointed his knife at Tom, "You get back, how the fuck did you get so…"

Laura spread her hands apart and grabbed the seat of her chair. When Bolt pointed his knife at Tom, she bounced the chair up and back. The feet of the chair came down on Bolt's insteps and then slid painfully off. Before he had a chance to register the scraping pain Tom sailed over Laura catching Bolt with a round house kick to the side of his head. Landing together, Tom is in a crouch and Bolt is unconscious. Tom moved to Laura and helped her to her feet. He tried untying her bindings but the knots were too tight. Laura pointed her chin toward a roll top desk in the corner. "Over there, in dad's roll top. There should be a knife he used as a letter opener." Tom rushed over and lifted the segmented desk cover as quickly as the old grooved pieces of wood would slide. He found the six-inch knife lying on the desk top. Laura turned around and Tom cut the damp dish cloth that they had used to truss Laura's wrists. She started rubbing them as Tom bent down to cut the dishrag that bound her ankles. "What should we do with studly over there?" She grimaced.

"I don't know, I promised to kill him if I ever saw him again."

"You know this guy! I mean it sounds like you do…I mean, it doesn't sound like you were friends or anything but when you were talking to him you two have history."

"He was there when Joy was killed."

"He should die then."

“I know he should Laura but I can’t be the one to do it. That would be cold-blooded murder in the name of vengeance.”

Tom was looking at the ground, seeing nothing, reliving everything. Laura stepped over to him and put her hand on his shoulder. She placed her other hand gently on his cheek and felt the tears, “I know.”

Bolt started coming around and made some groaning noises. Tom stepped over to him, bent down and grabbed each shoulder and yanked Bolt onto his feet and pushed him back against the wall. Bolt swayed and would have fallen except for the wall. “What are you going to do to me man? Please don’t paralyze me again man, I couldn’t hardly move for days after that.” He whined.

Tom looked at him with burning eyes, waves of powerful emotion rolling through him causing his narrowed stare to have an intensity that scared Bolt to his core. “Please don’t kill me man…please,” he whimpered.

Tom turned and began walking away from Bolt, worried by what his hands might do if he stayed too close. “I let you go…you could have gotten away…but you didn’t, you went right back to them doing their cursed work! I should end you!” Tom growled through gritted teeth.

Bolt saw Tom’s hesitation and like all bullies took it as weakness. His opponent’s weakness gave him bravado and he crowed, “You can’t kill me man. What about, *Thou shalt not kill.*”

In less time than it takes to blink Tom covered the distance between them. He grabbed Bolt’s neck in a vice and lifted him off his feet against the wall. Bolt kicked and struggled for a moment until he realized that the end of his life was but a squeeze of this man’s fingers. Tom let Bolt’s feet come back down to the ground and he allowed Bolt to breath, “Be very careful Mr. Bolt, the commandment says, *Thou shalt do no murder*, it makes no reference to taking out the trash.” He peered into Bolt’s dull eyes looking for any recognition of a lesson learned. Tom released his grip and Bolt sagged to the floor clutching his neck, his breath rasping.

Outside there was the muted screech of tires on asphalt, then, car doors slamming.

Tom looked quickly at Laura. “Shit.”

“You done for now asshole,” shrieked Bolt. “McPhee called in when we got the bitch. I’m gonna enjoy watchin’ you die!”

Tom jumped to the front door and bolted it tight. “Out the back Laura…NOW!” He started toward her and she ran to the back door, looking back as she opened it. He was standing there, one foot in front of the other, frozen in midstride, half a smile on his lips. He opened his mouth to speak and fell forward, Jorgen's knife sticking out of his back. Laura cried out. Bolt was finishing his follow through after throwing the knife he'd grabbed from the floor. He was laughing and leering at the same time.

"Maybe I'll get to keep you when they're finished with you."

Laura closed quickly on him, all he could do was throw his arms up over his face. She drove a front kick into his liver. He buckled but the force of Laura's kick propelled him backward and he bounced off the wall sending him forward into Laura's high roundhouse kick that dropped him to the floor. She wanted to finish him but Tom's prone figure recaptured her attention.

She turned quickly, "Tom, Oh God Tom, Oh God, Oh God please no!" She fell to her knees wrapping her arms around Tom's shoulders, burying her face in the new grown curls on the back of his head.

The front door handle was jiggled hard and then three loud knocks banged on the door. "Hey McPhee…open up, it's us!"

"Oh Tom," Laura cried as she whispered his name.

"Man…feels like someone hit me in the back with a sledge hammer," Tom said as he tried to rise.

"Tom…you're not dead!"

"Jeez I hope not. I'm in too much pain for this to be heaven."

"Tom, hang on…you've got a knife sticking out of your back."

"Ya and we've got goons and God knows what else out front bangin' on the door. Pull it and let's get outta here." Hesitantly at first but with more force as the knife resisted, she withdrew the blade. She almost gagged at the slithery sucking sound it made as it slid out of Tom's flesh. When the point finally exited his back, pulling at the fabric of his tee shirt she threw it aside. Tom had not made a sound as the razor-sharp knife slid out of his flesh, but a huge shudder now went through his body and he sobbed through clenched teeth, "My good God that hurt."

"Can you get up," she sobbed as more banging came from the front door.

"Kinda hafta don't I," was all he said as he pushed himself to his feet. "Let's go!" They made it to the rear door of the house just as the double oak doors of the front hall blew inward and evaporated into tiny splinters that embedded themselves in the old plastered walls. They darted out into the small back yard, the perimeter of which was surrounded by a twelve-foot-high cedar hedge. "Where do we go now?" Tom asked, each breath a searing agony.

"This way!" Laura pointed to the far corner of the hedge that lay in a shadowed gloom. "In there…quick!" She whispered intently as she pushed him into a small hole in the hedge. It wasn't really a hole, two branches of the corner cedar overlapped and hid a space where a couple of limbs had been broken off years ago, making a small opening into the neighbor's adjoining back yard. They scooted through the space and made their way down the side yard and out onto the street.

"We'd better get off the street," Tom gritted through clenched teeth. "One of them may jump in their vehicle and come around the corner any second." They darted between two homes and moved between the buildings until they were well hidden.

"Are you okay Tom? Do you want to rest for a minute?"

"I'm okay to make it to the truck. Is there much blood?" He turned slightly so that his back was more toward Laura.

"There's some," she noted, "But not as much as I thought there would be. Most of it's dry. I was in E R for a short rotation and saw a couple of knife wounds. The docs always advise you leave the weapon in the wound until you get to a hospital. Most knife wounds bleed like crazy if the blade is simply pulled free, but…yours didn't."

"I'm pretty sure I'm getting help. Remember the beating I took from Lamont's three goons. I should've been laid up for a week. This isn't natural."

"Let's go then." Laura said. "I think if we go round this house and follow the side yard out to the street we'll be right across from the truck." In minutes they were staring out from behind a hedge at Tom's Sabre. They stayed put for a while, just watching for any activity on Meredith. "I'm glad you parked several houses down from my place," she said. "Those cedars kind of block our view, but they also block us from anyone looking out of the house. Let's try to make it to the truck."

"Okay," Tom grunted. "I'm grateful to be healing quickly, but I wish there was some pain relief to go along with it." He put his hand on Laura's shoulder and jerked his chin toward the almost invisible truck. "I don't think anyone would see the truck if they didn't know it was there."

They moved further up the street away from the direction of Laura's house and then doubled back to the F150.

"I don't think I can drive," said Tom weakly.

"Will the Sabre let me drive?" asked Laura.

"I dunno, let's ask." In a whisper Tom addressed the truck slowly. "Sunny…open doors, no lights please." There was a soft click, both doors swung slowly open as the truck lowered itself. Tom held the passenger door for support and slid onto the seat. Laura did the same on her side. No lights came on. As the truck resumed its normal clearance, across the street a neighborhood cat stared at the spot where she had just seen two humans apparently vanish.

"Hello Tom," a soothing female voice said. "You are not driving," it was more a statement than a question.

"New driver Sunny," answered Tom, "This is my friend Laura."

There was a soft whir as the driver's seat conformed to Laura's contours. "How is that Laura?"

"Oh my, that's wonderful," She looked over at Tom questioningly, "Sunny?"

"The truck's designation is, Sabre Prototype F150." He looked at her in the dim light, "SPF 150. Sunny is much more personable isn't it?"

"I like it," smiled Laura.

"So do I," answered the truck.

Surprised by the vehicles humanlike responses, which until now had not been evident to Laura, she asked Tom, "She almost sounds human, I mean the truck's responses seem human, I suppose its voice can be made to sound any way you want it to…can't it?"

"I think the truck's interface computer learns more about us during each conversation. I think she fine tunes herself each time to make our interactions more comfortable."

Sunny responded, "My voice and my responses could be completely mechanical in nature, or they could be non-verbal, just written instructions on the dashboard screens. Over the weeks of our interactions I have modified my responses to be more personable."

"I'm sure George had something to do with that." Tom grunted.

They sat for a few minutes watching the street for any activity. The residential neighborhood was deserted at this time of night in the middle of a work week. With nothing of concern within sight, they decided to move out.

"Start engine Sunny but leave lights off please," instructed Laura.

"Do you also mean dash lights?"

"Yes, thanks. No sources of illumination till we're outta this area. She's great Tom, I never would have thought of dimming the dash." There was no response from Tom. Laura looked over, he appeared to be sleeping, his body held upright by the racing harness, but his head was back and his eyes were closed. "Tom!" she blurted, panic in her voice. She had almost forgotten his stab wound. The last few minutes in the truck, watching for activity on the street and then before that talking amiably about the human qualities manifested in the Sabre had lulled her fears. Tom had not complained of his pain or discomfort and the fact that a little over thirty minutes ago someone had speared six inches of razor-sharp steel into Tom's back had ceased to be forefront in her mind.

Sunny's warm voice sounded around Laura, "I've been monitoring Tom's vitals since he became unconscious sixty-eight seconds ago. His breathing is shallow but steady, his heartbeat is elevated but still within a normal range for someone whose system has been flooded with dopamine and adrenaline. I will flatten his seat."

Laura listened to the quiet whir of the seat servos as she proceeded cautiously out of the vacant driveway. She turned away from her home and took the long way out to Mount Pleasant Road. She used every trick she could think of for spotting a tail and was positive no one followed them when she turned off Jarvis onto Horticulture Avenue. Just before reaching their turn she pulled over to allow three metro police cruisers with sirens blaring to speed past her going south. Tom had come to then, whether it was the wail of the sirens or the change in the truck's momentum, something had woken him.

"Hey there sleepy head," Laura joked, trying to make light of their situation. "We're almost back, do you think you can manage to walk from the townhouse to the church?"

"No problem," he croaked, his mouth and throat dry. He raised his seat back to normal and opened the center console to retrieve a bottle of water. Laura shook her head when he offered her first sip, so he unscrewed the top and drained the bottle. "That's better," he gasped as he took a deep breath. "I wonder what has the police so riled up? We'll have to check the news when we get in."

“When we get in, I’m going to look at that knife wound in your back. Then I’m going to clean it, bandage it and if I think it’s called for, I’m taking you to emergency.”

“No!” Exclaimed Tom a little too vehemently. “Sorry Laura, it’s just that they’re looking for us and the authorities are looking for me and I think our best bet is to stay here.”

“Let’s get you inside and taken care of, then we’ll see what’s up.”

Once the truck was parked and the garage door closed, she helped Tom into the church and through their concealed entrance. They came out at the top of the staircase and saw Gordon and Bill looking up at them. Gordon looked as if he were about to say something when Tom stumbled and Laura had to grab him to keep him from going head over heels down the stairs. Bill ran up the stairs to give Laura a hand. Fortunately, the stairs were wide enough for three people abreast and between them they managed to get a rapidly weakening Tom down the stairs.

Laura gave the two a quick briefing on the night’s activities as she and Bill half dragged, half walked Tom to his room. They laid him on his stomach while Laura grabbed some scissors and cut his shirt up the back, opening it like the front flaps of a tent. She instructed Gordon to hold the bedside lamp up and over the wound. Bill left to get an antiseptic wash and some bandages.

Without releasing the puckered wound from her intense inspection, she said to Gordon, “He should be dead Gordon! This man Bolt, a thug knife fighter, threw a blade at Tom almost point blank and buried six inches of steel in his back. Blindfolded he should have been able to hit something vital.”

“What do you mean Laura?”

“I mean…a surgeon with complete knowledge of human anatomy, could not have placed six inches of double-edged blade into a human back and done less damage than the knife thrown by Bolt.”

“I’m still not quite sure what you mean…Tom is lucky?”

“Luck’s not involved. We knew Tom was special. We knew even before we met him, when we read about the fire. We knew…that something was…was…” Her words petered out as she continued to examine Tom’s wound.

Gordon put his comforting hand on Laura’s shoulder. “I know what you’re thinking Laura. I also would have trouble putting those thoughts into words.”

Bill returned panting and out of breath to place a large glass bowl, antiseptic, clean cloths and bandages on the table by the bed. "Here," he said holding out a small magnifying glass. "I thought you might be able to use this."

Taking the handle of the magnifier she thanked Bill. "Okay you two…out. I don't need your foul breath on my patient."

"We'll put on some tea," said Gordon as he shut the door.

"Mmm huu," she mumbled, her attention already refocused on examining Tom's injury.

Half an hour later she walked out of the hallway and into the kitchen.

"How is your patient?" Bill asked sipping at his tea.

"He's fine. He wanted to come out and have tea with us, said he was famished. I told him to rest. I cleaned the wound and applied a dressing."

"Should he be stitched," asked Gordon who had seen his share of battlefield wounds.

Shaking her head, Laura replied, "Here's the thing. Tom should've bled after I pulled that knife out of his back, his truck seat should've been soaked in blood but it wasn't. He needed a surgeon to close that stab wound but when I finally had a chance to examine the wound the depth of the puncture didn't seem right. It was significantly shallower than the length of the blade that pierced him."

"How can you be sure Laura?" prodded Gordon. "Events were transpiring quickly, you were desperate for Tom and in a dreadful hurry, maybe the knife wasn't in as deeply as you thought."

"The man named Bolt threw dad's knife at Tom from four feet away. When I grabbed the handle, the blade was buried to the hilt. It took considerable strength to pull it out. No, there was no mistaking how deep the blade was in. By the time we returned here and I finished cleaning and disinfecting the puncture the underlying tissue had begun to close. His healing abilities are accelerated. I wouldn't be surprised if in the time it's taken to tell you this, Tom's wound has fully closed."

Just as Gordon was about to speak, Tom stuck his head into the kitchen. "Listen Laura, I know you said I should rest, but I have to eat. I am famished, I can't explain it but I don't think I've ever been this hungry in my life."

Bill jumped up, "Sit down Tom and we'll fix you something." He grabbed a Bartlett pear and tossed it to Tom. "You can start with this."

Tom consumed three more pears, two apples, and a bowl of seedless grapes while he waited. After the fruit he ate half a pound of cheese, six eggs scrambled, a pound of bacon, six more eggs and a half loaf of freshly baked bread as French toast, a piece of steak left over from the previous evening's meal and a full plate of leftover baked potatoes sliced thin and fried in butter. He washed it all down with a quart of milk and two large cups of blackberry tea and honey.

"In all my years I have never witnessed such a gastronomic feat Tom. That was amazing!"

"I think I could sleep now," Tom mumbled as his head began to droop.

"C'mon cowboy," laughed a relieved Laura. "Let me help you." Five minutes later she was back in the kitchen with Bill and Gordon. "I'd like to talk about what happened tonight but I think we need Tom's input. I'm pretty wiped also," she said. "I think I'll go to bed. See you guys tomorrow?"

"See you tomorrow," they both chimed in.

Chapter 6

Tom awoke without memory but a moment later the previous night came flooding back and reflexes arched his back. He wondered where the pain was. All he felt was a twinge of stiffness covering his right side. As he sat up on the edge of the bed, he rotated his shoulders to alleviate the discomfort. All things considered he didn't feel too bad. He noticed clean clothes laid out on the armchair beside his bed. He stripped off his shorts and dressed quickly. He thought about shaving but decided at this moment that breakfast was more important so he made up his bed, took the remainder of his soiled clothes and placed them in the small laundry hamper and headed toward the kitchen.

The spacious kitchen was empty and dark. He flipped on the undermount lights that illuminated the countertops. He could hear muffled voices along with an overlay of TV noise coming from the library slash reading room. Nothing about the noises emanating from the other room were overly concerning so he began to make breakfast. He started with coffee and once the beautifully deep chestnut liquid began dripping from the nozzle of the coffee maker and the aroma began filling the kitchen Tom went to the large side by side stainless steel refrigerator to see what his voracious attack on their supplies of the previous night had left them. It seemed that his depredations had been miraculously restored. As he juggled a couple of eggs, a bottle of cream, a slab of cheddar cheese and a stalk of celery, Laura came through the pass way from the library.

"I thought that might be you when I smelled the coffee brewing." All business now, "How do you feel?"

Putting his armload of fixings on the big kitchen table he rolled his shoulders and arched his back for Laura's benefit. "I feel pretty darned good considering."

"May I have a look before you do your descending horde of locust imitation again."

"Sure," answered Tom laughing, "I don't think I can do that again. I'm just normal hungry now."

"Glad to hear it. Okay then, turn around. Lean forward a bit and just support yourself on the counter edge okay. I'm going to raise your t shirt up to shoulder blade height. If you feel any pain or discomfort let me know."

"Sure thing doc."

"I'm not one yet Tom."

"Maybe not Laura but last night you got that knife out of my back, hauled my ass to safety patched me up and put me to bed. If it was up to me, you'd have your shingle."

"Thanks, you'll go in the books as my first patient. Now quiet while I have a look. Hmmm."

"You've got the hmmm down pretty good doc, what do you see?"

"Nothing," came her answer.

"Whadyamean?" he said in confusion.

"I mean that there is nothing on your back but a fresh-looking scar. A little pink, small piece of scab still stuck to the skin in places, but completely closed, clean and infection free."

"When I got up this morning I wondered if I'd be healed up."

"It's far from morning Tom, as a matter of fact it's late afternoon. We just finished dinner and were watching the news."

"I guess that's why the coffee pot was empty," Tom said.

"Grab yourself some coffee if you want Tom and I'll get you out the leftovers from supper. They're probably still warm, I covered a dish for you and put it in the oven."

"Thank you so much Laura, you've taken such good care of me since we met."

"You're important to me Tom and I bet that you and Joy would have taken good care of me if I'd been in your home."

Tom put his coffee mug down and stepped over to Laura. He put his arms around her and hugged her till he thought he might crack her ribs. "You are my family now," he whispered to her as he let her go. There was a tear in her eye as she quickly turned to the stove, oven mitt in hand. Tom sat down at the big table and watched Laura retrieve the still warm plate of food from one of the wall ovens. "What time is it?"

"It's just after six thirty. You must have slept for almost nineteen hours. The evidence would suggest that you need massive amounts of calories and long periods of rest to facilitate your accelerated healing." Tom took the offered plate and placed it on the table. He peeled back the tinfoil and breathed in the aroma of baked chicken, mashed potatoes and string beans.

"This smells absolutely delicious." That was the last thing Tom said until his plate was wiped clean. "You said before that you had been watching the news, anything interesting?"

"Ya…it seems like the riot planned for St. James Park is underway."

"Really? I thought we'd disrupted that when we plucked the councilwoman from the park. Without her death as a catalyst there should have been no reason to riot."

"Well Tom…we may have thrown their plans off by a day but it seems that these idiots don't need a reason to riot."

"Was that the reason for the police and emergency vehicles out last night?"

"That was the beginning of it. They set parts of the park on fire and it spread to St. James Cathedral and the outbuildings by this morning. It's gotten really nasty now, they're shooting at first responders. Reports from the park say thirty or so rioters are armed. The police say the protesters were checked for firearms before they were allowed to set up in the park but some reporters are speculating the original group had 3D printers brought in."

"Wow, you mean they made their own hand guns?"

"Ya. Scary huh?"

Tom was quiet for several minutes, gnawing on a thought that was stuck in his head. A face Tom was not familiar with came around the edge of the kitchen entry. "Laura…you should come and see this." He disappeared back into the library.

Tom grabbed his cup of coffee and he and Laura went into the mahogany and limestone room. Gordon and Bill, the man who had called Laura into the library and a woman that Tom didn't recognize were sitting and standing near the large screen TV watching a news event unfold. There was a black and white picture of Laura's father displayed in the upper right corner of the screen as the anchorwoman was saying, "…belonged to the late Dr. Jorgen Hoching. The home on Meredith Crescent in Rosedale was completely destroyed in the blaze. Firetrucks were unable to respond as they were at St. Jame's Park fighting the fires already underway there. Now over to Mirabella for the weather." Someone muted the sound on the large television and they all turned to Laura.

"What happened?" she asked in a flat monotone.

Gordon stood and came over to her. "It appears that there was an explosion at your dad's house this afternoon. The authorities are saying it was a gas explosion and are not ruling out arson. The house was consumed by fire before the first pumper truck could even get there. A lot of the crews from the south command were already fighting the blaze at St. Jame's Cathedral. Laura…they are asking for your whereabouts as a person of interest."

An angry thought blazed through Tom's mind, *Dammit Tom, you should not have gone with Laura to the university. What were you thinking? Go to a karate class; impress everyone with how good you are. You jackass Tom, you almost got Laura killed, you almost got yourself killed! Now she doesn't even have her father's house anymore!* "I'm so sorry Laura, this is all my fault. I should never have gone with you. I've only brought trouble to you. Now the police are looking for you and Lamont knows your identity. Dammit I don't know how I could have been so stupid." Everyone turned to look at Tom. No one said anything so Tom took their silence as agreement. He turned slowly and began to leave the room.

"Tom?" said the unknown woman. She was older than Tom by several years. She was slim and tall. She stood very straight; the years had yet to bow her. She was very articulate with a soft voice. "Tom…would you hear me for a moment." She paused. "I understand your sorrow on behalf of Laura and your fear for her, but none of what has befallen her may be attributed to your actions. Laura is an adult and has been part of our world for far longer than you. She is well aware of the dangers she faces, we are all aware of the dangers each and every one of us faces, how our actions affect everyone and everything we hold dear. The danger is aimed at us, not inherent in us. It does not matter if we run and hide, the threat will find us. It does not matter if we had never been introduced to the path, the threat would find us. I daresay that if any of us had run and hid ourselves away that we would already be dead." She gazed at Tom with an intensity that held him in a vice. "You have been told about our lives and how we are affected by the evil that walks the earth and is trying, has been trying for tens of thousands of years to destroy humanity. You know how we work every day against this evil, and we all do this with our eyes open. It is time for you to stop worrying that you are the cause of or the catalyst for the horrible things that can happen to any one of us. It is time for you to…" she smiled, "Cowboy up, so they say, and stop blaming yourself for the hurts this evil is perpetrating. We are the good guys; we are going to get hurt, deal with it." She loosed Tom from the strength of her gaze and he dropped his eyes.

My God, he thought, *these people are so strong, I don't know if I have any business being in their company.*

He looked back to the woman who had just spoken to him. He looked over at Laura and Gordon. All he saw revealed in their faces was love and acceptance. *It's not about me or my family or anything that has happened to me to this point, it's about protecting the immortal soul of man.* Tom shuddered at this thought. Intellectually he had accepted the enormity of what he had been taught by these people. He was just now learning how to deal with it emotionally. He stood in the warmth and golden light of the large study, surrounded by these almost incandescent warriors of God and he felt himself begin to fill up. As the heat of infinite life filled his spirit, he felt gravity diminish and he moved to hold onto an armchair.

"Don't worry Tom," said Gordon through smiling lips, "You won't float off into the air."

"What is this feeling," whispered Tom, as he felt like laughing, crying, running and jumping and hugging everyone in the room all at once.

"The only explanation we have for this sensation," said the woman whose name Tom still didn't know, "is that your mind, your body and your soul are all acknowledging and accepting together the enormity of God's love for you and the almost infinite power of life."

The giddiness soon passed, leaving Tom with a powerful feeling of lightness and strength. He also felt stripped of all doubt and second thoughts. Still looking at the woman who had spoken to him he asked her name.

"I am Benoite Bellami. I was the Chair of the Department of Psychiatry, Schulich Faculty of Medicine at the University of Western Ontario. I have been retired now for almost twelve years but I still lecture from time to time. I do not have the opportunity to visit Gordon and his sanctuary often, though I do plan to be here more in the future. I am what might be described as an operational observer and analyzer for Gordon, even though that is not quite the proper term. My brother Alaire, who was also a psychiatrist of note," she paused, "and I gathered information and made analysis for Gordon. We had been researching the physical and psychological effects on the human brain of collusion with the Twisted Lord."

"I noticed you said 'was' and 'had' when referring to your brother," said Tom.

Except for arching her eyebrow, Benoite's expression remained unchanged as her gaze moved from Tom to Gordon and back to Tom. "I came here today to report to Gordon that my brother Alaire was killed approximately three hours ago by agents of Doctor Darque. I am glad to see we are back to twenty-three."

"My condolences on the death of your brother Benoite…how was he killed…if you don't mind my asking?"

"I don't mind Tom. We here in this small group are closer than family. We have to be, we share knowledge that few people on earth know and we share dangers which you Tom have just now begun to understand. There is nothing than can or should be hidden or withheld from each other. It saddens and grieves me to my core that I shall now be without my brother's company but there is great consolation in knowing that his spirit now resides with our Father. We were tracking close associates of Doctor Darque's. We knew he was to be in Toronto soon, although we don't know the why or the when or the where."

Interrupting Benoite, Gordon said, "Excuse me Benoite, but I think we may be able to shed some light on the where and when, compliments of Tom."

"Interesting," she said. Collecting her thoughts, she continued, "We had followed them to the Metro Toronto Convention Center parking garage just off Front Street. There were three of them. Two moved out toward the exit and one stayed at the entrance, we thought maybe to meet with someone closer to Darque. I remained with the agent at the entrance and Alaire followed the other two. We were hoping only to overhear any conversations which might give us a clue to Darque's whereabouts or at the least his reason for coming to Toronto. Darque is a Group Commander, meaning he controls all of Eastern Canada and parts of the American Northeast. We were hoping he would lead us to the Territorial Commander. Darque is the highest ranking bent we have ever identified personally. If we could discover who the Territorial Commander is, we would be able to track that person and begin compiling information that might lead us to any number of Group Commanders in the U. S., or even the American Territorial Commander. We have never known the identities of the eight or so bent who inhabit the upper echelons of the Twisted Lords power bases in North America. Excuse me Tom, I am getting sidetracked. You will have to learn the administrative structures of the bent hierarchy later. Alaire and I observe their operations and then analyze the information. We don't generally carry out direct surveillance, but we had acted on some information that had just been made available to us and so…here we were. I don't know what took place, Alaire and I had separated, but he must have been discovered by the two bent he had been observing. When I found him, he had been wedged between the back of a large truck and the concrete wall of the garage. His neck had been broken." Benoite paused for a moment, her voice trembling. Her calmness and clinical demeanor resumed and she continued, "I wasn't able to free him so I put in a call to 911. I waited until they arrived and once they had the situation in hand I retreated here to the safety and security of Gordon's sanctuary."

Gordon stepped forward and placed his hand gently on Benoite's shoulder. "You know of course my dear that you are welcome to stay here for as long as you wish."

Tom saw a tenderness in Gordon's eyes that was reserved for this woman alone and when she turned to thank him Tom saw that feeling reciprocated.

"Thank you, Gordon. I think I will accept your kind offer." Silence reigned for a moment then Benoite said, "What was it you were saying earlier Gordon concerning Tom and some information he had about Darque's motives for being in Toronto?"

"Ahh," said Gordon, "Let me show you something."

Before Gordon could move though the other man in the room who was also unknown to Tom said, "I think I'd best get going Gordon. The sooner I get the information into our computers the better."

"Tom," said Gordon, "I have no manners whatsoever. Tom, let me introduce you to Jonathan Brandt. He is a data manager at City Hall. His haste is brought about by our need to oversee the information being entered into the city's computer system concerning Alaire." Gordon took Jonathan's hand, "Keep me informed, would you?" With that Jonathan was up the steps and out of the sanctuary. "Jonathan helps us keep a low profile within official government records." Gordon said to Tom. "Now, let's go and retrieve our map and its legend."

Soon Tom, Laura, Gordon and Benoite were huddled around one of the large reading tables. They stood close together looking down on the surface of the table, their shoulders supported by their straight arms placed along the tables edge, their necks and heads lowered toward the tabletop like caricatures of vultures patiently waiting for the lions to vacate their kill. Tom stepped back and stood up straight, arched his back and raised his arms into the air over his head. He groaned with the ecstasy of his mighty stretch.

"I'm sure the color of the dot is the key to what type of activity is planned. We don't know yet what all the different colors mean, but we do know that the blue color on the lower right quarter of the circle over the GTA has already happened. The color either describes Glenda Purdy being assassinated or the riot and fires at the park. Do you guys know how the situation at the park is, are the fires out yet?"

Gordon answered, "The fires are under control, but they have leveled two city blocks. There is still looting going on and several protestors have been rounded up for questioning. There have been a dozen deaths attributed directly to the fires and several police and firefighters were wounded during the shooting spree. The police and firefighters' unions have demanded investigations into the companies that manufacture the 3D printers that were used to fabricate the pistols. Several federal politicians have come out supporting an outright ban on all firearms in the country."

"Wow," replied Tom, "They aren't wasting any time, are they?"

Benoite said, "Their goal right now is to overload the system. This is the start. Once the system is near critical overload, and I think that can happen sooner than most people think, there will be some leaders or groups that appear to have some answers. The bent will ratchet down the violence and people will listen to these leaders. As everyone begins to believe that we have averted the crises the seemingly stable but still critically overloaded system will simply be nudged over the cliff by a few strategic disruptions and our system will descend into chaos."

"Lovely diagnosis Doc." Replied Tom.

"We know their plan Tom; have known for years that this was coming. Until now though, we have been reactive. This map legend may tip the scales in our favor now. We may not know specific actions, but we know the where and the when. I believe they start with r c in four days."

Gordon was still looking down at the tracing paper legend laying over the text book map. "There are thirty-seven colored circles on this legend, spread over Ontario with dates, we have surmised, beginning yesterday here at St.

James Park and covering the next eight months. That will take us into November. Why November. Why not plan things out until the end of the year at least. What is in November that these disruptions are aiming at?"

Tom was thinking furiously, about Gordon's earlier supposition concerning the forces of evil bringing about the downfall of the United States, and by extension the politically and socially free western democracies. "The midterm elections in the States are in November," he said. Everyone looked at him. "Depending on which way the election goes and how the people react will set the bent's future plans. Hell, these disruptions may force a non-confidence vote here and plunge us into an election. If this is what the bent are planning then I'm sure they are going to concentrate on disrupting and sabotaging the elections somehow. This format of tracing paper over a map may be a onetime thing. If a federal election is called here, I bet they already have a plan that will be automatically set in motion to somehow destroy our confidence in the electoral process. After that it would be easy to cause chaos by having segments of the population refuse to acknowledge the governments legitimacy."

"I believe your reasoning is sound Tom, would you and Laura put the Roger's Center under observation, starting tomorrow. There will only be you two for now. Benoite, we must bring George in on this and Jonathan also. I believe we can handle the planned occurrences in the GTA ourselves but we must make some of the other groups aware that…things are going to start going bump in the night."

"I will contact George and Jonathan immediately. Shall I have them report here or do you want to meet at George's secure office?"

Gordon thought for a moment. "Bring them here. Make sure that Jonathan has made all his arrangements for poor Alaire first. Then he can report in. From here on we only use scripted responses when speaking on cell phones or land lines. Also have Bill beef up our security protocols. I don't want anyone on the watch list loitering within fifty yards of here. Okay everyone, let's get started."

Laura and Tom walked over to one of the tables in the corner. Tom watched Benoite climb the stairs and exit the subterranean sanctuary. Gordon left the library and went back toward the kitchen.

"You guys seem like you know what you're doing."

"Not really," replied Laura. "This has never happened before as far as I know. We've had crises to work through but nothing like this. I don't recall

Gordon ever requesting extra security precautions and I've never known our group to coordinate with any of the other groups."

"I didn't know you knew any other groups. I thought you were all…independent of each other."

"We are for the most part. We share a lot of information but we've not worked together on one specific crisis before…that I know of. Over the years our group has come into contact with other Twenty Thirds. Our initial contacts with them were not sought by either group, they just happened. We don't keep in contact with these other groups after the original reason for the contact has been resolved, but we are pretty certain they are still out there. One of the groups I know has been around since 1776."

"I bet they've been involved in some interesting things?"

"You have no idea. When things are back to normal around here you should ask Gordon to give you a history lesson. It will change the way you perceive the world, and especially North America."

"So…do you think these other groups will be able to handle the disruptions being planned?"

"No, but there are more Twenty Thirds in Ontario than we know of. Each group that we know probably knows at least the same number of Twenty Thirds besides us. We don't have a central directory, but we do have a Director who knows where everything is." Laura's eyes looked heavenward when she said this. She smiled and said, "Mankind's poor usage of the gift of free will and the bent's meddling is always going to cause us trouble, but as long as the stalwart have the faith and courage to remain on the path that our Shepherd has ordained for us then mankind will continue to grow and learn and become closer to the enlightenment that God wants for us."

"That's pretty deep my dear, you've gotta remember I'm just a bricks and mortar guy," Tom said laughing.

"I'll take bricks and mortar over cap and gown any day Tom." Thinking for a moment Laura said, "Do you know what PhD stands for?"

"Doctor of Philosophy or something, isn't it?"

"Nope, piled higher and deeper."

Tom gave her a throaty chuckle and then got serious. "Do you think we should head down to Roger's Center now?"

"Ya, I do. It's about seven thirty now, by the time you get dressed and we get downtown it'll be closer to eight thirty, pretty dark by then. Listen, don't shave, we'll get you a ball cap from somewhere and we'll get your glasses out of your truck and Oh…I'll darken up your face with some makeup That should do for now to disguise you a bit. I'll wear my hoody and get some light tinted sunglasses. We don't want some gung-ho rookie on the force causing us trouble. Meet back here in ten."

Fifteen minutes later he and Laura were standing outside the streetcar kiosk in a comfortable silence, quietly allowing the foot and wheeled traffic to swirl around them. Tom felt like an island at peace in a frothing turbulence. He felt the vibrations of the streetcar coming before he noticed the high-pitched screech of its metal wheels on the steel tracks. It lurched to a stop and Laura and Tom stepped up into the car. Laura flipped two tokens into the glass box and they made their way to the middle of the full car. They stood and held onto the handrail. Tom looked around, assessing the passengers. There were young men seated all about the car, and many women, some older, some younger standing, holding onto the bars for support. Tom could only shake his head in embarrassment at the lowly state of masculine manners.

Conversations on the streetcar were muted but every once in a while, there erupted raucous laughter from some of the young men. As they approached a stop the streetcar slowed and Tom moved aside for an elderly woman readying herself to get off. Just as the car came to a full stop and the double doors rattled open, two young guys made to jump up and push past her with no regard for her safety. Tom shifted his body quickly to get between the older woman's back and the oncoming youths. He braced his feet and held onto the vertical bar by the exit and the two young men crashed into him like Volkswagens into the Berlin Wall. The elderly woman exited the streetcar without concern and walked off into the descending night. The doors closed and the streetcar screeched ahead. The other passengers melted away from Tom as much as the packed confines of the streetcar would allow as the two youths stood up. They were no bigger than Tom but their rudimentary math skills told them they outnumbered him.

"You made us miss our stop," hissed the one closest to Tom.

Tom smiled said pleasantly, "You may disembark at the next stop. You'll only have to walk back half a block, small price to pay for someone's grandmother getting home without injury."

"What the fuck man!" said the closer one again. "Are you stupid er sumthin'…I don't wanna hafta walk back halfa block." By this time he had worked up a head of steam and screamed in Tom's face, "Gimme cab fare, fuckhead." He drew out a wicked looking blade and made to press it against Tom's abdomen. Laura sensed everyone holding their collective breath. Tom smoothly turned aside, grabbed the wrist and pushed it hard into the one-inch diameter nickel plated support bar that ran vertically between the exit doors. Laura heard the fingers break and saw the knife skitter to the floor. Before the young thug could cry out Tom drove his face into the same bar that had just broken his fingers. He would have collapsed to the floor if Tom wasn't holding him upright. He grabbed the buddy by his neck and pulled him in fast and tight. The streetcar was coming to another stop and the doors were just beginning to rattle. Still speaking in a conversational tone Tom said, "Always remember dumbass, you never know who yer messin' with. Now hold onto your friend and you can get off here." With the doors open Tom made the second youth support his stunned friend and then escorted them off the streetcar. After the doors closed and he was standing again next to Laura he looked around at the other passengers who had been witness to the altercation. Any young men still seated nearby were silent and avoided eye contact. Men standing or sitting were looking around, some nervously, their thoughts a mystery to Tom but many of the women on board, young and old, would catch Tom's eye and offer shy smiles to convey their thanks. He thought sadly, wondering why men had given up on their responsibilities?

The streetcar arrived at their stop and the doors whisked open. Their feet had barely touched the roadbed when Laura said, "So much for keeping a low profile."

As they walked Tom shrugged his shoulders and quietly replied, "What could I do Laura, it was as if I could see everything that was going to happen. Those two would have barreled into her, knocking her from the top step down onto the pavement. If she was lucky, she would escape with bruises and stiff joints, if not…" He shrugged again. They turned toward the stairs that marked the subway entrance. "You're right of course Laura, that was foolish."

The air rushing up the open stairway almost blew Tom's ball cap off and was saved by his quick reflexes. He removed the hat for a second before he reset it and Laura looked at him. "Ya know…you do look totally different from even a couple of days ago. With your hair and beard coming in dark with no grey you look thirty-five. The police may have photos from before the fire and after the fire but those pictures will not resemble the way you are now. I don't think there was any harm done, those folks on the streetcar would never be able to identify you."

They were on the platform level now and Laura pointed the way to the southbound train. They gave their transfers to the attendant and walked through the turnstiles. "Which do you think is more important Laura, our mission, and by extension what the Twenty Thirds have been doing…or…standing up to evil when it's presented right in front of you?"

"Geez Tom, I hope they're not mutually exclusive."

Tom thought for a second, "Let's suppose there'd been a policeman on the streetcar and we hadn't seen him. He approaches me after the incident and somehow recognizes me from a picture and arrests me, or arrests you. Would it have been better, more right, to have let that lady get hurt and not interfere with our mission?"

"I don't know Tom. I think this falls into the category of doing what is right at the time and hoping for the best outcome. Protecting that elderly woman was the right thing to do. What those two prompted you to do and their resulting injuries is on them, you did not force that idiot to pull a knife on you. You probably could have anticipated their actions, being who they were, but is that a reason to sit back and do nothing? I think I'm now arguing for your original point of view."

"Thanks for proving my point Laura, I feel much better." He put his arm around her shoulder and gave her a squeeze. "Where to now?"

"South on this train to Union Station, six stops I think. We'll check the map inside the car."

The subway route map showed Laura to be right. The train was virtually empty so they sat down together and both relaxed into a cushioned seat as the train began to move. Random thoughts came and went with the swaying of the car and Tom allowed his mind to wander, drifting to something Laura had just said, he was a lot different than he had been before the fire. His enhanced speed, focus and healing abilities were undeniable. He felt different, felt sharper, able to grasp nuance more quickly. *My physical and mental abilities are superior to what they were, who knows by how much? What I could've done with these abilities before the fire. If I went back, I wonder what I could do. I bet if I went back to Coalman right now, I would be able to talk my way out of this mess. With my physical abilities it would be a simple matter to clean up on the tournament circuit, pocket some good money and open a kick ass dojo. I could easily win an election for council, hell I bet I could run for mayor, knock Putnam right out, I could run the show. Yes, you could Tom, you could and would have everything. Everyone would listen to you Tom and your influence would grow. Who knows how far you would go, how powerful you could be!* Tom sat bolt upright and grabbed Laura's forearm. "Whoa!" He exclaimed.

Laura looked at him, "What's up, I thought you'd nodded off for a sec, you looked like you were sleeping."

"God Laura, you wouldn't believe what just went through my head. I don't know if I was asleep and dreaming or just daydreaming?"

"Tell me what happened."

"Well I don't really know. I was just thinking about how different I was now from before. Then I started thinking about what I could do with my…what would you call it, enhanced abilities? I started thinking about Coalman and dojos and running for office again and then suddenly it was as if my own mind was telling me how powerful and influential I could become if I returned to Coalman. Then I felt trapped, suffocated and I jumped up to escape." He sat silent for a moment. "Does that make any sense to you, it doesn't to me."

"I think you've had your forty days encounter."

"My what?"

"Scripture says that Jesus went into the desert for forty days to meditate. During that time the devil came to him and tried to entice him to evil by showing him how he could rule the world. Long story short, the Son of God told the devil to take a flying leap. You've just been offered a glimpse of your power in the world if you follow the Twisted Lords path for you."

"Does this kind of thing happen often?"

"It happens to everyone alive Tom, to a greater or lesser degree. It's what happens when someone is faced with a decision that involves a choice between good or evil. In members of The Path it is a little stronger and the message is clearer, only because we are more in tune with the spiritual world, we have a certainty of its existence."

"How often does it happen and do you know it's happening?"

"It will likely never happen to you again. You know now what your dream was, direct communication from the Twisted Lord, a suggestion of malice and coercion. When you jumped up to escape the entrapment you shut the door to it permanently. Your mind is closed to it now, it can't get back in."

"Did this happen to you?"

"Yes."

"When?"

"Shortly after I met Gordon and learned the truth about the death of my mother and father."

"What were you offered?"

"Vengeance and retribution. It scared me to see how much the desire for vengeance was a part of me."

She looked off into the middle distance for a moment and then looked as if she might have more to say when there was a bell sound and the car announced, "Union Station next stop…Union Station."

"This is us, follow me."

The train came to a smooth stop ignoring the high-pitched squeal of the air brakes. Laura and Tom walked through the open doors onto the concrete platform, up a set of stairs and out through the exit turnstiles. One more set of wide concrete stairs and they were breathing fresh air. Turning west Laura said:

"Only a couple of blocks." It was an easy stroll; the sidewalks were empty of people and they were at John Street in a few minutes. Tom looked around the fairly deserted streets. "For a city of almost five and a half million there doesn't seem to be much bumping into pedestrians."

"Well it is a weeknight, but if you stay here till ten or eleven it will get crowded. The ball game will get out, the theaters will get out, the crazies will awaken and you know the Much Music studios are just up the street and there's always something going on up there. Once Much closes up, all the hipsters come down this way. It'll fill in quick." Rogers Center bulked large as they proceeded up the pedestrian bridge that went over the rail yards. "Which way?" she asked as the pedestrian mall split.

"Keep to the left," he said, "We'll go along the east side of the stadium down to the next street."

They were walking along the wide concourse passing the venue gates one by one and scanning the walkway. Laura looked up at Tom and said quietly, "I saw Memmy earlier today while you were sleeping. He was frantic with worry after seeing the news about my house burning down."

"Is everything all right?"

“He asked me to marry him, he said it wasn’t the most romantic time or setting but he was so worried about me he said all he wanted to do was help me and take care of me.” She fell silent.

“What did you say…hmmm, you don’t look too happy.”

“I am, exceedingly happy but worried to. I told him I needed a couple of days to consider…but I hear the way you speak of Joy, and I hear the love that’s still in your voice when you mention her name. I feel that for Memmy but I also know how much you miss Joy and how devastating it is to not have her with you now…I…”

“One day with the person you love is worth any heartache you feel when they’re gone.”

“I know that, I really do want to be with Memmy,” her smile started small but took no time at all to light up her face, “I want to marry him more than anything in the world.”

“Good then, call him as soon as we get back to the sanctuary.”

Laura hugged Tom in a crushing embrace and started jumping up and down, “God, it feels like a weight has been lifted off me.” She held Tom at arm’s length and looked up into his face, “I know this is out of the blue and Memmy and I haven’t done any planning yet but…would you give me away?”

Tom was surprised. “Laura, that’s a singular honor you’re offering me. You’ve known Gordon far longer than you’ve known me. What about uncles, did Jorgen have any brothers?”

“You forget Tom, I feel like I’ve known you since I was sixteen. My father spoke warmly and often of your friendship and since I’ve gotten to know you, I understand why. There is no one I would rather have substitute for my father than you.”

Tom could feel the emotions begin to swell inside him and all he could say through his breaking voice was, “I’d be honored Laura.” Just then, at the upper extent of his peripheral vision Tom saw movement. Too far away to be of immediate concern, yet the hairs on the back of his neck stood up. Quietly he said, “Don’t move.”

“What,” she replied remaining still.

Tom was watching two men on the lower concourse, walking toward one of the lower gates. “There are two men down there, pretty far away, but I swear I know one.”

“Let me look.” Laura swiveled away from Tom as if she were readjusting her posture to continue speaking to him. “God that looks like Lamont!”

“You’re kidding!”

“No…remember I told you after the fight at the Grand that I’d been trailing Lamont.”

“Ya.”

“Lamont was mine to study, follow and gather info on. We’d been pretty certain he was a player in Darque’s organization but had little real Intel on him. Last year we started getting inklings that something was in the air and Gordon assigned Lamont to me.”

“I thought he was head of some union?”

“He is, Toronto Union of Public Workers. He will soon head the national organization.” Tom whistled. The Union of Public Workers was the largest union in the country and one of the largest unions in the world. Boasting nearly one million members it carried formidable weight in any discussion concerning politics or the economy. Laura continued, “They have been on our radar for decades but they lacked the importance to devote manpower to. That changed last year when you ran afoul of the law in Coalmen and your Mayor, James Putnam began spending quality time with the president in waiting of the UPW. Our interest in you combined with our curiosity about Putnam and Lamont made our need for information important.”

“Coincidence maybe?”

“There are no coincidences in the affairs we deem important. Remember our adversaries, the ultimate master of lies, deceit and seemingly unimportant coincidences.”

“Understood,” Tom replied.

“I studied Lamont’s pictures and videos for hours, I’d know him anywhere, let’s go down and see what he’s doing and who he’s doing it with.”

They hustled down the wide stairs and observed Lamont going into Gate Seven. The ball game had started two hours earlier so the concourse and Gate were deserted. Looking through the glass doors Tom saw two security personnel. He pulled on the door but it was locked. He rapped on the glass and the female security officer waved him away. They both knocked politely and waved the guard over. With an air of disturbed importance, she unbolted the door top and bottom.

“Look you two,” she said sourly, “The game’ll be over soon and you’ll have to clear these doors.” Tom had moved halfway into the opening when the guard put her hand firmly on his shoulder, “That’s far enough buddy, you can’t come in here.”

“I just want to talk to Lamont, you let him in.”

“Mister Lamont doesn’t get refused entry anywhere and Mister Lamont doesn’t want to speak to you!” With that she pushed Tom out of the doorway and closed and bolted it.

Tom turned to Laura, “Well, we’ve established without a doubt that *Mister* Lamont has entered the building.” After a pause Tom asked, “What do you think we should do?”

“Track him! We need to know who the other person was. It could just be one of his cronies or…”

“Or what?” Tom asked not really wanting to know the answer.

“If it was talent, then it’s one of the ones that can pass for human. The type we’ve known can barely speak, let alone walk around in public without drawing undo attention. They’re used to intimidate humans, to scare them so utterly that withholding information would take an act of impossible willpower. They have an essence of cruelty and evil that wraps them like a cloak and is absorbed into any human that is close enough for contact. If it’s a demon and it’s in public then I believe it’s one of a type we have never dealt with. If they are on earth now, then this is a game changer.”

“Let’s get away from this gate Laura. If that security guard tells Lamont that someone was snooping, he might investigate. Let’s head back to the entrance, we’re too exposed here.”

“Okay, let’s go, but I don’t think we should leave yet. It’s dark, it’ll be easy to hide if we have to, lots of alcoves and shadowy areas near the front plus we can high tail it if we have to. Lots of witnesses, we should be safe.” On high alert they ascended the stairs toward the north end of the stadium, their eyes scanning for signs of pursuit or interception. “I wonder where Lamont is going? I mean, they wouldn’t be doing something as mundane as taking in a ballgame…would they?”

After a moment Tom replied, “From what you’ve told me, I don’t think they do mundane…their presence has a purpose, and that purpose has something to do with whatever will happen here in four days. The only reason for them to target this structure would be to create panic and disorder. If it’s a bomb, I bet it's already in place. The Yankees will be here in four days, that means fifty thousand people...a bomb, could you imagine?"

"No," she said cringing in horror at the thought.

"It would have to be a series of bombs, spaced around the stadium for maximum effect...although the more devices deployed, the more chance of discovery. I think they're here to go over the last of the details and they'll leave subordinates to carry out the plan. Laura...I think they're in the hotel having a meeting just like they were the night I discovered the map and legend."

"You mean the hotel here at Rogers Center?"

"That'd be it."

"Then we'll never find them, if they're in the hotel the front desk will never give us their room number...and besides, look at us, we're not exactly dressed for the upscale scene here are we?"

They were now approaching the front entrance to the Renaissance Hotel, the lights gleaming off the polished metal columns. Tom looked around, noticing how the parking attendants were scanning them. "You're right Laura, we'd never get through the front door. Let's use our appearance to our advantage. You go and see if they'll let you in to use the washroom. While they attend to you, I'll see if I can find a hiding spot and we'll stake out the entrance for a bit. That's all I can think of. You?"

"I think we're on the same page. All we need is a signal to shut this down and go home when the time comes."

"Okay Laura. I'll try to keep you in sight at all times, if you want to shut down, just leave and I'll hook up with you on the bridge. If I think it's time to go, I'll just walk past you. What do you think?"

"Good and simple."

"I'll be over by the exit arches." Tom turned to go as Laura turned the other way and started her approach to the hotel entrance. Tom had only gone halfway to the exit arches when he heard Laura's slightly slurred tirade begin.

"Aww c'mon you guysh...a girlsh gotta pee!"

Tom smiled to himself. *She's good*, he thought. The sound of her slurred words faded as he came up on the steps that left the hotel entrance. There was no one around so he jumped down into the gardens that encircled the cobblestone driveway. Crawling through the early spring shrubbery he found a position where he could remain unseen and his view of the hotel doors was unobstructed. He could see Laura, away to his left, slumped against a large square pillar as if she were sleeping one off. The two valets were deep in discussion, likely concerning the drunken woman, but they finished talking and didn't move to shoo her away. He was glad he had worn the heavier jacket Laura had given him. It was late and getting cooler and the moist ground was chilly. Tom wondered what Laura would do when the baseball crowd came out at game's end. No more had he thought this than the concourse began to fill with fans. He quickly looked over to Laura's position and saw her still slumped against the concrete pillar. An elderly woman passing by stopped and bent over to speak to her. Laura made arm movements that exclaimed, 'Go away!' He couldn't hear the exchange but knowing Laura could take care of herself he kept scanning the crowd. He turned his head slightly to the right to cover the hotel entrance. The crowd leaving the ballpark was dense but moving quickly. As the swirling mass of people flowed past the Renaissance entrance and eddied in and around the tall metal columns Tom concentrated on any traffic that might exit the hotel.

Lamont doesn't know we're here; he won't try to dodge us or use concealment to get away. If he's here, he'll just walk out normally. Damn…he probably has a car here, if so, they'd drive out behind me and we'd miss them. Damn he thought again, *I'd better grab Laura and see if we can find a better spot.*

He started to make his way out of the garden as unobtrusively as possible. He took a quick look over to where Laura was against the pillar but the tail end of the dense crowds obscured his view. He shook free of the last pieces of shrubbery and threw a quick glance over to the concrete pillar. For a second the moving crowd parted and he saw the pillar but no Laura, then the gap filled with moving bodies. *Shit.* Tom quickened his pace, dodging and wheeling to get around knots of people not sure of where they were going. Another sighting of the pillar through the milling throng, no Laura. He ran now, his legs driven by panic, not caring that he moved through the crowd like a linebacker through a marching band. He got to the pillar, dread like a punch to the stomach, frantically he looked for any sign of her.

The woman, his mind screamed, *the woman who spoke to Laura, the woman who had a neon blue blazer on over bright yellow slacks. She was headed to the bridge.* He tore off down the cobblestone concourse toward the wide pedestrian bridge that spanned the old rail yards. It was easier running now; the crowd had begun to spill out onto Front Street, the wide sidewalks of the long boulevard absorbing the crush of baseball fans. The blinding collision of neon blue and bright yellow lit by an overhead halogen snatched his anxious gaze. He accelerated down the sloping ramp desperate to catch her before she crossed the street.

"Ma'am...MA'AM!...excuse me ma'am." Tom thrust out his hand and touched her shoulder just before the large middle-aged woman stepped off the curb.

"I beg your pardon," she said, more put upon than afraid.

"Please ma'am, the young lady, leaning against the pillar, back by the stadium. Did she say anything to you, did she get up, did someone else come over to her?"

"Yes, poor dear, I asked if she needed help, she pushed me away and said no. Then two security people from the ballpark came over and said she'd have to move."

"What did they look like? Did they leave after they spoke to her, did they move her?"

"They had uniforms on; they weren't police though so I thought they were security people, you know, with the ballpark. There was a man and a woman and they both bent over to speak with her, then they lifted her up and headed back toward the stadium. I thought she may have been drunk. Young man, are you alright?"

Without a word Tom turned and shot up the ramp toward the bridge and Rogers Center.

Chapter 7

Laura felt the sting on her neck half a heartbeat before her head drooped. She didn't lose consciousness; she just lost the ability to move. Ungentle hands hauled her to her feet. Her arms were thrown over two uneven sets of shoulders and she was lugged back toward the lower gates. The crowds were behind them now, the concourse to the south all but empty. The pair of security guards had an easy time of it and were bouncing her dragging feet down the long set of stairs to the lower courtyard before she knew it. They turned right and entered the stadium through Gate Seven. She wasn't able to lift her head so all her unblinking eyes could see was the cold grey concrete of the floor. Her ears were unaffected by the drug and she heard a familiar voice say, "You two, over here!"

Blink, that felt good, another blink. *The drug acts fast but must metabolize quickly*. Laura could almost roll her head and her arms and legs were tingling. The almost familiar voice said, "Through here and down the stairs." She heard a door open and saw the bottom sides of the metal doorjamb as she was manhandled through the opening. A wide set of open steel steps was next and by her count they rounded three landings so they must be two full floors under the entrances to the southeast side of the stadium. As the guards grunted and groaned down the last flight Laura's senses reeled. The foul reek had her retching before a wave of fear and loathing consumed her.

"What the hell's the matter with her?" a female voice said as Laura's dry heaves gave way to violent shaking.

"Smell…can't…you…smell that?" she could speak now, "Don't you feel that?"

"Feel what?" said a male voice.

"Smell what?" said the female voice.

Laura's legs were stronger now and it was her hands and feet that tingled. She looked up and recognized the two security guards from earlier. Lamont was coming down the stairs behind them.

"Put her against the wall, she should be able to stand. Yeah…that's it. Okay you two; there'll be somethin' extra in yer envelope this week. Somethin' for helping me now, somethin' fer warnin' me about her and something fer keepin' quiet. Now find my guys and have them meet us at the top. Go!"

Laura looked around as Lamont was finishing his instructions. It was very dim, one single bulb in a pigtail lit the small landing. The ceiling, walls and floor were of roughly poured concrete and the only other feature down here besides the stairs was a steel door in the concrete wall. Scanning, her eyes finally found the cause of her sudden nausea and shaking. It looked like a man but Laura knew it wasn't. It had non-descript features but she noticed hard eyes and a cruel mouth. The body appeared neither tall nor short but there was a foreboding sense of mass to it. She identified the suffocating malevolence because of who she was and what she knew.

"Love the company you're keeping Lamont." She said as the creature turned its attention on her and she was engulfed in a new wave of nausea.

Lamont stepped in front of her as she vomited onto his shoes. "God dammit!" He yelled as he jumped back. He turned toward the man creature and said in a subdued voice, "Dial it down a bit please. She's gonna have me pukin' soon."

"We must go now if I am to question her, it cannot be done here." The voice issuing from the creature was human, just. It was deep and hoarse, each word seared into the meat of your memory. It was disturbing and Laura recognized a mounting fear within. She steadied herself with cleansing breaths and dampened her fears with thoughts of the people she held dear. She knew Tom would not give up looking for her. Lamont produced a plastic card and swiped it between the steel door and its jamb. The door clicked and he pushed it open. He reached inside and flipped an old toggle switch. Distant lights came on, revealing a small chamber on the other side of the door. Lamont drew a knife handle from inside his jacket and pressed on its spine. A nasty blade snicked into prominence its edge flickered in the pale light.

He looked into Laura's face, "I know I don't need this considering my friend here, but having it does give me comfort. It would be a shame, but try anything and I'll slice your face like a pizza and leave the rest for him."

The creature moved into the chamber first, followed by Laura and Lamont. Lamont kicked the rust pitted steel door closed and it locked automatically. The small chamber was cut out of solid rock, the floor an extension of the concrete from the other side of the door. Laura could make out two handrails that came up out of the depths of a gloomy abyss and curled forward and down to attach to the floor where they stood. The man shape threw its leg over the edge, grabbed each hand rail, turned toward them and stepped down into the gloom.

"You next," Lamont said pointing to the handrails with the knife. Laura walked over and peered down into the shadows. A large metal ladder with handrails, anchored to the face of the excavated stone, ran down thirty feet. Encircling bands of metal had been welded at intervals all the way down to provide fall protection. Laura climbed over the lip and started her descent, partway down she heard Lamont.

At the bottom she found herself standing in a tunnel that had only one direction. The bottom was flat and approximately five feet wide, the highest point at least six feet above Laura's head and strung with light bulbs dangling every fifteen feet, just enough illumination to keep from tripping. The floor was not level, it rose and fell with no regularity and was strewn with stones and rocks, from gravel to the size of a fist. The man thing led off with Laura following and Lamont and his switchblade bringing up the rear. She decided she must learn all she could. It would be useless to try to draw anything useful from the demon, but Lamont might talk, he had nothing to fear. "Where are we Lamont?"

"Shaddup!"

"Aw c'mon Lamont, you got nuthin' to fear from me. At least tell me where we're headed…hell maybe?"

There was a grunt from ahead and Lamont sneered, "Maybe for you, you're gonna get what you got comin'. I'm gonna get plenty, especially when you talk."

"So where are we Louise?"

"We're in some old subway tunnels. Abandoned exploration tunnels actually. Back in the early seventies they were gonna do a revitalization of Union Station. They were gonna build a new underground station with extra subway lines and a new metro center development. I was with the railroad union then and got to inspect the exploratory tunnels that were dug. The whole project got shitcanned but the tunnels were left, too expensive to fill them in. When the tower was built and then Skydome developed we had the union excavation crews and foundation guys connect some of the old tunnels to the new buildings, thought we might have a use for some secret access shit. Whaddya think, pretty cool huh?"

"Well," she replied, "Rats like tunnels." Laura thought for a second that she may have angered Lamont into silence but he loved the sound of his own voice and once she'd gotten him talking, he didn't want to stop.

"We're headed for the CN Tower now."

"Why?" Laura could kick herself. She had to learn to keep quiet and let Lamont spill everything in his own time.

"Whaddya mean why?"

"Well, what good does it do to be under the CN Tower?"

"We're not going to be under the tower you dull bitch; we're going into the tower. The tower's foundation goes down almost fifty feet, this tunnel is at forty-five feet, we'll intersect the tower five feet up from the first pour."

Laura couldn't help but ask, "You have secret tunnels into the CN Tower…why?"

"God damn you ask a lot of questions. I'm going to ask our friend there to make you a mute when he converts you. Ya…a mute slave for me." Lamont's evil smile made Laura shudder thinking about what thoughts concerning her would make Lamont smile like that. He continued, "When the tower was first planned, the chief design engineer at the time suspected the abandoned tunnels of the canceled subway line might intersect with the tower's foundation excavation. If it did, he had a contingency plan to accommodate an access from the tunnel into the base of the tower. What his purpose was I don't know. I never met the man but he was one of us. He also used his position to build a secret place for us under the microwave receivers located in the Radome just below the revolving restaurant. The organization didn't use these places much in the beginning but over the last ten years our friend up ahead has been using them as his headquarters. I'll tell you, they've come in pretty handy."

"Holy crap…you have a secret hideout, way to go bad guys. But it still begs the question; what good is it?"

"Ha. Surprised you haven't figured it out yet but I guess maybe you're not the brains of your operation, maybe yer only good fer killin' guys with yer stick."

“You mean the three knuckle draggers at the Grand? I can’t claim credit for all that, I did have help, and oh ya, I had help at my house too and he’s coming and you will never stop him!”

The man thing stopped ahead of them at the mention of Tom and Laura almost walked into it before she stopped herself. “I will be asking you some questions about that one,” the creature said in its grating, sickening voice. “I will enjoy breaking you. I think I will relish more though when you become one of us…if even for just a short time.”

“Never!” She hissed, “I’ll die first!”

“Yesss…you will.”

All were quiet after that as they continued down the stone passage. Doubt was worming its way into Laura’s thoughts; had Tom discovered she was missing yet. *He will find me*, she thought. They soon came to the end of the rough sided tunnel, stopped by a wall of concrete. A rectangular opening in the wall presented itself, it was a passageway that continued straight back for forty feet. She could not contain her curiosity, “What is this place?”

Lamont was all too happy to answer her. “This is the exterior face of the CN Tower foundation. When they started the tower in ’73 they poured nine thousand tons of concrete into this hole to a depth of twenty-two feet. Our people formed a passageway into the center of the foundation. From there we can access anywhere inside the tower.”

“What’s inside the tower, I thought it was concrete?”

“It is concrete, but it’s hollow. All the servicing goes up through the center and there is also an emergency stairwell that goes all the way to the top. It would take a half hour to climb those stairs to where we wanna go, but we have our own little service elevator. We put it in secretly about ten years ago when we decided to use the space we had up there.”

Laura hardly believed Lamont’s tale of all this secret stuff being done. “How is it nobody’s found out about any of this?”

“Oh, many people do know about it, but they are all, for the most part, with us and if they’re not, well then money and threats help them keep their mouths shut. Why do you think large construction projects, especially union ones, are always over budget. It’s not just bribes and corruption that cause overruns, often we add things to the projects. We have secret places all over the world. We got secret offices in the Vatican, the Capital Building in Washington and most of the major telecommunications centers in the world.”

“That’s why you have one here?”

“Ya, that’s right. Every major communications company, television, radio, cell phone and CSIS run their data streams through here and we monitor it all.”

They passed through the last of the concrete tunnel and walked into an almost empty room that measured twenty feet by twenty feet. Against the walls there were six large upright canisters, three on either side of the opening. The canisters were three feet in diameter and ten feet high. “What the heck are those,” Laura asked.

“Tell you later,” growled Lamont, “Get over there.” He motioned to an elevator whose doors had just opened. The demon stepped in followed by Laura, guided roughly from behind by Lamont with a hand on each shoulder. As the elevator began its ascent Lamont reached down and placed his open hand on Laura’s backside and squeezed. Laura jumped forward and was about to land a quick back kick to Lamont’s knee when the demon grabbed the side of her head and effortlessly lifted her off the ground, her head and neck pinned painfully against the elevator wall.

“That is forbidden. You will learn this first.”

Laura could feel a freezing cold begin in her neck and shoulders where the demon had its large hand next to her skin. The pain of the cold was immediate and she shrieked with surprise at its intensity.

“Please lord,” Lamont whined to the demon, “She is of no use to me damaged.”

The demon let her drop to the floor of the elevator. “She may be damaged further during her questioning.”

“I understand lord, but…maybe not too badly.”

Laura lay huddled on the elevator floor as it rose higher and higher. After several minutes she felt the car slow and come to a halt. The door slid open, Lamont reached down and pulled her to her feet. The demon pushed aside a metal grate and they walked into a very large hexagonal room. There were no windows and the lighting was poor. The farthest reaches of the room were in shadow and all Laura could make out were the banks of computers that lined the walls. The demon entered the shadows and became very still. Laura saw its head bow and the shadows grew darker around it.

“What are you going to do with me,” Laura asked?

“You’re going to be questioned, and don’t worry about trying to resist or lie, he will get out of you what he wants. Then he’ll convert you and the more you resist the more painful it will be. Then he'll give you to me and we can have some fun."

"Yuck! You're gonna make me puke again Lamont!"

Before he could respond the elevator jerked and began descending. "That must be my guys. It'll take a bit before they get here, too bad, they'll miss all the fun."

Lamont became quiet. Laura needed to get him talking again, she had to find out what they were planning. "Hey Lamont, what were those big metal canisters in the basement? You have a still down there?"

Lamont walked over to a cabinet against the wall. He collapsed the switchblade he'd been holding and put the handle back into his jacket pocket. He pulled open the cabinet door and produced a bottle of scotch from inside. He held it out toward Laura and gently rocked it back and forth. Laura shook her head no and Lamont said, "Suit yourself, it's eighteen years old and might help the next half hour go easier." He pulled out the cork, grabbed a tumbler off the shelf and poured himself two fingers. He swallowed the drink and poured another. He replaced the cork and put the bottle back in the cabinet. He took a sip this time and rolled it around in his mouth before he swallowed. "Those canisters will be the biggest bang to hit a Canadian city since Halifax in 1917."

The blood drained from Laura's face as the portent of Lamont's comment dawned on her. "You gotta bomb down there?"

"A bomb? We have six bombs down there," Lamont said laughing.

She shook her head; not wanting to believe, but knowing, if it were possible these things could...She had to keep Lamont talking, find out what she could and then escape, somehow. "There's an awful lot of concrete in that basement, even six bombs wouldn't do much more than knock out a coupla chunks."

Lamont was warming up to this subject now, he felt like boasting and why not, this was going to be big! "Maybe six run of the mill, homegrown terrorist bombs wouldn't hardly dent that mass of concrete but we ain't got six ordinary fertilizer bombs down there. Have you ever heard of bunker busters?"

"Yes," Laura moaned.

"Give the lady a prize!" Lamont piped as he tippled the last of his third tumbler. The eighteen-year-old scotch was numbing his brain now and Louise was feeling pretty good. He knew the effect this news was going to have on Laura so he would swagger a bit, watch the demon cauterize her mind and then, later, have his way with her. He was thoroughly enjoying himself and now became more animated as he continued with his tale. “We liberated six GBU 37 warheads from an airbase in New York State. Don’t ask me how they got them here but there ain’t much we can’t accomplish. Each one of those warheads has forty-seven hunnert pounds of extremely powerful high explosives in it and when they go off, they’ll pulverize the southwest side of that foundation. Then…oh ohhhh…the tower’s gonna get tipsy and fall right onta that ballfield where ther’sh gonna be fifty thousand er so people inna shtands. Whoa…I should maybe shlow down on the scotch.”

She had to act. The demon emerged from the shadows and she knew what was going to happen next. She allowed the fear she’d held at bay to flood into her. She jumped to Lamont’s side, cowering against him, pleading, “Louise, don’t let it take me…I’ll do anything you want; I’ll tell you anything you need to know, just don’t let it touch me.” She was begging now, almost hysterical.

Lamont reached over and put his empty tumbler back on the cabinet shelf. He was behind her and as the demon approached, she pushed herself back into him. He placed his hands firmly on Laura’s shoulders and bracing his feet slightly began to push against her backward movement. Suddenly Laura grabbed Lamont’s left hand on her shoulder. His reaction was to pull away but his left hand was trapped in a vice. Laura stepped forward with her right foot and snapped her entire body to the left. With Lamont’s hand and wrist trapped on her shoulder her violent twist ruptured the wrist and he howled in pain. As she twisted, she threw a shuto strike with her left hand hard into his exposed ribs cracking two of them. She pivoted down and around quickly, still holding his broken wrist and came up behind him. His arm was straight up and back and Laura pulled down on the broken wrist while her other hand pulled on the back of the raised upper arm. She stepped back and Lamont stumbled back with her, another quick step back, applying downward pressure, she slammed Lamont onto his back smashing his head on the concrete floor. She jumped over him and reached quickly into his jacket. In one fluid motion she retrieved his knife and released the razor-sharp blade. Lamont was trying to sit up and she spun around behind him, reached her arm around his neck in a choke hold, yanked him to his feet and placed the point of the switchblade hard against his jugular.

"Get back!" She screamed at the advancing demon with every bit of courage and resolve left in her. "One more step and I bury this blade in his neck!"

It advanced hissing, "Plunge your blade…I care not, we have many like him."

Laura stepped back again, pulling the dazed and blubbering Lamont with her, his weight beginning to pull her down. The radiating stench of the demon reached out and enveloped her and she began gagging uncontrollably. The demon leaped forward just as the elevator arrived, its mesh gate open to reveal Lamont's henchman.

Chapter 8

Tom raced back across the bridge toward the stadium, his panic mounting. *There are a dozen directions they could go. Dammit! If I go the wrong way...Dammit!* He refused to think that thought. From the corner of his eye he saw the valet attendants at the hotel entrance watching him run by. *They would have seen.* The thought snapped into his head and he changed direction in mid stride. Before the two valets could react, he was on them. He grabbed each one by the shirt collar and pulled them close. They felt like ragdolls in his grip. "Where did security take the girl?" he growled menacingly.

"What girl, man. What are you talking about?" squeaked one of the valets.

Tom shook them violently and tightened his grip, "I don't have time for this. I know you were watching her…WHERE DID THEY TAKE HER!"

"Okay man, okay…don't hurt me man. Those two, the X and Y team, they work gate number seven, that's all I saw man."

Tom released both men and started running out toward the concourse. He sprinted along the side of the huge structure and when he got to the long course of stairs that veered away from the bank of glass faced entry gates, he leapt over the concrete fall barrier and landed ten feet down in a bed of ornamental shrubs. He rolled to break his fall and tumbled off the raised planter onto the cobbled pedestrian mall. Seeing gate seven he launched himself toward it. The big plate glass door was locked. He could see the two security personnel inside, one woman and one man. They stopped in mid stride and looked at him, amusement on their faces. In desperation Tom grabbed a chrome stanchion and swung it with all his strength at the door. The glass shattered into ten thousand diamonds reflecting the light from inside. The uniformed pair hesitated and Tom was on them like a bowling ball on a two-pin split. He careened off the stocky female security guard who was knocked hard against the concrete block wall and slumped senseless to the floor. He caught the male guard by the back of his collar as he turned to run and yanked him down and around, losing his grip but sending the man into a twisting pirouette to spin out of control and land on his backside, his legs splayed out staring up at Tom.

Tom sprinted to him and grabbed his lapels with both hands. He swept him up in one motion and drove him into the block wall that seconds before had rendered his partner unconscious. "Where is she?" He removed his right hand and slapped the security guard hard across his cheek, blood flying out behind his open hand. "Don't lie to me, I know you took her!" Tom shoved his face forward until his nose squashed the other man's. His eyes blazing with righteous fury he said in a voice terrifying in its stressed intensity, "WHERE…IS…SHE?" He stepped back half a pace, still holding the man off the ground, his arms straight out. He saw a dark stain spread across the fabric covering the man's crotch.

"Please…don't kill me, I don't know anything about her…they just took her…Lamont did I mean, please, oh please don't kill me." He was almost crying now and Tom's wrath was quickly evaporating. He let the man's feet touch the floor and he relaxed his grip slightly.

"Just tell me where they took her. I won't hurt you…I promise."

The man jerked his head toward a door up the hall that had no handle on it. "In there…" He started to say when suddenly his eyes flicked to the side and got very large. Tom started turning when massive arms came down over him and wrapped around his chest. He was pinioned.

As soon as the guard saw Tom's helplessness he stepped forward and punched him in the stomach. When he drew back his fist to strike Tom again a large hand enveloped his fist and a deep voice said, "We'll take care of that. Where'd the boss go?"

The security guard, regaining his authority said, "Who the hell are you?"

The gorilla not holding Tom said, "We work for Mr. Lamont, we were told to meet him here."

"Oh…ya, sorry. They've, ahh, gone to the tower. You're to follow asap."

The two gorillas moved over to the featureless door. Tom didn't struggle, preferring to marshal his strength. Gorilla one, as Tom named him, took a plastic card out of his pocket and swiped it at the top of the door then pushed it open. Gorilla two lifted Tom easily and walked without effort into the gloom. Tom saw they were standing on a ten foot by ten-foot landing that had stairs descending from it down into the shadows. He wanted to do something but being held like this offered him no avenue of violent release. He would simply have to wait. His captor descended the stairs, easily carrying Tom. They descended four flights of switchback stairs and Tom calculated they had gone down two full floors. He prayed he was following Laura. They were presented with another steel door, older and grimier than the one above. It also opened to Gorilla one's key card. The three moved through the opening and Gorilla two pushed the door closed with his foot. In a rumbling voice he asked Gorilla one how they were going to get Tom down the ladder.

"I've got some zip tie's in my pocket, get him down the ladder and I'll truss him up," said Gorilla one as he went to the ladder.

Gorilla Two growled into Tom's ear, his chest and arms still in a vice, "Jonesy gonna go down that ladder first, then you're gonna go down nice like and Jonesy'll cuff you when you get down. If you're thinkin' of tryin' sumthin' then I could just send you over the edge right now. What's it gonna be?"

Tom judged the distance to Jonesy, "Neither!" He drove both feet into Jonesy who sailed backward off the ladder. Before Jonesy cleared the first rung Tom planted his left foot on the ground and stomped Two's instep with his other boot breaking Two's foot. He howled in pain as Tom dropped low and forced both his arms straight out, freeing himself from Two's embrace. Tom's right elbow struck back swiftly into Two's ribs crumpling the big man. He reached back and grabbed Two's neck, twisting his body left and down he threw Two forward, sending him soaring over the edge of the landing into darkness. Tom shot down the ladder and found Two lifeless, his neck broken. Looking up at the partially enclosed ladder he wondered if Jonesy had been able to catch one of the encircling steel bands. He may have been able to climb down safely and would now be moving ahead to warn the others.

There was only one direction to go. He took off at a sprint, disregarding the uneven and stony path in his need for speed. Without misstep he came to the end of the rocky passage and entered the rectangular concrete tunnel without slowing down. Quickly reaching its end he saw two large metal cylinders on either side of the entrance into what appeared to be a sizable chamber formed entirely out of concrete. He sidestepped quickly into the angle of the metal cylinder where it curved back against the wall. From this vantage he was mostly hidden, but his view of the chamber was also severely restricted. There was just enough room to shimmy between the metal cylinder and the concrete wall. Peering between the next two cylinders he could see more of the chamber but still not all of it. He wriggled past these. There was one more cylinder left so he squeezed past its closest point to the concrete wall and stole a peek out the other side. There against the wall, not ten feet from Tom was what appeared to be a cage, a housing made of rusted metal uprights with heavy metal screening welded to them. Jonesy stood there holding a heavy metal gate.

The big man was staring up at the ceiling contained within the housing, occasionally looking over his shoulder toward the single entrance to the chamber. After a minute, a section of the ceiling began to descend within the metal cage. The bottom section of an elevator was revealed as it continued to drop. Jonesy moved into the rickety elevator and pushed a button mounted on the back wall, the car lurched upward.

Tom had to move quickly. He covered the ground to the elevator in half a second and leaped onto Jonesy's back. Jonesy didn't react, nonplussed by the intruder attached to his back. Tom wrapped his legs around the big man's waist and slipped his forearm under Jonesy's chin but soon realized he'd have a better chance of choking out a rodeo bull. Jonesy started throwing himself against the elevator walls, crushing Tom between his own massive body and the wire cage of the elevator car. Twice Tom nearly blacked out from the impact yet doggedly hung on for dear life, knowing his best shot at survival was tightening his chokehold. He thought he'd succeeded when Jonesy's knees began to buckle, but the big man only flexed his mighty leg muscles and jumped straight up. His move caught Tom unprepared and drove his head and one shoulder into the galvanized metal ceiling.

When they hit the floor, Jonesy twisted around to land heavily on Tom, knocking the air from his lungs. Senses stumbling, Tom could feel the angry giant stagger to his feet. Through a mist Tom saw Jonesy loom over him and reach out his massive hand to crush Tom's throat. Desperate now to stay away from Jonesy's killing grasp Tom lashed out with a powerful up kick into the shadow and caught the man squarely on the chin. He was propelled backward only to bounce off the elevator cage and topple back toward Tom. He rolled to his side and the big man hit the floor. Jonesy heaved himself onto all fours and turned toward Tom who jumped up and put his back to the elevator wall. As Jonesy raised his immense frame Tom connected kicks and punches in a blurred fury. With his hands and arms free from the floor Jonesy could block some of Tom's combinations, but not all. He was suffering damage that would have killed another man, but Jonesy was unique.

At six six and powerfully built, Jonesy had played college football without distinction. He'd tried for the U.S. Olympic team but he'd used chemical help to put on muscle and had been caught. Blaming his trainers and anti-doping politics he had not left quietly and it was then that he had been approached by the bent. He had been offered a way back into the Olympics, but by the time the bent had begun their coercion all Jonesy wanted to do was hurt people. They offered him that chance and he took it. At three eighty he could hurt a lot of people. Tom was trapped in an eight by eight steel cage with a human monster.

Tom's strikes were dislocating fingers, knocking out teeth, breaking ribs and bruising forearms but all this did was enrage Jonesy. He got to his feet and started swinging at Tom with long looping punches. To Tom's hyper awareness these strikes appeared to be coming in slow motion and were easy to avoid, for now. Their battlefield's tight quarters made it only a matter of time before Jonesy planted one on Tom. When that happened, he wouldn't recover. He ducked a battering ram that distended the thick wire cage of the elevator wall and got under and behind the extended arm. For his size Jonesy was quick and twisted around to face Tom. As he turned Tom aimed a downward sidekick at Jonesy's knee, crumpling the joint, he recocked the leg and sent a powerful roundhouse into Jonesy's back targeting a kidney then immediately threw a kick at Jonesy's exposed neck, but as the high roundhouse connected it was with the chorded muscle at the side of Jonesy's neck rather than the vulnerable cartilage in front. Jonesy was hurt but now more dangerous than ever. Endorphins were killing the pain and adrenaline was speeding up his reflexes.

Tom was tiring, locked in deadly combat with this behemoth. He aimed a front kick at Jonesy's groin but was slow. Jonesy grabbed his leg and pushed him backward into the cage wall. He burst forward and clamped Tom in a steel trap bear hug. He lifted Tom clear of the ground and crushed Tom to him. Tom could feel his rib's bending, could feel his sternum rupturing, could feel his heart being squeezed within its pericardium. He knew he dare not exhale or he would never draw breath again. Jonesy's head was down protecting his lower face and neck so Tom attacked the temples, ears, and arteries. He hammered at every part of Jonesy's exposed face and head and struck the muscles at the back of the neck and the nerve bundles up the sides. Tom could feel Jonesy weakening under his onslaught, a stagger here a grunt there but it was not enough. Tom was fading quickly. The edges of his vision were dim and foggy, he could feel his every heartbeat, the rhythmic pumping in his head and neck. He had seconds left. He gouged his thumbs into the sockets of his killer's eyes forcing Jonesy's head back. Pushing with all his strength he could feel his thumbs breaking through into the ooze of tissue behind the monster's eyelids. Slowly, slowly Jonesy allowed the pressure and pain of Tom's daggered thumbs to force his head back. Slowly his chin came up. Tom's breath began to escape his bursting lungs like steam forced from a pressure cooker. Jonesy screamed as blood and vitreous humor gushed from his ruined eyes and he gave up his neck. Instantly Tom reached back and using every ounce of energy left to him drove a knuckle punch deep into the gristle of Jonesy's neck.

The elevator shrieked as it reached the top and Tom was dropped to the floor against the back wall. Jonesy's face, smeared with blood and fluid, a gurgling cry trapped in his broken throat, died turning and collapsed to his knees. As his huge body dropped from view Tom could see the beast, at once more dangerous than all the Jonesys in the world, hurtling through the air at Laura now bent and retching and without escape. Tom pushed off the wall and using Jonesy's falling body as a ramp rocketed himself into the air colliding with the demon a heartbeat from Laura.

"Tom!" She screamed hoarsely and collapsed under Lamont's weight.

From below, Laura looked up and beheld the impact of Tom and the demon that created shockwaves to rival colliding planets. Poor, human Tom had no hope of besting the beast and was nearly destroyed. His frail flesh and blood body spiraled away from the point of impact to land in a heap by a panel of digital recorders. His nearly fatal sacrifice had prevented the demon from landing on Laura, saving her from a crushing finish under its sheol mass. Kicking the stunned Lamont aside it seized Laura by the neck, pulling her to her feet. Her flesh in contact with the demon's hand felt pierced by ice cold knives. Her skin blistered and cracked as frozen tongues of pain swelled up the back of her neck threatening to shatter her mind.

"Lamont," commanded the beast, "On your feet!"

Jerking upright like a marionette he passed a trembling hand over his face, "Yes lord?"

"Bring him!"

Lamont limped over to Tom who had still not moved since crashing to the floor. He latched onto Tom's collar with his good hand and slowly dragged him closer to the creature.

"Wake him!"

Cradling his broken wrist in the fold between his waist and hip, Lamont bent down and pulled Tom to a sitting position and slapped his face. Tom grabbed Lamont's wrist as his hand descended for another slap.

"Stand!"

Lamont stood followed slowly by Tom.

"Beat him."

Lamont turned to look at the beast who still held Laura effortlessly by her neck.

"Beat him!"

Lamont threw a right hook that Tom swatted away.

"Do that again and she dies!" The beast squeezed Laura's neck harder and she tried to scream but only wheezed.

Lamont punched Tom in the stomach. He may as well have punched a tree trunk. Too many years of having other men do his work had made him soft, he couldn't hurt Tom.

Dropping Laura to the floor the demon went to the elevator and ripped the safety gate from its hinges. Holding the gate in one hand it broke a metal rod away from the frame and pitched the useless gate back into the elevator where it hit the control panel. The elevator whined to life and started its descent.

The demon tossed the steel rod to Lamont and resumed its hold on Laura's neck. She was lifted without a struggle.

"Resume!" Was all it said.

Lamont held up the steel rod, a gleam in his eye. He walked to Tom's side and walloped the inch-thick rod into Tom's midsection. Tom doubled over with a groan. The rod came down hard on Tom's back driving him to his knees. Lamont lifted the bar high, ready to cave in Tom's skull when the demon barked, "No! The killing blow must not come now! Show him what agonies can come before death!"

Lamont began striking Tom hard, on his shoulders, his back and his thighs. Lamont tired quickly and while he rested the demon commanded Tom to stand. "Where do you and the girl reside? Where are the others, give me their names!"

Through gritted teeth Tom laughed. “You mean Santa and the Easter Bunny. We all live at the North Pole.”

“Fool,” growled the demon, nodding at Lamont to continue. He swung the bar up and then down onto Tom’s trapezius. Tom’s arm down to his fingertips went numb. Lamont swung the bar sideways into Tom’s upper arm and the pain burst through him like fireworks as he felt his muscle pulp and the bone snap. He dropped to his knees, holding his left arm.

“Where do you hide!”

Tom’s head lolled, drool looping from his slack mouth.

The demon reached across and grabbed Laura’s neck with his other hand so he could turn her fully to look at Tom. “Lamont will beat him to death. Every bone will be broken, every muscle ruptured, he will scream out for the killing blow, tell me who the others are and where they hide?”

“Never!” Came the iron reply through clenched teeth and tears.

The demon sensed her resolve and knew she would never tell, but the man, the man had deep feelings of responsibility and protection toward this female. That made him weak. It lifted Laura and walked her back to the elevator shaft, now yawning empty as its sole car neared the ground twelve hundred feet down. “Bring him closer!”

Lamont pushed and prodded the halting Tom closer to the demon, taking every opportunity to strike Tom again and again with the iron bar.

“Enough!”

Tom swooned to his knees, his body radiating pain, his head drooping forward.

“Lamont, make him watch!”

Lamont came around behind Tom. He dropped the steel rod and put his hand into the sweaty curls of Tom’s hair. He grabbed tightly and yanked Tom’s head back to force his gaze up at the demon who held Laura nearer the shaft. A moan escaped Tom’s lips, “Noooo.”

“Tell me what I want to know!” The demon closed on the shaft, Laura’s heels now at the edge.

“TOM! NO!” She screamed.

The demon struck her hard with its free hand. Her mouth became a ruined pulp of ripped and ruptured flesh. Blood flowed down her chin and there were two gory stumps where her front teeth had broken. The creature shook her mightily, dangling her over the brink to torture Tom before bringing her feet back to flutter on the edge.

Tom was sobbing now; he was witnessing Joy's death again. "Please don't." He begged. He gazed at Laura, pleading for her understanding, "Forgive me," he began.

As if in slow motion Tom watched with terrible clarity. A gleaming sliver pierced the darkness low at her side as a blade slipped from her sleeve, her fingers closed on the handle before gravity snatched it down the shaft. She brought the knife up over her head in one smooth motion and laced her fingers together over the handle. With desperate strength and love she drove the knife down through the beast's forearm and into her chest, capturing the blade in her own flesh and locking herself to the hell spawn demon. With her heels dug into the lip of the empty shaft she pushed herself backward and took the beast with her into the void crying out, "The cylinders Tom!," and was gone.

Numb, his body turned to stone, Tom was frozen. He heard a distant mounting scream and realized it was him. An iron bar across his back brought him to life. He turned his head and saw Lamont raising anew the lethal piece of steel for a head shot and threw out a hurried side kick from his knees that caught Lamont on the hip. It pushed him backward but did little else. Lamont raised the bar again advancing. On his feet Tom aimed a snapping outside crescent kick but missed. Tom let the motion bring him around and he planted the foot pushing himself off the ground to come around in a flying back roundhouse. Tom's view of Lamont was obscured, the kick was blind, it missed. As Tom came fully around twisting in the air, he cocked his trailing leg and drove a spinning front roundhouse down into Lamont's neck. The powerful kick drove Lamont sideways. He moved his feet quickly trying to outrun gravity and within two strides was running hard. Lamont kept falling as he pedaled harder and never saw the wall he crashed into.

His body broken and his will to live gone down the elevator shaft, Tom stumbled and put both his hands out feeling for invisible support. Pain engulfed him in a blood red haze and he fell forward, uncaring.

Chapter 9

He lay on the floor, consciousness returning, but refused to open his eyes. Like a child, convinced that as long as his eyes didn't open the events which they had witnessed would not be real. He longed for the return of blessed oblivion, but try as he might he couldn't slip the truth. The world was back with pain and loss.

A moaning reached his ears from far away. He opened his eyes and took a long breath, heaving his tortured ribs. He rolled over and winced as the masses of overlapping bruises contacted the hard cement floor. He was surprised to find he could push himself up using the arm which had been broken. It supported him as he rested on his hands and knees, allowing his head to clear. Tom straightened up and put one foot out. Placing both hands on this knee he used it as a leverage point to help the rest of his body rise up. He stood swaying, looking around to get his bearings. His body must have been healing itself while he lay unconscious, otherwise how could he breathe, let alone stand. He heard the moaning again; it was coming from a large ragged hole in the wall.

Slowly at first but steadier with each step Tom walked to the hole in the wall. Broken gypsum board and loose pieces of insulation hung haphazardly across the opening. Gingerly he pulled pieces of debris away until his view was cleared. On the other side of the wall was a metal staircase. He followed the moaning and saw Lamont, lying on his back, one flight down. His arms and legs were bent oddly, as was his head. It wasn't natural.

Lamont's eyes fastened on Tom and he mumbled weakly, "Help me."

The only way Tom was willing to help Lamont was in leaving this life. That would be coming soon enough but for now he needed to at least confirm Laura's death. He returned to the elevator shaft and looked over the edge, his gaze met only gloom. He hung his head; all he wanted to do was melt down into the floor. If he could will himself to die, he would do it right now. He didn't want to go on; he was tired as he'd never been tired. He wanted to give up, give in – retreat from life. He sank to his knees and bent forward staring down into the empty shaft with empty eyes. *Lean forward…just a little bit and rest will come. COWARD!* His mind reeled at the power of the word, its connotations yanking his thoughts from death. *You stupid ungrateful fool, death would be the easy way out. Laura's sacrifice would be for nothing.* Tom's head snapped up. "God forgive me," he said aloud. "Forgive me Laura," he whispered.

Ignoring the massed pain of his body Tom rose to his feet and walked back to the hole in the wall with renewed purpose. He didn't hesitate once he reached the opening and stepped through onto the descending stairway. He stepped down to the next landing and stood beside Lamont's twisted body. Lamont looked up at him, his eyes begging for help. Tom knelt down, "Can you speak?"

"Yes," Lamont whispered hoarsely, "It's hard to breathe though…can't hardly get the words out."

"I will assist you, but you must answer some questions first."

"Anything," he groaned.

"Laura said something about cylinders before she…before she took that thing to its death. Was she talking about the big metal cylinders down in the basement?"

"Ya," came the wheezy reply.

"Why would she mention them? Why did she think they were important?"

"Will you…protect me…if I tell…you?" Lamont was having trouble getting the words out.

"I'll take you someplace they won't expect."

"The cylinders…encase bunker buster…bombs…they're set to…detonate…in four, no…three days."

"Damn," He whispered. "Are you trying to bring down the tower?"

"On top of Rogers Center." Lamont struggled with this information, hoping its implications wouldn't make Tom change his mind about helping him. "You're…you're still going…to help me?"

"Of course," said Tom. He gently placed his right hand under the back of Lamont's head holding the occipital lobe firmly.

"Careful," whined Lamont.

"Be brave for once in your life Lou," he said as he placed the heel of his left hand against Lamont's chin. "Give my regards to your master," and he pulled the back of Lamont's head up and toward him and drove the heel of his other hand around and down. Lamont slumped.

Tom rose and stepped over the body. He turned slightly and walked around the landing to the start of the next set of steps. He looked down, it was a long way, he couldn't even see the bottom. He had no way of knowing but he had seventeen hundred steps to negotiate. He knew this would be difficult and painful, but knew he must begin. Tom held the railing like a lifeline and took his first labored step.

A tortured hour later, Tom stood on the third to last tread. He stumbled and his grip on the railing fell away. He crashed to the floor, the open web steel tread ripped fabric and skin as his shins raked the last step. He lay at the base of the staircase and felt the blood soak into his pants. Without immediate sustenance Tom knew his body couldn't heal itself. He already knew that some of his injuries would have been fatal by themselves, let alone piled on top of others. He didn't have much left but knew what he had to do. He would go until he died. He struggled to his feet and moved toward the elevator. The roof was completely crushed, pushed down almost to the floor and twisted beyond recognition. This had pushed the walls out, wedging the car in the hoist way. Laura and the beast were still pinned together by Lamont's switchblade, wrapped in the twisted metal of the elevator roof.

Through tears of grief Tom climbed onto the mess of deformed metal. He was perched just above and to the side of Laura's broken body, draped across what was left of the beast. He worked his arm between two sections of ripped caging and placed his hand gently on the cold flesh of Laura's hands. It took a few minutes but he worked her fingers apart. He grasped the handle and drew the blade out, freeing Laura from her grisly tomb mate. He tossed the blade aside. He climbed off the misshapen mass of metal and came around to where the entrance to the elevator car used to be. He bent down and could see Laura's feet and legs just inside the wreck of the elevator car. Both feet were shoeless and Tom could see the light blush color of her toenails. It was almost more than he could bear. He took a deep breath and reached inside to tenderly grasp her ankles and begin to try and remove her from the snaring iron tendrils. It took much maneuvering but Tom finally freed her body. He sat down beside her and reached out to hold her. He held Laura's bruised and battered face against his chest and rocked slowly back and forth. The tears washed down his face and into Laura's rich auburn hair. He cried for this beautiful young woman who was his friend. He wept for the life she would never lead, and the children she would never have. His tears were also for the young man who loved her but knew nothing of her fate and his impending sorrow. He knew she was with her Father now, in a place where there was only great joy, but he also knew without doubt that God intended for man to live on this earth and revel in the experience of living and Laura had given that up so he could go on.

He lowered her back to the floor and gently crossed her arms over her chest. He wouldn't leave her here. He would carry her back to the church on Gerrard Street. He looked around, through the open links of a fence surrounding a storage area he saw tarpaulins of all sizes and colors. The gate was not padlocked so he proceeded to rummage around until he found one that would suit his need.

Returning to Laura he recalled her last words. Once The Path knew about the bombs, they would investigate. The elevator would never work again so that entrance was now useless. The only way to the sub-basement would be through the secret tunnel. He needed to retrieve Jonesy's pass card to be able to access the tunnel without drawing attention. The collapsing elevator roof had not pancaked and Jonesy's body was relatively free of encumbering wreckage. After pulling the huge corpse from the remains of the elevator, Tom searched until he found the access card and limped back to Laura.

He unfolded the clean, dark green tarpaulin on the floor beside Laura. He tenderly lifted her body and placed her in the middle of the tarp near to one side. He folded the top down over her head, the bottom up over her feet and legs and then gently rolled her up so that she was safely cocooned within the poly. He had the nylon tie cords and he loosely secured the tarp around her. He lifted his precious cargo and draped her over his shoulder. He headed toward the exit door and stepped out into Bobby Rosenfeld Park.

Tom took in his surroundings. It was still dark with little traffic. It was cold and a brisk wind from the lake gusted around him. He was invigorated and took a deep breath. Balancing his precious bundle, he turned and began to walk. His plan was simple, he would avoid the busier roads and stay to the shadows. He would either make it or he wouldn't, success or failure was not in his hands.

The vigor acquired from the bracing cold soon dissipated and he was left with only his will to go forward. He passed Lower Simcoe Street and could've headed north but didn't feel like passing the underground parking facility where Dr. Bellami's brother had been killed. He continued east until he turned left onto York Street and headed toward Front. He approached the tunnel which ran under the railroad tracks and the darkness there looked comforting. Tom was weak though and tiring quickly. Under normal circumstances he could have borne Laura's weight for miles, but this night he had been beaten nearly to death. His broken humerus was slowly knitting itself together but this was taking substantial amounts of energy leaving nothing for his other injuries. The massive bruising of muscle tissue, the broken vessels and ruptured organs were not healing and they were causing intense pain. Every step was agony. He focused intently on putting one foot in front of the other. He found it increasingly hard to breathe, it was as if there was a bubble around his head and he was breathing in his own spent air. His vision blurred and his ears buzzed as he put one foot in front of the other.

Tom almost made the end of the tunnel. His blurred vision pulsed red then purple. Through his blood-tinged view he heard a rushing whine overriding the buzzing in his brain. Still upright and trudging forward he concentrated harder on his goal. If he could make it out of the tunnel, he'd rest at the first bench he came to. *Yes*, he thought, *I'll do that; I'll find a bench and rest for a minute.*

"Hey old timer, whatcha got there?"

I'm hearing things, Tom thought. *I must be close to passing out.*

"Hold on a minute there sir."

Tom felt a hand on his shoulder.

"Easy old timer, I'm not gonna hurt you. Do you need help?"

"Don't...need...nuthin'." Tom struggled with his reply but kept moving forward.

"Got into some bad hooch?" The hand began to hold Tom's shoulder more firmly. He was forced to stop moving and he almost fell over when he turned his head to see what was interrupting his progress.

"Easy fella...easy there. Why don't you put the bundle down and we'll figure out how to help you?"

"NO!" the vehemence of his reply drained his remaining energy. "Leaf...me..." He tried to push away from the hand holding his shoulder but the effort pushed him to his knees. Tom looked up at his tormentor and into the shadowed face of a metro cop. *Crap,* he thought.

"Let me help you with that," the young policeman said. He wrapped his arms around the tarpaulin concealing Laura's body and with a sudden questioning look on his face he lowered the bundle to the ground. "Have a seat old timer," he said as he half guided half carried Tom to the back of the cruiser. Holding Tom up with one arm he opened the back door of the cruiser and gently helped Tom onto the back seat. Tom felt the softness of the cushioned seat surround him and gave in to gravity. Feeling himself about to pass out he fought desperately to stay conscious, he couldn't abandon Laura; he had to think of something to get them out of this. He turned his head to look out the window and saw the policeman opening the tarpaulin. *Dear God*, he thought, *it's over.* As soon as the policeman pulled the edge of the tarp back to reveal Laura's face, he turned to look at Tom in shock. Tom's eyes rolled up and he was gone.

He saw Laura's face first, not with the broken mouth, the face of pure joy when she told him of her choice to marry Memmy. This disappeared and he saw Joy. He cried out. Then it was Laura's face again, then Joy's. The two faces came and went. It was very pleasant for Tom, neither face spoke to him but they were wearing warm smiles and Tom felt nothing but love. Benoit's face, radiant with life and love hovered near him now. "You are so very beautiful," he said.

"Why thank you Tom…what a lovely thing to say."

It took him a moment but he soon realized he wasn't seeing Benoit's disembodied head conversing with him. It was Benoit in front of him, he just hadn't opened his eyes all the way. "Where am I?" He gasped out as memories shotgunned his brain.

"You're in a bedroom in the townhouse by the church," Benoit said quietly. "It was touch and go there for several hours; you were so badly hurt I really didn't think we'd get you back."

"How did I get here? The police…"

"He is one of us Tom. Gordon sensed something was wrong around three in the morning and you guys had failed to return. We contacted Colin who's a patrolman with the Metro force. He did a sweep of the Rogers Center roadways and found you around four thirty."

"Laura?"

"She's been taken to a funeral home we own. Colin listed her as a hit and run. He didn't know who you were until he opened the covering and saw Laura."

Tom put his head back and closed his eyes. Dr. Bellami reached out and put her hand on Tom's. He looked up at her, "Thanks Doc," he whispered. Stronger now he said, "Benoit, are Gordon or any of the others around, I need to talk to you all."

"George and Gordon just left a few minutes ago. They're down in the sanctuary studying your map. Bill's in the church and Colin and Jonathan are in the kitchen here grabbing a cup of coffee."

"This is important; can you get them all here right away?"

Benoit went to the desk phone near the bed. She picked it up from the cradle and pressed one button. "He's awake George…are you and Gordon able to come over right away. Fine, would you bring Bill with you? Good…in a minute then." She replaced the phone in its cradle.

"Direct line to the sanctuary?"

Benoit came back to his bedside. "Years ago, we put in a single line directly from this phone to another phone in the library. When Gordon's construction company originally renovated the church basement after the fire, he anticipated progress in electronics and communications among other things. He placed conduits of varying sizes in the ground around the sanctuary that could be accessed to add new services without causing undue attention. When these townhouses were built, we bought them and used one of the smaller conduits to run a dedicated phone line."

"Wouldn't it have been easier to use a cell phone or two-way radio or something?"

"Hacking them is too easy. We could use encryption programs but the downside is it attracts the attention of agencies that track those carriers. We must not only keep our communications secret, we must never allow any agency or individual or entity of any description from even suspecting our existence. We communicate as little as possible when not face to face. Excuse me Tom, I'll get the others." Benoit went to the top of the stairs and called down to Jonathan and Colin. The three of them walked into the room together.

Tom looked at the young policeman and said, "I owe you my thanks for getting me back here as quickly as you did. I was pretty far gone when you found me."

"From what I've heard of your martial prowess Mr. Joiner I'm glad you were in a weakened state. Once I saw…once I knew it was Laura that you had been carrying, I knew who you were and brought you here immediately. While

Gordon and Benoit were taking care of you, I took Laura's remains and had it written up as a hit and run. Jonathan helped with that part. As it was, it took us nearly the rest of the night and part of the next day."

"Please Colin, call me Tom." He looked at the young man closer and said, "You were in uniform when you stopped me, you must've been able to take some time to change?"

"Well, after Jonathan and I finished with the paperwork for…for…damn, I'm sorry Tom." The young man's voice broke at this. After taking a minute to compose himself, Colin continued, "After we processed her Jonathan went to work and I had the day off so I went home for a bit."

"What," Tom exploded, "What day is this, Benoit…how many days has it been since Laura and I left?"

"It has been two days Tom. You left with Laura late Tuesday afternoon, just after you and I had met, it was April 11th. You were picked up by Colin here in the early morning hours of Wednesday April 12th. You've been here in this room all day Wednesday and all day today, which is Thursday and it is nine o'clock at night. We've been pumping you full of supplements and vitamins through this IV for two days now. Why is this so important?"

There were noises downstairs as Gordon, George and Bill let themselves in. Tom kept quiet as the three new arrivals made their way upstairs. They were extremely happy to see Tom alive and awake, but it was tinged with great sadness at the loss of Laura. George pulled a chair over and sat beside Tom's bed. He put his hand on Tom's arm and squeezed. Gordon sat in a chair next to George and Benoit sat on the bed alongside Tom. The rest gathered around, not wanting to miss anything.

Tom looked at Gordon and began, "Gordon, you told me not so long ago that in the entire history of The Path, as far as your research has shown you, no human has ever defeated a demon."

Gordon nodded.

"Two nights ago, I witnessed the bravest person I will ever know kill a demon."

George held Tom's arm tighter while Gordon shook his downcast head. Tom heard several sharply indrawn breaths from his astonished audience.

"I thought it was impossible," whispered Benoit.

"It's not impossible," replied Tom, "But Laura paid the price."

Gordon, his head still down, tears trickling from the end of his long nose said in a voice breaking with sadness, "Tell us please what happened Tom."

Tom made his report as well as he could, not knowing Laura's part of the tale until they had been reunited in the tower room. "When Jonesy went down, I saw the demon getting ready to jump Laura who had Lamont in a choke with a knife against his neck. I ran at the thing and tried to throw a block into it…but it was too strong and I bounced off. I must have been dazed because the next thing I knew Lamont was dragging me toward the demon that had Laura by the neck." Tom stopped for a moment to collect his thoughts and calm his emotions. "That's when Lamont started beating me with the steel bar." Colin winced; he had seen firsthand the results of the beating Tom had taken. "The demon wanted names and locations. It must have thought that it could break Laura with the threat of my death. The beast had no idea the strength of her resolve. It figured that out though because it changed its tactic. It threatened Laura to try and get me to talk. I could feel myself weakening. The demon was holding Laura over the empty elevator shaft shaking her like a rag doll and I swear I could feel it in my head. Laura screamed at me not to say anything. I asked her to forgive me and at that moment I couldn't tell you with any certainty whether I was asking her forgiveness for letting her die or for giving up what I knew. She couldn't…wouldn't take that chance. I failed her when she needed me the most, but she had strength enough for the both of us. She must have hidden the knife she'd had at Lamont's throat up her sleeve. She used it to stab down through the demon's arm that was holding her and into her own chest…"

A strangled sob escaped Benoit's throat, Gordon shuddered and George just stared at Tom, his mouth open.

"With the demon pinned to her she pushed backward and the two of them went down the shaft."

Gordon raised his head and looked like he was about to speak but Tom held his hand out so he could continue.

"With her last breath she cried out to me, The Cylinders Tom!"

"What cylinders?" asked George quietly.

"When I first entered the sub-basement there were four very large upright metal cylinders, two on either side of the tunnel entrance. I thought nothing of them at the time; I was concentrating on getting to Jonesy. After Laura was gone, I asked Lamont what they were. He said they were four bunker buster bombs set to detonate on Saturday. They are set to bring the tower down onto Rogers Center, probably during the ballgame."

George looked at Gordon. "Do we know anyone that has experience with explosives or bombs?"

"No," replied Gordon. "Colin…what do you think?"

"I may be able to get a bomb squad down there but the administrative gymnastics might be beyond my capabilities. If I'm not able to swing it we may have to call in an anonymous tip. Not sure that would work though. I'll do whatever I can."

George was deep in thought and finally said, "No Colin. We don't want to jeopardize your position or career. You're too junior yet to be trying to swing this. I'll talk to the Chief; he owes me. I'll tell him our engineers were getting some strange readings in a sub-basement of the tower and we need an explosives expert there to backstop us. Tom, how are we to get into this lower basement? You said the elevator was wrecked."

"Get my jacket, the one I had on when Colin found me. There's a card key in the inner pocket. It'll get you into the tunnels. Here…let me write it out for you…whoa." Tom had sat up in bed and nearly collapsed. Benoit caught him before he pitched over.

"Tom…don't try to rise. Less than five hours ago your survival was in question. We have been pumping you full of nutrients but I suspect that you still need to eat solid food to get your body functioning properly. Jon, Colin…would you start bringing up some of the food we prepared?"

"You bet," Jon answered as he and Colin headed for the door.

George rose next, "I'd better start the ball rolling. Tom, tell me how to access the tunnels."

"In Gate 7, about halfway to the concourse on the right you'll see a steel door, flat with no hardware, grey I think. The card swipes between the jamb and the door near the top. Once inside there is only one direction. Down two full flights of stairs, through another steel door, same procedure as the first, down the ladder and straight ahead through the tunnel. You'll come out where the cylinders are."

George put his hand on Tom's shoulder, "I'll get word to you as soon as we know what's up."

"George…once you have things in hand, go up to the first section and find the elevator. See if the remains of that thing are still there."

George nodded.

Colin and Jon returned then carrying trays of food. Benoit looked around and said, “Okay, I think Tom needs some privacy. He needs to eat and rest so everyone has work to do, yes?” The room cleared out and Tom spent the next hour eating. When he was finally full Benoit asked Jon to clear the plates. “You need your rest now Tom. I will wake you if any news comes in.” Tom was asleep before she spoke the last word.

The sun was shining through the open drapes of the bedroom window when Tom opened his eyes. Benoit was standing next to the bed, bent slightly with her hand on Tom’s shoulder. “I’m sorry to have woken you Tom, but we have word from George.”

Tom rubbed the sleep from his eyes and through a mouth seemingly full of cotton mumbled, “What time is it…what day is it?”

“It’s Friday, afternoon,” she said. “Splash some water on your face and come down to the kitchen, I have fresh coffee on.” After a moment she asked with a touch of concern, “Do you think you can stand alright?”

Tom straightened up and swung his legs over the side of the bed. He felt stronger and his head was clear. “I think so Benoit…give me a couple of minutes and I’ll be right down.”

Benoit left the bedroom and Tom could hear her soft footsteps descending the stairs. He went into the ensuite located at the far end of the bedroom. He turned the left tap and let the water run in the sink until it was hot. He soaked a small hand towel and after wringing it out he pressed the steaming linen to his face. *God that feels good*, Tom thought as he felt his pores open and soothing heat seep into his face. He repeated this once more and then looked at himself in the mirror. The swelling was all but gone from his face although there were small areas under his eyes and on one cheek that were still showing some yellow from old bruising. He braced himself with cold water and rinsed out his mouth. He felt better. Tom’s bare feet enjoyed the softness of the broadloom as he walked back into the bedroom. He slid each foot into the backless slippers he saw on the floor beside the bed and put the robe on that was slung across a chair. Down the stairs and then followed his nose to the coffee.

Benoit was waiting for him, sitting in a kitchen chair beside a little table. She let him fill his cup and sit down before she gave him her news. “George called a little while ago. Two engineers, a couple of steel fabricators and an explosives expert from the OPP went into the tunnels with George this morning. They found the sub-basement and the four metal cylinders just inside the entrance."

Without quite knowing why, the calmness of Benoit's voice troubled Tom as he raised the cup for his first sip.

"They searched the entire area first before they focused their attention on the cylinders. George said they found nothing down there besides the cylinders. They examined the cylinders from top to bottom and found no external sign of an entrance or opening. The steel fabricators had brought their portable equipment with them so at that point they were able to cut a small opening in each cylinder for inspection of the interiors."

"I don't think I like where this story is headed," mused Tom.

"The cylinders were completely empty," replied Benoit. "No bombs, no explosives, no parts or pieces, only stale air."

A small itch of concern prickled at the edge of Tom's thoughts. "I'm relieved to hear there's no bomb, or bombs, but why would Lamont say there were when there weren't? I know these people, these bent, are evil and will lie…lie to mislead and lie to save their skins and lie because the truth will reveal them…but this lie, telling Laura and then me that there were bombs there, it serves no purpose. Were George and his team able to search the upper basement?"

"They were in the upper basement fifteen minutes ago when George called. Nothing there was out of place. The elevator was marked out of order, but there was no wreckage, no demon carcass and no Lamont. One of the engineers had climbed to the top of the stairs and had radioed back down to them. He hadn't found any evidence of a room under the Radome donut."

Tom sat for a long minute, drinking his coffee and thinking. Whoever had gotten to the tower after he'd left with Laura had expended an awful lot of energy wiping out all traces of their confrontation. This tower and its secrets were very, very important to the demons and their bent allies, but with all traces of the recent battle removed there was nothing more to be done. "What is George going to do?"

"He told me he would dismiss all the others except for Lincoln, one of the engineers and a member. They would check around a bit more and also try and put together a reason for George calling in a favor from the Chief. This is very important as we don't want to attract undo attention to George."

"Understood. If I left now do you think I could make it down there before they wrapped things up?"

"Forget it," said Benoit. "As your Doctor now." Tom raised a surprised eyebrow. "I cannot recommend you leaving the sanctuary at this time."

"You're my Doctor now?"

"Of course, I am. I have a medical degree and I had practiced emergency medicine before going into psychiatry." She looked long and hard at Tom. "You should be dead…and that is the second time that prognosis has been given to you this week. I know of your ability to heal; Laura and I spoke of it in depth after your encounter with the knife. I am aware of your need for tremendous amounts of nutrients during your healing process."

Tom interrupted, "I feel fine now, I just need something to eat."

"Did you know the humerus bone in your arm was shattered, not just broken, shattered? Your right clavicle was broken and the top of your right scapula was dented. Your spleen was ruptured; your bowel was herniated and you were bleeding internally. One of your kidneys was pulped and oh, your back was broken. T2 down to T7 were chipped or fractured and the intervertebral discs were herniated. You also had two broken ribs, one nearly punctured your lung, you had six broken or dislocated fingers, several torn muscles and serious bruising to over fifty percent of your body. If Colin hadn't found you when he did…you would not have made it another block."

Tom slumped back in the kitchen chair. "I knew Lamont had beaten me pretty well but I had no idea the injuries were so extensive."

"Tom…you should have died…you should have died from any number of the individual injuries that were inflicted on you. Added all together you should have died in the tower. From a medical standpoint you should not have been able to walk, let alone carry Laura's body almost a mile."

Tom could see the concern in Benoit's eyes and tried to ease her worry somewhat. "Well I survived the knife thrown by Bolt without complications. You mentioned that you and Laura had discussed the incident."

"That was a mosquito bite compared to what you endured three nights ago."

"So what are you saying Benoit?"

"I have no empirical data to study, only supposition based on what Laura told me and now watching you convalesce." She thought for a long moment, staring hard at Tom, but Tom knew she wasn't consciously looking at him…he just happened to be sitting in the way of her sharply focused unawareness. "I believe," she continued, "That you are getting stronger, that your healing abilities are improving…and along with that, though I have no means of knowing why or to what end it is serving, that your cognitive abilities are also improving."

"I understand about the ability to heal, that's pretty straightforward. What about my cognitive?"

"I'm not quite sure." She saw the puzzled expression on Tom's face and smiled. "I am sorry Tom; I'm not being very definitive am I."

"No, you're not and I don't see how you could be…but you did sound like you have a theory."

"I do. You came to us to learn of our group and to learn of the bent and their demon masters. You were not sent to join us."

"But I have joined you…haven't I?"

"You would be welcome here Tom you know this. I don't believe your path is to stay with us though, I believe you have other work to do."

"You mean like Gordon? He learned of the path from the preacher in Alabama but it wasn't his destiny to stay with them, he came north and began the building of this group?"

"No."

"Then you've lost me."

Benoit stood up and went to the kitchen counter. "Would you like more coffee?"

"Yes please."

"Why don't you get some of the food that has been prepared for you and I'll try and explain my thoughts."

They busied themselves for fifteen minutes preparing Tom's meal. They settled back into the chairs around the kitchen table and Tom began eating.

"You are aware of pieces of our history from speaking with Gordon?"

"Yes," he said with his mouth full, "er…pardon me."

She laughed, "That's alright Tom, I'm sure the desire to put calories and nutrients into your system seems overwhelming right now."

"It is. I had no idea until the food hit my lips how ravenous I was, but I also very much want to hear what you think."

"Fine then," she said, "You eat, I'll talk."

He gave her a thumbs up without missing a bite.

"The shepherd's Path came into being during the time of the First Crusade, a little over nine hundred years ago. What form the resistance to the demons had before then we do not know, we have theories but it is only guesswork. Since the time of Ademar de Petit Fleury we have been gatherers of information. We take little direct action. Oh, elements of our groups have fought in wars, marched in protests and organized resistance but those efforts have not been our main goals. We search for the bent, which helps us discover who and where the demons might be. We search for their effects on society, we track those effects. We search for patterns and hope those patterns lead us to understand when the large conflicts are to happen and what we might do to counteract them."

Between mouthfuls Tom was able to ask, "Where do I fit in?"

"Patience Tom, and I will tell you of my theories. Through the eight millennia of civilized humanity our major conflicts have been between nation states, deadly to the participants yes, but for the most part localized. Then in 1618 came the Thirty Years War. This conflict encompassed the entire European Continent as well as small areas of the New World and Asia. Combined with disease, this war may have reduced the entire population of Europe by fifteen percent, closer to forty in Central Europe. Being a religious war, it was a nasty, brutal affair. In pitting Protestants against Catholics, it allowed each adversary to believe that God was on its side and because it spilled out of Europe to include small parts of the rest of the world it had lost its localized aspect. After thirty years of butchery the leaders of Europe lost their lust for war. A hundred years later and all of Europe is at war again. In 1754 the Seven Years' War begins and it is different from all previous wars. The European adversaries had empires that spanned the globe and the war leached into India, North America, coastal Africa, the Caribbean and the Philippines. Most historians consider the Seven Years' War to be the first world war. Our wars were getting bigger and our technology more deadly.

"We have no foreknowledge of the twisted lord's planning, only its ultimate goal. Many of us though who study the bent have theorized that the twisted lord planned for its ascendancy with the commencement of the Great War in 1914. We believe that the unholy had surmised that a war brought to every continent and including all the different cultures on earth fighting and killing each other in vast numbers would bring about the downfall of all civilization and plunge humanity into the turmoil and desolation the demons desired to rule over. Fortunately for humanity this did not happen. Mankind reached its limit, had its fill of killing, wore itself out. Gordon was there, he watched it happen while participating in it. He can relate to you firsthand how man can descend into a hell of death and gore, where only the strength of the individual instinct to survive will separate the living from the dead, where there is no compassion, no love, no gentleness, only fear…but it seems…that mans' soul cannot dwell in that place indefinitely.

"After amassing thirty-seven-million casualties in four years it seemed humanity had lost its passion for killing. The historical record has many reasons for the end of the war in November of 1918 but nowhere will you see any mention of this, that the twisted lord had once again underestimated the strength of the human soul that God had gifted to man.

"Unfortunately for humanity, the unholy had a backup plan. I know that is a mundane phrase for something as heinous as the destruction of man but…" Here Benoit just shrugged her shoulders.

Tom said, "Don't worry about the language; I'm getting the gist of what you're telling me. Wars were getting bigger, more destruction on a world-wide scale, but there was something missing, something that the twisted lord needed to turn war into something that never ended, something that got into the core of man and wouldn't let go."

"Yes. From the carnage and xenophobia of the First World War the unholy sowed seeds of their own hellish design. Now it used fear combined with hatred at the nation state level and this produced a number of demon-guided bent the likes of which the world had not witnessed before. Joseph Stalin, Mao Zedong, Hideki Tojo, Arthur Seyss-Inquart, Benito Mussolini and the most virulent tyrant of the age, Adolph Hitler. These warped and twisted servants of the unholy would have waged war and genocide indefinitely but they were stopped. They were slowed in the beginning by the democratic countries of the west and were ultimately destroyed by the free people of the United States. It's interesting to note that the bent took part in both sides of the conflict. If the United States, which at the time was immersed in economic disaster and a malaise of character that nearly disabled it, had not been able to shake off the ideas of isolation and defeatism the bent would have ruled the day and pulled the world down into chaos. But this did not happen. The victors, led by England and Canada but mainly the United States would not let the remaining allies viciously carve up the defeated nations for reparation and revenge, thereby renewing the cycle of desperation and hatred. They aided the defeated countries and helped them become prosperous and democratic.

"We think at this point, with the failure of three world wars to plunge mankind into never-ending chaos, that the fallen began its plan to destroy the western democracies with its main goal the ruin of America. This had to be accomplished from the inside as these countries were much too powerful to be harmed from outside."

Finishing up the last morsels of his large meal, Tom dabbed at the corners of his mouth with his napkin and asked, "I agree with all you've said so far Benoit…but I still don't see how my role, would be any different than any other contributing member?"

"Something big is coming Tom. Subtle is over. The bent, guided by their masters have changed us. People are no longer independent and self-reliant as they used to be. Most people, in a crisis, are lost. How to fend for ourselves has been educated out of us. We have been conditioned to look to our governments for aid and answers, to make way for experts who will tell us what to do. When the crisis comes the people at large will be confused and helpless and they will do what they are told to do by whoever appears to be in control."

"Ya…but…"

Benoit held up her hand to forestall Tom. "I have tried to explain our thoughts to you as well as I understand them, but I admit I have painted this picture with pretty broad strokes. There is quite a bit more detail but I don't think I need go into that for your benefit. The group I've been working with has judged this to be a stepping off point in our history, a time when humanity needs…champions, to come forward and hold back the forces of hatred, fear and chaos." She reached across the table and took his hand and said in a hushed but nonetheless penetrating voice, "Tom…you are one of our champions."

Tom sat in stunned silence, his mind conjuring snippets of heroic tales. "No," he said. "I am no champion. I am just me." He looked at Benoit.

"Just you; is what we need," she said. "I can see the strength in you that will sustain us. You and the others, for there is and will be others, will either lead us through the coming darkness or the tales of your sacrifices will light the imaginations of coming generations and fuel their struggle for humanities freedom. We have no inkling of what is to come, a brief skirmish in our ages old war with the twisted lord or the coming of darkness and slavery for ten thousand years. It doesn't matter. It only matters that we keep faith…because…you see; we will never be truly defeated. One thing the twisted lord cannot comprehend is that in the ultimate end, we will be free of its influence for we are all the Children of God and you Tom, you are a champion of God."

Sitting in stunned silence Tom wasn't aware of Colin bursting into the ground floor kitchen. "Do you have the news on? Have you seen the news?"

Benoit turned toward Colin as he rushed in, "No…what is the…"

"A bomb!" He cried. "The Parliament Buildings…Ottawa!" He grabbed the TV remote and switched on the kitchen set.

"Oh my God," whispered Benoit as a live picture of Parliament Hill came into focus. Brown and grey smudges obscured the clear blue sky directly over what had once been the Peace Tower, the stone spire that anchored the Center Block of the country's Parliament Buildings. The bottom sixty feet of Nepean sandstone had been sheared completely away by the lateral force of a blast and the top four fifths of the tower had dropped almost straight down to stand drunkenly to the right of the main focus of devastation. A fire raged within the blasted masonry rubble to the left of the skewed sentry.

A local reporter and her crew had quickly set themselves up on the intersection of Wellington and Metcalf and the three cameramen were recording the scene in its horrific detail. Her producer, inside the portable studio, chose each shot carefully to give viewers a full panorama of events unfolding and to accompany the narration now being given by the young reporter.

"Official details of the blast have not been made available…our team is one of the first on site and the emergency response units have not arrived. The local police witnessed the explosion first hand but they have their hands full. Earlier reports put the initial explosion at around two fifteen this afternoon, approximately twenty minutes ago. It appears from our vantage here that the Peace Tower has been damaged and the section of the Center Block that housed the House of Commons has been almost completely destroyed. The House was in session, but we have had no list to this point of which members were in attendance."

Slowly now but gaining volume and separating from the background noise multiple sirens could be heard. Police officers could be seen trying to clear onlookers away from the roadways that approached the Hill. The news crew shots were showing fire trucks, ambulances and police vehicles of all sizes careening onto the approach roads to the burning building.

"We are going to attempt getting closer and maybe find someone to give us a statement. Until then this is Mindy Kwon reporting for CJAM news. Back to you Gene." The picture switched to a middle-aged man sitting behind a polished chrome and glass desk.

"Let's go down to the library," Benoit said. "Gordon might have further news."

"You guys go ahead," said Tom. "I've got to dress." Hurrying back upstairs he rooted around impatiently, not finding what he wanted. *My clothes must have been thrown out, so much blood.* He shivered at the memory and out of nowhere a thought came, *there will be so much more blood before this is over. I do have to leave.* As much as he wanted to stay, his place wasn't here. He must act or the augmented talents he'd been blessed with would be wasted. He made his decision and immediately felt better. He had the how and the why, the where and the when would soon be revealed.

He found some clothes. Dressing quickly, he left the bedroom and went downstairs. He exited the rear door and started walking toward the church. He could hear the muted wailing of sirens in the distance. He wondered if the sirens were associated with the last remnants of action at St. James Park or some new catastrophe. He'd have to find out. The date for the next occurrence was tomorrow and he needed to know if the riots at the park and their aftermath would somehow overlap. Tom toyed with the idea of doing some recon work at the park but then thought better of it. *Anyone of any value to the bent will have abandoned the park long ago. Going there would be a dead end.* He let himself into the basement and made his way through their secret maze. He keyed in the simple code for the door and stepped through when it opened. From the landing at the top of the stairs he could see Gordon, Bill, Colin and Benoit gathered around the large flat screen. Bill saw him first and waved for him to hurry down.

"They're starting to get some details," Bill said.

The onsite reporter, Mindy Kwon, was starting an interview. "We have with us Mr. Bhai Singh. Mr. Singh is with the custodial service of the National Capital Commission that administers the lands and buildings in Canada's National Capital Region. Mr. Singh, would you tell our viewers what you saw earlier?"

She stepped closer to the tall, slim man and held the microphone up to him. “Well…as I told you earlier, I left the basement of the West Block to have my lunch outside. I finished by the statue of Queen Victoria and was returning to work when I noticed a tour bus on the access road to the Center Block.”

The reporter interrupted, “What made you notice the bus?”

“There were no tour buses scheduled for this afternoon, as there were no custodians detailed to police the area after the buses leave and there had been no mention of a detail this afternoon. The bus was very large, one of those high buses with the extra cargo space underneath. It was also going too fast, there is a ten kilometer an hour speed limit here. The bus was accelerating after going around the very sharp turn at the corner of the West Block Building. By the time it passed me it had to be going twenty-five kilometers an hour and it didn’t slow down.” The man lowered his head then and brushed tears from his eyes and then he scrubbed at his face with both hands, nearly dislodging his turban. He looked back at the reporter and continued, “The bus had to be traveling nearly sixty when it struck the Tower. There was a huge explosion which knocked me down. I was dazed for a minute because when I regained my senses the explosion was over and the tower was already down and the fires were burning. I tried to run over…”

Just then two RCMP officers appeared onscreen. One of them put her hand over the lens of the camera and they could hear Mr. Singh being escorted away. The first officer then removed her hand from the camera lens and explained to Ms. Kwon and her viewers that Mr. Singh was an important eye witness and the RCMP needed to interview him and that she and her cameraman were too close to the fire and needed to go back down to Wellington Street where the police had set up a media information area. Mindy kept trying to ask the RCMP officer questions over her instructions to clear the area.

“Do you believe the bus had a bomb in it or was this just a horrendous accident?”

“No comment,” replied the officer.

“How do you explain the overriding odor of diesel fuel and ammonia?”

“No comment. You really must accompany me to the media area.”

The CJAM reporter protested and the RCMP officer had her escorted out. The picture quickly reverted to the studio where news anchor Gene Oakley looked as if he’d just made it back to his desk in time for the camera to go on.

"Thank you, Mindy. We'll be hearing more from Mindy once they get back up." The video screen behind Gene began showing live footage of the fire still raging in the west wing of the Center Block. "This bombing and I'm sure the experts will conclude it was a bomb and therefore a deliberate act, is unparalleled in Canadian history. Not since the Halifax explosion of 1917 have Canadians been witness to such devastation and the Halifax explosion was an accident. The consequences of this heinous attack will be felt by Canadians for years to come. The Commons was in session today and at this time we do not know how many of the three hundred and eight members were in attendance."

Gordon hit the mute button. "He doesn't know anything new." Gordon looked at the four others gathered with him around the table. "I think we are all thinking the same thing. This is the beginning of the push to topple the governments of the west." There were no dissenters at the table. "We need to bring everyone in on this. Bill…would you contact George please and have him start contacting our members. Colin you need to connect with Jonathan and put the word out to any other groups we are aware of." Bill and Colin took their leave.

"What are you going to do?" asked Tom.

Gently Gordon replied, "We are going to do what we have always done. We will gather information. If there are other groups out there which can use the information, we compile to their advantage we will supply it freely. If we are to serve another purpose later…" Gordon shrugged. "I do know that your purpose is not with us as I know Benoit and you have spoken."

"Do you know what my purpose is?"

"I can only guess," replied Gordon. "We gather information. Since I started this chapter in 1920 the information we have gathered has been recorded, written up as a history. This has been more or less true of all the chapters of our Path since its origination during the First Crusade. We have been keeping histories; accurate, written, day to day chronicles of what has been happening. If human civilization fails now, then mankind will need an accurate history of our time for two important reasons. One; to illustrate to later societies the heights the ideals of freedom and democracy may take you to and secondly; as a warning to show how far society can fall when human arrogance and hubris take over our lives. For as long as I have ever thought about our purpose, this has been it, but just because I say this is not your purpose it does not mean that you must leave. You are welcome here for as long as your path dictates…I hope you know that."

"Thank you, Gordon." There was a pause in the conversation. No one had anything to say, they were caught within the thoughts and concerns that this day was generating. Finally, Tom looked up at the television and asked Gordon to turn the sound back on. "Looks like they may have some new information," he said.

The political analyst and his team that the twenty-four-hour news channel had put together was beginning to try and make sense of what the bombing had done to the government and how it would function. "We have just learned that two hundred and eight of the three hundred and eight members of the House were in attendance today along with a packed balcony holding approximately five hundred. There is no official word at this juncture but it is not likely that any survived the blast and the ensuing collapse of that section of the building and the fire that still rages there. We don't have the names of the MPs in attendance, but we do know that the Governor General, the Prime Minister and most of his cabinet were there along with the Leader of the Opposition and most of her shadow cabinet."

At this point Gene Oakley interrupted the political analyst, "If the GG and the PM are unable to fulfill their duties by incapacitation or death, what is the path of succession?"

"Well," the analyst began, almost beginning his explanation as if it were an abstract lecture being given for a 'what if' scenario but then stopping and stuttering for a moment as the reality of this situation reasserted itself. "What we have here is a situation that is unprecedented. In the American system there is a descending order of succession laid out. The President, the Vice President, Speaker of the House, President pro tempore of the Senate, Secretary of State and so on down the list of eighteen. In the parliamentary system our Prime Minister is not elected separately, he is the leader of the party with the majority of elected members and is acquitted the confidence of the House to run the government. Under normal conditions if the Prime Minister is unable to fulfill his or her duties then the deputy Prime Minister assumes the role. The deputy PM is usually a member of the PM's cabinet. If no deputy has been appointed then the Governor General will appoint an interim Prime Minister until the party in power can hold a leadership convention. If the Governor General is incapacitated and cannot appoint an interim Prime Minister then the Chief

Justice of the Supreme Court of Canada takes over the duties of the Governor General and appoints the interim PM.

"The situation unfolding now has roughly two thirds of our elected government members gone. The Chief Justice, as far as we know, was not in the Center Block when this tragedy happened, therefore he can assume the duties of the Governor General…but who would he appoint interim PM. The cabinet is gone, we don't know if there are any senior members out there and of the one hundred MPs still alive, we don't even know what parties they belong to. There will obviously have to be elections held but that will take time. In my opinion, as of right now, we do not have a functioning federal government in Canada. I believe it is up to the Provincial Governments to assume the federal government's responsibilities and duties within the boundaries of their provinces until such time as the federal branch can be reconstituted."

Gene Oakley put his finger up to his ear and tilted his head slightly, listening to his earpiece. "Excuse me Derrick; ladies and gentlemen we are going back to Mindy Kwon on Parliament Hill for breaking news. Mindy?"

The picture switched to show the pretty but now somber young newscaster standing in front of a crowd of other journalists. "Thank you, Gene. The lead investigator for the RCMP is about to give a statement. We've been given no indication of what's been found to this point except for the numbers of MPs that were in the House this afternoon. We're going live now to the Chief Inspector."

A very large man with short cropped grey hair, wearing the everyday uniform of the Mounties stepped through the throng on the slightly raised platform that held the podium and several microphones. His cap, bearing the iconic badge displaying the buffalo head under the crown and the distinctive yellow ribbon, was under his arm and on his shoulder was a slip-on badge portraying a crown over crossed sword and red baton.

"Good afternoon Ladies and Gentlemen," he began. His voice was higher than his size would warrant and quite soft, making listeners pay attention. "I am Deputy Commissioner James McGregor of A Division, the National Division which incorporates the National Capital Region. Our investigation is only in its beginning stages and we have few facts to convey. Under normal circumstances The Force would not be releasing information this early in the investigation. The circumstances we face now as a nation are extraordinary and we believe that some information at this time will allow Canadians to understand what has happened, will allow the nation to know that the full weight and resources of the RCMP investigative powers are coming to bear on this situation and above all that there are no reasons for panic. Measures have been taken and protocols put in place to continue the uninterrupted running of our Federal Government." After a short pause to look at his audience, the Deputy Commissioner continued. "At approximately two ten this afternoon a transcontinental tour bus was driven at high speed into the Center Block of Parliament Hill. As to the ownership of the bus we have no information as yet. We do know the bus was empty of passengers on impact except for a driver. The bus collided with the building on the west face of the Peace Tower where it connects to the western wing of the building. This western wing contains the House of Commons Chamber and the upper gallery. The interior of the bus had been engineered to direct the full force of the explosive blast into its target. This accounts for the high level of damage inflicted on the tower and the west chamber. The type of explosive used is still being analyzed at this time.

"According to this morning's records there were two hundred and eleven Members of Parliament in attendance, including the Prime Minister, his full Cabinet, his staff from the PMO, the Speaker, the Leader of the Opposition and the leaders of the other two parties. There were also four hundred and ninety-seven citizens in the second-floor observation gallery. Identities of the members present can only be ascertained from the roll and the persons in the public gallery from the sign in sheets. Actual identification is impossible at this time."

Suddenly reporters started shouting questions at the Deputy Commissioner. The press briefing quickly took on an atmosphere of chaos, the reporters sounding and acting like onlookers at a third-grade recess fight, taunting and yelling at the combatants. The questions that seemed to coalesce out of the din were; who did this and why aren't you able to identify the victims?

The Deputy Commissioner stood at the podium waiting for the commotion to die down. When the reporters were quiet once again, he slowly turned to look up the Hill to where the reporters could just see the broken tower wreathed in smoke and flames. He turned back to them, his eyes full of grief and sorrow. "It's like walking into hell up there."

For the next several hours Tom watched the news coverage unfold. The commentators had nothing new to add to their meager supply of facts, but that didn't stop them from speaking. What kept Tom watching were the efforts of the firefighters to bring the white-hot blaze under control. There was an awful lot of flammable material within the center block, timbers and lumber dried out over a span of a hundred and fifty years, lacquers and paints, rubbing oils and waxes adding their chemical impetus to the flames, carpets and upholsteries burning and melting and flowing molten over everything. The heat generated soon melted steel and cracked stone. Tom was mesmerized by this video scene of hell on earth. Finally, after five hours of raining water and fire-retardant chemicals on the collapsed western wing of the Center Block the raging fires were subdued. Tom was pulled from his reverie by the sound of many voices. He'd been so deeply involved in the coverage of the fire that he had not noticed the members of The Path trickling in. Now, by early evening, the majority of the membership were in residence.

Tom recognized George, Benoit and Gordon but if in the course of the afternoon he'd been introduced to anyone else, their names eluded him. He noticed that the young policeman Colin McAllister and the church custodian Bill Ware were not around. Tom started toward George who was speaking to someone with their back to Tom. When he got closer to George, he recognized Jonathan Brandt, the young computer technician who worked at city hall.

"How are you Tom? You've been glued to the TV all afternoon. Jonathan tells me there may be a lead to the identity of the bombers." He turned from Tom back to Jonathan and nodded for him to explain.

"The Chief of the Metro Police received a request this afternoon on his secure email for all info they have pertaining to a group called Q, A, T. The acronym stands for 'Quebec Avant Tous', Quebec Before All. They're new players in domestic terrorism, taking over where the FLQ left off. Anyway…if this bombing in Ottawa is theirs then they have vaulted into the number one spot on the RCMP's ten most wanted list. Hell, this puts them in the first five places with no one else on the list."

Tom looked at George, "Do you think they are…"

"Bent? My guess would be yes, some of them anyway, the timing is just too coincidental. We all believe that this is the opening play in what's to come."

"Have you discovered anything more at the CN Tower?" Tom asked.

"No," replied George. "Lincoln, that's him over there speaking with Bill and Benoit, arrived back from the tower an hour ago and they've not found anything."

Tom shook his head slowly. "Lamont seemed so certain…there was no subterfuge in him. I can't figure out what his angle was in telling me that?"

George put his hand on Tom's shoulder, "Let's be glad we don't have to worry about something like that happening, Ottawa is horrific enough, right now no one seems to know who is running the country." George looked closely at Tom. "We're going to be sending out some of our members to make contact with the other groups we know about. We need to pass along the info we have on QAT and collect any news we don't have. I'll make sure they also have instructions to ask if the other groups have heard anything concerning the CN Tower or Rogers Center, anything at all, no matter how insignificant."

"Thanks George."

"Meanwhile Tom, you still look like you've been through world war three. There's nothing going on here that you don't already know about, why don't you get some rest."

It was eight thirty and Tom was all in. He caught Benoit's eye and she excused herself from Bill and Lincoln.

"How are you feeling Tom?"

"I'm still pretty bagged," he replied. "Nothing to be concerned about in that is there?"

"Not after what you've been through. I'd be concerned if you weren't tired. I will be staying here for at least a few more days, maybe longer. I'll look in on you later and if anything develops, I promise to wake you. If not, I shall see you in the morning."

"Thanks Benoit."

Tom did not sleep well. He dozed off quickly but was disturbed by unremembered dreams and a feeling of disquiet. He awoke with a start very early the next morning. He was in his old room in the sanctuary and he lay in bed for a few minutes thinking about the last week. Seven short days had passed since meeting Laura and Gordon yet it felt like years. When he thought about it, he rationalized that the experiences of the last week probably could have filled a year. He had no idea of his next move, where he would go or what he would do. Everyone now knew that the bent and their masters were putting their plans into motion. He felt irresponsible and out of sorts doing nothing.

He thought back to the night before he had first confronted the man nicknamed Bolt. He remembered how utterly lost and confused he had been and how the decision to find Bolt had given him purpose. He had no idea where Bolt would be now; all of his contacts had disappeared or, like Lamont, were dead. *I wonder where Putnam is. I wonder if he went back to Coalmen? Putnam probably thinks I'm dead, especially if Lamont had gotten word to him that Laura and I had been captured by the demon. It's been four days now since...since she died, wonder what was done. I wonder if there was a funeral or anything.* Tom heard noises coming from the direction of the kitchen. He got up, put on his robe and slippers and went out to the kitchen. No one was around but he noticed there was a fresh pot of coffee on the warmer. He poured himself a mug and wandered into the library. Benoit was alone, sitting in one of the comfortably overstuffed chairs looking up at the TV. Tom walked over and sat down beside her.

"Anything more on the bombing," he asked?

Benoit muted the sound. "A few things. The bus was stolen from a Chinese tour company. The company has been cleared of any complicity in the bombing. The QAT has been mentioned as a possible suspect group. Of the ninety-seven MPs that were absent yesterday from the House of Commons ninety have been found and seven are still missing. There has still been no word about reconstituting Parliament or how the government is to function. The RCMP hasn't released the names of the MPs yet or their party affiliations."

After a few minutes of staring at the soundless television picture Tom asked, "Do you know what's become of Laura?"

"Yes Tom," she said softly. "She was processed quickly by the metro police, written up as a hit and run. The body was released to George and he made arrangements for cremation and a small memorial service. She was buried next to her mother and father yesterday."

Tears came freely to Tom's eyes and for a minute he was unable to speak.

"Tom...you couldn't have gone to the service. Even if you hadn't been so badly hurt the risk of you being followed or even attacked would have been too great."

"I know Benoit, you're right of course. Were any of her friends able to attend?"

"All of her friends from school were there, Memmy of course. He was inconsolable, he loved her very much. Did you know that he had proposed to her?"

"Ya…she told me she was going to say yes."

"Poor Memmy. George and Bill attended along with various members of the Baptist Church, but no one else from The Path."

"I see. That must have been hard on everyone that knew her and couldn't pay their last respects."

"Yes," she said, "And hardest of all on Gordon."

"He cared for her a great deal, didn't he?"

Benoit contemplated for a moment and then spoke. "Gordon has been on earth for so many years and has seen so much that his wisdom is almost beyond belief. He has become surrogate father and grandfather to everyone here but his relationship with Laura was special. I think a lot of that had to do with how close Gordon had been to Laura's mother and father."

Tom asked, "You are close to Gordon also, aren't you?" Benoit lowered her eyes. "I'm sorry Benoit…I didn't mean to pry. It's none of my business…it just seemed…I've noticed an affection between you and Gordon whenever you're together."

Benoit looked up and smiled, then chuckled softly to herself. She smiled again at Tom and he noticed how her face transformed when she smiled. She reached across to Tom and caressed his cheek with her hand. The heat from her fingers and palm and the softness of her skin surprised Tom and as she withdrew her hand, he wished she wouldn't. "Gordon and I have great affection for each other," she said, "But the fullness of his affection was with my brother Alaire."

Tom sat there thinking of Benoit, not really contemplating what she had just said. When her words registered, he became confused. He looked at her and she just stared back at him with only the slightest little smile playing at the corners of her full mouth. "I'm sorry…did you just say…were Gordon and your brother…My God, poor Gordon, he must have been devastated when he got the news of your brother's death."

"He was," she replied.

"Had Gordon and your brother been together long?" Tom felt both foolish and prying when he asked the question but didn't know what else to say.

"Alaire and Gordon were never…together. I'm sorry Tom I must be confusing you. I'll start at the beginning. I first met Gordon in 1963. Both Alaire and I were twenty, we were fraternal twins. We had just finished our first two years of rotations at McGill and Alaire and I had chosen psychiatry as our specialties. We were very interested in the study of human deviations. Yes?"

"I didn't mean to interrupt."

"You had a quizzical look on your face."

"I just thought twenty was young to be half way through med school."

"It is; Alaire and I were quite gifted. We both graduated in the top one percentile when we received our science degrees, we had just turned seventeen."

"Were your parents doctors?" Tom asked.

"I don't know," she said. Benoit tugged her sleeve partway up her slender arm and held out her exposed forearm to Tom. Barely visible were a series of five numbers followed by an upside-down triangle in faded blue ink. Tom could feel himself draw air in much too quickly. "Alaire and I were born in Natzweiler-Struthof Concentration Camp in the spring of 1943. We were taken from our mother at the time of our birth; the Nazis were experimenting on twins at the time. The camp was liberated before Alaire and I were old enough for experimentation to have begun on us. We had been housed in a nursery with the rest of the younger children. Most of the adults had been force marched to Dachau in September of 1944. No one ever came to claim us after the camp was liberated that November so when we were older, we suspected that our parents had either perished on the march or at Dachau. Because we were Jewish and the countries of Europe had their own generation of orphans to take care of and Israel was not yet a country we were brought to an orphanage in the US. We were later adopted by a couple from Montreal who thankfully had hearts big enough for two waifs. Once we were older and learned about the Holocaust we began to study, reading everything we could about the Nazis; the founders, their rise to power and the institutionalizing of their final solution. Once we'd exhausted the library's resources concerning the Nazis, we broadened our study to encompass barbaric regimes throughout history and that brought us to question the role of evil in man's history. The written histories and biographies that we studied illustrated that, basically, evil men did evil things. We began to look at it from the opposite perspective. You know the saying, 'power corrupts and absolute power corrupts absolutely.' The other side of that argument is that power attracts the corruptible. We started thinking about evil and wondered if evil was a quantifiable historic constant attracting men and women to it.

"Throughout med school it was known where our interests lay and it was always known by our professors that Alaire and I would ultimately choose psychiatry as our discipline. Many derided our search for the evil that preyed on mankind as superstitious hokum, it now being an age of science and logic with no room for religious beliefs, but many came to us, quietly, with their stories. Medical professionals, laymen, soldiers who had lived through the carnage of war and many, many survivors of the Nazis. We were getting ready to publish, we had volumes of data gleaned from our years of interviews that we had refined into a publishable size. Our book would have been over eleven hundred pages and my brother and I believed it would have defined evil to a generation of scholars who disputed its existence and would have opened the eyes of western peoples as nothing had since the publication of the Bible.

"At this time, I had been seeing a middle-aged man… I see your raised eyebrows. I was seeing this man as part of my research. He had fascinating stories of the not so long ago past, stories he said he's gotten from his father and grandfather who he said had written extensive journals as they lived through events we now call history. I had also become this man's confidant as he was living a secret and needed someone to talk to. The man had grown up in a time when homosexuality was viewed as a gross deformity of character, a debased lifestyle choice that could ruin your life if discovered and possibly end your life. He had never acted on his sexual nature; he had served in the military and had many close male friends and compatriots who had never suspected. Through extensive research, deep thought and prayer he had come to the conclusion that God's grace and love belonged to homosexual men and women as much as to heterosexual men and women. What he needed my help with was his deep melancholy brought on by his loneliness. This wasn't just the loneliness he felt at that time, but the loneliness and isolation that he had felt all his life in not being able to tell his closest friends who he really was. Of course, you know I'm speaking of Gordon. He had no regrets concerning his life, in that regard anyway, and knew he was following to the best of his ability the path that was apportioned for him. He felt he had deceived his close friends and that also added to his melancholy.

"One afternoon Gordon and I were in my apartment office talking. He was fascinated with our thesis on evil…and of course he was because he already knew we had it right. What he was really interested in was our process and how it had shaped our thoughts. At this time, I had been meeting with Gordon for about six months but Alaire had as yet never met Gordon. There was a knock at my office door and Alaire let himself in. As soon as I introduced Gordon to Alaire I knew that there was a connection. I had always known that Alaire was gay, it had never really meant all that much to me, it was just part of who my brother was, his hair was black and his eyes were brown and he was gay. It wasn't until I was standing there looking at the wordless interaction between Alaire and Gordon that I had seen my brother interested in another human being other than as a study subject. Neither my brother or I were much for social pursuits. Our time was spent in study and correlating our findings. After that Gordon and Alaire became tremendously close; as friends more than anything, but friends that shared something on a very deep and emotional level. It wasn't long after that first meeting that Gordon revealed to us who he was and why he had sought me out. He knew that by publishing our study Alaire and I would be targeted for ridicule, marginalization and then death. He had learned of our study the year before and after finding out about some of our conclusions he had fostered a relationship with me to discern if our conclusions were accidental and without merit or we had truly uncovered the reality of pure evil in a quantifiable format. He brought us into The Path. We never published our paper, but we never stopped the study of evil."

"Did the relationship between Gordon and Alaire ever develop?" Tom asked.

"My brother and Gordon remained very close and their friendship never faltered or faded. Gordon told me that in his mind he couldn't overcome the age and experience difference. When Alaire was twenty-one, Gordon was already ninety years old, even though he had the energy and the look of someone in his thirties. He said there were too many things that Alaire had yet to discover about the world and his life that he needed to do at his own pace and with his own generation."

"I wonder if Gordon ever regretted his decision?" Tom mused.

"I don't think so," replied Benoit quietly. "He and Alaire had a comfortable closeness and Gordon once remarked that the passions that governed a younger man's needs had left him by the end of the First World War. His desire to follow The Path that he learned of in Alabama consumed all his energies once he returned to Toronto. What he had felt on meeting Alaire was to him just a memory of his youthful ardor."

They sat quietly for a few minutes, Tom's gaze drifting to the television set. "Turn the sound back on would you please…thanks."

"…baseball game will still be played today at its regular time. The National Hockey League has cancelled regularly scheduled games for the next two days out of respect for the devastation in Ottawa. It's not clear at this time how Major League Baseball is viewing the recent events in our nation's capital; after all they are an American organization and only have the one team in Canada. We haven't been able to reach the Office of the Commissioner of Baseball for a comment. In other news; the seven missing MPs are still unaccounted for. The RCMP has designated search teams for each of the seven Federal Ridings. An RCMP spokesperson says the force has not ruled out foul play but has as yet uncovered nothing suspicious. The remaining ninety MPs, whose identities have still not been released, have been sequestered at a secure building by the RCMP in the National Capital Region. CTV News has learned that certain government agencies are requesting the implementation of the Canadian Emergencies Act. Passed in 1988 it replaced the War Measures Act that was infamously implemented by then Prime Minister Pierre Trudeau during the October Crises in 1970. It has been reported that CSIS, the Canadian Security Intelligence Service, would interpret this crisis under Part II of the Act, namely a Public Order Emergency." Tom turned the sound down again. "That's a lot of words to describe the situation."

"What's that Tom?"

"It's started."

"Some of the older members have been anticipating this for years. We knew it would happen eventually, as an intellectual exercise we all knew this day was inevitable, but now that the events are beginning, we are all a little surprised." Benoit was quiet for a moment. "Gordon is out now but I expect him to return soon. I would imagine George and most of the others will be returning sometime this afternoon, hopefully with more information. Go do your morning routine and I'll prepare some food for us."

"Thanks Benoit." Tom turned and walked back to the kitchen. He poured another cup of their excellent coffee and returned to his room. He showered and shaved, brushed his teeth, dressed and returned to the kitchen in an hour.

Benoit had lunch prepared. Cold cuts sliced and laid out on a glass tray; crispy buns hot from the oven broken open with creamery butter just beginning to melt within the warm fluffy white interiors. Mustard and relish and mayonnaise arranged in small pots, cheeses slivered, wedged and sliced beside vinegared onions and tomatoes ready for a sandwich. Crispy bacon slices next to pickles and olives completed the arrangement.

"Wow," said Tom, "This looks great!"

"Let's eat then Tom, while the mood and opportunity are upon us."

For the next hour the two new friends sat in comfortable company, chatting amiably about small things while they ate their fill. Just as they finished clearing up the lunch dishes, they heard the upper door chime.

"That must be Gordon returning," Benoit said turning to look toward the stairs.

Gordon and George began the descent down the stairs. Greetings and hugs ensued and then Tom and Benoit went to the kitchen to bring back the coffee service for the four of them.

Once they sat down Benoit looked at George and asked, "What is happening in the capital?"

"It's an absolute mess," declared George. "I've been in contact with all the business leaders I trust, and some I don't. I've spoken with the RCMP Commissioner and the Chief Justice of the Supreme Court. No one, no agency has a clue as to what to do next. Oh, they all think they know. The business leaders are only worried about the economy and the consequences to their bottom lines. The Commissioner and the Chief Justice are worried about the continuity of our government but they both have differing ideas and differing protocols as to what needs to be done next.

"This hasn't made the news yet obviously…but three of the missing MPs were found dead, no details mentioned. Many on the force think they were assassinated. The other four still haven't been accounted for. The RCMP has the remaining ninety in protective custody and will not be releasing any news on them for a while. I was told in confidence that the majority of the MPs they are protecting do not belong to the party that had formed the government. They can't form a government with what they have now, there is no one qualified or with enough support to form even a coalition government to get the country through an election cycle. If the opposition parties try to form a government out of what's left of the MPs the populace will not react well. Without civilian authority the military is rudderless so the Provincial Police are contemplating quarantining the border with Quebec. There has been a haphazard censorship put in place by the OPP in conjunction with the RCMP as the national police force so you may or may not hear this on the local news. There have been riots and shootings in Montreal and Quebec City. Native groups, in solidarity with the QAT, have set up roadblocks throughout their territories and have brought road and rail traffic that intersects with their lands to a halt. Small gun battles have broken out between natives and pissed off truckers and the QPP won't get in the middle. News from New Brunswick and further east has been disrupted. Some cable and satellite microwave towers have been brought down so most of the reporting is coming through by telephone land lines."

"News from out west?" Tom asked.

George shook his head, "It seems quiet for now; I think law enforcement agencies there are just holding their breath, waiting for the other shoe to drop."

"What about Northern Ontario," Tom asked.

"Nothing…why?" replied George.

"You remember the map I'd found, well today's date and a symbol for what we believe is the Rogers Center was the first notation of anything to happen after the riot at St. James Park."

"Yes, I remember."

"Well after today there were notations we decrypted for things to start happening all over Ontario, mostly north of the Trans-Canada Highway. I also remember a notation closer to Coalmen…at an airbase west of Coalmen."

"Nothing has been reported, but the police are on high alert. It was also relayed to me that because the Feds aren't able to function, the individual provinces are going to be given temporary jurisdiction within their own borders, except for defense. The Chief of Defense Staff, General Ehrlich has ordered active-duty personnel to report in. The general rotation of service personnel will continue but non-essential personnel will not be allowed onto bases. The assets of the Canadian Forces will be locked down until a Minister of Defense can be appointed. The military command is worried about the status of the bases in Quebec though. There are two army bases and one air force base within Quebec and they are not one hundred percent sure that the lockdown of the bases' assets will be honored by the Quebec Provincial Legislature. If the separatists within the legislature were able to wrest control of the province from the majority Liberals while the country has no federal government and if they could access the army base assets and personnel then their goal of separation from the rest of Canada becomes a fait accompli and by the time we have a reconstituted federal government it will be without Quebec."

Tom looked at his brother-in-law. "You're talking civil war?"

"Maybe," replied George, "But I don't know."

"I think what is coming will make us all forget about what Quebec will do," interjected Benoit.

With a stretch, Tom stood up from his chair and turned toward the kitchen. The floor shifted under Tom, followed by a low frequency rumble that emanated from the very walls of the sanctuary. Tiny motes of dust filtered down between the lights as Tom looked at George who mouthed the question, earthquake? Tom shifted his eyes to the television. The video feed was frozen with lines of interference streaking across the picture. The ground around them rumbled again as if a distant artillery barrage was commencing. It lasted mere seconds and ended. Again, fine dust hung in the air. Tom was staring at a blank and darkened television screen. "Skydome," he muttered. The four stared at the dead screen until Tom tore his gaze away. Raising his voice to cut through the horror of the moment, Tom commanded Gordon and George, "Find your people, get them here to safety, this is it!" He turned his gaze to Benoit and in a slightly calmer voice said, "Pack my stuff up would you please?" With that he ran up the stairs and was gone.

Traffic was snarled and unmoving. Pedestrians gaped nervously trying to find a reason for the rumbling ground, ignoring angry horns. Tom ran south, moving into the street finding it easier to dodge idling cars than dazed pedestrians, his feet tore at the pavement. He strained to see to the southwest but only sky presented itself above the burned and scarred trees of St. James Park. He turned right onto Adelaide and ran west. Traffic began to move slowly and pedestrians quickly forgot why they had stopped in the street. Tom hit Church Street and had to stop to allow a streetcar passage. He gulped air and leaped across the road, refusing to look back toward the burned-out hulk of the once magnificent Cathedral Church of Saint James. Citizens seemed to be back in their cocoon of canyon living, not taking much notice of what was going on around them, moving from one high banked avenue to the next, their blinkered vistas small. Tom's lungs were burning by the time he barreled through Yonge Street and that's when he heard the first siren's wail. Throughout his run, his eyes had gazed south, desperate to see the tower. No luck as he flew west. The flashes of bright sky poking between the soaring buildings as he passed through the intersections at Bay, then York and then University Avenue offered no sight of the tower, his only sense that revealed anything was his hearing. The wailing of sirens was everywhere and people stopped to take notice. Just as he thought he'd pass out, his cramping legs froze in mid stride. He peered south past an old parking lot and the low rent apartment buildings tucked in behind. Off in the distance, past the newly constructed mirrored glass and steel condos of Toronto's newest homeowners, an angry and violent pall of smoke and dust was churning into the sky.

"Dear God," Tom moaned quietly.

People were beginning to point, some were screaming, some were running, most though just stared, pinned like bugs on a board, transfixed by the impossible becoming believable. Unlike most of these people Tom knew what had, and what was, happening. Recovering, he sprinted to the next street over, where chaos ruled. Ambulances and police cars careened south weaving in and around abandoned passenger vehicles, taxis and jammed up busses, sometimes leaping the sidewalks and scattering the masses of people escaping north. The backdrop to this kaleidoscopic helter skelter was a roiling boiling churning mass of grey and brown and black fume expanding and billowing out in its inexorable rush up John Street, swallowing the smaller buildings and leaving the tops of the skyscrapers like islands in a rushing, muddy torrent.

For a moment his mind had a vision of another street, in New York, on an awful morning in September, and now, other cities came into his mind with dust and panic and death. He knew this was the end, nothing would ever be the same, and he knew what he had to do.